Land *of* Enchantment

Cacophony. Courtesy of Philip Rosenthal, PhilipRosenthalPaintings.com.

Land *of* Enchantment

Liza Wieland

Syracuse University Press

Syracuse University Press
Syracuse, New York 13244-5290

All Rights Reserved

First Edition 2015

15   16   17   18   19   20   6   5   4   3   2   1

Grateful acknowledgment is made to *Sou'wester*, in which a portion of this novel previously appeared.

∞ The paper used in this publication meets the minimum requirements of the American National Standard for Information Sciences—Permanence of Paper for Printed Library Materials, ANSI Z39.48-1992.

For a listing of books published and distributed by Syracuse University Press,
visit www.SyracuseUniversityPress.syr.edu.

ISBN: 978-0-8156-1046-5 (cloth)   978-0-8156-5313-4 (e-book)

Library of Congress Cataloging-in-Publication Data
Wieland, Liza.
Land of enchantment / Liza Wieland. — First edition.
pages ; cm
ISBN 978-0-8156-1046-5 (hardcover : acid-free paper) — ISBN 978-0-8156-5313-4 (ebook)
I. Title.
PS3573.I344L36 2015
813'.54—dc23   2014043512

Manufactured in the United States of America

for my own Georgia

We have art in order not to die of the truth.

     —Friedrich Nietzsche

Liza Wieland is the author of *Quickening*, *A Watch of Nightingales*, *Near Alcatraz*, *Bombshell*, *You Can Sleep While I Drive*, *Discovering America*, and *The Names of the Lost*. She was raised in Atlanta, Georgia, and educated at Harvard College and Columbia University. Her work has been awarded two Pushcart Prizes and the Michigan Literary Fiction Award, as well as fellowships from the National Endowment for the Arts, the Christopher Isherwood Foundation, and the North Carolina Arts Council. She teaches at East Carolina University and lives near Oriental, North Carolina, with her husband and daughter.

Acknowledgments

My heartfelt thanks to the following:

First to Suzanne Guiod for her tireless support and encouragement, and Kelly Balenske, Deborah Manion, and Lisa Kuerbis for their help with the manuscript. To Ann Youmans for her patient and insightful editing.

Dear friends who read versions of this novel along the way and made excellent suggestions: Linnea Alexander, Connie Hales, Alexis Khoury, Brian Lampkin, Kathie Lang, Kat Meads, Tanya Nichols, and Carrie Thies.

My colleagues in the English Department at East Carolina University.

My students past and present, especially for those times when we were all writing quietly together, and the room hummed with discovery and grace.

Inspiration from visual artists Joan Mansfield, Franny Levine, Philip Rosenthal, and my mother, Barbara Wieland, as well as from filmmaker Mary Kate Monahan, and conversations about filmmaking with the late Van Neely.

Others whose affection and support of my work have sustained me during the writing of this book: my family, Jeff Aydelette, John Barlow, Grace Cordts, Tom DeMarchi, Kathy Fagan Grandinetti, John Hales, Christy Hallberg and the late Bill Hallberg, Cheryl Huff, Jill Jennings, Lee and Jeffrey Johnson, Franny and Philip Levine, Derek Maher, Dan Marcucci, Flora Moorman, Wendy Osserman, Barry and Susan Saunders, Jane Saunders, the Fabulous Starlight Women, Karen Tolchin, Dympna Ugwu-oju, and Vance Wilson.

Dan for space to work, for love and patience.

And finally, in memoriam, my father, Lee Wieland (1927–2010).

Land *of* Enchantment

Brigid Long Night

1985

You can talk about most things, so they don't need to be painted. You can talk about a horse flying along the rim of the canyon above Taos, New Mexico, in stark moonlight. You can almost talk about a woman speaking to the edge of the universe and then waiting for the echo. But the smell of piñon? The rub of three small stones inside your boot? The sigh of Proterozoic feldspar, schist, and gneiss? The float of the baby inside you, the father long gone? A Navajo man in the doorway of the bar and his entrance into the noon sun. The cant of his drunk walk, the nearly *can't*, as if one leg were shorter, as if he's entertaining some muscle memory of tribal dance, leaning toward the fire, balancing a crown of feathers, the palsy in his wrist the old shake of beads inside a gourd. Follow him down the sidewalk to the blue truck where he stands a wavering moment, contemplating his image in the side mirror, and the shadow of the woman behind him. Her. Brigid Long Night. His daughter. His pregnant daughter.

"Those pictures she makes," his friend Fuentes said. "She's got a gift."

Her father spat in the dirt outside the post office, where he sorted the mail, and Fuentes carried it to the houses. "What she's got is a baby."

"It's in the air," Fuentes said. Then he looked into his empty mailbag. "I mean the gift."

In the air, in the water, in the amphibolite earth that stretched between her house and Miss Georgia O'Keeffe's house, three miles north. Brigid knew her by sight, walking with a companion on the far edges of her ranch. At night, sometimes Brigid heard music from the phonograph, slow violins, the high notes that traveled farthest.

Not in the air, Brigid thought. Inside me.

Her father in the bar, shaking his head, grey braid shivering, turning to look at her. Don't paint this. His eyes close slowly, and then open. The eyes are green, which she's always thought was crazy, wonderful, a sign. For an instant, the pink light in the bar turns silver, a wash of it, like an effect she's seen in black and white photographs, everything in the picture glazed as though the sun were shining on it hard, creating a shattering brightness, a silvery aura, as if the souls of people and objects were laid bare. Brigid leans over and touches the beer her father is drinking, draws her index finger across the label, spelling INERTIA in the condensation. "Save me from that," she whispers. "Indian inertia."

Her father raises his left hand, *how*, then folds the fingers down, a fist, a warning, a pledge, rage. He wants to know who the baby's father is. He asks her every day, the owl of his voice going *who, who, who*, but Brigid won't listen. She's too awed, frightened, and in love to tell him. And what would the name mean to him anyway, a white man he met once in the bar, the gringo friend of the famous painter?

Brigid saw first his reflection, shining in the shard of mirror balanced beside her easel.

Julian Granger, the painter from New York, invited by Miss O'Keeffe in the last year of her life, slipped like a knife into the room, in a flash of silver and black. He stopped behind her. He was very tall—she thought this at the time, though she later realized what she saw was the reach of his shadow. She was in the high school, in the art room, working on a painting of a red-haired woman in Hopi dress, seated below a window, the woman's head turned away from the light, so it shone not on the face but on the silver ring in the woman's ear.

Julian Granger asked quietly, "Why would Vermeer want to come to New Mexico?"

Brigid wondered how to answer such a question. What else am I supposed to paint, she thought, in this class, in this school, in this town?

She could say, *Vermeer's here because he likes the light.*

Or, *I don't copy anyone.*

She felt a sudden longing for her father, who would say the same thing, in his own vernacular. "That ain't a want. That's a need," he'd say.

"Nothing new under the sun." "A thing don't fix itself." Brigid knew her father was across town, in the United States Post Office, sorting mail in the cool back room, where the windows were small rectangles the size of bricks, very high up and tinted a light green. He was in some way responsible for Julian Granger's correspondence with Miss O'Keeffe. Her father had brought him here, as if all three of them had communicated through unopened letters, a language of touch and order. Her father had brought Julian Granger to New Mexico, and if Brigid saw it through, if she fixed things the right way, Julian Granger would help her escape.

And so that was why Brigid said to Julian Granger, "It's not a want. It's a need."

He stepped closer and his arm brushed hers, electricity moving along the points of contact. How to paint that? The crackle of attraction, the impossible chemistry.

"She's a redhead," he said. "That's unusual."

"It's my mother. German family. Schumann," Brigid said. "I wish we lived in a place where children can take the mother's name."

"You do," he said. "Show me some more."

Brigid brought another canvas from the storage closet.

"The color is spectacular. The purple and red. It assaults. It's an assault."

"Yes."

"The woman's face is a skull."

"It is."

"But there's something else wrong with her. What is it?"

"She's drunk."

"She's Indian. The braids. The body and legs. Like an apple on two sticks. The feathers around her waist, the amulets."

"She's Piuye."

"And she's drunk."

"She is."

Julian Granger turned from the canvas. He was smiling. "Why do you want to paint?" he said.

"I don't know. I'm trying to figure that out."

"You will. Right now, you have a lot of nerve," he said, and then he laughed. "You're going to get yourself in all sorts of trouble now, aren't you?"

"I might," Brigid said.

Sasha Hernandez

2001

Everybody in New York City remembered exactly what they were doing when the planes hit, and how they came to be doing it. Everyone had a story. Sasha's began the evening before in her dorm room, with its tenth-floor view of Broadway to Riverside Park, to the Hudson. Three sentences:

My biological mother is Brigid Schumann, the painter. She lived with us for two years when I was a baby, but I didn't know who she was, and then she left. I remember that she taught me the names of certain colors.

I can't write it, she said to Jennie, her roommate. Why do they need a life story? It's all in the application.

You can't not do the first assignment of your college career, Jennie said. Go talk to Fisk, the resident adviser. He'll help you.

She's your mother? Aaron Fisk said. Brigid Schumann is really your mother?

So I was told.

So write about her work.

I've never seen her work. Except in books. Or on a computer screen.

Then go see something. Tomorrow's supposed to be a beautiful day. Go see that big moving piece downtown, at the World Trade Center, on the plaza.

Red Sky/White Doe.

That one. Take your camera.

Sasha and Jennie could hear the sirens underground at the Chambers Street station, and sounds that might be human voices but might not be. Even so, they were enclosed in a kind of stillness, the subway train shut down, its doors frozen open, passengers moving through in an orderly fashion, out and in and out again, slowly, like sleepwalkers. Above ground, people stood in the street, gazing upward, appearing to talk on cell phones but not making any sound, their bags and briefcases dropped on the pavement. Jennie borrowed a phone and pressed it to her ear, thumb punching the redial button over and over. She said she knew her father was dead. She could tell by looking—what floors the plane went in and blew out as fire on the other side, blew her dad out as ash.

"We can't get any closer," Sasha said. "They won't let us."

"Who won't?" Jennie said and then she shouted into her phone, "Pick up, god damn it! Please pick up!" She held Sasha's hand and Sasha gripped hers.

"Are you calling your mom or your dad?" Sasha asked. Her voice rang too loudly all over the street and down into the black hole of the subway stairs, where it was lost.

"Both," Jennie told her. "Why don't they answer?"

Sasha wondered who she should call. She knew everyone was safe in Santa Fe, probably still in bed, except her uncle Edgardo who would be wide awake, praying his morning devotions, working on a sermon. He would have heard the news on NPR.

"They're jumping," a woman whispered beside them. "Oh my God." She began to moan and would not stop even after Sasha touched her arm and held her hand.

Jennie's dad would come to get her. Sasha remembered now that Jennie had said that last night. *On Tuesday my dad will come uptown for lunch. He said meet me at 116th and Broadway.* Jennie was on her hands and knees, beating the pavement with her fists, like the sidewalk was a door, and she could get it to open that way and let herself in. Or let her dad out. Her knuckles were bleeding, and when Sasha saw this, she knelt down too and put her arms around Jennie to keep her still. There was blood in Jennie's hair, on the tips of her blonde bangs, where she'd pushed them out of her eyes. A man stopped and looked at them, shook his head and moved on, north. A woman passed them, talking into a phone, saying she would walk to the Cloisters and that should be far enough. "But who knows," she cried. "Maybe they'll get us there too." No one screamed. The time for that seemed to have passed or not yet arrived. Instead, Sasha saw round empty eyes and round gaping mouths. These aren't really people, she thought. We aren't people. We are something else now, all of us. She stood and pulled her camera out of the bag, flicked the on switch, raised the camera to cover her face. She thought the phrase, I can catch them on film.

Nancy Diamond

1 9 9 6

You can see me in all the networks' videotapes, holding Alice Hawthorne in my arms while her daughter screams. If you look closely, you can see part of the nail that flew into her head, out of the pipe bomb, out of the backpack, out of the night in Centennial Park. It's the Olympics in Atlanta, and you'd think everybody was a track medalist, sprinting to the exits. But I caught her, I caught Alice as she fell, and there's a weird happiness racing through me. I think maybe I can save her life. "Henry!" I'm yelling to my brother. "Look at the map! How do we get out of here?" I'm lifting Alice up off of the bricks. She's light as a feather. Her daughter is saying, "Mom, Mom, Mom. Oh God, Mom. I love you, I love you." Henry is unfolding the map, but it's really too dark to see. "This way," he shouts, gathering Alice, gathering her daughter and me. We're all carrying and being carried, all one inside the same body.

I'm seeing it like an odd kind of play. This is how I tended to see the world: outside of time, two people talking. People who can't really, wouldn't normally talk to each other.

Alice Hawthorne, please speak to me.

Oh honey, Alice says, I'm done in. I'm done. But this. This here is my little girl. Hold her hand. It's got to be some magic. Take her hand. Open up your hand, honeychild. Her hand goes here.

After that, I saw Alice everywhere, even in myself, and it came to be that I couldn't quite understand my own face anymore, like it was dipped in the shadow of Alice. I thought maybe I had what my parents, an architect and a painter, would call a vision problem. Faces seemed to change overnight, grow longer or shorter like in a funhouse mirror, or darker, like someone had turned off a light. My mother, for instance. Changed. She had recently become interested in wearing makeup. She had been fitted for contact lenses, too, after having worn glasses for ten years, and she struggled through months of adjustments, Optilense, Accuvue, hard lenses, soft, disposable, dailies, admitting she didn't see as well, but maybe that would be good for her painting. I had to say my mother looked both prettier and younger. She could be our older sister, Henry's and mine, but he was eighteen and I was seventeen, so we had absolutely no interest in a sibling mother.

Her work was changing too, starting to get more attention. She was a part of little group shows all over Atlanta. A critic in the *Journal-Constitution* wrote that one of her paintings was the love child of Jan Vermeer and Georgia O'Keeffe. I could see this going on in her still lifes, the ones she called *Obsolescence*, as if Vermeer had been less interested in the women he painted than in the flowers on the tables beside them, poppy and calla lily, morning glory and Dutch iris blooming out of huge canvases, all lit from an invisible window above and to the left. "Love child" was a good word for it, that electric conjunction, like marriage but with a hitch, a stumble.

After this review, she had her most important show in one of the new galleries on Tenth Street. Mostly it was the work of her old friend Simon Anderson, who looked exactly like an Asian Arthur Ashe, the tennis player, and painted birds in ornate Victorian-seeming cages. Dad stayed home, alone in the house, which was a geodesic dome of his own designing. Henry and I rode in the limo Simon rented for her, and we pretended that she was the star and we were her glowing acolytes. She drank too much wine and ignored us. Henry, who had started painting himself and really was her disciple, wandered away into another room at the heart of the gallery. I followed him into this space, into a surreal and beautiful quiet, though the canvases appeared to be shouting. Most had large black words stenciled on them, like signs in restricted or unsafe places. "Wow," Henry said. "Not my thing," and he turned back to Mom's show. I couldn't move, though, captured by a painting of an American Indian, all purples and reds and yellowy-oranges. He was holding up a bottle of beer with the word INERTIA on the label, offering it to the viewer. The next canvas depicted the Lone Ranger and Tonto. Above the Lone Ranger's head, large black letters read TONTO, GO TO TOWN. Above Tonto's head, the letters read KISS MY ASS. I loved how she did that, this painter named Brigid Schumann. She became my mantra, *Brigid Schumann, Brigid Schumann,* and my muse, the way she made up speech for people who couldn't or wouldn't say those things.

> *The setting is Heaven or a place very like it. Jan Vermeer and Georgia O'Keeffe enter from opposite sides of the stage, dressed alike in back trousers and billowing white shirts. They are backlit, in such a way that their shadows stretch out and cover the audience. The stage, though bare, is painted the medium blue of O'Keeffe's* From the Faraway Nearby.

VERMEER AND GEORGIA (*in unison*): What did she say? The love
    child?
G: Well, can you believe that?
V: Nice to meet you too.
G: After all these years.
V: How many?
G: 311, but who's counting?
V: How have you been?
G: Quiet. And you?
V: Lonely.

My early plays, like my life, are long on prologue and short on denouement. I wanted, more than anything, to fix that imbalance of time, but it's not easy, as you, the living, must surely know. A play can only go forward. If you're seeing it, you can't look back. I want to look back, capture that moment the viewer can't have and has already forgotten. I want to live in that escaped moment. Be it. Think of Orpheus before he caused his wife to fall into hell, Orpheus in the moment between turning to look and seeing. Orpheus before the loud noise—what was the shape or sound it made? Was it a crack of thunder or a din of bells? Or was it the kind of whine that only dogs can hear. How could you stage it?

And maybe I want to be his wife too, Eurydice, because she must have seen all colors, all shapes, all contrast, all ecstatic movement before she spun back underground. I'd like to see that too, take in that enormous vision, and then have eternity to sort it out.

Which makes me think of other hell-bound girls. Persephone, for instance, and her anticipation, a whir and warmth beginning in her feet, her ankles, up her smooth calves, making a splash in the whirlpool of her knees, drifting up her white thighs like fingers. To where. To where Hades is, will be.

Persephone because, like me, she must surely be compensated for all that darkness and lost youth.

So I wanted to put them in a play, Eurydice and Persephone. I liked the idea of bringing together people who never dreamed of being able to talk to each other. What would they say?

EURYDICE: How do we get back?
PERSEPHONE: Where's the map?

Henry would know. My brother, Henry Diamond, is the last true cartographer on earth. He paints maps. He says there's a map inside of everyone. He can make the old dead map inside you come alive again. He paints maps people don't even know they need, maps of places that can't be seen with the naked eye or any other kind of eye.

Your soul, for instance.

Henry started painting maps because he liked to tell people where to go. Who doesn't? But mostly he loved land, places you could get to and see, or when that wasn't possible, touch gently with your finger, the raised ridges on a globe, which he said felt alive to him. That year, 1996, he started to keep a list of words that began or ended in *land*. He wrote them on scraps of paper or on the chalkboard our mother hung in the kitchen to remind her what to forget or ignore. Singly or in pairs, these words took on larger life. Bottomland, homeland, dreamland. Or they made a small, secret poem: wetland, Shetland, hinterland, winterland. For a couple of weeks, the name Scott Weiland hung in the air, and Dad asked us at dinner, "What is a stone temple pilot?" The roller skating rink in Atlanta was called Playland, and out loud Henry wondered why. "But it sounds like your kind of place, Nance. Your kind of heaven. Playland," he told me, though I was a terrible skater. "It's all work and no play at Playland," I used to say until one day a boy I knew invited me into the darkened storage room, deep and warm, enchanted. Buckets of wood soap and dis-embodied skate wheels, bags of hot chocolate mix and popcorn kernels. Now find your way out, he whispered, stepping closer. I said I didn't think I wanted to. I wanted to stay where I was in this deep heart of Playland and take my chances.

Brigid

People talked about her gift at the bar in Española too, most Saturday nights, when she arrived to take her father home. Everybody said she was a good daughter even in trouble like she was. They all wished for such a child, but got only boys or nothing at all. Then Fuentes, whose wife was a year dead, asked Brigid to marry him. She stood between her father and Fuentes, waiting for her father to finish his last beer, drink up the last shot, running her thumb along the wooden rim of the bar. The whole place seemed softly joyous, the little light there gone pearly in the haze of cigarette smoke. The radio music was turned lower than usual. Fuentes wore a pale blue denim shirt with amber snaps. His hair was combed back and held with a leather tie. Since his wife's death, he'd let his hair grow, and it now reached to the middle of his back. But tonight he was coming out of mourning—he leaned over and whispered this in Brigid's ear, and damn she looked beautiful, even in her condition, and would she marry him? He would be a good father, he said. Yes, he said, he would save her from inertia.

Fuentes waited, and she looked at him, his wind-worn face. He had a daughter in her class at school. He was already a good father. He carried the mail all over town and never missed a day of work and knew everybody. His wife had assisted at home births, working beside the priest Father Edgardo in kitchens and bedrooms to clean and bless the newborns, and so her death was a shock, a kind of injustice, an affront to all of Española. At her funeral, even Father Edgardo had seemed angry. In the middle of the eulogy, he lost sight of the words and swore. Fuentes was standing beside him at the pulpit. He reached over and put his hand on Father Edgardo's shoulder, as if to steady him. Father Edgardo recovered, found his place. That was Fuentes' gift: he was a walking map. He could help you find out where you were. But Brigid didn't want a map. She knew where she was. She wanted a ticket.

Someone called to Fuentes, and he looked away from Brigid, struck up a new conversation. His proposal hung in the air, also silvery, exposed, shimmering. Like the Holy Ghost, she thought, or the presence of Fuentes' dead wife, drifting here, waiting without voice or intent, to see what Brigid would do. She turned to her father, slung her right arm around his shoulders. She pressed her cheek against his and told him it was time to go home.

"You damn kids," Brigid's father said, pushing her away. "Look at you. You get yourselves in trouble. You and your brother both. You don't care about nothing. You don't know this place. You won't learn the language. You don't even look like us."

"That's not their fault," Fuentes said, laughing. "You married a red-headed German. You watered them down."

"What're you taking her side for?" her father said. "What you got to do with it anyway?"

"Nothing," Fuentes said, "except I've seen her all my life, and she's a good girl."

"And just how do you come to know if she's a good girl? Just what are you saying there?"

"Dad," Brigid said.

"And her mother too," Fuentes told him. "Damn fine women."

"Take me home," Brigid's father said.

"Let me," Fuentes said and offered his arm.

"Enough of you," Brigid's father said. He shoved Fuentes back against the bar. "Ain't you done enough harm already?"

"He hasn't done anything," Brigid said.

"Oh yeah? I think he done plenty."

The rest of that night comes back to her as if they were acting in a play. A play is a kind of magic. Watching it, you're dragged along. You can't go back and undo the action, change the cause. You have to get it all the first time, the only time. Brigid's father and mother, and Fuentes, the three colors of them. Her father dark as cherrywood; her mother's light skin, her red hair going to gray; Fuentes, the Mexican, coffee with cream. But the darkest thing in the room is the pistol her father takes from the kitchen drawer, black and large in his hand, a puzzle of potential, like a coiled snake.

Then there is shouting. Her father accuses Fuentes, and her mother laughs. Her father strides across the room, weaves, hesitates. He takes aim at Fuentes, and then slaps her mother. Fuentes lunges forward—Brigid is sure her father never intended to shoot, but he does, and Fuentes is on the floor, his face torn open.

"You get out of here," her mother cries, "Get out. Go on."

Her father starts toward the door, turns back. "This is my house," he says and fires again.

Her mother moves away, her hands crossed on her breastbone and blossoming red. At first, Brigid thinks it's her mother's tubercular lungs finally giving out, but then she registers the second shot. Her mother shouts something, a foreign sound. Maybe it isn't words in any language, maybe it's just pure meaning, and her father looks at his wife, at Fuentes, looks at the gun in his hand as if it's something he will never be able to recognize. He's like a child, Brigid thinks and feels a small breath of relief until her father's gaze swings toward her, and his eyes say, remember how a child first knows the world, and he opens his mouth and puts the barrel of the gun inside and pulls the trigger.

Brigid and her brother Theo are watching this play. Theo is wearing a plum-colored cotton shirt, and Brigid will remember that shirt like a ribbon moving about the room, trying to tie up all the spilt and broken parts of his parents.

Paint that. Go on. Her mother's last words. Paint. It's the only way to understand anything.

She hardly left the house before the baby came, and always she felt a vague, small sense of companionship. She believed the baby inside her was a girl and talked to her quietly, all day long, calling her "Sasha." This had disturbed Theo until he finally asked Brigid to stop, saying all the conversation would make it harder to give the baby up. And when the time came for that, Father Edgardo arranged it, and brought Brigid to the rectory to meet a lawyer and sign the papers. She wrote her name on the line they pointed to. The words on the pages were a sad monotony, a blur. The next morning, before sunrise, the baby was born at home, in the kitchen where her mother and father and Fuentes had died, another awful rush of blood and fear. But not crying. The baby entered the world silently. She took a breath and opened her eyes and did not make a sound.

"A girl," the midwife said. "Just like you thought."

"Is she alive?" Brigid asked. "Is she all right?"

"She's one of the quiet ones. It doesn't happen very often, but sometimes."

"Her hair's gold," Theo said, tracing the circumference of the baby's head with his fingertip. "I have to get to work."

"You don't want to be here when they come?"

"I don't think I could stand it."

That afternoon, the husband's eyes filled with tears as he took Sasha out of Brigid's arms. His wife, Sasha's new mother, didn't trust herself to hold a baby. She'd said that, but Brigid didn't believe her. She believed it was something else, some other feeling, a kindness, to make a man stand in between the two mothers. The woman's dress was pale yellow and loose around her thin body, almost a nightgown, as if she'd woken into her own dream of having a child. Her hair, too, a little mussed, her face creased as if she'd been asleep. And maybe she had been. The woman's name was Beatriz and the man's name was Francisco, a name that suited him, delicate, saintly. Brigid liked it that Sasha's new mother's name also began with B, that her new father had the name of the famous protector of animals, the saint whose body had never corrupted. He held the baby very carefully, the pink bundle of her, and Sasha still did not make a sound. Brigid thought she must be holding her breath, waiting to see what would happen next. Against the dark suit Francisco wore, and in his brown hands, the bundle of Sasha looked like an opening into his body, a gaping hole. Something large could pass through there. He needed Sasha to fill him in.

Francisco did not hand the baby to Beatriz until they were outside the house, about to get into their car. First Beatriz bent and disappeared inside, and then Sasha. The car door closed. Francisco walked around to the driver's side door. He looked back at the house. Brigid did not know if he could see her standing beside the front window—he couldn't, she believed at first, because it was afternoon, and the light silvered the window, seemed to set it on fire. Even though he could not see her, Francisco looked directly at the window. Then he did the most extraordinary thing. He blew a kiss, one and then another, and finally a third.

When Francisco and Beatriz drove away with Sasha, Brigid was alone for the first time in nearly a year, and she felt a searing, frantic emptiness. Hunger, she thought, feels like this and brings a certain clear vision. The sky looked unbearably bright, the sun a yellow mouth that might swallow her. She stared at the patch of ground where Francisco had stood, and it seemed his kisses still hung in the air, strange blooms where the brightness grew pink or multicolored and wavering, like the rainbow oil makes on the road. She was overcome by dizziness, as if she were floating. The mountains deepened into an uneven purple, jagged at the edges, a child's drawing. Someday Sasha would color mountains this way, and the patchy green sagebrush below. Brigid imagined her child's concentration and perfect imprecision. She stood still at the window, trying to see the world Sasha would make.

And all at once it came to her, what she was waiting for. She was waiting for the car to return. She was waiting for Francisco and Beatriz to realize the shattering thing they had done, the crime they had committed, turn their car around and bring Sasha back. She could see it, not quite a movie going backwards, not the halting, comical reversal, but a kind of overpainting. The first canvas had been wrong, bad, ugly, not what the assignment required. It must be painted over, so that no one would see anything of the first attempt. She stood waiting for their car until the sun set.

When the house was lost in total darkness, and Theo had not returned, she opened the front door and stepped outside. The night was clear, and a gibbous moon hung over the mountains, like a belly, she thought, and touched her own. She would walk to the fence at Miss O'Keeffe's. This moon would light the path.

Just then a vehicle turned into the driveway. Brigid hated to think what her face must look like, caught in the headlights, and then her heart blossomed—it felt that way, a muscle opening, revealing itself to be full of small, secret parts. She took a breath and recognized the angry rattle of Theo's truck. And so there was nothing to do but stand and wait for his frank glance at her, and then, later, around the house, into the small cradle Sasha had used, his horrible *making sure*. She waited for Theo to get out, come up close and ask if she were all right, but he stayed where he was.

Brigid went to the truck. Theo had rolled down the window, and his elbow lay on the door like the point of an arrow. In that moment, the wrong phrase appeared in her mind: *the point of an error*. The confusion made her smile, and Theo smiled back. He reached out and touched Brigid's shoulder.

"It's too hard," he said. "Mama felt bad. She said it was part her fault for not keeping a closer eye on you."

"I miss her," Brigid said. "I don't think I can let her go." Theo nodded. She leaned her forehead on his arm. Tears leaked out of her eyes. They came and came, silently, until Theo's sleeve was soaked. They listened to the night, the gasp of birds' wings, questions from the coyotes, two of them on opposite sides of the canyon, a faint scurrying across the gravel behind the truck. A little wind trying to be larger.

"You think you'll hear her, don't you?" Theo said. Brigid nodded into her brother's arm. "You think if you listen long enough and hard enough, you'll hear her crying, wherever she is, and you'll go find her, and then she'll stop."

"Yes," Brigid whispered.

"But that won't happen, Brij. And you know why it won't happen?"

"Why?"

"Because she's not crying," Theo said. "She's asleep. And she's warm, and in a good place with people who love her already. You won't hear her because she's not crying."

"How could you let me give her away?"

"I'm moving you along," Theo said. "Remember that word you like, *inertia*? I'm saving us from that."

The painting came to her then, almost complete, including the color, which had been flickering off to the side of her vision for days. A vivid cranberry, blood with purple in it. An Indian, two braids, his shirt made out of an American flag, his face a grinning skull, a death's head. He was walking down a street, at the edge of the curb, one foot balanced, unbalanced, over the gutter. He gripped a beer bottle. The name of the beer, visible on the label, was INERTIA, in stencil, or maybe letters like on a soup can.

This painting would not make her popular, or else it would.

Nancy

The shadow of Alice Hawthorne grew large enough to hang over our whole house. Our father had been the chief architect of Centennial Park, responsible, he liked to say, for making the city of Atlanta beautiful, for covering all of Atlanta's hatred and racism with flowers, shrubs, grass that neither grew nor died, trees from every nation on earth.

"But now," he said, "all anyone will remember is that the poor woman died there."

"And in a way, that's fitting," our mother said. "Black people in Atlanta have the authentic experience."

"What do you mean?" our father said. He dropped the newspaper in his lap and brought his fists down on it. The paper made a sound like breaking glass. Henry and I heard this out in the kitchen where we were doing homework. We took note.

"It's what Simon's paintings are about," she said.

"Simon paints colored birds in cages."

"Exactly. Slaves of one kind or another have always made this city possible."

"That's a disturbing thought, Ella."

"Art was made to disturb people. But then what you do—measuring, angles, mathematics—reassures them. Until they find out that's made up too."

"So you paint to disturb?"

"I paint so I can forget life. The only time I'm alive is when I'm painting."

"You're not making any sense."

"The enemy of creativity is good sense."

"Fuck this."

"And you know what else? Blasphemy and prayer are the same thing because they make God real."

"Aren't you afraid you'll go to hell?" our father said.

"Not a bit."

"You should be."

Then he accused her of having an affair. Simon, he said. He used the word *again*. In the kitchen, Henry and I made ourselves very small and still. We listened, even though we really didn't want to.

"Mark," our mother said. "You have to stop."

"Simon the painter?" I whispered and Henry nodded.

We hoped our parents would just ignore us, maybe for the rest of our lives. We prayed to be forgotten, each one, quietly. Please God. Then our father answered, as if he heard our little blasphemes, as if he were the big Our Father.

"You know I can't forget. Nancy. . . . You know. The hair. And the eyes."

Our mother didn't even tell him to keep his voice down. I wrote Henry a note in the margin of the newspaper: What's the deal? What about the eyes?

"Sometimes I think I might want to become a stylite," Henry said. "These saints who lived on pillars, about six feet wide at the top. They could sort of watch over everything. Think of the view."

"Henry," I said, "I feel a painting coming on." That's how he worked. He found out about something obscure, and obsessed about it. Then he disappeared into his room for a few days. A huge part of me hated it, that he seemed to forget I was around. "But what about the eyes?"

Henry stood up from the kitchen table. He looked at me as if he were deciding something momentous, then he turned and walked down the hall. I heard the door to his room click shut.

Our father got up and walked into the kitchen. He poured himself another scotch.

"Nancy," he asked, shouting the question so our mother could hear, "are you afraid of going to hell?"

"I am," I said. It seemed like the best answer, the answer he wanted.

"See?" our father said.

And so it was decided: we should know the difference between blasphemy and prayer. Henry and I could use some religious training. Our father enrolled us in the youth group at the Catholic church, Our Lady of the Assumption. Youth group met on Sunday nights at the leader's house, people actually named Christensen. We attended once, ate the Cheetos and drank the Cokes, said the prayers, listened to the other kids talk about how much they loved Jesus.

"I call bullshit," I said as soon as we got to—not even in—the car. "I go to school with those kids. I know what they love, and it's not Jesus. I'm not going back."

"But we have to," Henry said.

"Why?" It wasn't really a question. Henry was quiet. I knew he was getting with the program, into the spirit, as it were.

"We'll get in trouble, Nance."

"Not if we don't get caught." We didn't talk about it again.

At 6:30 the next Sunday evening, I yelled to Henry that we had to get going. We left the house in a little bit of a rush, called good-bye to our mother, painting in her studio, waved to our father, who was reading the newspaper in his halo of lamplight. We got in the car. I was driving, even though Henry was older. He was a terrible driver, too easily distracted by road signs, by whatever flashed into his peripheral vision. The youth group leader's house was at the other end of our neighborhood. You could get to the house directly or, actually faster, by leaving the neighborhood, traveling down Peachtree Road and turning left back into the clutch of houses off Ashford-Dunwoody. I headed for Peachtree.

Henry said, "So you decided to go after all."

"Watch," I said.

I turned left across from Cherokee Plaza, where one day in the future there would be a Starbucks and a gay bookstore, drove north on Peachtree, past the next two strip malls, which would one day transform themselves into a condominium neighborhood called "Neighborhood." I made a left into the parking lot of Burger King.

"Do you want fries with that?" I asked Henry, anticipating by some years the joke about excess. Henry nodded, dumbstruck and deeply frightened. We ate in silence, shared a Coke—which we both detested—in order to get the proper scent of adult-supervised teenage group activity. I dabbed a little behind my ears.

At 8 p.m., we disposed of the evidence and headed home. "We're back!" I called, as I opened the kitchen door. Henry followed, cringing, expecting a shriek from our mother and the silent menace of our dad.

"How was it?" our mother sang back from the living room, where she sat, now enshrined in her own halo. She was sketching something odd: a woman holding a puppy on her lap.

"Fine," I said.

"Okay," Henry said.

Later, as she turned off the light in my room, my mother asked again. "Really, now. How was it?" and then, less welcome, "What did you do?"

"Not much," I said, glad for the darkness. "Kids lie about how much they love Jesus."

"Hmmm," my mother said. She lingered, sat down on the edge of my bed. "Do *you*? Because you know, that's all right. Everybody does it."

"No way," I said. "I just listen."

My mother seemed relieved and wished me a good night.

All the next week, Henry and I observed a code of silence. Even though we had ample opportunity to discuss and plan, we didn't. We exchanged no meaningful glances. If anything, we spoke to each other less than usual. On Sunday at dinner, our father asked if we had any youth group homework. We looked at each other, really for the first time in days, baffled, until our mother said, "Now Mark, why would they have youth group homework? What would it be, read the Bible? Can you see any teenagers doing that?"

Our father nodded in sad agreement. "You're right," he said. "What the hell was I thinking?"

By 7:15, Henry and I were settled in the Burger King parking lot with a large Coke and a bag of fries.

"That was interesting at dinner," Henry said. "Maybe we should just tell them we don't want to go."

"Do you want to go?" I said.

"No. Why?" Henry flicked a burnt fry out the window.

"I'm just checking, Henry. I don't want to decide for you."

"That's okay," Henry said, and I wondered, forever after, if he meant it was okay for me to decide for him.

That night back at home, it was the same as the week before: vague questions, vague answers, our parents somewhere else even while their bodies were present.

All that week, our father often followed his second scotch with a third. Wednesday night he yelled at our mother about something he remembered she'd said ten years before, a comment that sounded to me rather sweet and sympathetic. On Friday night, he started an argument about taking her picture, how it was obvious she didn't really like any of the photos he'd taken of her, even though she always used them for publicity. "You loved the ones Simon took, Ella," he said.

"Yes," she told him. "I did. Note the past tense, Mark."

The weeks of missed youth group turned into a month and a half. Henry and I got to be regulars at Burger King, fries and a Coke, same every time. One week the burger jockey said to me, "He kiss you yet?"

I felt the world spin off its axis for a moment. "He's my brother," I said, my nose and mouth suddenly filling with the scent of grease, as if I were drowning in it

"That right?" the burger flipper said. "You here every week like you on a *date* with that white boy."

Henry was waiting outside, hunched down in the car in case someone we knew drove in or passed by. I wondered about the appearances of things. White boy? How could Henry and I ever be mistaken for two people on a date? Later I would know exactly what the burger jockey saw: our intensity, the aura of fear and betrayal that must have surrounded us. That one of us was leading the other astray. That I was other than white.

I read this David Mamet play called *Bobby Gould in Hell*. Bobby Gould is consigned to Hell, and he has to be interviewed to find out how long he's going to spend there. The Devil is called back from a fishing trip to interview Bobby Gould. And so the Devil is there, the Assistant Devil is there, and Bobby Gould. And the Devil finally says to Bobby Gould, "You're a very bad man." And Bobby Gould says, "Nothing's black and white." And the Devil says, "Nothing's black and white, nothing's black and white—what about a panda? What about a panda, you dumb fuck! What about a fucking panda!"

I can't believe I didn't get it. You get it already, don't you? Nothing's black and white? Nothing's black and white? What about a love child?

I started work on a play about a meeting that may or may not have taken place between Emily Dickinson and Louisa May Alcott. Somehow being in Atlanta in 1996 made me imagine western Massachusetts, in 1885. I considered calling it "Stairway to Heaven," which would be the punch line of a joke Lou tells Emily. It was a play about women who loved their fathers way too much and also didn't quite know who they were. It was not autobiographical, not exactly. I'd had the last lines in my head for years.

EMILY: Lou. You have to tell me the truth. Did I miss anything?
LOU *(beat, tilts her head into a bright light)*: No. *(beat)* Nothing.

Sasha

At first, she believed her film of bodies falling from the World Trade Center would have to be silent. Whose voice could you put behind images like these? What could you say anyway? The only words Sasha could think of were "Please help me." Too little, too late. Jennie was gone, home to Long Island to be with her mother, to wait for her father, to hope, to realize he was dead, and then to try to plan a funeral without a body. Sasha stayed up at night in the computer lab, transferring the video to DVD, stabilizing, playing with speed, slowing everything down. It felt like falling backward into a world without speech, a soft bed, the embrace of her mother. Beatriz. Not Brigid Schumann. We are all living in fiction, she told herself. We are in some imaginary world. There is no reality. Columbia's classes began over. No one seemed to take attendance, no calling out of names—too much absence already. So you could wander into a lecture you hadn't registered for, sit awhile, leave if the spirit moved you or moved out of you. The Intro to Film class wasn't open to first-year students, but Sasha went anyway. Cinema loves the surface of things, the professor said. And it's a sort of hyperreality. We're drawn to films because we want to know a thing really happened. Because we spend so much of our lives in uncertainty.

Why are you drawn to these scenes, the last performances of other people? the film teacher in high school had asked her. Why do you want to film this stuff, Sasha, this unspeakable? You have so much talent. That eagle eye. But the subject. Cavalier. His name was Wayne, and he let the kids call him that. He was obviously the smartest person in the whole school, that movie-book-computer smart combination that threatened at any moment to collapse into full-scale geek but never did. Or never in public. He had escaped from a tiny godforsaken town, he said, to the big city, *La Ciudad del Dio,* he called Santa Fe. At graduation, he gave Sasha a hug and said, Now get the hell to the real big city and do something unspeakable.

Unspeakable.

That's exactly why somebody would be drawn to the final moments, to make it all say something.

Two months before, when it was clear that her mother wouldn't live, Sasha set up the video camera, the Sony DCR-TRV11 they gave her for graduation. Her mother in bed, her father's voice in the background, "What are you doing?" But not angry, not even really interested in the answer to his question. "We'll want this," Sasha's voice says, though she's not onscreen either. Her mother, eyes closed, seems to wake then, turns her head slowly toward the camera. "What is it?" she says. The camera zooms in, so that her face fills the frame. Sasha asks questions, which she will edit out later, most of them, causing the first part of the film to run like a monologue. She leaves the edits rough, as jumps in the video, so that it seems her mother twitches between questions. It's not pretty, but Sasha wants this. It's never pretty, the end.

I had no life before you, her mother says. I worked in this hotel, and then I married the owner's son. His first son. Then I owned the hotel too, the place where I used to clean the toilets. I owned the toilets! Her mother laughs. She had a wonderful laugh, complicated, spoons in pottery bowls and glasses touching at the rims. We drove up in the mountains above Taos to get you, and I didn't want to hold you at first because I was afraid. And you never made a sound, and that scared me too. But then I finally did hold you, and I never got tired of it. And you did talk, and I never got tired of that either. Remember when you were in elementary school, and we'd get there early and sit in the car and you'd get in my lap even though you were too big and the steering wheel was in the way?

At home by myself, I would miss you all day. No, that's not true. I would miss you for a minute walking out of the school building, but then whole hours would pass and I wouldn't have a single thought about you. I don't know what I did all day. We were in a talking movie, and then when I left you, after the last flash of your little red head, I would go to silence, and then at three o'clock when you walked out of the school, I would go back to sound, noise, conversation. I baked bread sometimes. I did the laundry. I made our beds.

Yes, yes, yes.

Sasha's mother lifts her hands from her sides and curls the fingers away into fists. I put my hands into soft things trying to find out where you were. That's what I did in silence before you brought the sound back in.

Where was I? Sasha's father's voice asks.

Here. There. Nowhere. Counting. Fixing. Reading. Driving away.

That's me all right, Sasha's father says.

Church? No, that was your brother. That little church in Taos.

After this, there is no talking for a while. Sasha's mother looks into the camera, blinks sometimes, looks away without turning her head. Two full minutes of no talking, which is a long time in film. Am I dying? her mother asks. No one answers, but she says, I thought so.

What else, Mom? Sasha asks.

Nothing, her mother says.

Sasha turned off the camera and crawled into bed beside her mother. She lay with her head on her mother's chest. Her father sat down on the other side of the bed half turned away from them. He reached back to take his wife's hand. Sasha listened to her mother's breathing. The sound seemed to come from a cave deep inside the earth where there is the life of heat and rock. You know this cave is there but also you know that you could never reach it. She lifted her head then, to look at her mother's face, memorize it. There were pictures, she reminded herself, video-tapes, and she lowered her head again so that her left cheekbone pressed against her mother's sternum. Bone to bone, it felt like, the beginning of dust to dust.

Beatriz exhaled. Stillness then, and Sasha said, Mom! Her mother inhaled. For five minutes, Sasha told her mother to breathe in this way, and Beatriz did. Exhale. Command. Resume. The startled intake of air.

Sasha, her father said. You have to let her. Sasha turned her head slightly to look up at him.

I can't let her, she said. She has to do it. Her father nodded. Dad, she said. Turn the camera back on.

Her father shook his head, the smallest gesture, like palsy.

Please, Sasha whispered, and a hiss came into her mother's breathing.

Her father leaned away, flicked the on switch with his index finger. The camera hummed.

Mom! Sasha said, and her mother breathed. A shadow trembled on the wall behind the camera. Sasha counted. One more breath. One more. And then none. Her mother's body let go, and then seemed to press upward against Sasha's cheek. Loss of gravity, she thought. The old laws no longer apply. Oh, she said, oh Mom, don't go. Please don't go.

Sasha, her father said, and reached to turn off the camera. But all he did, in fact, was shut off the microphone. So there was more to see when Sasha finally felt brave enough to play the tape. Some fifteen minutes of Sasha and her father saying good-bye to Beatriz. Two bodies, one dark, one light, both living, attempting to—it appeared—climb inside a darker body that was not.

Sasha wondered if she should forget about college, stay home and take care of her father, but he told her no, there was nothing new for her in Santa Fe. But after a long afternoon of silent drinking, he asked Sasha, "Why do you want to go so far away?"

"I won't leave," Sasha said.

"That was the booze talking," her father said later. "Maybe now I think I want you close by, but in a few weeks I'll regret it. You'll regret it. Maybe not today."

"*Casablanca*," Sasha said.

"You know," her father said, "that's exactly why you have to go." He smiled in the sad, conspiratorial way his brother Edgardo used for assigning penance. And then he said the really crazy thing. "You know your mother's in New York."

At first, Sasha thought he'd lost his mind. She wanted to slap him, knock him back into this world. "My mother's not in New York. How can you say that? My mother's not anywhere."

Then it all came out. Who her mother was, Brigid Schumann. Who she had been. Brigid Long Night, that was her Navajo name. Navajo. And how close she had been: working on her first paintings in the hotel, holding little Sasha in her arms.

"The painter?"

Her father nodded.

Sasha knew her: under forty but already famous for paintings with words on them, sculpture that moved or balanced, as if defying gravity. "She needed to get out of Española," her father said.

"Española?" Sasha repeated.

"It was my brother's idea."

"And how fucked up is that?" Sasha said. Swearing at her own father, she heard herself, away from herself. Worse than swearing. Obscenity.

Her father bowed his head. He tried to take hold of Sasha's hand, but she wouldn't let him. "We thought it made sense then," he said. "Edgardo and I. I don't quite understand now, but it did make sense at the time."

"Is that the best you can do?" Sasha yelled. "That's fucking lame. Fucking halt and fucking lame. There's language Uncle Edgardo can understand."

So, she thought. So. So. So. Like a pause in the universe, an empty space she would have to fill. Or a place erased waiting to be redrawn. So. So. So. Her mind skipped and caught, a rough film, images blipping, piling on top of one another. This lasted for hours, for days, she wasn't sure. It didn't matter. Two mothers. One. Two. Two mothers. Both missing.

So. So, now that it turns out I'm a little Indian, I'll be a good little Indian, do like they do. She drove her father's car to the grocery and picked out a big jug of wine, the cheapest there was, the ugliest label. Then she put it back, in favor of beauty, a label like a work of art, a painting of a Navajo woman, long dark hair flowing past her face, transformed into calla lilies over her chest. And a higher alcohol content. She stuffed the bottle in her backpack and drove straight to the high school, toted her pack into the library. And it was the greatest feeling, she thought, wine in the library, and it ain't in a book, ain't a word, ain't in the dictionary. She passed through fiction and reference, back, back, into the hole-in-the-wall cave of Wayne's A/V room. She shut the door.

Wayne looked up from his computer screen, not surprised, Sasha noticed, but curious, appreciative in a way, ready. He'd told her his mom died when he was Sasha's age. He said he remembered how it felt, that the worst of it hits you later.

"So guess what, Wayne?"

"Trouble," he said. "More trouble."

And she told him, all the while making a show, easing the backpack off one shoulder and then the other, fumbling with the zippers, reaching in and drawing the wine out slowly. She observed a moment when he thought she might have a weapon, but it was interesting, watching Wayne think in that geek way of his, like a ticker tape running at the bottom of a screen, but not horizontal. More like columns that add up and add up and add up, and Wayne was waiting patiently for the sum.

"Oh, shit," she said.

And he knew. "No corkscrew?" Sasha nodded. "I have one. But here's the deal. You can use it if you stay here until you're done, and then we assess."

Sasha said all right. Wayne opened the drawer of his desk and drew out a Swiss Army knife. "Every tool you could ever want. Totally geek." He held out his hand for the bottle.

"I can do it," she said.

Wayne watched silently. Sasha knew she looked ridiculous as she struggled with the cork, holding the bottle between her feet for leverage. When the bottle was open, she realized she'd also forgotten about a cup, so she held it to her lips and tipped it up. The wine tasted better than she thought it would, better than Uncle Edgardo's communion vintage, which was like old syrup. Wayne reached into the cabinet beside his desk and brought out a coffee mug.

"*Land of Enchantment*, it says here. Perfect."

Sasha poured and drank. Without students, the school seemed to make a kind of purring sound.

"Let me see that bottle," Wayne said.

"No way. No Wayne."

"I'll give it back. Have I ever lied to you?"

"No. But there's always a first time."

"There isn't always a first time, Sasha. Really. Come on. I just want to test your senses." She gave him the bottle, and waited while he read the label. He handed the bottle back. "Okay, take a sip, a little sip. Then tell me what you taste."

Sasha took a mouthful of wine, held it, swallowed. "Cake," she said. "Breakfast."

"Not bad," Wayne said. "They call it vanilla. Anything else?"

Sasha drank again. "Like fruit salad. The kind in the can."

"Pear," Wayne said. "You're pretty good."

They were quiet for a little while. Wayne opened his desk again and pulled out a package of cheese crackers, and lobbed it at Sasha.

"Wine and cheese," he said. "I understand back east, they call these 'Nabs.'"

"What?" Sasha said. "That's ridiculous."

"It is," Wayne agreed. "All these crackers are made by Nabisco. Hence, Nabs. Like all carbonated drinks are 'Coke.' Take, eat, as your uncle would say."

"How do you know my uncle?"

"Everybody knows your uncle. Think about it, Sasha. This is Santa Fe, New Mexico. We've got all the priests on speed-dial. Plus, I grew up in Española."

Sasha started to laugh, but then an odd thought gripped her. "If you know my uncle, did you know my . . . Brigid? In Española? Did you know about me?"

Now Wayne looked sad. "I had an idea. About your mother. I was in college, but when I came home for Christmas that year, Brigid Long Night was. . . ."

"Knocked up," Sasha said. She liked the feel of the words in her mouth.

Wayne nodded. "First she was gone. Then she was back. It wasn't hard to figure out. But I had no idea that baby was you."

"Well, it was."

Wayne turned back to his big, geeky computer. "Let's find her."

"My dad says she's in New York."

And in less than a minute, there she was, Brigid Schumann all over the place, *Art News*, *Art World*, the Venice Bienniale, Rockefeller Center, New York Public Library, World Trade Center Plaza, Guggenheim Museum, Bilbao, the Tate Collection in London, the Berlin Prize, a medal from the French government. And all the words for her: provocative, masterful, elegant, cynical, genius, shocking, precocious, oracular, incoherent, radiant. About a billion Who's Who listings. "Who's Who?" Sasha screeched, and Wayne shushed her. "That's a good one," she whispered, tears gathering behind her eyes, in her throat. If there was anybody she could cry in front of, it would be Wayne. He wouldn't look at her or try to gauge her level of discomfort. He stared at the computer screen.

"She has a show running in New York through the first of next year. Called *The Mad Tea Party*. Here's the address. You can go see it."

"What if she's there?"

"Well, you'd have to recognize her, I guess. How about a picture?" he asked. "Are you ready for that?"

"I've probably seen one. But I don't remember."

"You should think for a minute. What do you want from a picture? Do you want to make her real? That's something pictures do. Do you want to look like her? You don't actually, in the obvious way. But I haven't seen her in a long time. So you might. And you've got a father out there somewhere too, you know."

Sasha stared at Wayne, taking in his round face, the bowl cut of his hair. Not him, she thought. This was one reason she had to get away now. She knew she would spend too much time studying men in their forties, or older men, or all men, waiting for that flash, for the glint of the mirror looking back.

Wayne typed some more, clicked the mouse, paused, sat back. "*Voilà*," he said. "*Tu madre*. I'm going to make some coffee in my lab. I'll be right back."

And so Sasha and Brigid were alone, staring at each other. Sasha's first thought was, I have two brown mothers. Who on earth am I?

Brigid

After one week without Sasha, Brigid made her way across the arroyo to Miss O'Keeffe's fence where there was a broken rail and loose wire. She crept very close to the house, too close, and kicked a rock or a branch that skittered into view. Miss O'Keeffe turned, and Brigid could see the glow of her white hair, like a moon pierced and leaking out around a face. "Who are you?" Miss O'Keeffe said, though her companion insisted they had heard an animal. Brigid said nothing, did not move. She thought Miss O'Keeffe must hear her breathing. She stayed still until the two women went inside, and then stayed even later, concentrating on the pale glow where Miss O'Keeffe had been. It's the darkness turned inside out, she told herself, and she felt her parents nearby. She knew the place was called Ghost Ranch.

The next night, Brigid went back. The two women sat again under the stars, their phonograph music like fireworks without fire. This time she walked closer, until she stood before Miss O'Keeffe, just inside the shadows.

"It's a child," Miss O'Keeffe said, not gently. "What do you want? How did you get in?" Brigid told her: a broken spot in the fence.

"She lives with her brother," the companion said. "Down the road. You know. The parents. . . ."

Miss O'Keeffe asked that another chair be brought. "How old are you?" she said and then, after Brigid answered, "How is it to be eighteen?"

Brigid thought a long time before answering. She wanted to say something brilliant and true. She felt the night around them, the pure dark of it inside her head, and that was how it was to be eighteen. But finally she said, "There are a lot of rules."

"And you want to go around them?" Miss O'Keefe's companion said.

"I want to paint," Brigid said.

"That will mean going around rules." Brigid thought that Miss O'Keeffe was smiling as she said this. A hand touched hers, and in that touch, a spark, a twang, a violin note flew up her arm, it seemed.

"Jerrie," Miss O'Keeffe said to her companion, "is there anything I can do to get you to stay?" and Jerrie's voice shook as she said no, nothing you can do.

They met the next morning by the low place in the fence. Brigid knew Miss O'Keeffe would want to see how her property might be breached, and that Brigid herself would be expected to appear, to be waiting. The day was only a thin orange line over the mountains. Brigid placed her hand on the wire and pressed down to show how she had been able to get over. Miss O'Keeffe smiled and lay her own hand just beside, so they saw the two together, remarkably similar, brown and strong, not thin. Useful hands.

"I know nothing about children," Miss O'Keeffe said. "I don't think I like them."

Brigid believed she had not been a child for a very long time, but what she said was, "Sometimes you miss them."

"You can help me," Miss O'Keeffe said and explained how she had just lost her companion over money, and she had learned a good lesson from it. Miss O'Keeffe looked at Brigid severely, her face closed but also eager, like a fox's. She wore a gray jacket over a blindingly white shirt, and a man's black trousers. Red mud caked her boots—or maybe it's paint, Brigid thought, the color of earth in some of the famous landscapes, in which the hills look like the hide of a great beast, prehistoric, or not yet dreamed of.

She stepped over the fence and onto Miss O'Keeffe's property.

"Don't you have to go to school?" Miss O'Keeffe asked.

"No. I've been out of school. Last year, I learned at home."

"Ah, then you're not a child." Miss O'Keeffe smiled. "At least they don't send you away. My mother and father sent me away. To the Catholics. So many rules."

"Your own parents sent you away?"

A stranger might have believed they were mother and child—from a distance this might be the perception, from this angle, the low morning light lengthening the shadows behind them, erasing lines on Miss O'Keeffe's face and deepening the hollows below Brigid's cheekbones, along her throat. The space between their bodies, too, geometric, a theorem about lines and planes and what parts rest gently upon others to make structure, depth and meaning, relation. Miss O'Keeffe turned, walked on ahead toward her house, and Brigid followed, but unsteadily, slipping over small rocks, catching the hem of her dress on the low scrub. She wondered how, just the night before, she had moved so easily in the dark.

"You can come to me when you're ready," Miss O'Keeffe said.

Brigid felt a kind of rising and opening in her chest. "I'm ready now," she said.

To Miss O'Keeffe's house, she brought one box of clothes and one box of paints and all of her own work. She knew she would be embarrassed if anyone at Ghost Ranch saw these few tubes and brushes, the one stained cloth, the single palette knife, the outsize bottle of turpentine, her sad colors, a dried blend of yellows and reds and blues. Salmon, her favorite, as if a fish might leap out of the tube and swim away before she could make anything of it. White, which was hard for her to use, the way it sat on the canvas, waiting, criticizing, daring her to make ruin. One tube had never been opened. Ochre. The name made Brigid afraid, the block letters OCHRE reminded her of teeth in a grinning death's head. A rictus of color.

Theo drove her in the truck, through the front gate and up the drive. He would not enter the house, even though he was invited by Miss O'Keeffe's voice over the speaker by the door. He glanced at Brigid and tried to smile. "I know I've forgotten something," she said, to calm him. "I'll have to come back Saturday." He said it was all right, and she wanted to ask which he meant, her going or her coming back in a few days. "I'll be gone anyway," he said. He told her he'd found work with a traveling crew of grapple trucks that follow natural disasters. Ice storms, hurricanes, tornadoes. "People are always glad to see you," he said. "That part sounds pretty good to me."

Miss O'Keeffe's front door opened into cool shadow. They saw the housekeeper standing just beyond the threshold in her white uniform, a ghost. A tremor ran out through Theo's arms and into the box he was just handing over. The tubes and brushes rattled as if they'd come alive, and Brigid felt it in her hands and up to her elbows. She steadied the box, released it to the housekeeper, along with the other, her dresses, skirts, trousers, shirts, and she and Theo watched as all of it was taken in, taken away.

"Tell them next time I come, I'll stop in," Theo said. He ran his left arm over Brigid's shoulder, withdrew it, patted her hair. Brigid bowed her head and closed her eyes against his shirt. She felt she might never see him again, even though she knew it was ridiculous—between jobs, he would return to their parents' house, three miles away.

Behind them came the sound of a body turning in a chair, the creak of human bones against wood. A woman's cough, a small voice: "Is that you?" Theo stepped back into the sunlight and the housekeeper closed the front door. "Come and sit down," Miss O'Keeffe said. Brigid moved toward the voice. She felt rather than saw a slash through the air and a blind opened, a shaft of light fell across Miss O'Keeffe's shoulders, arms, her famous hands, fists now, like knots on pine. Work hands, her father would have said.

Her father would not have let her come here, into this uncertain light, to sit before Miss O'Keeffe in her hard but beautiful chair, metal and wood with a woven seat. "It's the most uncomfortable thing I have," she said. "It was a gift and the giver tends to visit."

"It's not so bad," Brigid said. "Anyway, you'd never fall asleep in it."

Miss O'Keeffe laughed. Then they fell silent. The housekeeper brought in a tray of small white objects, like lights in the gloom: cups of coffee, a pitcher of milk, a sugar bowl. Brigid poured milk in her coffee, carefully. She knew Miss O'Keeffe was watching. She tried to think what to say first, gazing up to the tall fireplace, the large canvas above it and the others on the walls. She could not tell which they were, paintings or photographs, white and silver, colors that picked up light, held light, drew light from where it could not possibly come. Her eyes were adjusting to this world, ready to admit complexities: now she could see a dining table, a shallow blue bowl at its center inside which sat an orange. Fruit that is a color, a color that is a thing. Like pink is a flower, and blue is a sadness. She thought of Miss O'Keeffe's whole life devoted to effect. She knew she should say something.

"What will I do here?" Her voice rang hoarse and raucous.

"I'm not sure yet. You can learn Jerrie's jobs right away. What did you do at home?"

"Everything. My brother and I divided the work. Mine was inside, and his was outside. My father worked in town, and my mother wasn't able to do much."

"Consumption, we heard."

"Yes. But really, she lost interest in housekeeping when we were small."

"A wise woman."

"She was, in her way."

"Jerrie looked after my correspondence, among other things. I think you could take that over."

"Do you get a lot of letters?"

"Yes." Miss O'Keeffe frowned and then she went still and closed her eyes.

Brigid could stare then at the famous face, a mask loosening, the brown skin like leather pulled taut over stone and now coming undone. She listened for breath, felt afraid in the silence. She moved her hands to the arms of the chair. She would get up now, call for the housekeeper.

Then suddenly Miss O'Keeffe opened her eyes. "And most of the letters are about money. Jerrie didn't want to handle the money talk, and I don't blame her. You won't either. You want to paint, you said. But we'll see how it turns out. I expect you'll go away in the fall, to college. New York is the one place you must go if you have any talent. We'll see about that too." Miss O'Keeffe paused. "Now I'm going to put on my boots and take a walk. I don't generally talk much on these walks. I've talked enough right now to last a week."

Just past ten o'clock, they set out with long sticks and a canteen of water. Brigid could discern no path, and it was work to walk beside a person when you didn't know where you were going. Apprentice, she thought. The air was empty, different, even three miles from her parents' house. Every waft of it felt new, invented just the moment before they walked through. Miss O'Keeffe did not speak, though sometimes she pointed at the ground with her walking stick—at a flower or animal tracks. Brigid was never quite sure what Miss O'Keeffe was looking at or what she herself should see.

After an hour, the house came into view, but from another angle. Miss O'Keeffe sighed. "Someday I will keep walking toward the mountains and never come back." She reached for Brigid's arm, leaned heavily. "Later," she said, "you will show me your work."

"What is that?" Miss O'Keefe asked, opening her hand toward the canvas.

"A kachina doll. Pour Water Woman."

"The Earth Mother. What happened to her head?"

"It came off."

"Why?"

"Because she hated it."

"Ah." Miss O'Keeffe stood looking at the painting for a long time. "The force must have been extraordinary. And violent."

"It was," Brigid said.

"Is that meant to be blood?"

"Maybe. Or happiness. Or relief."

"It was hard being her, yes? Nourishing the whole world. Taking care of everybody. All those children crawling on her all the time."

"All of that," Brigid said.

"Do you mix your own colors?" Miss O'Keeffe said.

"Sometimes. I can't afford very much."

"No, of course not." Miss O'Keeffe turned to the second canvas and brought her left index finger very close to the paint, then stopped. She seemed to shake herself out of some thought, turned back toward Brigid. "May I?"

"I think it's dry."

Miss O'Keeffe extended all the fingers of her left hand. The sight was frightening, as if the fingers had lengthened suddenly of their own accord. You wouldn't put it past those fingers, Brigid thought, to have some power like that.

"Very thick. Did you paint over something else?"

"Probably," Brigid said. "I've worked on this a long time, so I don't remember exactly."

There was more painting, a lot more, on paper and heavy poster board. "These are good," Miss O'Keeffe said of the landscapes, which Brigid did not care very much about. They were the work she made herself do. She lingered over a sketch of a Pueblo woman sitting by a fire.

"This is what people will buy," she said finally. "This is what will make you money."

"Everyone paints that," Brigid said. "You can buy something like it in any little shop in Taos."

"I hate Taos. Taos is the fall of civilization. But the money is there."

Brigid felt a stab of betrayal, in her legs, as real as physical pain. She wanted to sit down, or run out of the studio. "But you don't care about money!"

"I can afford not to."

There was a silence between them, but still Miss O'Keeffe smiled.

"I'm sorry," Brigid said.

"Never be sorry. Your work is too strange for this place. You should go to New York. Start there. You're too young to wither away here."

"I don't have any money. I don't know anyone in New York."

"Well, I'm paying you, so you'll have money soon enough. As for the other, your work will have to speak. I know people, but I dislike that method of introduction. And what if you turn out to be better at drinking than at painting?"

"I paint that." Brigid pointed to the Piuye woman. "I paint that as a warning to myself."

"Make a painting a day," Miss O'Keeffe said. "Paint quickly. Decisively. Don't think about it. I'll give you canvas. Use a canvas over and over until it gets too slick, and then I'll give you another. Don't think so hard about Indians. In fact, don't think about them at all. Think about the brush stroke. Yours tries to be bold, but it's really just wide. No one has ever watched you work. Now I will, as if you were a model, except I won't paint you."

"All right."

"And there's another thing. When you go to New York, in a year or so, don't let them paint you. They will want to. They'll do it to make you smaller. They want to make you the subject, not the creator. Men and women both. Don't let them."

"I won't."

Miss O'Keeffe stared at her. "I know you from somewhere."

"Española."

"What happened to your mother?"

"She died."

"And your father?"

"Same."

"There's more to this story," Miss O'Keeffe said, "but I won't bring it up again if you don't like me to." She moved back to the stack of canvases. "This one, for instance."

She held up a watercolor, in blues and grays, of a girl in an empty room. Sunlight comes through a window outside the edge of the scene and falls in shafts across the girl's left shoulder and chest. She appears to be behind the bars of light, delicately imprisoned. The girl herself has no human face, only a red spatter where her features would be.

"This suggests knowledge," Miss O'Keeffe said. "As if you tried to kill Vermeer. It also suggests you have no talent for abstract work. At least not now. Later maybe."

Brigid stood and faced away, knowing it was the first time she had deliberately turned her back on Miss O'Keeffe. She felt something in the room clench and relax, as if the atmosphere were a fist.

Miss O'Keeffe sighed. "Turn around," she said. "You're angry about something. I don't need to know what it is. But I want you to understand you will be safe with me. And then we will get you to New York. Maybe farther." Together they gazed out the window, at the low scrub beyond the house, the mountains in the distance. "You don't belong here. You're not very western, really. You're something different. But we don't know what yet, do we? Now what's this last one?"

"The Dog Woman."

"This is something," Miss O'Keeffe said, staring at the canvas. "Every woman's a dog woman, isn't that so? A half-breed. Like you. Not broken but powerful. To be brutish is good. It's about the body. Eating, drinking, snapping of jaws, baring of teeth, all of that."

"All of it," Brigid said. "Thank you for the safety."

"You're welcome. Now. I'll show you the correspondence, and then I'll leave you alone for a while to do what you like. There's a small room left empty in Jerrie's part of the house. It gets good north light. Jerrie never knew what to do with it, so it's just . . . waiting. The waiting room!" Miss O'Keeffe laughed. "Just listen to me. On and on like an old bat. I'm really very sensible."

"I know you are," Brigid said.

"I want you to paint flowers. I want you to paint a different one every day. Walk the ranch and find them. Not a different kind, but a different one. See them at first on the ground, living, and that will help you understand them after you've come inside. See them first and then paint what's in your head. Paint what you see in there."

There were probably thirty long envelopes tossed carelessly on the desk, on top of a layer of other papers. Bills, requests, letters from admirers and strangers. Black and white, Brigid thought, there it is, Miss O'Keeffe's life in words and numbers.

"Looks worse than it is," Miss O'Keeffe said and then she left, closing the door firmly behind her.

The room was small and spare, not a single window. No distractions. The desk was impressive though, cinnamon-colored wood, seven drawers to investigate. The chair looked uncomfortable: black molded plastic, invented by a boss plagued with sleepy workers. Four tall filing cabinets, the alphabet divided among one of them. Brigid opened the second drawer and found what she wanted in "G," five envelopes marked with Julian Granger's return address. She ticked off the edges with her finger but did not read them. Not yet. She would wait to see if Miss O'Keeffe brought up the subject. She glanced at her wristwatch. Two o'clock.

By four o'clock, the desk was half-cleared and Brigid had collected a box full of correspondence needing Miss O'Keeffe's attention. She sat back in the unforgiving chair, trying to think how to explain. She could do this work, but not every day. It was either dull or heartbreaking: all these letters asking for time, attention, money. *I am a young woman who has just begun to paint.* Brigid saw that she might spend her entire life writing back, how kindly she would learn to say no, no thank you, good luck with your work, best wishes, don't give up. But then she would be a writer, not a painter.

She stood and stepped again to the first file cabinet, picked back through the files to "G." She told herself again to wait, but finally she couldn't. One letter, just one. She lifted it from the paper folder and turned back to the desk to read. This must be the first, dated a year and a half ago. *Dear Georgia, I'll see you next week. The high school art teacher wrote to me as you said she would. She wants me to meet her students. Oh well. Best, Julian.*

Oh well?

Nancy

Something Henry said or might have said as we hid out at the Atlanta Burger King in the fall of 1996: life doesn't move forward, not really. It accumulates. He was thinking of paint on canvas, the way it worked for him. It was hard to explain, he said. A painting didn't really have a beginning and an end. It didn't start with "If it was fine, they would go to the lighthouse," and end with she had had her vision. Although it did. End with vision, I mean. But it's also true that there's a beginning. There was that moment, Henry said, when you began to stretch the canvas or unscrewed the cap on the tube of gesso, and then there was the moment you put down the brush for the last time—or sold the painting. But in between, it didn't go from left to right like words on a page. You laid down some paint here and here and then more on top of that, and then you stood there for a while smoking and thinking and then you scraped paint away, almost down to the pure canvas and then you said *shit* and smoked some more and laid down more paint. But this time, it was a different color, a color you'd been afraid of your entire life. Really. Your hand shook when you touched that color. But this was the moment, Henry said. This was it. So that was another beginning too. An accumulation of beginnings.

On the tenth week of youth group—we said it that way, half singing, like the Christmas carol—I considered buying a six-pack of beer. I could get away with it at the package store on the corner of Peachtree and Osborne.

Jan Vermeer and Georgia O'Keeffe enter from opposite sides of the stage, which is again bare, but painted the yellow of the woman's blouse in Vermeer's The Procuress. *O'Keeffe is carrying a large black satchel, which she sets on the floor between them. She reaches in and*

*draws forth a six-pack of beer in cans, labeled LIGHT. She pulls a can
off the pack and offers it to Vermeer.*

V: Not again. They'll smell it on our breath.
    *O'Keeffe shrugs, opens the beer, takes a long swallow. Vermeer
    strides offstage. A cash register bell rings. He returns with two
    Cokes, two bags of fries.*
V: We're going to get caught.
G: I know.
V: And I've been meaning to ask you, Boss. *(Vermeer is angry.)*
    When we do get caught, what should we say?
G: You mean, should we lie or tell the truth?
V: Or should we tell them we've been here so long we don't remem-
    ber what the difference is?
G: You do too remember.
V: We should tell the truth.
G: Which part? The true part or the angry part?
V: I never thought of it that way. But I'm not the one who's angry.
G: You're not?

Henry shook his head. "I'm not angry. And you're the wheels, Nance.
I go where you go."

I thought about that. *I go where you go.* True. All our lives, like twins.
And when would it not be true? Next year for sure. All of college, probably. Marriage. Everything after that. Utterly incomprehensible, to be not
together all the time. People did it, though. Even twins did it. So simple.
But the realization was heavy and painful, like dropping a brick on your
foot. I glanced over at Henry, who was licking salt from the tips of his fingers. "Can you help me not to be so angry?" I said.

"Why are you angry?"

"What do you know about Mom's friend Simon?"

"Dad hates him."

"Why?"

Henry went still for a moment and stared straight ahead, as if he'd
caught a strange, distant sound. Then he spoke. "You know why these fries

are so good, Nance? I heard this somewhere, I don't remember. They're coated with this stuff—it's mostly salt, but then they add a little sugar. It's weird, but apparently, it's irresistible."

The Sunday after Thanksgiving, the third-to-last week of youth group, I felt an immanence, a foreboding, a dark shape just up ahead of us, the loom of discovery and punishment. The weather turned against us too. The fall had been so mild we could sit in the car at Burger King without turning on the heat. But suddenly the temperature dropped twenty degrees, and there was talk of snow. We shivered in the car. We drank coffee instead of Coke.

"You realize what's coming," I said.

"Christmas?" Henry said.

"No. The end."

"I know. So." Henry poured another pouch of sugar into his coffee. "What do you want to do with your life?"

He'd never asked me anything like that before. This, I thought, must be how the condemned talk to each other. Death row jabber.

"I want to write plays," I said. "How about you?"

"I'm not going to college. I'm going to New York next fall."

This was news. "We'd be really far apart," I said. "You might not like that."

"It'd be okay," Henry said. "I'd learn to live with it."

"It's a good place for somebody like you who hates to drive."

Henry seemed to think about this. A hard shiver convulsed his chest.

"Cold?" I said. I reached to turn the key in the ignition.

Henry grasped my arm. "Do you ever think you're going to do something great?" he said. "Something really important?"

"Do you?"

"I do. It's almost scary, to feel it waiting out there. Like this"—here he pointed at the dashboard to signify our present predicament—"is nothing. This is a blip on the radar. This is a grain of sand on the beach."

"What is it, do you think, this great thing? Will you be famous?"

Henry shook his head. "Maybe. It feels different though. Not about me. Something like save people in a train wreck or a burning building."

And so, finally, the thirteenth week of youth group. We should have known, lucky thirteen. Really, really cold for Atlanta, Christmas bearing down on a house full of unbelievers. When I said this, Henry said I was nuts. Wasn't that why we were hiding out from the stupid youth group, because our parents were believers?

"I don't think they are," I said. "I think they're kind of lost."

What was Christmas, I asked him, when your children knew the truth about the guy in the red suit? What was the point of Christmas morning? No throwing open of doors, no more of that harsh light from the movie camera. No ripping of paper, searching for batteries, eating all the candy pills in the doctor kit before breakfast. No breakfast. Our mother was on a diet because she thought maybe if she lost some weight, her husband would treat her better.

Henry was a solutions guy. "Well," he said, "maybe it's mystery. We don't know what they're giving us, right? They don't know what we're giving them. The same for you and me."

"True," I said. "So what do you want anyway?"

"Paints," Henry said. "I can't get enough. I like having a huge drawer full of those little tubes. I like the names of the colors."

"Have you been using Mom's?"

"No. You know how she is about her stuff."

"How about brushes? More canvas?"

"All of that."

"You're expensive," I said.

"So what do you want?"

"Let me think about it." I said. I turned the key in the ignition. "Back to reality."

Reality was sitting at the kitchen table, waiting for us. Youth group had an end-of-the-year Christmas party, parents invited. The Christensens were surprised to see the Diamonds, to say the least.

"Whose idea was this?" our dad wanted to know.

"Mine," I said. "Really. Henry had nothing to do with it."

"Well, I'm not surprised," he said. "You're just like your mother."

For Christmas, Henry and I didn't get anything, except what we gave each other. The glorious names of paints: *burnt sienna, cadmium yellow light, red ochre, rose madder, quinacridone magenta, jaune brilliant, raw umber.* Henry bought me the Riverside Shakespeare. Our parents gave us the silent treatment, the cold shoulder. They slept late, kept their bedroom door locked. They left us at home and went on long drives together, returning hours later, flushed, tipsy, their arms full of packages from after-Christmas sales, none of it for us. Later, Henry and I would realize we had become a force against which our parents could unite. Some people need that, a common enemy. We had, in fact, saved our parents' marriage by not going to youth group.

At dinner on New Year's Day, our mother said, "I hope you both become Buddhists."

"Or maybe Swedenborgians," our father said. That sounded promising, the religion of Johnny Appleseed and Helen Keller, fans of a guy who said crazy shit like *the sky is an enormous man.*

"Okay," Henry said. "But first I should tell you, I'm going to New York in the fall."

"Absolutely," our parents said. "By all means."

"You've figured it out about Simon, right?" Henry said.

"Figured what out?" I said. "Yes. But tell me anyway."

And then he told me so I could tell it my own way: two people who never dreamed they'd be able to talk to each other. Again.

DAD: Is it over with Simon?

MOM: It's over.

D: Henry needs you to come back. He's barely a year old.

M: I know.

D: Do you want to come back?

M: I do.

D: You said that once before, in a church. Remember?

M: I *want* to come *back*.

D: But . . . ?

M: I have a little friend.

D: What the hell are you talking about?

M: I'm going to have a baby.

D: Oh, God.

M: I don't know what I was doing. Henry needs me to come back.

D: Whose?

M: His.

D: Are you sure?

M: Yes.

So I got it. Finally. Duh, Nancy. Talk about mixed up.

"How do you know?" I asked Henry.

"I asked Simon."

"What if he's lying?"

"I asked Mom."

This was in the woods behind our house, rolling joints, preparing for the second great deception, more subtle than the first, not actually a lie, more like contraband. We were to drive with our parents to a cousin's wedding at the Citadel, in Charleston, bringing with us four joints and a camera film container of pot and a packet of rolling papers. And so, the next day, in the car heading east on I-20, I stared at the backs of my parents' heads, wondering if they'd ever planned to tell me, if they were leaving it up to Henry. I loved and hated them, in quick succession, like good dramatic dialogue, really fast, overlapping almost, like two characters trying to drown each other out, their voices so loud that everything else was erased. That was it: I felt rubbed out, like I could almost see the pink eraser hovering over the family picture, then hear the squeak of it moving back and forth over my face. Whited out. That's a good one, isn't it? But I began to be grateful for the weed in my bag. Each time a cop passed us on the highway, I came back to being a body in a car. I broke into a cold sweat. I knew I was there. Trouble to get into became happy affirmation of my existence.

As we drove, Henry counted the *George Washington Slept Here* markers. Sometimes there were two or three within a few feet of each other, lined up, like people waiting politely for a bus that never comes. The two hundredth anniversary of George Washington's southern tour had passed a few years before and you could still find maps of the whole journey, with all the markers.

"If you look at the whole map," Henry said, "it's a bird upside down, the beak in Savannah and a long, trailing tail stretching up to Albany, New York."

"How is that a southern tour?" Mom said.

"How is anything southern?" Dad said.

"Passion, magnolias, the scent of gardenias, thunderstorms in summer."

"Basements that never dry out. Dirt roads."

This was the way they talked to each other now, as if their heads had suddenly sprung a leak, just a pinprick, a small, odd ooze of thought.

Then we were crossing the bridge from Charleston to Mt. Pleasant, the confluence of three bodies of water, the Cooper River, the Wandoo River, and the Atlantic Ocean. This was mid-March, that first burst of spring. The air felt newly clean, just shaken out, like a bed sheet, just for us. All that water below, finding itself joined, made new, gleamed and sparkled like . . . one of us would have to say it.

"Diamonds." Our mother stared down, over the side of the bridge. "Like us." She turned to Dad. "You know, a diamond is a mineral. The four properties of minerals are hardness, color, streak, and luster. Luster is the way light bounces off something. There are four ways to describe it: glossy, greasy, dull, or shiny. That's what we are. Isn't it beautiful?"

All plays are about lies. I think Mamet said something like this. All plays are about something that's hidden. A play starts because a situation becomes imbalanced by a lie. The lie may be something we tell each other or something we think about ourselves. If you're cheating on your husband, that secret puts things out of balance; or if you're someone you think you're not, that disturbed vision takes over your life and you're totally unhinged by it until you're cleansed. At the end of a play, the lie is revealed. The better the play, the more surprising and inevitable the lie is.

Sasha

In the computer lab, the film seemed to be nothing but fragments. It was September 21, ten days after. Sasha could assemble the images randomly, move them around, run them backwards, put people back in the building, take away the fire. It made the people into objects, little playthings. There was this rhythm to the progression of the stills, what the film professor called "lyric impression," though it was hard to know exactly what was taking place. It was a poem without context. The viewer would think what every ninth grader says in English class reading Shakespeare: I don't get it. But still, Sasha thought, there are so many ways to know what actually happened, like maybe a couple thousand or so. That was the number the news people were reporting: 2,819. No, no, no. It was an insane number. And wrong. Because there was a new total every day. You couldn't keep up with it changing like that. But everyone did. Everyone wanted to have the last word, the current tally, the facts. Sasha tried to see the point of it. She watched people falling and falling and falling, and she decided her film wasn't going to be about getting that kind of information. It wasn't about making an argument or solving a problem. It was about light and sound. The film professor talked about Abel Gance's *La Roue*. From 1923. This film is the poetic evocation of power and speed, he said. It builds up speed and hurtles toward an unspecified destination. The editing stresses rhythm and form, not reality or truth. When she ran her film, Sasha saw bodies as mass and volume and color. And this terrible, outlandish grace. It was like looking at a body as if you'd never seen one before. A body was a revelation, the kind of thing that forced people into speech. So what do you say in the face of such a phenomenon? To locate it, to *ground* it. Oh my god, Sasha thought. To make it comprehensible. The professor showed a film about the Jews driven away by the Germans and Germans driven away by the Russians, *Danube Exodus*. In the background, voices recite diary entries. "This morning the sky is clear and blue. The summer's heat has finally broken." It's a war film, he said, but it redefines the genre. It's trying to get at mood rather than at history. It's a bit of a relief that way, he said, and the whole class knew what he was talking about.

Sasha walked by the Indian twice in the Carman lobby that morning on her way out to class and back. She remembered the dust on his clothes, in his long black braid, and how that frightened her, like he'd taken shape out of dust. Then just before noon, Aaron Fisk, the RA, was standing beside this man, calling her name, beckoning, a strange rapid opening and closing of his right hand, like the beating wing of a frantic bird. The man stood up then, and dust drifted away from him, tangled in the light and disappeared. Aaron didn't move. The man seemed not to be breathing. He's stuck, Sasha thought. He needs CPR.

"Sasha," the man said. He held out his hand, empty palm turned up. "I'm Theo Long Night. Brigid Schumann's brother."

Sasha felt dizzy, frozen, and looked at Aaron, who understood the thought before she could put it into words. "It's not bad news," Aaron said quickly. And then, "He's who he says he is. I checked. He's working downtown."

Theo had come here, he told Sasha, as part of a construction crew for rescue and recovery. He drove a grapple truck, every day, seven-hour shifts, over to Staten Island and back. He was union. He was worried about his sister. They'd been out of touch, he didn't have a number, but he'd called a family friend, a priest.

"Uncle Edgardo," Sasha said.

Theo nodded. "He told me where you were."

"Did you find her?" Sasha glanced around the lobby. Maybe he'd brought Brigid Schumann, and she'd tucked herself into the shadows, waiting for some sign, some horrible perfect moment.

"She's away. I went to the gallery where she shows her work. They didn't know when she would be back. Or where she'd gone. Or for how long." Theo shook his head. He tried to smile, but it didn't quite work. "Or her address."

His voice wavered and broke, as if he couldn't get enough air or didn't trust himself to speak. Shell-shocked, Sasha thought. He sounds like the kind of person you wouldn't give information to, a person on the edge of something bad. Knocked way off kilter. Numb. That peculiar numb that's waiting for the next awful thing to happen. Really, he sounds just like everybody else. Sasha tried to make herself stop staring, though that wasn't precisely what she was doing. She was moving her eyes, taking in his features one by one, noting the resemblances. He was Brigid Schumann grown large, more Navajo. The skin on his face was drawn very tight, molded around his cheekbones, the hawkish bridge of his nose seeming about to poke through.

"If you want to talk," Aaron was saying. He turned his head toward the door of the resident's suite.

"If you do," Sasha said to Theo, and he nodded, and they went in.

"I have coffee." Aaron was already moving away, toward his tiny kitchen.

"That'd be good," Theo said. "I've been living on it."

"Coffee is like snowflakes," Aaron said, and laughed, too loudly. He seemed nervous. "No two cups are the same."

"True," Theo said. He seemed to consider. "A lot of things are like that," he said quietly.

Aaron brought in the mugs, a carton of milk, a handful of sugar packets, two spoons. "I'll be right outside," he said. "Take your time." He looked at Sasha. "Let me know if you need anything."

"You're all grown up," Theo said when they were alone. "I can't really believe I'm seeing you."

Sasha wondered what to say to this, but no words came to her.

"You look so much like my mother," Theo said. "Your hair."

"Would she want to see me?"

Theo winced, then shook his head. "I thought you meant . . ." he said. "But you mean Brigid. Would she want to see you? I wish I could say yes. I'd like to say yes, but I really don't know."

"She left me twice."

"She didn't leave you the first time. I was there. She hated it. I can promise you that."

"What about the second time?"

"You have to ask her."

"Sometimes I think it might be better if I made it up for myself."

"It might be."

They each picked up a mug and drank. Aaron Fisk's window looked out on 114th Street. They watched a man carrying a guitar go into a building across the street. "Music," Theo said. The tone of his voice was admiring, awestruck, full of longing. "I guess I should ask if you like it here, but that seems like a stupid question."

"If you asked me two weeks ago. . . ."

"Yeah," Theo said. He gazed into his coffee mug.

He's not too good at this, Sasha thought. She told Theo about Jennie, that they'd been downtown just after the planes hit, and why, and what she'd filmed. Theo listened intently, leaning forward, like he was waiting for a particular piece of information.

"You must have been so scared," he said.

"Then we ran. But we couldn't get far enough before the . . . first it was a black cloud, then gray and then ash . . . just . . . surrounded us. We followed people into a building. I thought it was the end. Everybody did."

"I know," Theo said. "I'm sorry. He pressed his right hand on top of his head. Sasha saw his forearm and bicep tense. "Oh man, oh man," he said. "All of this *I'm sorry, I'm sorry.* I say it all day long. It never ends. I drive the debris to a place called Fresh Kills. Can you believe that? And everybody knows it's not debris. This guy I drive with, Dennis, he said the other day, what I am is a hearse. And that's it. You're up top working the grapple arm, and you can see what's in your load, and it's. . . . It doesn't make sense."

"No," Sasha said.

"But you're here." Theo gazed around the bare walls of Aaron's room as if he was trying to see through them. "He must have just moved in too." He looked at Sasha, looked away. "I'm glad to meet you anyway. Meet you again."

"How long will you be working?"

"It's a three-month contract."

"What's after that?"

"I go to the next thing."

"Is there always a next thing?"

"For me there is. I can count on it."

God, Sasha thought, what a weird way to be hopeful.

"You get there after they've cried all they can and shouted at God. That's what one lady in Florida said: 'Good thing you weren't here yesterday and trying to load up my stuff. I would have cut off your head with the last rusty knife.' That was Hurricane Andrew. 'But now I'm just numb,' she said. 'Haul it all away, Mister Indian.'" Theo set his mug gently on Aaron's low table and stood up. "I've got to get back downtown now. It's a seven–hour shift. I just asked for a little time off."

Sasha stood too. She was surprised by what she felt, that she didn't want Theo Long Night to leave. "Can you come back?"

"That would be good," Theo said.

"Let me give you my phone number." Sasha opened her backpack, drew out a notebook, tore a page from the end.

"Math," Theo said, reading the cover. "The only subject I was good at. And then it's just like kids say. You never use it again." He smiled a little, shook his head. "Except maybe geometry. The other day, I got lost again, for like the fifth time. I can't seem to remember the route. I can't visualize it. And those streets down there, they don't run straight. And I radioed the dispatcher, and he told me just keep making lefts, and I had to tell him that would be going in a circle."

Sasha wrote her number, folded the notebook page and handed it to Theo. "I'll walk you out," she said.

"The last thing I heard about you," Theo said, "was that you couldn't talk. You got to be three years old and you didn't say anything. But now you seem fine. You seem perfectly normal."

Sasha tried for a laugh. "What's normal?"

Just beside the door to his suite, Aaron Fisk sat like a sentry. He looked up at Sasha and Theo. He had a slow, deliberate way of seeing. Gazing. Sasha had noticed this right away, eleven days ago when she asked him what to do about the autobiography assignment. It was as if there was no breath in his body sometimes, no bones, no dimension to him. He lost himself, utterly, when he was looking at a problem.

"Come back if you want to talk," Aaron said, and he seemed to be speaking to both of them as they left the dorm.

"What are you going to do with that film you took?" Theo said.

"I'm not sure," Sasha told him.

"Nobody's going to want to see it, you know," Theo said. "Even though they should." He turned toward Broadway. "I think I'll walk a few blocks. You want to come along?"

"I have class. Otherwise, I would."

"Okay." Still Theo did not walk away. Sasha waited. "You know," he began, "I remember—I was so afraid. For Brigid. I never felt anything like that. Like in my gut. Like *pain*. I called all the numbers I had for her and there was no answer. I said out loud in my house, 'I can't find her, I can't find her. Where is she? I bet today she decided to paint her goddamn World Trade Center painting.' My only relative in the world. And then I find out *you* were the one who was right there."

"Maybe your other only relative."

"That's right," Theo said. He looked around, across Broadway, toward the Hudson. "No one would believe it to look at us. My mother used to say that as a joke. You kids make me whiter. You kids clean me right up."

Aaron was waiting for her in the Carman lobby. "You okay?" he said.

"I'm fine," Sasha told him.

"Then you're the only one in this whole city."

"Yeah, I bet."

"They didn't really prepare me for any of this in RA orientation."

"I guess not."

"I did some calling around, but like I said, he's okay."

"Thanks for doing that." Sasha shifted her backpack. She had an odd urge to hug Aaron Fisk. He was a graduate student in linguistics and art history, but he looked more like he should be carrying a surfboard down a beach in southern California, which gave him an air of confusion. "You seem sort of, well, freaked out."

"I am. I'm also mildly freaked out that your mother is Brigid Schumann."

"Believe me, I am too."

"I was planning to talk about her work in my section of Art Hum. But now I don't know what I'm going to do with that class. They're practically hysterical. Nobody has a filter anymore. If they think it, they say it. This morning, a student asked if we noticed that a lot of the virgin Marys in the Italian Renaissance seem to be looking out at the viewer and saying 'O.K. I'm a virgin. I have this baby. Deal with it!' People cracked up. I kept putting up the slides, Raphael, Giotto, Masaccio, the whole bunch of them, and the class kept yelling, 'Deal with it!' and laughing itself silly."

"I wish I'd been there."

"Anytime. Just wander in."

Deal with it, that's right, Sasha thought, but how? First, there were facts. At least 200 people exited visibly through the windows. The fall took ten seconds. The bodies fell at an average rate of 150 miles an hour, depending on weight and distance traveled. This speed was not fast enough to lose consciousness. When a body hits the ground at this speed, it is obliterated. And Theo was right: living people can't stand to look. But they have to, Sasha thought. Look at what is unspeakable. The film could tell them to look, in a voice like God's, where God is a professionally trained man, objective but omniscient, speaking from an undisclosed location. Heaven. Judging the world but not caught up in it. The pictures are from hell, but the voice would say these people are not killing themselves. They are being killed. This is only common sense. But what does that mean these days, common sense?

She spent a lot of time in the diners between 96th and 116th Streets, drinking coffee and thinking about this, pretty much by herself, not talking. School is weird enough, she thought, not for the first time. There are all these people around you, every minute, even in your sleep. And still there's really nobody. Everybody is missing in some way. Why is that? And now, there's this private fear too. People froze when an airplane roared overhead. In her dorm, women talked in their sleep or cried but couldn't speak about it when they were awakened. This odd silence. Everyone was frightened and lonely, deep down where sound originates, like the inner ear of the soul. Way in there. Ordinarily, she'd like this, this quiet, this isolation that was usually pretty safe. The way nobody noticed you, even right here in the middle of the fourth-largest city in the world. Why is *that*? And inside her, another question, like an ache, but she didn't know exactly what it was, only that it had to do with missing people, missing her mother, Beatriz. Wayne was right: it hits you later. The way Beatriz held her, kissed her awake in the morning, little kisses all over her cheeks until Sasha had to say, Mom, stop eating my face. The way they talked, like friends, and Beatriz said, I think I'm grooming you to be my companion in old age. And then she never got there, old age. Maybe old age, Sasha thought, was when she was going to tell me about Brigid Schumann.

And already missing Theo Long Night, even though she barely knew him.

Probably some of the people in the air were missing. Sasha knew she would have to find these people's families and ask their permission. But a lot of the families themselves didn't want to be found. They had their reasons: religious belief, life insurance, which somehow amounted to the same thing, right? She enlarged the images until they became meaningless, looking for the significant detail. She began to understand something about these particular last moments, which is that they were entirely different from any other path to the end, completely private, independent, unmoored, magic. She thought of Beatriz, filmed in this moment too. Her mother had been captured, taken prisoner on film, for Sasha, for the living. Not so with these people in the air. They belong only to themselves. They are caught up in this work. What they are doing requires their full attention. They have no room for the living, even the two women holding on to each other. Even those two are looking away, toward a place no one else can see.

She discovered that a lot of photographers had the same footage she did, video and stills, that it was published and then suppressed. Some of the families said why do we need to see this? Why do you need to see this? Why is it so fascinating to you? You're disgusting. Leave us alone. Why did you stop there? one mother asked. Why not show the landing, the pavement, the blood on the windows? The shreds of clothing clinging to the wreckage? Others, though, wanted to be sure, wanted to have in the air what they couldn't have on the ground, which was a body intact. A man took out an ad in the *Times,* asking if anyone had filmed or photographed his sister. She was in the eleventh window on the ninety-third floor of the North Tower. He had talked to her on a cell phone from Greenwich Street and then he was pretty sure he saw her go. But only pretty sure. He thought she had on a long skirt because that's what she liked in the summer. She wore a man's watch, really much too big, on her left wrist. Maybe you could see it if you enlarged the image, enhanced it. She had dark curly hair, a mass of it flying all over. She would have looked maybe Asian. She would have looked young if you could get that close. Her eyes would have been open. His ad ran every day for two weeks and then it was gone, so Sasha figured someone must have answered, supplied the information he wanted. Of course, it was possible that no one replied or he ran out of money. But it stuck with her, that last sentence about the sister's eyes. She felt a vague desire to ask the man why or how, how he knew that about his sister, what it meant, that she would be looking, watching, at the end.

When Sasha walked in to Aaron Fisk's Art Humanities section, she understood at once that the class had, just like he said, turned into something of a circus. Students squirmed in their seats like toddlers. A few huddled in the back of the lecture hall, smoking and drinking coffee beside the sign prohibiting these activities. Aaron smiled when he saw her and rolled his eyes and huffed out a here-goes-nothing kind of breath.

"So," he said to the class, "I'm just going to give in to it. Art jokes, anyone?"

One student called out, "What did the artist say to the dentist?"

"What?" the class called out in perfect unison, as if they'd been rehearsing.

"Matisse hurt."

Another said, "What do you call an art history dropout?"

"What?"

"A performance artist."

"Ouch," Aaron said. "That's close to home."

He told the class a story about Picasso. A wealthy man commissioned Pablo Picasso to paint a portrait of his wife. Startled by the nonrepresentational image on the final canvas, the woman's husband complained that it wasn't how she really looked. When asked by Picasso how she really looked, the man produced a photograph from his wallet. Returning the photograph, Picasso observed, "Small, isn't she?"

A young woman raised her hand. "Are we getting anything out of this? I mean, what does it have to do with the lecture?"

"Well," Aaron said, "you'll be ready for the Freud readings in Contemporary Civ. Dreams and jokes."

"That's way next *year*," the woman said, her voice a cry. The room seemed to tremble.

"I know," Aaron said, "but we'll get there. I promise. We'll get to spring semester. I *swear* we will. Now look at this." He put up another slide. "This is the *Virgin and Child Enthroned*, by the Master of Bigallo, who is probably a painter named Bernardo Daddi or one of his pupils. What do you think of this one?"

"Jesus," a student said, "I mean . . . well. That Jesus looks just like Quentin Tarantino. Our Holy Mother of Quentin Tarantino."

"You know what they call a cheeseburger in Bethlehem?" Aaron said.

The class went on like this. Petulant Jesus, nervous Jesus, Jesus grumpy, Jesus worried. A Jesus that seemed to be channeling Axel Rose's snake dance. Sasha laughed so hard she didn't know if she was laughing or crying.

"Maybe I'll get back to the syllabus next week," Aaron said as they walked out of the classroom. "But maybe not."

"Seems like it's good to laugh," Sasha said. "I mean, it can't hurt."

"And I wonder," Aaron began, "if part of laughing at these paintings is making fun of God. Laughing at God. Because they're angry. We're all angry. Jokes can be aggressive that way. These students are thinking something like, 'Okay, God, where were you? Why weren't you paying attention? You're a jerk, God. You're a fool. How could you let that happen?' I know I'm thinking it. Maybe I shouldn't be, but I am."

Brigid

Most remarkable were the books in Miss O'Keeffe's house. Heavy as cement bricks, thick as shoe boxes. Shiny covers, blinding even in certain kinds of light. At first, Brigid could not bring herself to touch them, but then she had to, because they were everywhere, on every flat surface, table and shelves, the seats of chairs, piled on the floor too, the dining room table, one end of the kitchen counter. Often these books had to be moved aside so someone could sit down, prepare a meal, open a door, serve a guest. It was like gathering some kind of large, glossy flower, Brigid thought: you picked them up, carried them somewhere else, and made another pleasing arrangement.

One afternoon, a week into her life at Ghost Ranch, Brigid opened a book that wasn't devoted to Miss O'Keeffe's work. Pierre Bonnard, a lover of wallpaper evidently, and soft colors, patterns and windows. Sailboats too. Brigid had never seen a real sailboat. She said this, blurted it out, when Miss O'Keeffe found her paging through the Bonnard, after apologizing and promising next time to ask to see the books.

"No, no." Miss O'Keeffe held up her beautiful hands as if to push someone away. "Look as much as you like. That's what they're for. But how have you never seen a boat on water?"

"It's the desert. I haven't been anywhere else."

"Do you like it, the desert?"

"Emptiness. I like that."

"And don't you think the emptiness makes everything seem possible?"

"Maybe," Brigid said. "But sometimes there can be too much of it."

Miss O'Keeffe nodded. "I remember when I was teaching in Amarillo. That part of Texas looked to me like a big bowl. And the sky was the same big bowl. I liked that. You could get away, off by yourself. I needed that, more and more. But you." She clapped her hands together once, as if to stop herself. "I'll arrange for you to see a sailboat. Though I can't think where that might be."

But first to paint one. This seemed like a fine notion, to paint something you've never seen in life, and the idea caught fire in Brigid's mind. She started on paper, with geometry: two triangles and a thin rectangle below. A child's boat. Many children who had never seen boats must have drawn them, on rippling water, with mountains, also represented by triangles, in the background. But the sketch was ugly, flat, an embarrassment. She turned the paper over so she wouldn't have to look at it.

Julian Granger's face, Brigid recalled, was that shape, only inverted, wide at the cheekbones, tapering to his pointed beard. His face was a sail, a way to move his body. Her father once said that, faces were for moving bodies around. He was talking about having a pretty face and where you could go with it. So she gave up on the boat and sketched Julian Granger, from memory, expecting that Miss O'Keeffe would appear silently behind her chair and recognize her friend's face.

But when Miss O'Keeffe did see the sketch, she asked why she was drawing a man. She said a man made a very odd boat. And Brigid thought, yes, Julian Granger was an odd boat. He didn't take me anywhere, he couldn't hold me up. Still, he was always racing this way and that with the wind. He was beautiful to watch, thrilling. *How could a person paint water in this horrible place?* Julian had said to Brigid one day, after he took her to a motel outside Taos. And then he was gone. She looked at her sketch of his face, then folded it up and put it in her shirt pocket, where it made a small weight over her heart. Do I draw what I want, she wondered, or do I draw what I see?

At dinner that night, Miss O'Keeffe ate in silence. The soup in the bright bowls seemed dull. Too much spice and no taste, she said, and that was all. The water glasses had not been washed properly. Nothing they ate had come from the garden. After two bites, Miss O'Keeffe dropped her spoon, and the bell of it was a warning. She looked up slowly from the bowl, and Brigid looked away. At first Miss O'Keeffe spoke very softly, and Brigid could barely make out the words. "Pardon me?" she said and leaned closer. Miss O'Keeffe's shoulders were shaking. The cook stood behind her, horrified.

"You're just going to get married, aren't you?"

Brigid tried to laugh. "Who would I marry? Who's here to marry?"

"And then have a child."

"I'm too young," Brigid said and glanced at the cook, who probably knew better.

Miss O'Keeffe said nothing, and took up her spoon again. She reached for the sugar bowl and mixed a spoonful into the soup. "Lightening the spice," she told them.

After dinner, Miss O'Keeffe brought out another large book of reproductions. "When you want babies," she said, "there's always this. Mary Cassatt. Round naked babies, round pink women. But I prefer the furniture. That blue chair is beautiful. People should choose to live beautifully."

"They should," Brigid said.

"In your studio. You'll see canvas tomorrow. I've left it for you."

That night, Brigid woke suddenly from a dream she did not remember, not at all, except for the atmosphere, the air, like a spring afternoon before a storm, full of resigned anticipation: *This will happen. I have no umbrella. I will get very wet.* She lay in bed, and the dark was so total that she touched her face to see if the blanket covered her eyes. Then a fine pink line stretched along the bottom of the window shade. Not like a ribbon but like a strip of flesh, as if a naked person were standing outside, pressed against the glass. Perfect unblemished pink, balanced on the darkness, stretched between darknesses, now turning to blue as dawn came on. And then she knew she should put a baby in the boat, a round, fat, soft baby. This was the answer to a question she did not realize had been asked.

In the morning, Brigid went into the studio and began to paint the odd boat. She brought the Mary Cassatt book with her, and tried first to get the blue of the beautiful chair. She stood still for nearly an hour, and then she painted the baby, well before the boat was even sketched in, so that the baby appeared to be floating on the water, Moses without the basket, just riding the waves, this perfectly formed, astonishing baby, legs in the air, arms held out for balance. But when she saw it, Miss O'Keeffe said, "Ah, so you're a surrealist now, is that it? We make quite a household, goat skulls and now this charming *puti*. Who would believe us, eh? Such strange goings-on."

Brigid sometimes let herself think about it, the moment Julian Granger stepped up behind her in the art room at school. She understood at once that he was important, that he was looking for something—how did she explain it to herself?—to control. Something he might buy. She learned all the words later, but *imperious* was the one she liked best, a shine about him, some kind of gold gleaming behind his body.

The man who kept the grounds at Ghost Ranch, the one Miss O'Keeffe called Juan, was singing. Brigid could hear the tune rising from the bottom of the arroyo. She knew the singer but not the song, though she thought it sounded spiritual, what her mother would have called "churchy." The pitch was high for a man—almost girlish, which made her start to laugh—this voice out of that body. And then there he was, up the rise in front of her. He stopped, fell dead silent. Brigid saw he was much younger than she'd thought, maybe just a year or two older than she was.

"Oh!" he said, as if something had pierced and deflated him, a briar, a thorn in his shoe. "I didn't know you were out here. Pardon me, Miss. . . ."

"Brigid."

"Brigid. I was just. . . ."

"Singing. I was enjoying your singing."

"Well, I'm not much of a singer. The rest of my family, though, they're nice to listen to. It just gets me from place to place."

"I had a friend when I was little," Brigid said, surprised at her own desire to talk to this stranger, but she kept going. "She did that. She sang all the time. She moved herself though the world by singing. I always knew where she was."

Juan looked at her. His teeth were very white. "My mother and daddy and my brothers, they're all singers. They play guitar and piano too. Not me. But I'm the only poet."

"Really?" Brigid said.

"Well, I scribble a bit. A little." He glanced off behind Brigid toward Miss O'Keeffe's house. "You work for the Great Lady now, don't you? Do the letters and all that?" He laughed. "You're like me on the inside."

What a thing to say, Brigid marveled. But that was a poet for you. Juan stepped back and apologized for taking up her time. She saw he was missing a tooth—maybe two. It made his face strange now, too colorful: suntanned skin, lips burnt pink, all those white teeth, and then that darkness just beyond, like a quiet threat. He moved past her, toward the garage, in long, almost comical strides, as if he were making fun of walking.

Like me on the inside. Brigid repeated the phrase as she let herself in the windowless office and locked the door. She opened the second drawer in the file cabinet and shuffled through to "G." This time she removed it, the folder marked Julian Granger. Later she might read the letters in order, but now she only wanted to have a look at the most recent.

Typed, she saw, with a handwritten note added at the bottom, dated February 19, six months ago. Her eyes lit on the word "August," and she felt sick, breathless. She forced herself to go back to the first line, read through the friendly salutation, the references to people she did not know, the two sentences about winter in New York, the one sentence about his work. And then: *delighted accept invitation visit.* Words like grimacing, gritted teeth on the page. Again the promise to stay with friends. She wondered if Julian Granger thought of her as one of these friends. She doubted he thought of her at all.

She could pretend to be sick. She could say Theo needed her. But she'd just come here and got started on this work. If she left, Miss O'Keeffe might not have her back. And he could find her in town if he wanted to. Brigid knew she had to think about this more carefully, read the other letters. Maybe there was some mention of her, and then she would know what to do. She closed her eyes, listened to the house, which seemed to have gone very still. Miss O'Keeffe was napping. The cook and the housekeeper had gone to Taos for groceries. She carried the folder to the desk and sat down, adjusted the lamplight, opened the folder, moved the first letter off to the side. The second, dated the month after Julian Granger's visit, whined with apologies and fawning. Delay to thank her for such a wonderful visit, perhaps overstayed the welcome. Spent so much time in town. Charming place, though not my usual scene. Hard to adjust to life in New York after such vistas as yours. Such extraordinary conversation. And so on.

"The day after tomorrow," Miss O'Keeffe said at dinner, "we'll have a guest for a couple of days. A painter from New York named Julian Granger." Brigid nodded, and Miss O'Keeffe raised her eyebrows. "You know him?"

"He came to a class I took at the high school. About a year ago."

Miss O'Keeffe looked at her for a long time. "Did he like your work?" she asked finally. The tone of the question, Brigid noticed, was peevish, embarrassed, jealous. The green-eyed monster. She remembered that from high school too, but imperfectly, an image. Miss O'Keeffe as a dragon, as the medusa.

"Not very much."

"I can imagine."

"Should I stay with my brother?"

"Why would you do that?"

"To make room for him."

"He'll stay in Taos, I'm sure. Did he say anything specific about your work?"

"He thought it was too much imitation." Brigid tried to guess what the next question would be, and prepare her answer. No, I never saw him after that. A lie. But Miss O'Keeffe didn't ask. She handed over the day's mail.

Brigid walked back to her little office the long way, from outside the house. The air was still and thin with the scent of rain, like bleach. A storm coming. Julian Granger would bring a storm with him, a deluge of talk, and it would all be fascinating and brash, conversation and gossip, the woe and exhilaration of life in New York. As soon as he arrived, the skies would open, and they would all be caught together. No one could escape.

"I don't recall using the word *trespass*, Brigid," Julian Granger was saying. "I think all I said was that you ought to meet her." He had seated himself across from Brigid at Miss O'Keeffe's dining table. A roast chicken sat between them, looking, Brigid thought, like a naked, headless baby. She could not drive this notion away. Julian poured wine for the three of them, and they admired its color, a deep, friendly magenta, a hue that looked like it should have a voice.

"When was this?" Miss O'Keeffe asked.

"I told you about each other more than a year ago," Julian said.

"Really?" Miss O'Keeffe said. "I must have forgotten."

The two of them turned to Brigid. She smiled and shrugged, took a mouthful of wine. Too much.

"Not so fast," Julian said quietly. Miss O'Keeffe watched them over the rim of her wineglass. Her expression was closed, as if she were a drawing of herself.

The meal was very good—bread that Miss O'Keeffe had made, the chicken with runner beans and tomatoes she had grown. They ate without much conversation until Julian noticed Brigid had not touched her chicken and asked why and Brigid told them.

"I had a baby one summer," Miss O'Keeffe said. She waited then for the effect.

Julian smiled. "I've heard that story," he said. "The woman who worked for you."

Brigid thought she would faint, but then her breath came back, and she realized she was almost frantic for this story. It was a way to see how Miss O'Keeffe would treat her if the truth ever came out.

"The summer of 1945," Miss O'Keeffe said. "She refused to admit she was pregnant, and I had to take her to the hospital. And when I went back to get her, she claimed there was no baby, even though I knew it was in the nursery. She said, over and over, There is no husband. There can be no baby. But we found the father, in a mining camp in Colorado. And we had a wedding. It took me an entire summer to get that baby married."

"What a good sport you were, Georgia," Julian said.

"What else could I do?"

"Throw the baggage out!"

How could you paint this? Brigid wondered. History repeating itself. Maybe you would have to use the words themselves, stencil them on the canvas. But then, why bother with the paint? She listened to Miss O'Keeffe and Julian Granger talk about people they knew in New York, artists who had made bad marriages, struggled with children. Now and then he glanced across the table at Brigid, but without feeling, as if he were checking the time, looking at the face of a clock. It came to her very clearly she would never tell him about the baby, because this exact expression would greet that revelation. If she said, we made a golden-haired girl, Julian Granger would look at his watch.

Miss O'Keeffe went to bed earlier than usual, something quiet and defeated in her manner. Julian whispered the question, "Is she all right?"

"We make her feel old," Brigid said after they heard the bedroom door click shut. She led Julian outside to the patio, lit the candles on the table. "She tells me every few days to stop making her feel old and useless."

They settled into chairs and Julian repeated the word, *old, old, old.* "You're what, now, nineteen? What are you doing here? Your parents—I remember I met your father. Not for very long, but. . . ."

"He's dead."

"I know. I heard about it." Julian Granger shielded his eyes. An odd gesture for sympathy, Brigid thought.

"What did you hear?"

Julian Granger looked away, out into the darkness surrounding them. "That it was unpleasant."

"It was," she said. "Ugly." She saw it again, the ruined bodies, the bleeding everywhere. Theo's plum-colored shirt darkening with their parents' blood.

"And your brother?"

"He's working. And trying not to be a drunk Indian."

"Like your father."

"Yes."

"How's it going for him?"

Brigid gazed into the candle flame, then brought her left hand very close to it. "He's a lot like our father," she said, "but I think he'll be okay."

Julian nodded, watched her hand, wincing. "You should paint more Indian," he said after a while. "Your father actually said that, in the bar that night before you showed up to haul him away." He looked up away into the night sky. "And he left with you so peacefully. Why was that? I mean, how did you do it?"

Brigid shrugged.

Julian waited, but then he seemed to understand she wasn't going to explain. "Your father said, she paints like a white girl. I told him you were partly a white girl, and that's when you walked in."

"Looking like a white girl," Brigid said. "I'm not a white girl though."

"I remember that necklace you wore."

"I buried it with my mother."

"Why?"

"I'm not sure. Because it was a white girl necklace. I think I wanted her to have something of mine. Wherever she was going. She might need to trade it for safe passage."

"Fair trade," Julian said. He got up and let himself back into the house. Brigid wondered if he was gone for the night, to bed, to his rental car, a grand conveyance, a barge on wheels. Certainly she would hear its great door slam, its engine roar to life, the tires slipping on the gravel. That was how he'd left last time. Dropped her off at her house, practically in the middle of a conversation.

But no. Now he was back, with the wine bottle and their glasses. "There's money in it," he said, towering above her, the bottle and glasses gleaming in the candlelight. Brigid could see prints on the glasses, his fingers ghostly, her lips on the rim. "If you paint more Indian, you stand to make a lot more money."

"What's more Indian?"

"William Garrett."

"All those shapeless women. They look like ponds. Ponds of color with heads attached to them. Women staring at nothing. Clutching a feather or an ear of corn. It's pathetic."

"It sells."

"It sells *here*," Brigid said.

Julian kicked the footstool closer and sat down in front of her. Their knees almost touched. He held out the wine glasses and she took hers with its kissed rim. By the light of the candle, his hands seemed immense, his fingers casting long, thick shadows. The darkness enclosed the two of them, like a tent. "You're too young to know what sells where," Julian said as he poured a little wine into her glass, more into his own.

"It's just what the white people want," Brigid said. "It's not about the subject."

"The white people have the money," Julian said. "You should have some too. And by the way, it's never about the subject. It's about the artist. If you leave here and go anywhere thinking otherwise, you'll be eaten alive."

"So where should I go?"

"New York is the only place that matters."

They sat in silence. A voice in Brigid's head whispered *paint the wine in the mouth, paint the taste on the tongue.* She didn't know what it meant or whose voice it was. She leaned forward. "Who buys your work?"

"Everyone," he said. "All kinds. A boutique hotel in Paris, in the Marais."

Brigid didn't know what the Marais was. "I'd like to go to Paris," she said.

"So paint more Indian."

She realized he hadn't understood what she meant, or he pasted his own meaning over the top of hers. She wanted to go to Paris as a painter, but he would have her go as a woman who could afford to, as a tourist. She touched his knee, intending to explain. He flinched, barely a shiver, and she moved her hand back quickly, settled it as a fist in her lap.

"I should tell you I got married," he said. "In June. Just so you know."

"Oh," Brigid said.

"She's an actress."

"Oh," she said again. She pictured Doris Day, and the thought made her laugh out loud.

"You seem happy about it," Julian said.

"I am." She knew he was waiting for her to say more, explain this odd happiness. "I should give you a wedding present, then," she said, thinking of the two canvases in her studio, the drunk Indian and the bright hills. The drunk Indian would show him, show Julian Granger she could paint what she was. What he believed she was. And so she understood, finally, there in the dark, what he'd thought of her all along, which was a kind of slave, a low-class piece of flesh. That's what *paint more Indian* meant: don't get above yourself. Don't start acting as if you're a white woman.

White women are for marrying. Women like you are for screwing in cheap motel rooms outside Taos.

It was heart-stopping, breathtaking, this truth.

Paint that.

Brigid saw the words stenciled along the bottom of a canvas, *Women like you are for screwing in cheap motel rooms outside Taos.* And above the words? Maybe the words should go at the top? The image that came to Brigid right there, with Julian Granger staring at her, was the Mona Lisa, but in American dream-of-Indian dress: beads, buckskins, a feather in her hair.

"You should come to New York," Julian was saying. He drained his glass, poured more. He tipped the bottle toward Brigid's glass, a question, but she lay her palm over the rim. "Go to art school. You could stay with us. Anne has a huge apartment in the Village. Huge for New York. He gazed up over her shoulder at Miss O'Keeffe's house. "Not huge like this. Plenty of room though."

That would be great. Brigid heard the tone in which she might say the words. *A little harem. Your women together under one roof. Perfect.* For the first time and all of a sudden, she felt glad about the baby, a deep contentment, flooding the marrow of her bones. She had something Julian Granger couldn't take back, couldn't take away, even though she didn't actually have the baby. Pain seared in her chest. Red. It felt red, as if she might be able to see it. This would be the baby's first birthday. Brigid had to remind herself. No. This *is* the baby's first birthday, the tiny girl she named Sasha, living somewhere, somewhere with that dark woman, darkly beautiful, darker than Miss O'Keeffe. Even if she was sleeping happily in another woman's arms, Sasha still belonged to Brigid. Julian would never know. That would be his loss. He should have a loss too.

Nancy

Our cousin's wedding at the Citadel went off in the usual way, though Henry was worried by all the swords the groomsmen carried and unsheathed in front of the departing bride and groom. He was relieved then, when it proved to be only a ruse to get the couple to kiss. Still, I thought, what a horrible way to approach affection, to demand it publicly with weapons not intended for this specific use. I wanted to share this notion with someone, particularly one of the many handsome cadets, but Henry led me away from the reception hall to the surrounding woods and their half-hidden meandering trails. We remarked about how much time we'd spent lately amidst the flora and the fauna. We used the word *amidst*. Henry wondered if either of us would grow up to be a botanist. "Cannabist," I said. We felt we were extraordinarily clever, but of course we weren't. "This is my first wedding," I told Henry, "and I'm totally shit-faced."

We were discovered by one of the groomsmen, an older alumni the others called White Bob, even though he wasn't white and his name was Rodney. This seemed hilarious. I thought maybe I should call myself White Nancy, but I had enough sense not to say it out loud. He said he'd keep our secret if we'd share the weed, and that seemed a small enough price. Henry asked about his name, and White Bob said it was a lot better than Black Rod. He said this so matter-of-factly that I didn't even laugh.

"That's cool," White Bob said. "You're too young to get the joke. You're too sweet."

"Not sweet," I said, "not even a little." We told White Bob the story of youth group.

"Youth group is a completely fucked up idea," White Bob said. "It's a totally lazy white person thing. No colored momma I ever met would let some other adult introduce her child to the Savior. Maybe she'd allow her sister if she was handy, but not a stranger. That's like. . . ." But White Bob couldn't think of anything it was like. "They also probably listen to your opinions." He spat the word, like it was an obscenity. "Like you'd be old enough to have any." He looked into my eyes. "But I guess you are, because you done opinionated not to go to youth group." Then he sat down in the middle of the trail, pulled his knees to his chest, hugged his arms around them. "Lord," he said, "listen to me. I am one changed motherfucker."

Later, after we'd gone back in to the reception, I noticed that White Bob was the only black person in the room, apart from the women carrying trays of tiny appetizers and the men behind the bar. I wondered how this could happen in the last years of the twentieth century, and then had to remind myself it didn't implicate the entire armed services. I planned to ask my cousin's new husband about it later. The DJ played "Beast of Burden," and White Bob asked if I wanted to dance. I did. I tried to locate my parents in the sea of faces, gauge their reaction, but they were nowhere to be found.

"Beast of Burden" is one of those songs you can't figure out. Is it fast or slow, do you hold on or step back? White Bob thought it was slow. He seemed in fact to think the lyrics and music constituted an entire drama of affection and betrayal. Am I tough enough? Am I rich enough? I'm not too blind to see. He held me gently but awkwardly, as if we were in one of those terrible high school dance classes. Worse than youth group, because lying wasn't possible—you were just so completely exposed, badly dressed and poorly coordinated. Except White Bob was totally graceful, in his dress uniform and hipster moves. I had two strange, cool thoughts: first that my skin was more like his than it was like anyone else's on the dance floor. And second: our dark bodies were made of taffy or that beautiful fondant icing and a cosmic spoon was twirling us into complex and astonishing shapes.

"A cosmic spoon?" White Bob repeated, a little too loudly. Another of the groomsmen turned and gave us a huge, theatrical wink, which White Bob returned. "So what are you gonna do with your life, Miss Nancy Diamond? You're too young to be a full-time stoner."

"Not sure," I said. "What about you?"

"Finish med school," White Bob said, "up in New York. Live on Governor's Island, my childhood home. Be with my own kind."

"What do you mean, your own kind?" I said, but White Bob didn't answer. Henry was right then dancing past us with our cousin, the bride, stepping on her dress, though she seemed not to notice. "My brother's going to New York too. You should hang out." Over White Bob's shoulder, I thought I saw my father's face, clouded. Or maybe just blurry.

"Stormy weather, aft," the bride said to White Bob. "My uncle."

"Beast of Burden" ended, and the DJ oozed right into "Stairway to Heaven." White Bob pulled me closer. "We will hang out," he said. "I like your bro." White Bob smelled really good, I decided. He smelled like a cliché: Old Spice.

"Oh no," Henry said. "Here comes Dad."

"Gotta go," White Bob said. "Time to perform."

White Bob, I recalled, was the best man, and in charge, therefore, of the rituals. First the bride's bouquet: a short, purposeful lob to her maid of honor. Then the bride sat down and drew her dress—I saw the mark of Henry's shoes on the hem—up over her knees, while the groom reached up farther to retrieve the garter. The DJ spun "Bolero" and theatrics ensued, the groom wiping sweat from his brow, the bride managing to look like both a nun and a harlot. How did she do that? I wondered. Maybe it was the look of brides everywhere. I wanted to think about this.

Eventually the groom captured the garter and stood up, triumphant. He stretched the garter over his head between his index fingers and let fly, aiming carefully at White Bob, who, with his head turned in conversation, reached up and caught it. The room exploded into cheering, so perfectly timed was this move. I knew we'd just seen the most wondrous moment of the entire wedding, and that I would never forget it.

White Bob looked right at me as he pulled his fistful of garter out of the air and began to move through the crowd toward the maid of honor. The DJ cued "Bolero" again. I wasn't sure I could watch this last lurch of ritual and White Bob's hands on the maid of honor's leg. But I did. I moved around Henry for an unobstructed view. It was glorious and hor-rible, the pale, freckled leg, the sky blue garter, the black hands working their way up. I felt envy and hopelessness as a kind of cavern yawning inside me. Where my lungs should be, there was suddenly empty space. I wanted to run outside into the bright, breezy oblivion of Charleston and never come back. My parents and Henry would find me, we'd go back to our motel, and in the morning begin the drive home. But White Bob did it again, looked up at me with his hands under another woman's dress. Then he helped this woman to her feet, handed her a glass of champagne, took one for himself.

Spoons yammered on glasses. White Bob began to speak. It was astonishing: gone was the backwoods black boy with his momma and his curious syntax. He was from Virginia suddenly, or some cultured outpost in North Carolina, Asheville maybe. Henry stepped in close and whispered in my ear, "Is that the same guy?" White Bob was quoting from the Book of Ruth, "Where you lead I'll follow," and the army wives laughed softly, making a collective sound more like muffled crying. White Bob went on to assure our cousin that her new husband was a good leader, a born leader, so she was lucky there if she was going to be following. He wished them children and grandchildren. He pulled a square of paper out of his jacket, unfolded it and read a poem about what the bride and groom would want for their journey. His mother wrote it, he said, and it had been read at many weddings, and all those other couples were still married. "Swimming the shallows, rowing the deeps, knowing the difference." That was my favorite line. I loved the sound of White Bob's other voice, his new voice, curling around the words of the poem. I hoped it was one of those endless poems, like *Paradise Lost*, so he could go on reading for a long time.

Afterwards, he was mobbed by wedding guests I didn't know. Henry took my arm and led me outside, back into the trails for another smoke. "He's a little strange," I said to Henry, "but he said he lives in New York."

Henry said, "Who?" and I figured it was best not to answer. We wandered off the trail and into the campus. Henry wanted to find the art studio. He wondered what kind of art army guys made. We stood below the clock tower for a while. We wandered back to the reception hall, where our parents were looking for us. Our uncle, our father's brother, said, "AWOL again, you two?"

"We've got them on a short leash these days," our father said. He was happily drunk. "Time to go, my heathen children."

I wanted to find White Bob, but then I wondered what I would say to him. Thanks for the dance? Good luck in New York? Take care of Henry?

Call me sometime? I was seventeen and he was—well, I didn't know exactly—maybe twenty-three? The years between stood like a barrier high as the clock tower. The clock's hands went around and around, unreachable, unstoppable.

He found me, though, at the very last minute, my parents and Henry already in the parking lot, my father turned away to unlock the car door. He held my elbow gently, like I was the old I'll never be.

"You take care now. Don't smoke too much of that stuff. Stay out of youth group."

"Okay," I said. "You too. Henry will find you."

"Tell him I live on Governor's Island. But I'll find him first." Then a kiss somewhere in the vicinity of my ear, White Bob's cheek soft and warm against mine. Old Spice. And these last words, whispered slowly so I would make no mistake about them later. *I can find you too when I want to.* Not if. When.

When was five months later, after Henry had left for New York too, to live with friends, work as a waiter, try to paint his bird's-eye maps. *When* came in the form of a postcard. *Finally got in touch with Henry. Hope this finds you far away from youth group. Where are you going to college?* I didn't know the answer yet, but there was no way to tell White Bob, since he didn't include a return address. But really, I thought, how big could Governor's Island be? How many Rodney Jacksons could live there? The public library had telephone books, zip code listings. By Monday, my letter was on its way. By the next week, White Bob had written back. There was so much mail coming into the Diamond household from colleges, banks, and credit card companies that no one noticed White Bob's hand, small as typing, on the legal-sized envelopes.

Our letters were brief, a weather report, a med school story, a high school story. All the important stuff was missing on purpose. Omissions were securely *there*, secrets, little jokes, allusions, all of it an explanation of how White Bob was a changed man and I was not exactly what I appeared to be. And so, but still, I never told him about Simon Anderson. In the eyes of this black man, who called himself White Bob, I could pass. It was ridiculous, awful. The world had turned and turned again and arrived at this improbable place.

Henry too, was a changed man. He had found himself a cheap car and drove it all over the five boroughs. He waited tables at night, took an art class when he could afford it, and painted during the day in a loft in the Bowery. He told me he was doing a kind of portrait now: like an actor's head shot, but instead of the face, he painted a map of the person's hometown. Poughkeepsie, Missoula, San Diego, Charlottesville. He made the most of Dad's connections, and, through Mom, Simon Anderson's. People found jobs for him. Lately, he'd got on with a sign company, designing banners, making a lot of money. "My best work hangs in that fine gallery called Madison Square Garden," he said, "seen by more people than will gaze upon the *Mona Lisa* in a single year."

He met up with White Bob every month or so. They drank in McSorley's then swung through the trees in Central Park. They presided over Governor's Island. These letters persisted, twice a month, twining with Henry's phone calls and visits home, through the second half of my senior year in high school and into the summer.

College was going to be Clemson, my father's alma mater. I knew already that I would hate it, the adorable little college town and probably most of the people. But it would be away. And away was the point.

I'm one changed motherfucker, Rodney had said. Everybody knows that feeling. But I wondered, did anybody ever want to get back to that unchanged self, age fifteen or maybe eighteen, before the world and all its distractions came rushing at you, into you? Or did change come thick and fast and more and bigger so that it seemed your whole life was change?

Jan Vermeer and Georgia O'Keeffe enter from upstage center, seeming to come up from under the horizon, as if taking a curtain call. They walk purposefully toward the edge of the stage. They stare out into the audience. They do not look at each other when they speak.

GEORGIA: What do you remember?
VERMEER: I have a dim memory of the room suddenly going dark.

G: Dim . . . dark. Very funny.

V: And the people sitting there with me stopped talking. What about you?

G: I remember that I could see again.

V: Bright light at the end of a tunnel?

G: Something like that.

V: I don't remember childhood.

G: I don't remember school.

V: Except that nothing they taught you was very useful.

G: When I think back on all the crap I learned in high school, it's a wonder I can think at all.

V: That's a song about a camera. Film, actually.

G: You've kept up, haven't you?

V: Not much else to do.

White Bob asked if he could come to Clemson to visit, and I said no. It was too small a place, too much like a crazy family. Everybody watches everybody else. Are you ashamed of me? White Bob wanted to know. I wasn't. It was that college had made me feel suddenly old, reasonable, prescient, brutally honest. Or out there, Henry said. College has taken you to the edge of the known world, he said, though I was sure his wild life in New York had done the same to Henry. I told White Bob the absolute truth: you know what's going to happen between us. I don't think I want to have it happen in a dorm room. Even a nice dorm room like this. Right, White Bob said. Gotcha. I should have thought of that. You'd prefer my place. I would, I said, I really, really, really would prefer that.

His place was the house he was raised in, on Governor's Island, in Upper New York Bay. His father had been in the Coast Guard. His mother had died six years ago and his father moved over to Long Island and remarried. White Bob didn't much like his stepmother. Not exactly evil, he said, just . . . wrong.

"Wrong?" I wished I could peer through the miles of telephone line and see his face.

"For one thing, she's too young for him."

"Ahem," I said.

"I know," White Bob said, "but she acts young. You at least have that *gravitas.*"

I had to consult a dictionary for *gravitas,* I'm ashamed to admit.

I said good-bye and called Henry to talk about a trip to New York.

"You should come up and see the Macy's parade," he said. "Like really see it, you know, not on TV, but up close. Feel the breath of Bart Simpson on your face." Henry had a job working the floats, Bart Simpson's handler, he called himself, the person who took care of the wires that kept Bart from drifting away, over to Brooklyn or New Jersey, depending on the wind.

"You could ride along," Henry said. "When's the last time you were in a parade?"

"1970. July 4." I remembered exactly. "I rode a bike with red, white, and blue streamers. Lester Maddox was the governor. He rode a bike too, backwards, and then he handed out dollar bills."

"This will be different," Henry said.

So the dream I had that night in my nice dorm room didn't come completely out of nowhere: me, larger than life, bulbous, floating above Fifth Avenue, tethered to the earth by a long, slender string clutched— though I could barely see this—in the dark fist of White Bob. The dream was unusually alive with sound, a swirl of voices from the street below, plomp, plomp of tuba-heavy marching bands, Katie Couric's endless commentary. In the dream, I worried that parade-goers could see up my skirt, but then an out-of-body view showed I was wearing trousers. Immediately, though, another difficulty presented itself: I had to give White Bob a message, though I didn't, for a moment, know what I was supposed to say. I shouted down to him, but he didn't look up, or else he looked up when I wasn't saying anything.

Finally, the floating me cupped her large, round hands around her huge mouth and yelled. The message was *When can I start calling you Rodney?*

On the phone the next morning, I told White Bob my dream. "Can I call you that?" I asked him.

"Sure. Just so you call me."

"That's an old line."

"I'm an old guy now. I live alone on an island. I've aged two years since I last saw you."

"So have I."

"But I bet it looks better on you. I'll see for myself next week."

Thus it was arranged. I would fly to New York the day before Thanksgiving. Rodney was at grand rounds, and Henry was working, so I would take the bus from La Guardia and the ferry to Governor's Island. The key was under the mat. I didn't know anything about grand rounds, but I appreciated the sound of it: a square dance grand finale. One of those crazy calls like *Wrong Way Promenade* or *Wrong Way Thar*.

Which was how I found myself in Rodney's childhood bedroom, contemplating his bookcase. The books made a funny collection: *Lucifer's Hammer*, *Zen and the Art of Motorcycle Maintenance*, *The Little Prince*, an ancient collected Shakespeare, its spine broken. "Antoinette Lee" written at the top of the flyleaf, the ink faded. Below this, I saw a much more recent dedication: "For my son Rodney, 1992. To see you through."

I lifted the book carefully and crossed the room to Rodney's bed. I pulled my T-shirt over my knees and opened the book on top of it, bent my head and sniffed, taking in the scents of libraries, cardboard boxes, and hospital rooms. The copyright year was 1942, the editors two professors from Smith College who wrote an introduction about apostrophes and brackets, and full of claims of merits and shortcomings, poems in honor of Shakespeare, long, long commentaries. I sighed. No wonder there were so few English majors anymore. I had been looking forward to a course in Shakespeare, but not all these . . . I thought the word "condiments." No marginalia to help either, not for more than a thousand pages until— and here I gasped, actually put my hand over my mouth—*Othello*. And then no more after that until—really, it was unbelievable—*Antony and Cleopatra*.

What words did Antoinette Lee leave for herself and the reader who would turn out to be her son? In the introduction to *Othello*, she underlined *no comic relief, his credulity seems monstrous, force of shattered idealism, leaving only unfathomable sorrow*. Her first comment is "Hmmmm?"

in a tiny, upward-slanting hand, using thin-tipped black pen. She was responding—indicated with an arrow—to the sentence "His suicide is a kind of atonement." Later, she's circled the word "circumscription" and written beside it "love represents loss of power." In other notes, she seems obsessed with truth, asking questions like "how does one know the truth?" and at the very end of the play, this small essay: "How much true self-knowledge of protagonist at the end of any tragedy? Maybe profound but not necessarily true?" And then, "How much truth can humans bear?"

In *Antony and Cleopatra*, I thought I heard a different voice from Antoinette Lee, her real voice. The comments were funny, saucy, sarcastic. Where Caesar says to Pompey, "Our gravest business frowns at this levity," she'd written "kill joy." Beside a line about "Lepidus troubled with the green sickness," she'd written "I'll bet he is." When Canidius says to Caesar, "I will render," she completed the line "what is Caesar's."

I woke to the sight of Rodney sitting on the bed beside me. He was shaking me gently awake. His face looked old in the trembling glow of early morning, ancient, lined with sleep and worry. The light behind him had a pearly quality to it, and silvery, as if objects in the room were covered in frost.

"You fell asleep with Shakespeare," he said.

I tapped the book. "With your mom talking."

"It's amazing, some of it. Like she knew the future."

"The future wasn't so terrible," I said.

"Except that there was no Mom. Did you see in *Macbeth* how she didn't annotate anything but drew all these pictures of knives?"

"I missed that."

"It's where the witches ask for a wind," Rodney said. "She made all kinds of little dark drawings in that play." Rodney stared out the window. "I still don't know what she was thinking."

"Do you know what I'm thinking?"

"I believe I do," he said.

Sasha

Jennie was still gone, at home in Long Beach, for the rest of September, then October. They talked every day, though, like a married couple, as Aaron Fisk observed, though mostly Jennie talked and cried. "The day I can get through one of these calls without crying," she told Sasha, "I know I can come back to school."

Sasha nodded, though of course Jennie couldn't see her. She had a funny urge to pet the phone, as she would Jennie's hand while she talked.

"I try not to read the paper," Jennie said. "'The Portraits of Grief.' And I know some of it's bullshit, maybe a lot of it. All these people can't have been such saints. Guys were smug assholes. Women yelled at their kids."

"But not your dad," Sasha said. She meant it. She'd met Jennie's dad on move-in day. He leaked nice from every pore.

"No, not my dad. He hardly ever raised his voice." Jennie started to cry.

Not today, Sasha thought. This isn't the day she can come back.

"I'd give anything if he'd walk in right now and start shouting."

Later, Jennie heard that when the North Tower collapsed, her father was actually in a stairwell, maybe around the twentieth floor, after he'd helped people get out of the building and then tried to get back up to the Marsh offices. "For fuck's sake," Jennie's mother had said, over and over, then because she couldn't stop saying it, she rearranged the words: "For the sake of fuck." She'd stopped drinking an entire bottle of wine every night, but after this piece of news, she started again. She'd gone in to work for one day, finally, at NBC where she was a writer, and then the anthrax letter to Tom Brokaw arrived, and she came home at noon and never went back. Jennie said most of the time she was either scared to death or furious. But Sasha knew it was hard to be angry with the dead. They didn't fight back. They just stood in front of you with their eyes closed and their heads hung down.

"Do you want me to come out there?" Sasha asked. "To visit. To bring your homework."

"I think I do," Jennie said. "But not the homework. Please." She went quiet for a while. "Sasha, I think we really need you."

Theo came to see her again, arranging the visit formally through Aaron Fisk, even though he could have called Sasha. Aaron invited them for coffee in his suite like before, but this time he stayed to listen.

"Do you want to know about her?" Theo asked Sasha. "I mean if I were you, I would."

Sasha nodded, but then all the questions made a kind of train wreck in her mind. She glanced at Aaron. "What do I want to know?"

"How did she figure out that she wanted to be an artist?" Aaron said

"It seems like she always knew," Theo said. "But I remember this one time. We used to go see Dad's mother in the Navajo home in Colorado. There's movies of this, actually. I wonder where they are."

This grandmother was very old, Theo said, but still full of life and mischief. He and Brigid loved her, the patchwork skirts she wore, her long, gray braids. One year, she gave them a sketchbook and a pack of colored pencils and asked them to draw her portrait.

"I didn't want to," Theo said, "but Mom and Dad made us both sit there and draw."

"Are your parents—" Sasha began.

"Died," Theo said. "Before you were born." He looked away from Sasha.

"I'm sorry," she said.

"It's okay. It wasn't okay for a long time. But it pushed my sister to . . . something. I'm not sure how to explain it. Away from something maybe."

"You should write this down," Aaron said. "People would read it."

"I know. I should do a lot of things where she's concerned. I'd hate to look like I was trying to make a buck off my sister."

"That's not what I mean," Aaron said. "A lot of people want to know about her work."

Something's going wrong here, Sasha thought. Maybe because I'm not filming it. Maybe sometimes filming keeps people on their good behavior.

"*I* want to know," Sasha said.

Theo seemed to soften, deflate. "I remember the exact words Granny said to my sister. Something like, 'Don't draw this.' She was looking around at the other women in the room. She was pointing at the other women and their beadwork and weaving, the paintings on the walls, braves on horseback, a coyote howling to the sky, a campfire, a tipi. 'Draw me another way,' she said.

"We asked why she couldn't come to live with us in New Mexico, and she said she would die of boredom and tourism. Too many white people. She didn't like most white people, though she thought my mom was all right. She used to say my mom was smart like the Navajo because she was German, another trickster people. She said she only let Dad marry a white person to know the enemy."

"But I'm—" Sasha began.

"You aren't, though," Theo said.

"What about the words in her paintings?" Aaron asked.

"No clue," Theo said.

"Did you speak Navajo?"

"Our dad tried to get us to learn, but we never did. I never did. Maybe she learned."

"There's this idea," Aaron said, "about her language, the words in her paintings. In the scholarship. People working on art history and linguistics."

"Like you," Theo said.

"Like me."

"What do they say?" Theo asked.

"Verbs in the Navajo language," Aaron began. "They're used according to the physical properties of their objects. Parts of a sentence move from most animate to least animate. Humans and lightning come before infants and big animals, which come before medium-size animals, which come before small animals, which precede insects, which come before natural forces, which come before inanimate objects and plants, which come before abstractions."

"Whew," Theo said. "So what does all that prove?"

"There's a hierarchy," Aaron said. "And abstractions are useless."

Theo grinned. "I was right to stay out of college. But you." Here he slapped Aaron on the back. "You, it's good for."

"It is," Aaron said. There was a note in his voice, humility, surprise, relief, that filled the empty room with warmth. "I'm lucky that way. I found my groove."

"Not everybody has that," Theo said.

"I think almost nobody," Aaron said.

After Theo left, Sasha helped Aaron wash the coffee things. For a few minutes, they didn't talk.

"I like him," Sasha said finally.

"Me too. I think it means a lot to him to see you."

"Thanks for having us in here."

"No sweat. But I have to say, it's strange too. Like the painting's come alive."

"What painting?"

"An early one, *The Point of an Error*. I can show you."

Aaron opened a closet and dragged out a heavy box. He sat down on the floor, lifted the lid off the box and began sorting through the contents. Sasha dried her hands and went to stand behind him. He came to a large anthology, *Visions and Voices*, flipped to the index, found the page. "Look. It's him."

And there he was, Theo Long Night, sitting in a pickup truck, left arm out the window, holding a bunch of arrows, his arm bent as if he's going to throw them, but the arrows are pointing the wrong way, behind him.

"It's like he's giving up," Sasha said. "Like he's saying the hell with this."

"Look inside the truck."

A bundle of something. Pink. Sasha could just barely make it out, a cushion, a pile of rags. Then, as if she'd put on glasses, the image took shape: a swaddled baby sleeping on the seat.

"And maybe that's you," Aaron said.

"No," Sasha said, but she knew he was right. "Can I take this upstairs? I feel like I want to look at it for a while. I'll bring it back."

"Sure," Aaron said. "No problem. But listen, as your RA I have to ask. Are you okay up there by yourself?"

"I'm okay. But for a room that small, it gets pretty lonely."

"I trust that won't get you into trouble." Sasha tried to understand what Aaron meant. He was good in this job, she thought. *Motherly.* The word surprised her, its little ache.

"Not likely," Sasha said. "And anyway, I'm going out to see Jennie this weekend."

"Ah," Aaron said. He reached for her hand and held it. "Be careful."

Sasha packed up a couple of days' worth of clothes, her math textbook, *The Harbrace Guide to English Grammar and Usage.* In Lit Hum, they'd just started *Medea.* She wondered if it might be horrible for Jennie and her mother if she arrived with a video camera, but then she banished the thought, slung the bag over her shoulder. She rode the elevator downstairs and walked through campus to the 116th Street subway.

It was darker underground than she'd remembered, and nobody was playing any music. That seemed odd. There wasn't, in fact, anyone else waiting. The train arrived nearly empty, and stayed that way to Penn Station. Sasha imagined most people were avoiding spaces they couldn't get out of quickly. She thought maybe she understood how the people in her film felt: did you want your clothes full of fire or full of air? Did you want death on some stranger's terms or on your own? Did you want to have one last go at flight, at magic, at miracles? She knew people would hate her for making up these questions. But she thought they were pretty close to what those people asked themselves as they stood at the windows, holding hands or punching numbers on their phones.

Sasha knew she wouldn't be able to say any of this to Jennie or Jennie's mother. They didn't care about the people in the air. They had a whole different category to contemplate: reentry. The people who went back in or back up when they didn't have to. These people wouldn't stop to call their loved ones. How would they explain? And anyway, they'd left their phones behind. Where was Jennie's dad's cell phone, for instance? In his briefcase, Jennie thought, which he probably left beside his desk or in an elevator. Jennie hoped they would find his wedding ring. She thought that might calm her mother down some.

In Penn Station, Sasha had a half hour before her train. She opened the camera bag and set up the video camera beside a kiosk covered with missing persons flyers. She pressed the on button and stepped away. In a few minutes a young man, maybe in his mid-twenties walked over and asked what she was doing. He smiled, seemed curious, nice, Sasha thought.

"Will you ask me that on camera?" she said.

He seemed suddenly exasperated, and then close to tears. She wondered if he would raise his left hand, which was curled into a fist, and hit her. "Okay," he said, finally, and Sasha eased him into position in front of the camera. "Why are you filming here?" he said.

"I'm not really sure," Sasha said, off camera.

"Well," he said, quite angry now. "You need to be sure. This is private."

"No. It isn't. It's a kiosk in a public place." Her voice broke and dropped to a whisper. "Not private."

The man began to cry. "I know," he said through his tears. "I know. It's hard to figure out what to do about this." He flung his hand toward the kiosk. "Nobody's missing," he said. "It's been too long. We all know what's happened to them." And then he walked away.

In the next twenty minutes, four other people stopped to look at the missing persons flyers. Sasha filmed them all. One man, maybe Jennie's dad's age, walked away without noticing her, and a woman, middle aged, heavyset, stood and wept. When she understood she was being filmed, she clapped her hands to her face and half ran, half stumbled out of the frame. Sasha followed her with the lens until she melted into a cluster of people. Another woman, much younger, stopped to read the flyers, and Sasha asked, from behind the camera, who she was looking for. This woman didn't turn around but spoke slowly and carefully, Sasha thought, as if she were just learning English, although she had no discernible foreign accent. "I don't know. I'm not even from New York City. I'm from Montana. I just happened to be here, visiting my sister. But now I can't make myself get on an airplane to go home. And I don't want to leave my sister. I'm going to have to quit my job. I'm an accountant at the university, in Missoula. The budget office. I'm pretty much losing my mind. My sister made me go outside today. This is my first trip away from East Eighty-fifth Street." She turned then to face the camera. "I'm scared shitless. Can you help me?" Then she reached for Sasha, to embrace her, to hang on, blocking the camera lens. There would be no picture, but the audio would work, recording their heartbeats.

The last person she filmed before she had to get on the LIRR was a black man in a business suit. He carried a cement-colored raincoat. Putty-colored, Sasha corrected herself. At first she wasn't sure why. *My mom would say putty*, a tiny voice told her, and she felt a clenching in her heart, a ripple in her lungs. Which mom? Where was her mom? Gone, her dad would say. Away, Theo had said. The man peered at the flyers and the photographs, moving slowly around the kiosk. His lips moved and his eyes closed and opened, as if he were learning the names, memorizing them. Sasha asked who he was looking for.

He laughed, just a little, and exhaled a long breath, as if he'd been holding it for some time. "Me," he said. "I think I'm looking for myself." He glanced at Sasha, but the camera beside her seemed not to make any impression on him. It was like he took it in as a part of her face. "How about you?"

"My mother."

"Where'd you last see her?"

Sasha shook her head.

"Ah," the man said, "so it's like that."

"Like what?"

"You let her go and now you want her back."

Sasha slid the camera off the tripod. "Maybe. I have to catch a train now."

"Where are you going?"

"Long Beach."

"Me too," the man said.

Sasha had no idea whether he was telling the truth. *No earthly idea*, she thought the words, saw them in her head, *no earthly*. He seemed like that, this man, something not of this world. She let him take the camera bag and lead her to platform gate and down the stairs to the waiting train.

Seconds after they boarded, the doors whooshed closed. Sasha saw they were nearly alone in the car, but still she did not feel afraid. She felt nothing, maybe a vague curiosity, as if she were watching television, as if mentioning her mother had created a kind of vacuum. They sat side by side, the man still grasping Sasha's bag. The train began to move and Sasha was relieved to notice he had chosen forward-facing seats. Almost immediately, the man said, "I get sick if I ride looking backwards." He took off his suit coat. Sasha smiled and nodded. "Do you live in Long Beach?" he said.

"No, no. I'm visiting a friend." She thought the man must be waiting for her to ask him the same question, but she couldn't bring herself to say the words. She believed somehow he would tell her what she needed to know.

When the train broke into daylight, Sasha was surprised to remember it was early afternoon, warm for October, the sun burning off that brownish tinge. Tan, somebody in her dorm had called it, skin-colored, and somebody else asked "Whose skin?" And then there was shouting, a fight, nearly to blows, but Aaron Fisk turned up just in time. Doors slammed. Everyone felt sad again, for a few days, and frightened, alone in their dorms rooms on the tenth floor, too high up.

"I'm a therapist," the man said suddenly. "I'm living with my parents in Long Beach because my place was. . . . It was on Church Street. It was my office too, so that's a problem." He made a terrible face and crossed his arms over his chest. "It hurts to think about it, but I can't stop. My dad has a restaurant in Long Beach, and I'm working there. But sometimes I just need to go back into the city." His voice trailed off.

"I'm at Columbia."

"Let me guess. Film student."

"Something like that."

They rode in silence for a while. The names come last, Sasha thought, and wondered why. Maybe like a title. You have to see what you are before you can call it something. See what you made or are made of.

"I'm Rodney Jackson," the man said and offered his hand. Sasha held it for a moment. His hand was very cold, perfectly manicured, smooth, a mannequin hand.

"I'm Sasha Hernandez," she said.

"Your name goes shhh," he said.

Now he's going to ask me all those other questions, Sasha thought, and I'm going to tell him. I'm going to keep going.

But that wasn't what happened. Rodney Jackson, it seemed, wanted to do the talking, even though it appeared to cause him acute physical pain. He clutched his belly and leaned forward as he spoke. Sasha wondered if he would be sick. His father's wife worked at Windows on the World, he said. And there was another friend.

Sasha watched herself do it: she patted his back. This complete stranger.

"You probably want to film me saying that," he said, "But you can't, and I'll tell you why. Because it wouldn't be spontaneous. That's what you're after, isn't it? A moment that's never happened before and never will again."

"I guess that's right."

"What will you do when we get to Long Beach?" Rodney Jackson asked.

"My friend is supposed to be waiting for me."

"Well, if he's not there—"

"She."

"If she's not there, I could drive you. My car's at the station."

"Thanks, but I have no idea where she lives."

"It's a small town."

"Her name's Jennie Burgett. Her dad. . . ."

"I know," Rodney said. "They're neighbors. We're a pretty sad lot on Oak Street."

Sasha didn't know what to say to this. She felt tears gathering and prickling in her eyes. Rodney Jackson probably had enough of that. She waited a minute.

"Do your patients ever make you cry?" Sasha asked. She spoke to the long, flat expanse of Rodney Jackson' back. He was still bent double, hugging his knees. His shirt was white, linen, Sasha saw, not the usual no-iron business attire. His shoulder blades pressed against the fabric. She could see the curve of his rib cage. "In front of them, I mean. Like right as they're talking."

The question made him twitch, noticeably, as if he'd heard a sudden, loud sound. "Not a lot," he said. "Not full-out weeping. Sometimes

I tear up. Usually they're busy crying, wiping their eyes, so I have time to recover."

"How is it working in your dad's restaurant?"

"It's all right. I don't wait tables. I'm the one who brings salad and bread and refills water glasses. I don't talk."

"Like your other job," Sasha said.

Rodney Jackson unbent himself slowly, sat up and smiled at her. "I think about it that way too."

The train eased into the Long Beach station. Rodney lifted Sasha's bag and followed her out of the car. Just past the platform, Sasha saw Jennie leaning on a Jeep, and she waved. Jennie didn't move, though her gaze drifted momentarily to Rodney.

"Hello neighbor," Jennie said when they reached her. She had dyed her hair a flat, false black. She held Sasha in a long hug. The chemical smell of the dye was fierce.

"This is new," Sasha whispered.

"Just this morning. Stop staring, Rodney."

"Jen," Rodney said. "I found a friend of yours."

"I guess you met Sasha," Jennie said. She looked at the bag he carried. "Or else you were stealing her stuff."

"Actually," Sasha said, "he'd be stealing mostly *your* stuff."

Rodney handed the bag to Jennie, who took it, slung it on her shoulder, and shook his hand. "Come over and visit Mom again. She appreciated it."

"I will," Rodney said. "Your hair's incredible." He moved closer to embrace Jennie and then Sasha.

"That's the look I was hoping for," Jennie said.

Sasha watched him go, his wandering gait, his head turning slowly left and right, as if he might find his car in the parking lot, but then again, he might not.

They got into the Jeep. "He's nice," Jennie said. "He used to babysit me. You heard about his stepmom, I guess."

"He said 'father's wife.'"

"God, we're fucked up," she said. "Totally mad."

Jennie had lost weight, Sasha saw. Her breastbone stood out beneath her sweater. She seemed exhausted by the act of turning the key in the Jeep's ignition. "Did you bring your camera?" Sasha nodded. "Mom's got a project for you." She pulled to the parking lot entrance. To their right, about a hundred yards away, Rodney stood, leaning over a Chevy Malibu, his palms flat on the hood, elbows locked, head lowered.

"Should we go talk to him?" Sasha said.

Jennie shook her head no. "I think I make it worse," she said and pulled out into traffic.

The Burgetts' house on Oak Street was white with modest columns, a green yard recently mowed, tall hardwoods on either side of the property and in the back. It looked, Sasha thought, like a house into which no sadness could come—so closed and disciplined and cared for that sadness would slink past, holding its breath. Jennie pressed a button and the garage door opened, revealing more discipline and order. Three bikes hung on one wall, gardening supplies stood on shelves in precise rows, five labeled file boxes were stacked neatly. "Christmas," one read. "Miscellaneous Holidays," said another. Jennie pulled in next to a white Ford Taurus. Beside the door, a refrigerator hummed contentedly.

This door opened into the kitchen. Mrs. Burgett sat at the kitchen table. She was bringing a glass to her lips. A can of Diet Coke sat at her elbow. She did not turn to look at her daughter or Sasha until they came to stand right beside her.

"Mom," Jennie said, her voice slightly raised, "I'm back. Remember Sasha?"

Jennie's mother gazed up at them. Sasha had never seen anything like Mrs. Burgett's eyes, which were light green and completely empty, the way blind people are sometimes shown in the movies.

"Sasha," Mrs. Burgett said. Her voice cracked, and she cleared her throat. She held out her hand but took it back before Sasha could hold it. "I know I met you on move-in day, but I didn't remember. I do now, though. Your hair. Of course it's you." She turned her head away again. "Move-in day." Sasha thought she must be speaking to Jennie. "I'd like to think about move-in day for a while. Did you know Dad cried when we left?"

Jennie went to stand behind her mother's chair but did not touch her. "I know," she said.

Mrs. Burgett nodded and took a drink out of her glass. Jennie led Sasha out of the kitchen. They passed a living room that was completely white, a dark study, and a small bedroom, before climbing the stairs. The house was immaculate, neat as a pin. Sasha thought the phrase was perfect for the Burgetts, that its neatness would hurt if you got too close, that it did hurt. Surfaces were completely bare—coffee tables, side tables, desks, even the mantle over the fireplace. It occurred to Sasha that maybe the Burgetts hadn't lived here very long, but then she thought she remembered Jennie saying something about the same house her whole life.

Upstairs, Jennie paused in the middle of the hallway between three bedrooms. "You can have the guest room," she said, "or we can share." She smiled. "Like before."

"You pick," Sasha said.

"Share. I miss your snoring."

Sasha laughed. The joke, for the six nights they shared a room: Jennie snored and talked in her sleep and sometimes wandered around until Sasha heard her and gently guided her back to bed. "Do you still . . . ?"

Jennie nodded and bent to roll up her pant leg. Green bruises bloomed along her shin. "The other leg's worse. Mom caught me on the landing, where the stairs turn. It was pitch black, but she heard me. She just happened to be coming up. Lucky."

Jennie's bedroom was as neatly kept as the rest of the house, twin beds carefully made, books tight and straight in their shelves, the tops of the desk, dresser, and nightstand bare except for a digital clock. The walls were alarming though, painted white, no decoration.

"Was your room always like this?" Sasha said.

"Not always. I got weird in high school. I didn't want any distraction—or feeling, really. I'd had all the Monet water lilies for years, you know the posters and the sheets on the bed, and it was very soothing. But one day, I thought you won't get anywhere being soothed every time you look up from your homework."

"You're hard on yourself," Sasha said.

"I know." They were quiet for a minute. "I think my mom's headed for a big crash."

Sasha dropped the bag on the bed and opened it. "Here's your—"

"No," Jennie said. "That can wait. Mom needs to go for a walk. If I don't take her, she never leaves the house. You ready?" Sasha pointed toward the bathroom. "Right," Jennie said. "Meet you downstairs."

Spotless, empty bathroom, though the scent of hair dye hung in the air, an almost visible haze. No soap, no towels, no shampoo in the shower. Sasha gazed at her reflection. "Under the sink," Jennie said just then, her mouth very close to the door on the other side. Sure enough, Sasha found a stack of towels, a bottle of tangerine liquid soap, lime shampoo, raspberry conditioner, toilet paper, tampons, arranged in a basket. "You run a tight ship," Sasha called, in case Jennie was still standing outside, but there was no reply. She washed her hands with the soap, which smelled like both summer and Christmas. When she shook out a towel, she saw it was covered with black fingerprints, and sometimes the impression of an entire palm, like a child's art project. The towel below this one was marked in the same way, and the towel under that one too, the whole stack of ruined towels neatly folded.

Brigid

A week after Julian Granger's visit, Miss O'Keeffe simply said it: Do you ever think about art school?

Art school. No one had even mentioned college. No, she should admit that wasn't true. College had always been the real subject whenever her parents had talked about money. There was no money, not for books, clothes, getting there, living there. No matter where *there* was. No money. Go talk to someone, Mrs. Silva the art teacher had said the year before, but when Brigid asked who, Mrs. Silva went blank. If you could get down to Santa Fe, Theo always said. The museum, the university. They must have art teachers. They would know.

But right now Brigid was afraid to talk to Miss O'Keeffe, who would think she wanted to leave. And she didn't want to leave. Ghost Ranch was so safe. A hilarious truth in this: no ghosts at Ghost Ranch. It was the safest place on earth. How to paint that? Like a prison is safe. Three meals a day, out of the weather, the warden's watchful eye, a bed, darkness at night, quiet. Prisons probably were never dark or quiet at night.

"I do, but it also scares me."

"All right," Miss O'Keeffe said. "I won't mention it again unless you bring it up."

Five minutes passed. They were in the kitchen, washing tomatoes from the garden. The light in the room seemed to come from inside the fruit.

"What was it like?" Brigid said. "Your school."

"Daunting," Miss O'Keeffe said. "Full of men, which I loved. But I was not taken very seriously because I liked to have fun. Because I was friendly. I learned more by working on my own, at my own speed." She stopped talking, brought a tomato close to her face, sniffed. "That's not true. I learned a great deal from the teachers, Chase in particular. But it was in opposition that I came to understand my own mind."

The rules are fine to know, she explained to Brigid. Necessary really. Composition. You don't know any of that now. You're just lucky with the brush. You have a good strong stroke, a sense of color, a different vision. School can't teach you this. School will in fact make you feel quite like an odd duck. I don't know this for certain, but I do suspect it, that you're already an odd duck. You wouldn't be here otherwise. You'd be married, working in the grocery or the post office. Babies on the way. Color, though, that was the skill to have.

Color. Brigid already knew something about that. Color was electricity. It made things work. Made *you* work. Color could knock you off your feet or turn you blind when you got hold of it. But that was the only way to stay alive: hold on to the color. Certain shades promised eternal life. No shades promised certain death, but some shades guaranteed boredom, and that was worse. So you had to find the good ones. Sometimes it was all a horrible mess and ooze, like the way your feet feel on the bottom of a lake. Bad, and the next move could be worse. Sometimes you just took a swipe at the canvas the way a man did in a drunken rage. And the canvas was the woman. And the canvas was your mother. The sound of glass breaking in the background. How to paint that?

Or else color was trapped inside, inside rocks, buried there, and you had to smash the rock against another rock. Sometimes it was in a tube, and then it was expensive. Sometimes the color was all in your head. Sometimes it was on the edge of a shirt worn by a man in a disappearing car. The most perfect hue. You've longed for it all your life. That man in the car. Where was he going? You had to paint him to find out.

Miss O'Keeffe gave Brigid the rat ends of tubes, powder clumped in jars. The powder and the oil made an odd thing happen, a sort of texture, a slick, what happens when unlike meet but don't mind. What would you call such a meeting? The first years of marriage? Brigid tried not to think about Julian Granger and his actress wife, a woman always working to become a different woman. How could you live with someone like that? Who was she really? Brigid gazed across the dinner table at Miss O'Keeffe. Who was she? Miss O'Keeffe had stopped baking bread, so their meals seemed flat and thin, cloudless. The bread had been the clouds.

Brigid would have to learn how to bake bread; otherwise they would die of exposure.

These were the kinds of ideas she had: a thing was not itself but more dangerous. She wondered if she were going just a bit crazy, or going backwards somehow, to childhood. This was how she felt after the awful deaths of Fuentes and her parents, after Sasha was gone, the ebbing away of sanity. She thought of the sacred heart, that picture at the back of the church. Jesus pointing to his heart, which was visible inside his chest, and on fire. His expression so serene. Or so ignorant. Didn't he know anything about synapses, electrical impulses, that a spark from his heart could blow him to bits? Thousands of artists had copied that original image, but it was always the same: calm, stupid Jesus, in every church in America. Brigid thought there had to be better representations in France and Spain, those rabid Catholic countries.

Did she really think the words *stupid Jesus, rabid Catholic?*

Art can't be taught, Julian Granger said, a long time ago it seemed. Art can only be practiced, imitated and practiced, until one day you realize all that screaming is coming from you. Is you. That's how he put it: all that screaming. She loved him for that.

She was the stupid one. She had listened to the wrong words. The important part of what he said was that art can't be taught.

So Brigid hoped Miss O'Keeffe would live forever. Then she would not have to go anywhere. This was school enough for what couldn't be taught anyway, this light, drawing it perfectly out of the air, through a veil or a tunnel of color and out the other side. And getting it imperfectly too. Some days, Miss O'Keeffe said, about Brigid's paintings, Well, I never quite saw it *that* way, and quickly left, slamming the studio door. Brigid knew Miss O'Keeffe had gone off to think about why she *hadn't* ever seen it that way, to brood about it. A half hour later, she might see the dark figure, 200 yards in the distance, staring at the mountain, trying to see. At this distance, Miss O'Keeffe looked tiny, a forgotten child, a little lost girl, and the sight made Brigid's heart bunch like a fist.

But the end of bread baking was not a good sign. More of the garden was left to go to weeds. Sometimes Miss O'Keeffe seemed not to hear

Brigid come into the room. At the dinner table, there was a constant clatter of things knocking against other things, because Miss O'Keeffe couldn't see well enough. Dinner was the only meal they took together. Miss O'Keeffe spent much of the day sitting in her room, her face turned toward the window, as if she were breathing the light. More and more, she asked Brigid to sit with her and hold her hand. After an hour or so when Brigid stood to leave, Miss O'Keeffe often said, "Please don't go." And Brigid would stay.

As the weeks passed, September into October, the relatives began to arrive. Vultures. A nephew from Chicago, with his elderly father, married to one of Miss O'Keeffe's sisters, who was herself too ill to travel. A second cousin, a third cousin once removed. All of them gathered in Miss O'Keeffe's bedroom, talking at full volume until Brigid couldn't stand it.

"You don't have to yell at her," she said.

"But she's deaf," the nephew said.

"Not *that* deaf."

The elderly brother-in-law, Fred, was almost bearable. He had what seemed to be endless patience for the hand-holding, a crystalline memory, and a pleasant, low voice. He spoke to Miss O'Keeffe about her childhood as if he had been there. "We didn't like the state of Virginia," he said, in the persona of his wife. Brigid heard his voice rise, almost an octave. "Too humid. And the people were odd." A kind of female lilt came into his speech. "They were very soft, the people of Virginia. We didn't understand how things worked between neighbors. There were rules everybody else already knew."

"They didn't grow anything," Miss O'Keeffe said. "Not by themselves, in gardens."

"You taught the girls at school to play poker, Georgia." he said. "Remember?"

"That I did."

Fred liked to walk, and so Brigid led him on tours of the ranch, naming the plants and darting animals, the moods and whims of the landscape. On the fourth day of his visit, on one of the walks, he stopped and grasped her arm, hard, not in a cruel way, Brigid reasoned later, but as old people will when an idea strikes them.

"We've been trying to discover," he said, "what exactly you do here."

"I was hired to attend to the correspondence."

"That's all?"

"All?" Brigid laughed. "Sometimes there are a hundred letters in a week."

"Is there legal work?"

"Some. But I don't do that."

"Of course not."

"I learned early on that what she really wanted was a companion."

"And you paint, I know."

Brigid nodded.

And then he asked a question she could hardly believe. "Do you paint for her? Do you work on her paintings?"

"No." Brigid tried to keep her voice settled, even. "And she doesn't work much these days."

"So you're the painter in the house now."

Brigid wondered what she should explain, why this mattered to him, what he was getting at. "Some days, I'm the only one painting," she said. "Some days no one in the house paints."

"Do you think she's not painting because you are?"

It was an odd idea. She would have to think about it.

"You can go home for Christmas," he said. "She doesn't really need you."

"I will," Brigid said. "But you know she doesn't really need anybody."

Theo chose an enormous fir tree, loaded it into his truck and brought it home. Brigid helped him carry it inside and trim the trunk to fit the metal stand. The tree seemed extraordinarily thirsty. Every morning Brigid lay under the lowest branches to pour more water into the reservoir. They talked about stringing lights and hanging ornaments.

"Do you miss them?" Theo asked.

"The decorations?" Brigid said.

"No."

"Sometimes I can't remember them," Brigid said, "or Fuentes."

"Everybody's lost without Fuentes. You hear that all the time in town."

"I wonder where they are."

"I think they're all together." Theo nodded toward the fire. "Their ashes mixed up."

That fire would have been blue with orange at its center, the whole spectrum of light contained invisibly, red to violet. So often Brigid had imagined that progression of color as cold, arcing high in the airless sky or in the lifeless pages of her science textbook, or the poster on the block wall in the art room at school. But this time it would be hot, blazing around their three shattered bodies, her father, her mother, Fuentes. Brigid did not want to see it, but she thought she should have had to, for some kind of resolution, an answer, the darkening curl of flesh, the shrinking of a person to the darkest, hardest kernel, and then to powder. How to paint that, that kind of disappearance? Reduce it to two dimensions, she told herself, or paint in layers, an accumulation of texture to show the opposite, a body going to dust. Stand back from the canvas and flick the brush forward to make a wild spattering. Or lay the canvas on the ground, stand over it, and weep paint.

Later, Christmas night, they decided to paint the room their parents left behind. Originally their mother had done it in white: smooth white walls, white lace curtains, white bedcovers, white pillowcases. Later she painted the wood floor white, so that the only color was what the day made through the window, or clothes pooled sometimes on the floor. Or blood coughed into a handkerchief but quickly hidden.

Brigid's first impulse was black lacquer, a swath down the middle of the room, to divide, she believed. But then: divide from what? What from what? Or half black and half white, that division, day and night, here and there, is and not. She would find the cans buried deep in the shed, black paint their father used for the shutters, for inside barrels. This was the joke—he liked to look into a barrel of water and see black all the way down, like a hole in the earth, a tunnel to nowhere. Anyway. The black was available, *to hand*, their mother would say. They talked about it, but then Theo fell asleep in his chair, and the idea of black faded, like a dream goes to image, the way you remember the stripe of someone's necktie, the gleam of a coin in the street. Brigid began to think of stars, a row along the top of the wall. Silver paint on the white, wintry but not cold. Or a glittery blue-green, like a bottle fly, the piñon when the sun strikes it hard.

This room must be painted. She heard the words in her mother's voice, the harsh command. A spot of red on the pillow beside her mouth. The dry air isn't helping, her father had said two days before he shot her. Could you paint me better air? Her mother had never thought to ask this. Better lungs? She could paint those. She had tried to. Brigid slid her hand under her mother's white pillow, bleached now, starched, lace edging stiff as cardboard. It was still there, the little watercolor she'd made her mother, the human lungs on each side of the bronchial stem, brilliant blue, veined and pendant, like sweet peas. Six more of these paintings in the kitchen, where her mother could see them, wish on them, show them off. Sometimes in front of company, she'd say, Look what my girl can do. But in private, she sang a different tune.

Theo snored, coughed, opened his eyes.

"I'm going to change my name," Brigid said.

"To what?"

"Schumann."

"Why?"

"To make her love me."

"She loved you in her own way."

"Remember the thing about praise?"

When Brigid was sixteen, Mrs. Silva had agreed to pay the tuition for Saturday art classes, if her parents would let her go. When Brigid announced this at home, her mother said, "You get too much praise." Then she left the room. It was the dead of winter, January, and school had just begun again after Christmas vacation. Brigid stood quite still in the middle of her bedroom. Her first impulse was to call after her mother, "Does that mean yes?" but she found the voice would not rise out of her throat, as if she were trying to scream in a nightmare. Late afternoon. The sun seemed to dilute rather than set. Brigid thought her room might fill up with some sort of liquid. She patted her cheeks. Dry. Well, it wouldn't fill with tears. Not from her.

Her mother called her for supper, and she went. They ate in silence, all four of them, some sort of stew. Gray punctured by a pale knuckle of potato. Tasteless, as her mother's stews always were. As she spooned the food into her mouth and swallowed, Brigid rolled the sentence over in her head. What could it mean, to get too much praise? How much was *too much*? Who kept count? As far as she knew, she had never received praise in her mother's presence. Sometimes at the bar. She glanced quickly at Theo. He had finished eating and was staring at the blank wall above their father's head. Why had nothing been hung on that wall? Her brother's profile was astonishing, she saw. He had a nose like their father's, a *hatchet*, she had heard it called, though the shape was more like a butte, a nearly right angle out from between his eyes, dropping away to another right angle. A precipitous nose, as in precipice. An equally sharp chin below beautiful, full lips. He stared at the wall and did not flinch, as if he knew Brigid was studying him. He would make a good model, she thought. Maybe he should come to class on Saturdays. Their parents finished eating, pushed back their bowls, rose from the table. Theo stayed with Brigid. When they were alone, she asked him if he thought she got too much praise, and he said, no, she didn't get enough.

Brigid took the class, and later that year, in May, Mrs. Silva entered one of her paintings in the junior art show in Taos, where it won first prize. The painting was called *Arroyo*, but there was a play on words in the title, *roi*, French for king, though Americans said "roy": the mountains made the shape of a crown. Brigid thought no one would understand—she didn't really know what she'd meant. There was a ceremony, and a man from the Chamber of Commerce handed Brigid a check for $100. It seemed like a small fortune. Mrs. Silva was there, and the school counselor. Not her parents. Not Theo.

At home, Brigid hugged her mother, and her mother hugged her back. It was nine o'clock, so her father was at the bar. Her mother stood beside the table as Brigid ate. The kitchen was bright and warm. The windows were open, and the loamy promise of the changing season wafted and swirled about them. A yellow cloth covered the table, and Brigid imagined a jar of flowers though there wasn't one. She wished she'd bought a bouquet in Taos. Then her mother cleared her throat. "Well," she said. She dropped her hands heavily into her apron pockets. Brigid felt the weight of this gesture. Her mother huffed out a breath. And then she said it: "It's not like you invented a cure for cancer."

"She can't love you," Theo said now. "She can't love anybody anymore."

"I think she can," Brigid said. "I think there's some magic out there, flying around. It's hard to explain."

"So you'll paint it then."

Theo went back to work the day after Christmas, driving east again, to Louisiana where people were still digging out after Hurricane Juan. You don't chatter, he told Brigid. You don't look them in the eye. Guys who chatter get sent to the front office in Kansas City to work dispatching. You lift all their stuff. You get to the last couch cushion and you're full and you climb down, duck in behind the wheel, and start to drive off. You don't want to look in the rearview, but you can't help yourself. And there she is, this lone woman, staring at that cushion with this awful look on her face. Not the look you see at a funeral, but worse. Tired, empty, something even less.

"Someday I want to get to understand it, that look. Maybe that's why I keep on signing up for these jobs," he said. He drove trucks that lift roof trusses from the ground into the sky and swing them into place, or dig beneath a house and raise it eighteen feet into the air, high above any threat you could name. He did not come back for her birthday in January. He sent a check for $500, made out to Brigid Schumann.

The feast of Saint Valentine gave people something to look forward to in the dead of winter, Miss O'Keeffe told her. She said it was invented to cancel out the pagan holiday Lupercalia, on which day men sacrificed goats and then ran through the streets wearing their bloodied skins. If a woman wanted to get pregnant or deliver a baby safely, she stood where these revelers might jostle her. So Valentine is a civilizing force, Miss O'Keeffe said. Brigid stared out the window at an idea, a form seeming to take shape just beyond Miss O'Keeffe's fence.

She began work on a strange image: a she-wolf suckling a human baby, the Lupercal, which had her mother's face and the human child had Brigid's, but the colors were reversed: dark fur and pale skin. Brigid did not know what this meant. She understood it was not her business to know, only to paint. To know, Julian Granger had said, would make painting unnecessary. We work in the dark, he said. She thought some day she would do that, literally, enter a darkened room, maybe even pitch black, the paints where she could reach them, her only guide the memory of what had been there, in what order, before she shut off the light. She'd done it with words, making notes in the dark about her dreams, and then she loved the sight of her handwriting the next morning: spidery, angled up the page as if climbing out of the valley of sleep. The words never made much sense, and in a way that was the point. Sense was overrated anyway. Maybe Julian Granger had said that too.

The Lupercal, though, seemed to ask for some understanding, some view inside. In the painting, her face is fierce, but the mouth hangs slightly open as if she will speak soon, explain her brokenness, but then suffer a long silence after her child is taken away. She has one paw raised to touch the child, who lies nestled into her. Together they make a curved world, light skin and dark fur. The child's eyes are closed, the skin over her eyelids pearly. The Lupercal's eyes have just snapped open in alarm, and her brown fur is matted and dank-seeming.

"Mother," Brigid whispered to the painting, "you look terrified."

Two weeks later, she borrowed Miss O'Keefe's car and drove to Father Edgardo's church, to the graveyard where she and Theo had buried their parents' ashes. Snow fell on the graves, and this made them look clean. There is no one here, Brigid thought. Is that the point of graves? A stone with her mother's name, next to her husband's stone. Name on a stone, stone in the snow. This snowfall on the first of March was unexpected, alarming, wet. Profound. Brigid remembered walking in the snow with her mother. She was eight. Her mother said, "It's snowing down," instead of "It's slowing down." They doubled over laughing. The snow seemed to come harder and at an angle, as if to defy her mother's statement. And Brigid realized then, for the first time, that her mother didn't have power over anything.

This graveyard ran down a hill and ended at a sharp drop-off. People call this an arroyo, that play on crown, Brigid thought, but it had more the crack-in-the-earth feel of the word *ravine*. She wondered if she really knew anything about geography she couldn't see. What did she know about *prairie* or about *ocean*? "Ocean," she said out loud, over her parents' graves. The sound of the word, here in the snow, brought with it a particular, piercing knowledge: it was time to go away. "I'm Brigid Schumann now," she said to the gravestones, "All that power you didn't have. I've got it now, and I'm leaving."

She would see Miss O'Keeffe through this last failing, and then she would go. To New York. But first she would have to ask a hard question.

Nancy

Afterwards, Rodney and I got dressed and rode the ferry to South Street Seaport for dinner, and that was all right, and watching television with Rodney in his empty house on Governor's Island was all right. Listening to him talk about the anesthesiology rotation, and about his specialty, which would be psychiatry, all of it, just fine. Thanksgiving loomed before us, a different emptiness. Like the cavity of a turkey, I told Henry when he called, and he repeated the phrase he used to describe me sometimes, Out there, he said. Way, way out there. I realized, hearing Henry's voice, that all I wanted was to go see him, but he was still at work, waiting tables in midtown. Double shifts the day before Thanksgiving. While most people in America were at home cooking, New Yorkers were dining out. And I think now Henry didn't want to see me, not right away. I would look too changed, too, well, *fucked.*

The next morning, we found ourselves in what Henry called the Belly of the Bart, a Humvee with a professional driver, traveling at about five miles per hour down Sixth Avenue. The driver looked almost exactly like Rob Lowe when this was beginning to be a good thing again. I found it hard to take my eyes off him, but Henry and Rodney didn't notice, as they were giving their full attention to a video screen that tracked Bart's every drift and glide. Every so often, Henry had to adjust a cable, move Bart's arm so that he appeared to be waving, all the while keeping up an obscenity-laced but otherwise mostly incomprehensible exchange with Rodney, referring to someone named Jack. Once Henry asked if I wanted to make Bart move, but I didn't.

"Who's Jack?" I asked when there was a half-second of silence.

Henry's eyes got huge, and he looked at Rodney, aghast. "You mean you haven't told her?" Rodney shook his head with great solemnity. "That's harsh, man." Henry turned in his control seat so he could release Bart's wave and put his hand on my knee. "It's his dad's name. Walter Jackson. Admiral Jack."

I thought they were having a joke at my expense. "Admiral?"

"Actually," Rodney said, "he was a ship's cook."

"I'm missing something here," I said.

"Shit, Bart, get back in your lane!" Henry yelled.

Rodney looked out at the cheering crowd. "How's the sign business these days?" he asked without turning his head.

"Good. Signs are in demand."

"He changes lives," Rodney said, still staring out the window. "He'll tell you."

"That's right," Henry said. "You read my sign, you realize you want a Coke, you want those Nikes, you want all that stuff. And you don't forget once you leave the Garden. All the marketing research shows this. You go buy it. I make you who you are."

"You make me what I buy," the driver said.

"Same thing," Henry said.

It occurred to me that men in Humvees probably all talked this way, about their power to make you who you were.

The parade ended in the Meadowlands parking lot. The floats arrived in succession and their air valves were popped open. Rodney, Henry, and I stepped from the Humvee into a huge surreal landscape, row after row of cartoon characters bent, falling, facedown and hissing. It reminded me of the depot scene in *Gone with the Wind*, when the camera pans back to show the thousands of wounded waiting to be helped, to be moved, to die. A crime scene. The humans seemed shrunk too, even more than a couple of hours before when they were marching underneath all these crazy pumped-up cartoons suspended on top of their disbelief. The day went dark, losing itself. Small planes buzzed overhead, and Henry said it was the weirdest thing about the parade, that people paid money to be flown over this.

"Like looking at a car wreck," Rodney said.

"Some people get off on that," Henry said. "Like nothing's really fun unless there's carnage and devastation at the end."

Henry had left his car at the Meadowlands, and he offered us a ride. He said any other day we'd get wasted someplace downtown, but since it was Thanksgiving, well. Here he looked directly at Rodney. "A son has to do what a son has to do," he said.

"Me?" Rodney said.

I was missing something else. Suddenly I felt sick, as if I had a mental hangover, a kind of flu of the spirit.

"Wait," Henry said. "Aren't you going to the Admiral's?"

Rodney didn't move, didn't blink, didn't acknowledge Henry's question in any way.

Henry turned to me. "Tell me you're going to the Admiral's. Please."

He was actually begging me, I realized. He was heartbroken. I shook my head. I opened my mouth to speak, croaked out the words. "He hasn't said anything about that."

Henry moved to stand in front of Rodney, grasped him by the shoulders and shook him, hard. Too hard, I thought. "What are you doing, man?" he said to Rodney. "You just got back in touch. I know they invited you. Tell me they didn't invite you." Henry shook Rodney again, shook out the words, a whisper.

"They invited me."

"And you're not going? You're not taking Nancy?"

"I can't," Rodney whispered again, as if he were hoping I couldn't hear him, right there, holding his hand. "I mean, look at her. Look at *us*."

Henry turned and walked away from whatever *us* was. He unlocked his car and got in, cranked the engine, and I thought, great, stranded at the Meadowlands on Thanksgiving Day. I dropped Rodney's hand, turned to survey the wreckage, the wheezing cartoon characters, revealed now as all hot air. This was not what I bargained for. This was so *stupid*. Henry started the engine, stared straight ahead for a moment, then rolled down his window. "Do it for your mom," he said. He waited. I thought I heard a kind of broken hiccup. I felt Rodney's hand on the back of my neck, under my hair.

"Okay," he said. "Nance? I've got to go see the Admiral." He walked to the car and opened the passenger side door, offered me the seat next to Henry. I started to protest, but then thought better of it. Rodney seemed to be moving slowly, tenuously along a narrow wire, high above some dangerous abyss. So I sat down, glanced at Henry for explanation or help, saw I wouldn't be getting any, not right then. Rodney got in the back and we drove him to the PATH station. "There's lots of food at my place," he said. "See you guys tomorrow."

"He didn't like his dad getting married to a white woman," Henry said. "He complained about it. He was pretty awful one time, and then he didn't ever go see them."

"That's funny, isn't it?" I said. "I get it now, what he meant by 'look at her.' But. . . . I guess you never told him about *my* father."

"I thought about it. But I figured it was your story to tell."

People have these complicated histories. How could you ever really get to know anybody, all the way down? People act like the words *Rodney's mother died and his father remarried* can explain any of it. Well, they can't. I stared out the window. The only person I could ever possibly know was Henry, but all I knew was that I was falling out of his life.

"I can drive straight to the ferry if you want," Henry was saying quietly, "but I was thinking about a little gallery hop. You need art."

"I know I need something," I said.

"One of my teachers has this installation in Chelsea. Multimedia, performance, I'm not sure what to call it. I think she's there today."

"Suck up," I said.

"Actually," Henry said, "wait until you see her."

I laughed a little. "What does she teach you?"

"Film. Technique. She said at the beginning of the course, you're going to leave here with a third eye. It sounds weird, but I swear sometimes I feel it growing in the middle of my forehead. She's been getting me reviewing work too."

We were in lower Manhattan now, heading north and west. All of New York City seemed to be outside, shopping, holding hands, laughing. Even the serious punks around Tompkins Square Park—all smiles. Henry parked off Twelfth Street, a block past the Strand Bookstore. The morning had darkened toward noon, and now, as we climbed out of the car, snow began to fall, but lightly, softly, an idea almost, the inside of some spell.

The snow came harder as we walked north up Broadway to Twenty-third Street. There was a moment of meteorologic critical mass when I felt as if large, soft mittens had covered my ears, and all sound slipped away, a wisp under a door, breath out of a body. I spoke, but the words got lost before Henry heard them. Sound was not possible, or maybe there was too much of it. This snow was very wet, and soon my hair was soaked, dripping into the collar of my coat and down my back, like sweat. We were laughing though, in a way that seemed to me overly boisterous, forced, the warning of breakdown. A clanging cymbal.

I remembered something Henry had said earlier. He had asked Rodney, "Don't you think it's strange that they left *you* behind?" And now I understood the eerie quiet on Governor's Island. People were never coming back. The military chose Rodney to stay behind as a watchdog and a symbol. One lonely black man with nothing to do, watch over nothing, patrol and welcome the tourists. For show. To do the bow and shuffle. He was an entertainer. He was one changed motherfucker, but really not changed at all. Changed back.

So what I wanted to do right then, on the corner of Broadway and Twenty-third Street, was turn around, find a cab, wave to Henry, and race back to the ferry. Hightail it back to Governor's Island, knowing, now, there wouldn't be anyone else there. Ever. Rodney would come back, and it would be Eden in winter. We could wander the whole island. The forbidden fruit was already ripening in our hands. That was how I needed to find Rodney again, not in this big white world, but in that small one. I almost said it, I'm going back. But by then we had arrived, dripping wet, at the door to Cheim and Meyer Gallery, and Henry's teacher was there too, waving us inside, smiling, her eyes locked with Henry's, a force I recognized burning between them.

After five minutes of conversation, I realized this teacher, Ann Elderburgh, was exactly the sort of person who would think to film scenes from Shakespeare in the lobbies of banks all over Manhattan, in front of the ATM machines during business hours, so that *people who wanted money* became actors, audience, and metaphor. It was brilliant. As I watched the film play the third time, I thought about Rodney's mother's Shakespeare. I thought about a book, how people believed, when they read the last word and closed the cover, it was over. When the last student made the last comment about Prospero's last word, everybody could nod off. But then along came Ann Elderburgh to kick you awake. Ann Elderburgh had no patience for sleepers, for small talk, for what she was calling *Chablis critique*. Though she held a glass of wine, she never took a sip. She was one of those people who needed something to do with her hands. Her eyes worked just as restlessly. *"New York Times,"* she whispered to Henry, "in the doorway. And to his left. No idea about that one, but obviously *sent*." Henry looked so pleased to be in her presence that I thought he might start to vibrate. "From Boston," he whispered back to her. "Looks provincial." Ann Elderburgh laughed and touched his arm with her fingertips. If they hadn't already slept together, they would soon.

I left them and found myself in a different installation, and I recognized the style before I saw her name on the wall: Brigid Schumann. I'd loved her work in Atlanta: the Indian, the bottle of beer, the label that shouted INERTIA. Most of these canvases also had words painted on them, the same large black lettering, the size and style of signs in nuclear waste disposals and arms factories.

CASINO read the first, which depicted an American Indian behind the wheel of a pickup truck, hair blown over his face, so that you could almost see the open window and feel the great speed. KACHINA, KA-CHING screamed the next, and the scene was a ratty gift shop in the desert, an Indian woman extending her hand, palm open. CREATION MYTH depicted the first Thanksgiving, the Indians bowing before Pilgrim men and offering ears of corn. Its companion piece, THANKS A LOT, showed a Pilgrim man bending an Indian woman over a table loaded with turkey, pumpkins, ears of corn, dishes of blood-colored cranberries.

"This woman is angry," Henry said.

"That woman?" I pointed to the painting.

"No," Henry began, "but. . . ." He glanced to the wall by the doorway, a photograph of the artist. "Maybe. This is a self-portrait." I saw it then, the unmistakable resemblance between the painter and the woman splayed over the bounteous feast. "These are hard to look at," he said.

"But you can't look away either. Seems like that's what she's after."

Henry gazed at me, *adoringly* really was the right word to describe that expression. "How did you end up where you are, Nance?"

"Lucky, I guess."

"You understand everything," Henry said. "You know what it all means. You totally get it."

"You can't always get what you want," I said.

"But if you try sometimes. . . . Ann wants to take us to lunch." Henry was practically dancing with happiness, anticipation. "She said they'll give us a table by the fireplace. She said, tell your shivering sister."

It was another forty minutes before Ann could leave her show, and in that time, I drank two more little cups of wine. I thought of my mother at her show with Simon, drinking like this for courage. I thought I should have the courage to ask Rodney a question or two. Why was his whole life invented: the Admiral wasn't an admiral. Rodney wasn't white or named Bob. Were there other inventions I needed to know about? Did it hurt the Admiral's feelings to be called that when in truth he was a cook? Did the name White Bob have anything to do with his father's new wife? Harder questions: did Rodney love me? Or anything approaching love? Did we have any kind of future together? What would that future look like? What *color* would it be?

Did I really, deep in my heart of hearts, want to know the answers to any of these questions? Didn't I know them already?

I would never ask. I let Henry leave to find me another little plastic cup of wine. I stared into the face of the painter, Brigid Schumann, and then into the eyes of the Indian woman, the victim of Pilgrim appetite. A strange thought came into my head then, Chablis-fueled, a pair of thoughts actually. I wanted to meet this painter. I wanted Brigid Schumann to walk into her exhibit right now and stare at my face and then paint it. Then I could look at what she made and know for once and for all who I really was.

Jan Vermeer and Georgia O'Keeffe enter from doors at the back of the theater. They climb onstage from the left and right aisles. They are real. It's really them, so this play will be difficult to stage. You just need to know that going in.

VERMEER: Do you ever want to come back?

GEORGIA: I am back. You?

V: No. I did all the work I could do. I had a feeling I was about to start repeating myself. How many paintings did you make?

G: 2,029.

V: But who's counting.

G: I think you are. I painted things again because I saw them again. Differently. Or because I was different. I was one changed. . . .

V (*overlapping*): All right, all right, I know. I've been listening.

G: Anyway it's apples and oranges, your 37 to my 2,029. And you died young and you had all those children. Not in that order.

V: There was a kind of frenzy at the end, but something inside my head was very calm. You have used up your vision, a voice said. You have used all the available light.

It didn't take me long to flunk out of Clemson. Just under nine months, one year in college years, like dog years, only shorter. A lot of good reasons, had I. Too hard. Too much pot, too readily available. Not enough school spirit. Hated the color orange, and not fond of tigers. Spooked by the two brick towers in the middle of campus that look like the ovens at Birkenau. Crazy roommates. Lack of interest. Lack of Rodney. Lack of Henry. Lack. Lackadaisical. Which means what, exactly?

Moved back to Atlanta, lived with Mom and Dad, tried not to smoke so much weed. Failed. I'm realizing these are only notes to a life, but that's how it was. I couldn't get between the lines, fill myself in, flesh myself out, complete the sentences. Halting. Eviscerated. Dad got me a job in production at a radio station where he knew the owner. WPCH. Peach. Get it? It was all right for about two weeks, learning my way around the warren of a studio, making coffee, fetching lunch, dry cleaner pickup. But then they wanted me to actually do something in Radioland, make tapes off of Reuters, short news pieces. I remember that the tapes were color coded but not why. My first tape: made it, handed it over to the producer. He stuck it into the machine, pressed play, and . . . nothing. Dead air, the cardinal sin of radio.

From there, I descended to breakfast shift at McDonald's. You get to eat the stuff that doesn't come out right, stuff left over in the walk-in. Once there was a birthday cake with blue icing—our tongues and lips were blue, our fingertips. It woke people up, I have to say, especially at the drive-thru window. Or maybe they thought we were an extension of their dreams. I spent all my pay on blow. The assistant manager handed me my check, and I handed it right back to him, more or less. Those little spoons on the end of the coffee stirrers. You know why all the franchises stopped using them, right? You know why we came out of the walk-in with runny noses? Not because it was cold. The service was brisk, speedy you might say. I think we won some kind of award for pep and verve, purpose and industry. Our store—management wanted us to call it that—was so shiny! We loved each other, we were the real Breakfast Club. We had nicknames. Mine was Miss Korea.

Henry's work was evolving, Ann Elderburg pronounced. He used maps and aerial photographs, and colored them by hand, so that the place became a shape, repetition, like what you see in a kaleidoscope. Some of the maps were people's faces. It would be hard to say which came first, he told me, the map or the face. Ann was getting him other kinds of work too, like he said, interviews and reviews for decent magazines. Sometimes he was too busy to paint. He'd met a woman, named Paula, a nurse. Rodney introduced them.

Rodney wrote sometimes. Never phoned. He was finishing up at Columbia, thinking about his residency. The Match, they called it. You and a school or a hospital, wed for life pretty much. And then he did call, to say he wasn't ready for a permanent match. There are six- month fellowships in psychiatry, he said. You'll never guess where.

"Where?"

"Emory. Henry's coming too. He needs to get some place quiet and just paint."

"I'll be really glad to see you."

"Henry says you're adrift."

I thought, no, not adrift. That would imply I was going somewhere. "I'm working on a play."

"That's good, Nancy. I'll be glad to see you too."

"I think I'm getting my inner life and my outer life confused."

"What do you mean?"

What I told him:

I dreamed I watched Georgia O'Keeffe go flying off a ladder and into the clouds. No, I think that was Henry's dream and he told me about it.

I was considering buying a plane ticket to Paris. One way. All the problems that would arise.

I've been gathering all the house paint swatches in Henry's room, under his bed, and making a kind of quilt on the wall.

What I didn't tell Rodney:

That I really loved him, even though we'd spent only a few days together, and surely we didn't know the worst things about each other.

I wanted to keep quiet, to become invisible. Whenever possible to be the least interesting person in the room.

The past and the future: Nancy, Age 7, Speaks to Nancy, Age 21.

N7: How did you get there?

N21: I grew up.

N7: What were you smoking?

N21: Pot. We smoked joints in a rowboat on the East River before the play. The boat appeared magically. I remember being profoundly hungry and eating fish and chips.

N7: I will someday learn that's called the munchies.

N21: Quit getting ahead of yourself. You're supposed to stay young. Otherwise this conversation won't work.

N7: Sorry. I want to ask you something though. This just happened at school. I was in a play. I said the lines the way I understood them, and I was very funny. How did I do that? It was such a shock, all those people smiling and laughing. At me.

N21: And then you discovered you really liked it. Am I right?

N7: I did. I almost didn't know what I was feeling.

N21: Like your first orgasm.

N7: My first what?

N21: Never mind. Did you try to be funny after that?

N7: I don't know yet. Did I?

N21: As much, as often as you could. Then that wasn't really enough, so you made up people in your head who talked to each other, said humorous things, made the audience laugh. But at some point, about ten years later, the conversations got serious. You had a revelation. You realized that all speech comes from desire, that people only talk to each other because they want something.

N7: You're talking about the future like it's already happened.

N21: Because that's the something that I want. A long and glorious future.

Sasha

In Long Beach, they could walk to the ocean from the Burgetts' house. It was one of the only places Mrs. Burgett would go. She had a hard time, Jennie explained, with almost anywhere outside, and especially anywhere she'd been with her husband. The beach, though, was all right because she'd spent so much time there alone, before her marriage. "She'll tell you all this," Jennie said while her mother went to get a coat. "The ocean does something for her. But pretend you don't know." And sure enough, once they'd walked the three blocks to the beach and stepped down onto the sand, Mrs. Burgett—call me Lisa, please, she'd said to Sasha, please, please, as if she were begging for her very life—Lisa did begin to talk. She recounted how, in the summers of 1980 and 1981, she wrote pretty much most of her dissertation right here, on her belly in the sand, in pencil, on the backs of handouts from her composition classes. "I wrote straight across the page in my little tiny handwriting, until I came to sand, and then—*ding!*—like a typewriter. Automatic. I was a machine."

She had so much to say about American literature, Lisa told Jennie and Sasha, about Washington Irving and Henry David Thoreau and Nathaniel Hawthorne. She wrote about *mediate space,* as she called it, places that weren't quite civilized and weren't quite wilderness and somehow made magic by that. She wrote a lot about *The Scarlet Letter,* the way Hester Prynne lived on the edges of worlds, between worlds. "I had no idea what I was talking about," Lisa said, kicking through the sand. "Now I do have some notion, believe it or not." This dissertation, she continued, ran to nearly four hundred pages, which were followed by nine endnotes.

"Nine! That's not enough, Mom," Jennie said. From the tone, Sasha understood this was the thing Jennie always said, the thing her mother needed her to say in order to move her on to the next part of the story.

"My advisers were the two oldest professors in the Columbia English Department. One of them was a true pacifist, the dean they called in during the SDS riots. Together these professors had probably fought their way through ten thousand footnotes. They were grateful for a break. So for once in my life I was in the right place at the right time."

This thought caused Lisa Burgett to lose her breath and stumble into the surf. Jennie caught her arm and the two of them stopped walking. Sasha wondered if she should go on ahead, but Lisa reached for her hand and gave it a hard squeeze, so she stayed with them. Then Jennie took her mother in her arms. Sasha thought she heard Jennie say *It's okay. It'll be all right*, words she imagined they didn't really believe. A moment later, they were moving again, and Lisa was talking about how by the end of this writing on the beach, that second summer, she was so big with Jennie that she had to lie on her side. And then she got married. "I didn't know this Tim Burgett very well," she said, "even though I was having his baby. And it turns out. . . ." Her voice trailed off over the surf.

"Mom," Jennie said. "Please don't."

"I didn't know him at all," Lisa said.

Behind her mother, Jennie was shaking her head, no, no no.

"It was something he needed to do. Right after the first plane hit. He said he had to. He called me," Lisa was saying, "but the connection was bad. So I called him back. And I heard it clearly that time, his voice saying he had to go in. He said it was his duty. And I said what about his duty here? But he didn't answer, and he went."

Lisa stopped walking, turned to face the ocean. "I need to go back now, Jen. I think I need to lie down."

"How was the family service?" Sasha asked after Lisa had disappeared into her bedroom and shut the door.

"I kept looking for him. I caught myself thinking, 'Where's Dad?'"

"How are you? Really?"

"Well, for starters, I'm afraid. I'm afraid of hallways. I'm afraid of loud noises. I'm afraid of feeling. I'm afraid of thinking. People keep saying you go through it and come out on the other side. The other side. Where's that? I don't think it happens. I don't think I know what that means really. I have this image of falling sometimes, headfirst into a shallow hole. At night, sometimes I have to go in and sleep with my mother and kind of hang on to her body. We go to this grief class. That's what Mom calls it. But I think we have to stop. Or I do. You wouldn't believe what people say about their so-called loved ones. I just can't say that stuff. Or listen to it. My dad never hurt me. I hurt *him*. Once when I was five, I was trying to get into the car like Batman, and Dad closed my fingers in the door. He said last summer he still thought about doing that and it caused him intense pain. Like he could feel it in his own hand.

"The other night I had this dream: I was in a hospital, recovering from something, drifting in and out of consciousness but sitting up. A woman came in, and I asked her for coffee. Then three of my cousins arrived, and I realized a whole day had gone by, and it was 6:30 in the evening. My cousins were all happy and excited and wanted to go see a movie. I went with them, and we waited in a long line. I didn't really want to see a movie. I realized suddenly I needed to find my mother. I found her not very far away, looking for a gift shop in a church that had no walls, just an open courtyard and a crucifix. She started to wander away, and then a big bus pulled up. Inside were two Tilt-A-Whirls. It looked like those play spaces in McDonald's."

"Oh, Jennie," Sasha said. She tried not to laugh.

"It's okay. It's funny. Sometimes my dreams are the best part of the day. Anyway, Mom wanted to get on a Tilt-A-Whirl, and I thought that was okay. When the ride ended, people got out, and I realized she was gone. We followed these streets and at the end came to a body of water. Mom came out of a side street and asked if we were looking for her and said now I could help her carry her bags—she pointed to them on the ground—a long wicker basket, sand colored, and a suit bag, the kind you hang up. Inside we could see a pair of Dad's wool pants with the belt still in and some golf clubs just strewn about—no golf bag—and she said she always liked to take that stuff with her, and I got the sense she wanted to give people the impression that she still had a husband. There were also two manila file folders that I knew contained pictures of her and Dad, and I knew that she had done something to Dad's face in the pictures—put tape over it or blacked it out and I didn't want to look. Then I woke up."

"That's a wild dream."

"They're all like that. And it feels like there's always another dream coming for me. Something about knives and killing. And then this crazy one about heaven, where heaven was just a row of stores. I mean there was a Staples and a Target and a Burger King, and I was walking along, and I had the strangest thought. I thought, hey, heaven is the same as here except that we make better choices.

"I just want to know where he is. But you know, sometimes, I hope they don't find anything. I don't want parts. I want him back whole so we can sit someplace and I can hug him."

The real art is in the editing. That's what Wayne always said. Any idiot can set up a video camera and push the on button. But it turned out this wasn't what Lisa and Jennie wanted anyway. They didn't want to sit on a couch and talk. They wanted to go places. Lisa thought she could manage this, a sentimental journey all over Manhattan, Brooklyn, and Long Island. They wanted to go to Cambridge, Massachusetts, and Burlington, Vermont. They wanted to go to a lot of churches. Eventually, they wanted to go to Paris, but not until June 21, the summer solstice but also *La Fête de la Musique*. They would do all this, too, Sasha understood. They would try to outrun their grief in one of these places only to find it somewhere else.

But they began, the next day, back in Manhattan at the Caliente Cab Co., where in 1983 Tim Burgett proposed marriage to Lisa Giovanni, at the bar. They each had a glass of champagne, Lisa, Jennie, and Sasha, who took one sip, put down the glass, and took up her camera. Lisa talked and Jennie looked at her, adoring and crying, though it was not a particularly remarkable story. Tim had a ring in his pocket and he brought it forth without fanfare or knee-bending, which at the bar would have been awkward. Lisa was eight months pregnant and about to defend her four-hundred-page, nine-endnote dissertation. Tim had just started a degree program at John Jay, in criminal justice, which he wasn't sure he'd enjoy or finish.

"He said," Lisa recalled, "that he was definitely sure about me and the baby, and I said, 'Sure we're not criminals?' and somehow that was funny."

It was a slow night, so the bartender could stand and watch the filming. "You're going to put me out of business," he said to Sasha. "People are supposed to tell their stories to me. This may change bar-keeping completely."

"You could rent me," Sasha said.

The bartender laughed and winked. "I'll bet you're expensive." The camera was still running and trained on Lisa, who glared at him.

"You leave this girl alone."

"Yes, ma'am," he said and winked again.

They stayed at the bar and ordered beers and food. "We want the extra hot everything," Lisa told the bartender, who gave her the thumbs-up. "It'll make you cry," he said. "For a change." He brought a basket of tortilla chips and set it in front of them. "Chips can be kind of calming," he said.

"Once Tim and I did this," Lisa said. She took chips from the basket and laid them out roughly in the shape of the United States. "Where do you want to go? Eat the places you don't want to go." Sasha ate the entire Midwest. Lisa ate the southeast, below Virginia. Jennie ate Texas and Arizona. The bartender, who was listening with obvious admiration, brought them another round on the house and shots of tequila, a salt shaker, a dish of lime wedges. Then he brought their food: huge, steaming plates of enchiladas, burritos, rice, beans, oozing cheese. They ate and burned their tongues and swore.

Suddenly, Lisa put down her fork and gripped Jennie's arm. She was still chewing. Then she started to laugh. But something happened and her laugh was gone, her face a rictus of mirth and suffocation. The bartender caught it all, calmly wiped his hands on his apron, moved around the end of the bar and positioned himself behind Lisa. Sasha lifted her camera, turned it on.

"It won't hurt," the bartender said. Then he gripped his hands below Lisa's ribcage and pressed in and up. Lisa clawed at her throat and the bartender did it again, his perfect Heimlich. They all heard a sound, like the opening of a soda can. Lisa relaxed. Tears streamed from her eyes.

"I'm not crying," she whispered. She pulled the bartender's arms more tightly around her body. "You just earned yourself a very large tip."

"No sweat," the bartender said. "At least you didn't pee in your shoes like my wife did once. Now she won't eat steak but she still wears those damn shoes." He turned to Sasha. "I can't believe you filmed that."

"Me neither," Sasha said.

"Would you have kept on filming?" the bartender asked. "If it didn't work?"

"Probably not to the very end," Sasha said, "but I don't know."

"What would that be, really? The *very* end?" Jennie asked.

"Don't think I'll be watching it," Lisa said.

But some people would, Sasha thought. They would watch it over and over because they want to see it's possible for the living to do this, pull others back from the edge, but before that, how the daughters are too stunned to save the mothers, or can't save them, how the survivors get on with it. If I need to know all this, Sasha thought, other people must need to know it too.

"Can I film you talking about it?" Sasha asked when Theo came to see her again.

"Working downtown?" he said. "Not now."

"Something else. About work. Something strange that's happened."

"Strange," Theo said, and Sasha turned on the camera. She focused on his face, his left eye, the braid fallen over his shoulder. He didn't speak for a long time.

"Okay," he said finally. "I know."

This was strange, all right. This was cleanup after what people called the Storm of the Century in 1993. Me and my crew drove to Alabama, where there had been a foot of snow. Then I got sent on to Georgia, to Atlanta, up I-75 to neighborhoods beside the Chattahoochee River, which was frozen in a few places and snow-covered, so it was hard to believe I was in the south. The cold was stunning, even for me, a windy, humid chill. The first neighborhood was called Vinings, like the plant life, all of it growing steeply uphill, away from the river, all this snow-dusted ivy choking the trees. You could see why people would be terrified, why they stood at the bottoms of their 6 percent grade driveways, flagging you down, begging for news. No power for days. The landscape looked sort of tilted, like just a breath of wind would make it all slide into the river. Avalanche! you'd find yourself shouting to nobody. Landslide!

I kept going down to the river. I'm not sure why. The water was brown, tired-looking, just wanting to get on with itself, a few rocky parts, not very dangerous. I walked down there with my thermos of coffee, and that's when I discovered the couple in their car, a ten-year-old buff-colored Cadillac. They were pouring from a cocktail shaker into silver cups. They were perfectly fine, only a little buzzed. They'd had no power in their house for a week. The car was the warmest spot they could find.

"I know you can't have a whole one," the man said to me, "but I bet you'd like a little sip."

I wasn't sure what came over me, but I opened the rear passenger door and slid into the backseat. And then the man poured out a martini and handed me the silver cup, and I took it because it seemed rude to refuse. The man introduced himself as Lee. There was an L engraved in script on the cup. I took one sip.

"This is Barbara," Lee said.

"But you can call me Barb," the woman said.

I told them my name, and the woman laughed happily. She had a nice laugh, like little bells there in the cold. She laughed a lot. The more she drank, the more she laughed, but the sound of it stayed exactly the same.

"Theo is my brother's name," Barb said. "He's in Florida. He left Chicago to escape this very thing." She pointed out the window at the snow.

"So did we," Lee said. "Remember?"

Barb nodded, and I watched their faces mask over, go waxy, like they'd been called back somewhere. They seemed to forget I was in the car with them. Lee held the cocktail shaker away from his chest, then drew it closer, looking at his reflection in the silver. It was a very nice shaker, polished to a kind of crazy gleam and engraved, the initial L in the same script.

"I'm not going to survive another one of these," Lee said suddenly. I wanted to ask if he meant the storm or the martini. Lee turned away to look out the front windshield. "I am going to die in snow," he said, "and come back as a dog."

Barb looked at me, rolled her eyes heavenward. She reached for the shaker and poured more martini into her cup. "Where are you from, Theo?" she asked.

I told her, and she said I must not see much snow. I told her I did, in the mountains. And she said she didn't like the mountains, she preferred water. But, she added, she preferred it to be thawed.

I thought I should thank them and go, get back to work hauling pine trees out of people's yards, but I felt hypnotized. It was so familiar, like riding in the car with my mom and dad, Dad talking about the weather, Mom rolling her eyes. I didn't want to leave it behind again. I wondered if somehow, this was actually them, that I'd found them back in the world. They'd come back, and some heaven had made them white people. Or maybe they'd come to get me.

That was when I got really scared. I'd just spent weeks—years, really, if you counted my whole life—using a chainsaw and walking under half-fallen trees that could collapse on me any minute, live power lines whipping past my head. Lee and Barb, though, they really got to me, got way down there where true fear lives. I closed my eyes.

"That's right," I heard Barb say. "You just take a nice rest here."

"I might not wake up," I said.

Lee laughed. "We all have to go sometime," he said.

I heard the jangle of keys and the crank of the car's ignition. Still I didn't open my eyes. I felt bone-tired. The car's heater purred.

"Just warming it up a little in here," Lee said. "Though another body does help hold the heat."

Another body, I thought. The words repeated inside my head, echoing. I knew I was falling asleep. I woke up because the car had started to move, and I heard the click of a seat belt. I said "Hey!" and Barb said, "Lee never wears a seat belt. He's such a daredevil."

I asked where we were going, and Lee said they were taking me to my truck. I told them no, it was still icy, too dangerous to drive, and Lee said, hell, he'd learned to drive in Chicago, in the winter. This was nothing.

And slowly we made our way up the hill. I asked Lee how he knew where my truck was, and he said he'd noticed the direction I came from.

"After you drop me," I said, "You should go home. The roads are okay now, but this slush is going to freeze up again."

"I think we'll do a little sight-seeing," Lee said.

"We should go check on Sandra and Harry," Barb said. "They have all those big trees in their yard."

"Now don't be doing that," I said, even though I had no idea where these people lived. "There's power lines down everywhere. Some roads you can't get through."

"We'll take our chances," Lee said.

"Right," Barb said. "This is the most fun we've had in a long time."

Lee found my truck, but I didn't want to get out. Barb offered me another pour from the martini shaker, and I took it. I leaned my head back.

When I woke up, Lee and Barb were asleep. He had turned off the engine, and they'd let their heads fall back and their mouths drop open. In the chill of the car, their separate breaths made little wisps in the air.

My dad used to say you could see people's dreams that way, if they fell asleep in the cold.

When I opened the car door, Lee and Barb woke up and said goodbye, wished me luck. When I tried to return the silver cup, Lee said I should keep it. He said, "Son, that's your initial too." I didn't remember telling them my last name.

Theo paused, looked hard into the camera as if he were searching for a person inside the lens.

"That's all," he said. "That's my strange little story."

Sasha thought maybe she could undo the falling. You can't undo it, Jennie said. Everybody knows what happened. But Sasha thought she actually could. It's just a construct, a representation. The camera might just as easily *mis*represent. The editing program could do it, run the film backwards. It was that easy. Or she might film something else; actors and bungees cords, to fly back up. Or give thoughts to all those people in the air. Like *Wings of Desire*. Or edit in shots of other people filming alongside her. No, what would that do but break the narrative line? Are you making a documentary? Aaron asked. Or a fiction? Neither, Sasha had answered. Both. I want to make it strange. It is strange, Aaron said. I want to invent a different strange, Sasha told him. The world is bigger than what we see. I want to go into that place between what happened and what might have happened. Maybe that's what all adopted children want, Aaron said. Yes, Sasha said, that's it, that's right. Perfect. I want to think about it a different way.

And then she saw the disappearing woman. Somehow she'd missed this detail, that one of the two women holding on to each other flew out of view. Sasha looked at the footage over and over, trying to understand what had happened. There were possibilities at first: the camera angle caused the woman on the right to fade into the silver of the building, or her light skin caused this, or her clothing. Or maybe her jacket, which was long, like a lab coat, had caught on a spar of the tower and stopped her fall, as Sasha continued to film the other woman's descent. It was possible, but no one else filming or taking still photographs had captured this. Her companion seemed to notice—her head turned and her right hand seemed to grope in the air, and then this same hand went up, over the woman's head, waving. And as she studied this image, Sasha realized she was seeing the sister of the man who placed the *Times* ad. It was all visible, just as he wrote: the long skirt, which opened below her like a fin—if she were to make a landing in water, she could glide to shore. The oversized watch, the hair a black mass undulating, turning in the air as if it were some other kind of fire. Her skin darker than the white blouse she wore. And the eyes, wide open, gazing toward the camera, giving to her whole face the impression of a person about to say something of great importance.

She went to the library and searched back through old issues of the *Times* until she found the brother's ad. Henry, the ad read, and a phone number. She called but there was no answer, so she left a message, telling him what she had and asking if he felt he wanted to see it.

"In private," he said when he called back. "Would you send me a copy?" He gave her an address.

"Henry Diamond the art person?" Sasha asked. She heard a little puff of air that might have been laughter.

"I like that. The art person. Like there's only one."

"You interviewed Brigid Schumann a couple of years ago."

"I did."

She wanted to say it, tell him, *She's my mother,* but no. This was about something else. There might be time for that later. "It was good."

"Thank you."

"So I should tell you that this video is . . . made into something. It's edited. There's a soundtrack."

"Oh, Jesus. Are you kidding me? Can't you just send me the clip?"

"No."

"Who are you?"

"It doesn't matter."

But Henry Diamond said that it did in fact matter, given what horrible things arrived in the mail these days, and so Sasha told him, Sasha Hernandez, but of course her name meant nothing.

So now the soundtrack, since she'd promised one. Eight minutes into the fourth movement of Dvorak's Symphony no. 9. If you took one-second audio clips, three seconds apart and spliced them together, you got the cymbals, very quietly, like punctuation, the notice of a specific pause. *The New World* broken into bits, Henry Diamond said when he wrote back. It's awful, he wrote, but I recognize my sister. It's ugly and terrible, he wrote. I never want to watch it again. Not ever. But I know I will. Her name's Nancy. She wanted to write plays. Did write them, I think. And you've sort of produced her. Can I call you?

"Henry Diamond," Aaron said. "I read that interview. You know where all this is headed, don't you, Sasha?"

Sasha nodded. "Brigid."

"I can see it," Aaron said. "Like connect the dots. Or more focused. A straight line. An arrow."

When he phoned, Henry Diamond said, "It's kind of sick I know, but you've given her a stage. And the woman with her. It makes me feel better to know she wasn't alone. Like she had a guardian angel or something."

Sasha could tell Henry Diamond was crying, but then he laughed his way out. "I'm the art person, that's what you said, but making art out of this would never have crossed my mind. I don't know if it's great. It may be pretty childish in a way. *Jejeune* is the critic's word. But you've given her back to me. That's all I really care about."

Brigid

Miss O'Keeffe lay in bed, in a white nightgown. Her eyes were closed, her face both set and slack. Brigid did not think this could be possible in life, and she gasped and put her hand to her mouth. But then Miss O'Keeffe turned her head toward the doorway and opened first one eye, then the other. Her face stretched into a smile, the lines of skin moving up like a venetian blind. She looks like a ranch hand, Brigid thought suddenly, an old ranch hand caught sleeping on the job. Miss O'Keeffe moved her left hand out from under the blankets and motioned Brigid into the room, towards the one chair. "Bring it here," Miss O'Keeffe whispered, and Brigid did. Miss O'Keeffe held Brigid's hand and closed her eyes.

"I want to ask you again . . ." Brigid began.

"School," Miss O'Keeffe said, her voice like a string spinning off a spool.

"Yes. I'm going to go—"

"Not yet. Not yet."

"No, not yet. I won't leave you." She felt Miss O'Keeffe squeeze her hand as if to stop her from saying any more. "I have savings." Miss O'Keeffe squeezed her hand again, longer this time. "But I'm afraid I might not have enough."

Miss O'Keeffe opened her eyes very wide, as if she were frightened, as if she'd realized she'd forgotten something. "It's already done," she said.

Neither one of them could have said whose idea it was to make the handprints. Brigid thought at first Miss O'Keeffe was talking in her sleep when she said, "Paint my hands vermilion and press them on cloth." Brigid brought the pigment on a tray, along with water and refined linseed oil, and made the mixture exactly as Miss O'Keeffe specified, mixing small quantities of oil into the pigment with a wide palette knife. While Brigid did this, Miss O'Keeffe kept her eyes closed, and at times appeared to be asleep—her breathing steadied into an even, delicate whistle. This pigment Miss O'Keeffe had ground herself, from the red rock of the mountains. It was years old, and Brigid wondered if anything would come of it. But soon enough the oil began to take hold and lighten the color to a familiar shade.

"Is this it?" Brigid asked.

Miss O'Keeffe nodded, though she did not open her eyes. "It's timing. Long enough."

"What cloth?"

"Towel."

"I brought a white one from the studio."

"Put it on the tray."

She picked up the broad brush and reached for Miss O'Keeffe's hand, opened the palm, brushed on the color, then pressed it gently into the cloth.

"Hold your breath, Brigid."

"I am."

"I've always liked your name. It sounds like a crossing, a place to cross over."

"It does."

Miss O'Keeffe raised her hand away from the cloth. The print was perfect, and a little frightening. She cleaned Miss O'Keeffe's hand carefully with solvent, but the color lay deep in the creases of her palm.

"Now the right hand?" Brigid asked.

"So everyone will know I had one of each."

When it was done, Brigid helped Miss O'Keeffe sit up in bed. Together, they stared at the cloth. Brigid thought Miss O'Keeffe could not see it very clearly, and maybe that was good, because it looked a little as if a murder had been committed.

"Now put on one of my shirts," Miss O'Keeffe said. Brigid stood and went to the closet, took a long white shirt from the rack.

"This one?"

"They're all the same. You know that."

Brigid turned away, unbuttoned her own blouse and slipped it off. Miss O'Keeffe's shirt felt like clean bed linens.

"Hands again, Brigid."

This time Brigid painted both at once, wondering where they would go. Miss O'Keeffe gestured for Brigid to move the tray and lean in close. For a moment, Brigid thought Miss O'Keeffe would touch her cheeks with the painted hands. Instead, the hands found their place high on Brigid's chest, almost reaching over her shoulders.

"There," Miss O'Keeffe said. "Enough."

Brigid took off the shirt. The prints looked as if Miss O'Keeffe were pushing her away. She hung the shirt over the back of the chair and went into the bathroom and filled a basin with warm water. She cleaned Miss O'Keeffe's hands and then helped her lie down. She sat on the bed and bent to rest her head, lightly, on the old woman's chest. Miss O'Keeffe brought her right hand up and moved over Brigid's hair, long, heavy strokes. "You're painting me," Brigid said, and Miss O'Keeffe sighed, a low noise in her throat.

The room was very white and still, though the early spring light seemed like a kind of madness, careening through the window, lighting the wall just above Miss O'Keeffe's head. That famous *Pieta*, Brigid thought, but tilted, off-balance. The old images were supposed to be changed anyway, as the world moved, spun, wobbled.

Miss O'Keeffe's breathing deepened into a gentle snore. Her hand dropped halfway out of Brigid's hair. Brigid reached over to hold that hand too, and raised her head. Out the window, she saw the snowy peaks of the Sangre de Cristos, falling from blue to purple as the sun dropped behind them. The window was so clean as to appear absent. Or no, she thought, it's fully there, a waiting presence, waiting to be made absent, waiting to open when the time came to release Miss O'Keeffe's spirit.

Now there was nothing to do but sit and try not to think outside this room. Watch. See what body and spirit did at the end, their final, beautiful untangling. Or, rather *this* body and spirit. She knew it would be different from the other dying she had seen, that violent, bloody wrenching. This is not for the faint of heart, Father Edgardo had said, examining her father's corpse, after blessing her mother's and Fuentes' bodies. He had put his breviary into the pocket of his cassock. Brigid remembered that he paused for what seemed like a long time, deciding. He drew the breviary out, paused again, his hand opening and closing around the little book. This waiting was like that, even though her father was already dead, suspension inside a moment. That room was also filled with sunshine that dimmed as they waited, Brigid and Theo. Even as he opened the prayer book and searched for the page, they weren't sure he would do it. And then he did. Father Edgardo blessed her father on his way, in spite of the way itself.

On the morning of March 5, Miss O'Keeffe sat up and announced that she intended to take a drive to Santa Fe. Then she threw back the duvet and the sheet and swung her thin legs out of bed and settled her feet on the floor. She appeared to Brigid to be made of something other than flesh and bones, ice maybe—she appeared to be a kind of snow queen, imperious and irresistible inside the swirled white of the bed linens and her night dress. Or some kind of flower, her face the center, the stigma, like *The White Calico Flower*, a painting from the forties. Brigid went to see about the car while Miss O'Keeffe dressed. But when she returned, she found Miss O'Keeffe lying down, tucked inside the duvet, as if she'd never moved.

She reached for Brigid's hand. "You should have gone without me."

"I couldn't do that," Brigid said.

"You will."

But that night, when Brigid brought her a cup of tea, Miss O'Keeffe had more to say. "There's going to be a lot of trouble," she whispered. "Look in your file." Brigid did not know what she meant, not exactly, though she understood it would take some time to settle the will.

There is one breath that is the last. The last breath, hidden in the lungs, inside the body, all those years, waiting its turn. Not so different from the last painting, *The Sky Above the Clouds*, finished more than twenty years before.

"So this was your trip to Santa Fe." Brigid said the words out loud to the still form in the bed. She turned then and opened the window. The air outside St. Vincent's was cool and still and then a breeze rose out of nowhere. She crossed the room and clicked off all the lights but one. A gibbous moon hung in the narrow window, as if it had stopped to look in on the scene. The man in the moon had a round open mouth, the cartoon face of surprise. "Go away," Brigid said. The moon slowly obeyed, to be replaced by a dipper, a belt, a chair, seven sisters, all of them leaning in for a last glimpse. Outside the hospital, a car paused, then raced off, tires squealing. The headlamps shone into the room. Miss O'Keeffe's right eye stood open, while the left remained closed, and for a moment she remembered her mother, confused the two women.

She and Theo had stayed with the bodies and the darkness grew around them, but neither got up to call the police. At three o'clock, Brigid thought she might cross the room and sit by her mother, whisper *Sorry*, put her head on her mother's torn chest. She thought about this for some time, imagined the various approaches—quickly, slowly, silently, calling *oh, Mama* until she felt delirious. She might have fallen asleep. Finally a resolve came into her body, and she rose from the chair. Her mother seemed a piece of darkness on the floor, and Brigid moved toward it. She sat down. Her mother was utterly still and very cold.

For an hour, maybe longer, Brigid sat beside her mother. Cold seeped into her skin all along the left side of her body. She reached up once to touch her mother's face, felt the open eyes and gently closed them. One stayed closed, but the other drifted open again, and relief shot through Brigid's chest like a blast of air, relief that this room was dark, that she would never see her mother's sinister wink.

After a while, the windows turned from inky black to gray, then to a silvery blue. The change was imperceptible, but real, impossible to stop, the way heat slips out of a building or a body. Brigid reached up and closed her mother's left eye, ran her finger firmly along the eyelid, as if sealing an envelope. She wished then she could see her mother's eyes open one last time. She knew that in a minute or two she would be able to see the outline of her mother's body next to her own. Her mother would *take shape*. Brigid felt exhausted, emptied, as if she had worked all night on her mother's new shape, as if she had brought her mother into being out of pigment or clay or stone, minerals and paper. In a moment, she would see what she had wrought.

She moved to close Miss O'Keeffe's eye, but then she changed her mind, staring down into the blank, black disc. "You can still see me," Brigid whispered, and then a nurse came for the body.

Miss O'Keeffe had made a file for Brigid, and in it she found a manila envelope that contained forty $100 bills.

"Scatter" is the wrong word for it. In fact the whole idea is ridiculous: that the living go out into the open and actually *do* something. The wind does it, Brigid saw, always the wind, no matter where the living supposed the dead wanted to be. Open water, a high mountain, beside the new shoots in the garden. In the end, the wind got to decide, the wind and the ashes themselves.

The nephew carried the urn, a golden metal cube, followed by his family and a few friends from New York. Julian Granger could not be there, but sent his condolences and—of all the ironic gestures—flowers, lilies, that deathly cliché. Brigid couldn't believe it, and then she decided he must have put the actress wife to work on the task of honoring Miss O'Keeffe. She shook her head over this, walking behind the gaggle of them, wondering why they couldn't stop talking. The nephew at least was silent, far up ahead. The family had wanted a priest, so Father Edgardo followed, but at a distance, as if he were on some other, private errand.

After he'd gone a hundred yards from the house, the nephew stopped, turned, and signaled to Brigid, using the urn, like Father Edgardo raising the chalice at Mass. At first she misunderstood, thinking he meant some sort of offertory to Ghost Ranch, but he looked right at her and raised his eyebrows. "Farther," Brigid called. "Toward the mountains." She quickened her pace and moved past the others, past the nephew and kept going. She wished she were carrying the ashes. She wanted to find a way to keep some for herself. She would have to think quickly. The wind blew her coat open, whipped at her dress.

She came to a place where the mountains seemed to settle around Ghost Ranch and then rise like a cupped hand, the sign for *come here,* the hand like a small oar. The nephew caught up, and then the others did. Most of them wore the wrong shoes for this terrain, Brigid saw. The nephew lifted the lid off the urn and handed it to Brigid. A clump of ashes had gathered in one corner and this she scooped into her left hand and held it inside her closed fist. The nephew invited the relatives to reach in for a handful of ash, and so they did. Then they flung their arms wide and called Miss O'Keeffe's name, as if they were searching for her, as if she'd got lost somewhere on her own property and must be found. Their voices rang with a mindless hysteria, and Brigid thought it was a terrible thing to do, to get rid of someone this way. But it was what Miss O'Keeffe had wanted.

The wind changed, and ashes flew against Brigid's cheek, along her lips. She opened her mouth to let them in. She tasted and swallowed. She imagined this bit of Miss O'Keeffe traveling down her throat, the length of her esophagus, and into her stomach, where it would be absorbed into the tiny blood vessels and spread throughout her body. A kind of magic would happen, and this little bit of ash would be everywhere inside her, for as long as she lived. For a moment, Brigid felt something like happiness, but then just as suddenly she remembered Miss O'Keeffe was dead, and she would be alone and homeless. Ghost Ranch would be sold or placed in trust. No one would live here. It was horrible what happened in empty houses, animals got in and ruined everything, or the house itself came slowly to understand the owners weren't coming back and finally collapsed in grief.

Brigid gazed out at the land toward the Sangre de Cristos and tried to see it with Miss O'Keeffe's eyes. She remembered those eyes, dark and clear. Even as the sight failed, the eyes never grew milky or strange, though they would sometimes fly open if Miss O'Keeffe knew Brigid had come into the room. She was seized again by the horror of cremation, that those eyes might have flown open just that way as the body was being sent into the fire. You can't imagine it, Brigid told herself. You can't ever see like she did, you can't expect to. Do something different! Julian Granger had shouted at Brigid's class. For God's sake, stop copying!

Brigid followed the family back inside. Theo would be coming for her in an hour, and after that the family would divide itself and get into cars and drive away. She knew they wanted her gone first. They wanted to lock the door on Miss O'Keeffe's things until their lawyers came back later to argue about the will. Brigid went into the office, took an envelope from the box on the desk and uncurled her hand full of ashes into it, licked the seal, pressed the envelope closed. She wrote the date on the front. Something clenched inside her, a contraction, as if Sasha had returned to her old first home. Brigid wondered if Miss O'Keeffe's ashes inside her would fill in the places that Sasha had left empty.

At that moment hard knuckles sounded on the door. Brigid knew it was Father Edgardo and also that he would come in without being asked. He hated to waste time with pleasantries or convention. Sometimes this was useful. "No sense waiting," he had said as he was preparing to baptize Sasha, right after she was born. "Bad enough that she doesn't have a father." "She has a father," Brigid said, but Father Edgardo didn't answer.

Now he crossed the office quickly and took hold of Brigid's hand. He smiled and squeezed her fingers. "I was waiting for a sign," he said. "The heavens to open or the ground to burst into flame."

"She wouldn't have wanted you there."

"No, but she's subtle. That was her great strength."

"One of them."

Father Edgardo turned to look around the office. "Will you finish up here?"

"I'm finished. My brother will come for me in a little while."

"Where will you go?"

"I was thinking about New York, but now I don't know if I'm that brave."

"Oh, but you are. I'm quite sure of that." He shook his head. "But it's so far, New York. Do you know about the Indian art school? I've heard it's a terrific place."

"I've heard that too," Brigid said, "but I don't want any more Indian."

"Ah," Father Edgardo said. "Well, let me know what you decide."

Brigid promised that she would. When he'd crossed again to the office door, Father Edgardo turned back.

"Do you know how she is?" she asked. "Sasha. The baby."

Father Edgardo looked down at his shoes. His face collapsed into a terrible grimace. "I don't hear anything."

"So I guess that means she's fine."

"Yes. I'm sure she is. She was so beautiful. They are good people, I understand."

"Is," Brigid said.

"What do you mean?"

"Is beautiful."

Father Edgardo nodded, whispered that he was sorry. They stood still for a moment, and Brigid felt dizzy, as if time were about to change direction, start rushing backward. Then she told him she had to pack her things, and he said good-bye.

Last to go into the suitcase were the letters, ten of them, exactly the same but for the salutation, *letters of introduction*, Miss O'Keeffe had said as she dictated the language and then signed each page of onionskin. Three of the letters were addressed "Dear Director of Admissions." Then eight terse sentences explained Brigid's connection to her, described her work and ended with the endorsement, "She will not disappoint," followed by "warm regards" and the unmistakable signature. As she signed the tenth letter, Miss O'Keeffe had whispered, "I don't think these regards will be so warm." Then she laughed, a small, rough chuckle like rattling stones against a boot. Brigid laughed too. She thought later how morbid it was, this last joke they shared.

So she had three chances at school, three schools. Brigid believed with all her soul that these letters were golden tickets. Miss O'Keeffe said she had never written such a letter for anyone else. Brigid believed that too.

She closed the suitcase and carried it to the front door where she nearly tripped over four other bags lined up in the entryway. The nephew stood beside them, smiling in his grim, embarrassed way.

"You're leaving too?" Brigid said.

"No, no. These are yours."

When Brigid began to protest, he waved his hand very close to her face. She thought his fingers would stab into her eyes, and reached up to stop him. He caught her hand and held it, would not let go.

"These are my aunt's. Her clothes." He glanced away from Brigid's face, down the length of her body, and she felt frightened. Where was Theo?

Father Edgardo? Where were the others? "You're about her size, aren't you? Some of her things have paint on them, so I thought you could. . . ." He let go of her hand and made the gesture of painting on an easel.

Brigid started to say she did not want his aunt's clothes, but suddenly she knew just how much she did want them, the black trousers and impossibly white shirts, the long, dark coats, the shapeless dresses, inside which the body could be utterly forgotten. This was better than the ashes. She smiled at the nephew, looked him in the eye, tried to see to the depths of him, find out what else he might be willing to give her.

"Did you steal her things?" Theo asked, and then he just stared at his sister, who gazed straight ahead, through the windshield. "Or did you steal *her*?"

Brigid had wondered if that would be the effect, dressed in these clothes, her hair pulled back in a knot, the way Miss O'Keeffe had worn hers. They had the same high forehead and dark eyes, sharp nose, thin lips. This had been remarked upon before, by Julian Granger last summer.

"I didn't steal anything," she said to Theo. When he moved to start the car, she put her hand on his arm. "I don't want to leave."

"It will be dark soon," Theo said. "You could sneak back in, I guess."

A fierce gust of wind rose out of nowhere and shook the car. "I can't tell what she wants me to do," Brigid said.

"It's not what she wants you to do. Not anymore. It's what you want to do."

Brigid nodded, believing he meant move back into their house, teach art at the elementary school, give private art lessons, cook, clean, live with him in polite harmony until he decided to bring in a wife.

"I'm going to Denver," he said.

"Denver?"

"There's a lot of work there. Steady work. Construction. I've had enough of moving all over, and I'm sick of coming back to this place and talk about nothing and drunks."

Brigid thought he might cry. "You'll come back. You'll want to. You hate anything steady."

"If I don't go, I'm going to end up like Dad. The house is sold."

"Sold? Who bought that house? Who would want it?"

"Father Edgardo."

"I just saw him. He didn't say anything about that."

"I asked him not to. And he bought everything in it. He paid extra for the paintings. Cash. That's all yours. And half what he paid for the house."

Brigid remembered Father Edgardo in the house the day he baptized Sasha. She imagined him now, purifying the rooms, secretly with the censer borrowed from the church. Then he would invite the pueblo to perform their own ceremony with burning sticks of sage. He would want it that way, the Christian and the pagan together, but the Christian first.

"So where are we going to live before you go?"

"Not we. You. My stuff is already in Denver."

He was going to make her ask again. There was some strange cruelty in his manner, a new hardness. "Where am I going to live?"

"With Father Edgardo."

"No," Brigid said. They were still parked in front of Miss O'Keeffe's house.

"They would probably let you stay another couple of days," Theo said. "And they're leaving tonight. Didn't you trespass the first time?"

"They'll come back. Or somebody will. To catalog her things."

"What about her summer house?"

"It hasn't been opened yet."

"Perfect."

"Why are you doing this to me?"

"I'm moving us along. That's what I do. The world doesn't need another drunk Indian. The world doesn't need another twenty-four-year-old mother of five little Indians."

A light came on inside Miss O'Keeffe's house. In a moment, the nephew would surely appear, his brow furrowed, a studied look of concern spread over his features, barely masking irritation. He was an actor, too, Brigid remembered, the lawyer kind. He strutted in courtrooms, Miss O'Keeffe once said. He would know exactly how to make her leave.

"All right," she said to Theo. "Take me away."

Nancy

While I waited for Rodney and Henry to get to Atlanta, I worked some more on the play about Emily Dickinson and Louisa May Alcott.

> LOU: Weren't you hot in that dress—
> How could you not think of the wedding you'd miss—
> What about stains? What a pain
> To bleach in a bucket. And where's the pocket
> To keep paper? And why eleven buttons—I'd like to know—
> All those pleats you had to iron—and starch closed—
> EMILY: Very funny.
> LOU: And what did your father think?
> EMILY: Which one?
> LOU: Heavenly.
> EMILY: He approved.
> LOU: The other?
> EMILY: Wondered where I came from.

Henry and Rodney rented the largest U-Haul available, 26 feet, enough space for a small circus, and filled it with brand new furniture. Rodney had envisioned a big white house with a screened porch and a short walk to the medical center. Henry wanted a one-bedroom apartment in Virginia Highlands, north-facing for the light, upstairs, a balcony, street noise okay. Both would be disappointed.

When Rodney climbed down from the driver's side, he looked first at my mother. She had come out of the house because the U-Haul's giant cartoon of Mount Rushmore suddenly blocked the light in her studio, even the high windows. My mother was wearing a pair of jeans and a red T-shirt. "First Thing We Do, Let's Kill All the Lawyers," it read, in black script, Elizabethan-looking. The font is called Old English Bold, Henry once told her, but she said no, it was called French Style, and then they argued over it for a while. The sight of that shirt still provoked Henry. My mother looked dazed. I could smell the cigarettes from ten feet away, where I had been sitting on the front steps, waiting for Henry and Rodney, half-hidden by boxwood.

"You?" my mother said to Rodney. "The best man?"

"Mom. I told you who he was." This was Henry, from the other side of the truck.

"I was imagining someone else," she said. "But oh well. Come over here, Henry, and let me hug you."

I thought I would just sit there for a minute and listen, not give myself away quite yet. Henry seemed to look right through the boxwood branches and find me. I thought he winked. "Where's Nancy?" he said.

"Around here somewhere," my mother said. She called my name, half-heartedly I thought, though I couldn't see her face. She'd stepped back inside her studio. "You can't park here for very long, you know."

"We know, Mom." Henry sounded exasperated.

Suddenly I believed that they would climb back into the U-Haul and leave, abandon me. Still, I couldn't move.

"Where *is* that Nancy?" my mother asked the air.

I wished I had a joint. I wondered how I could have been so stupid to think I could face this moment without reinforcements? Girlfriend's little helper? Something else became clear right then: that Rodney hadn't chosen Emory because of me. Why, I wondered, didn't humans have the ability to transmigrate, blink themselves hundreds of miles away? Or five miles. I calculated that was about the distance from my parents' house to the walk-in refrigerator at McDonald's. There was a dime bag under the bottom carton of Happy Meal toys. Imagine the manager's surprise.

You can't escape, of course, at least not that easily. You walk around the green scrim of boxwood and hug the brother, kiss the lover, mindful of the mother in her confrontational and exuberantly splotched attire. And by that afternoon you're flat on your back in the Extended Stay America, courtesy of Emory University Medical School, making love that is wonderful and doomed. You try to leave, but the man you love keeps taking off your pants before you can get both legs back in.

"When are you going back to college?" Rodney asked.

"In a few months," I said. But I knew I'd never go back.

Rodney had a fifth-floor suite so we could keep the curtains open all the time with no fear that anyone could look in, see us hard at work. Possibly the patients in the Medical Center rooms across the street.

What's on the fifth floor over there, Rodney?

I.C.U.

That's funny.

All that light. Morning light. I woke with it, and turned to face my sleeping lover, learning him. The third morning, I realized what I was waiting for as the sun rose higher over the hospital. I was waiting for Rodney to lighten, to emerge from the shadow of his own body. What happens to everyone as daylight eases over us. And when it didn't come to pass, I thought how misguided all metaphor is. Even the most elemental figures of speech don't apply to more than half the people in this world. So I moved closer, put my false not-quite-white-enough body near then next to then over his. I wanted to melt into his skin. Not to change it, not to possess it, but almost. Close. The lines where our bodies met—I wanted them to blur, our chests and bellies and hips, my legs locked around his. But they never did. I seemed to get whiter. The contrast became stark. Piano keys. That music, made by fingers. All he had to do was touch me. Probably the least interesting line I've ever written, but maybe the truest.

This was half of the month of July and most of August. I don't remember what we did during the day, though I *know.* We didn't do anything because Rodney was at the hospital. I quit my ridiculous job at McDonald's and stayed in the suite and worked on my play. Rodney came back in the evening and we cooked something on the two-burner stove, opened a bottle of wine. It was very peaceful in that doomed kind of way. I realize I've used that word twice now to describe life with Rodney. I'm betting I'll use it again, and soon.

Sometimes we went out with Henry. But my memory of Henry from those days is the back of his head, his shoulders, his body turned away. He'd stopped cutting his hair in New York, and now he wore it in a long braid, dark, glossy, alive with perception and interests. I am talking about the braid here, which moved as my brother moved, echoed his life. He looked Mexican sometimes, which is to say he looked more like me, until you got him in the right light, and then he could be American Indian or far eastern Slavic, high cheek bones, a face shaped like a shield. Women drifted around him, mesmerized. I picture him walking away from me toward a crowd of women, or standing at the bar in the Five Points Grill. I'm behind him, at a table with Rodney, a pitcher of beer sweating between us. Henry is flanked by two women, and really that's what he's become, their flanks, because their two bodies are pressed so tightly to his. For a split second, I wish he would step back, step out of this picture, and cause them to crash into each other, but then I feel sorry for them, their two impending broken hearts. Henry's girlfriend Paula—who followed him to Atlanta and will soon become his wife—is sitting at the table too, laughing, shouting to Henry, *Go for it, Loverboy.*

Georgia O'Keeffe and Jan Vermeer. Heaven or someplace very like it.

GEORGIA: Finally, I have to say it: I like your work.

VERMEER: I haven't seen yours.

G: Not yet or not ever?

V: Yes.

G: I have some questions for you.

V: Questions?

G: About light.

V: Shoot.

G: It's flatter than you think.

V: That's not a question.

G: People think you're all about light, but really you're all about shadow.

V: So why do you think they're so easily confused?

G: People?

V: Light and shadow.

G: I—

V: It's one of those unanswerable questions. Maybe because they're next to each other. Adjacent entities are troubling.

G: *Adjacent entities?*

V: It sounds better in Dutch. Anyway. Think countries and their borders.

G: Think men and their servant girls.

V: I was, actually.

G: She was pretty.

V: I didn't do her justice.

G: What do you mean by "do her justice"?

V: What do *you* mean?

G: Paint her, you old goat.

V: Well, I guess you know something about old goats.

G: I can get inside their heads.

V: I always wondered if she was uncomfortable in that dress. If she hated sitting for so long, if at the end of it all, she hated me. I wondered about women's work—what they did—how they did it all, made those stinking clothes wearable again. My clothes too. I thought I should know that in order to make the paintings breathe.

G: You think that now.

V: Yes, but I thought it then. Not all the time. Or, yes. Really, all the time. You can ask her. *I* asked her. I did. "What do you do all day?" I said. She didn't much like the question. I suppose she knew where it would lead. But—it's the other lives I want to see. Really to understand them—or something like that. I'm not sure. And now I'm too dead to know.

G: Me too. Too dead.

V: Shall we tell them what it feels like?

G: They'd never believe us.

The Em and Lou play was better. I understand that now, the gap, the space between the play you want to write and the play you write.

Somewhere in there is "can." The play you can write. Plays that can't, teach. A play saved is a play earned. The closest play may be behind you.

Rodney and Henry. They loved each other so much. They loved how they could never understand what the other one did. How do you make color and order come out of your hand? Rodney said to Henry. How do you make comfort come out of your mouth? Henry asked in return. Your eyes? Your breath across the room? The lift and fall of your chest? The faint sigh of your chair when you move to signal the end of the therapeutic hour? I don't know, man, they both said. Ask Paula. Ask Nancy. Paula and I were sitting at the table with the sweating pitchers of beer, or we were making a pan of enchiladas. Or we were waiting in line for tickets to see Bruce Springsteen, his acoustic show, *The Ghost of Tom Joad*. The point is we were barely there, or never there. For a while, we were the same kind of absent. But then Paula began to gain substance, put on emotional flesh. She got more distinct. She increased in volume. Her voice made real words, talk beyond *mmmhmmm, yep, sure.*

Henry gave her a diamond, a tiny chip on a stem. She wore it first in her nose, until she found a job. Then the diamond went in her left earlobe. Maybe Rodney thought that because I was a diamond, I didn't need one.

At the end of September, we moved out of Extended Stay America and into a house on Candler Road. A rental, but still. Three bedrooms, three baths, a formal dining room, a huge kitchen, a real library, full of the landlord's books. This vast forest of a yard, part of which was a neglected, overgrown, and perhaps secret garden, full of exotic perennials: asparagus, rhubarb, sorrel, powerfully spicy arugula. I spent so much time out there that I started to think about exterior scenes, but I couldn't write them, not people in daylight. It was so much easier to write darkness. Because the theater is dark. I thought about dark exterior scenes: the ghost of Hamlet's father on the parapet. This led to other questions. For instance, why didn't anyone jump? You got a parapet? Somebody has to go off it in the third act.

I thought my dad would hate the idea of me living with Rodney, but he never said a word about it. I think he lived in fear of the question I would ask him: *Do you disapprove because he's black?*

"Think of it as my practicing on you," Rodney said.

"I thought that's what you were doing."

"I don't mean sex."

"Oh."

"I mean your. . . ."

"My what?"

"Problem. Addiction."

"It's not an addiction."

"Nance, you smoke every day."

"It's not an addiction. It's a ritual. You know. Something you do in the same way, usually at the same time, for some kind of—what would you call it?"

"Addiction."

"Comfort. Like people going to church. Like the Mass."

We were having this conversation in bed, early morning, the light pearly gray, like the wing of a dove. I thought again about how Rodney was visible—his darkness a rent in the gray, a place where the gray had been erased—and I was probably not visible. I could just barely see the details of our lives: our two digital clocks, my small stack of magazines, Rodney's taller stacks of books, the high-backed rocking chair we never sat in but hung clothes from, a basket overflowing with laundry. Notice the props surrounding the people, one of my textbooks said. No wonder they're called props, these objects. They prop you up, keep you steady, nail you to the cross of the world.

"You don't go to Mass," Rodney said.

"I'm saving it for when I have children."

"All I'm saying is that I'd like to talk to you about it."

"You mean listen while I talk about it."

"Yes. That's what I mean."

"Is this the psychopharmacology rotation?"

"Actually, it is."

I suddenly knew Rodney would be a very good therapist. He was a human depository for pain. He captured it and kept it to himself. His patients could go to him to visit their pain, like that Civil War general who had his leg amputated. I remembered the story because it was so odd: the surgeon donated the preserved leg to a museum, and from time to time, the general went to visit it. A funny thing to do—and what for? To prove you'd got over the loss, the trauma? That Simon and Garfunkel song. *Hello darkness, my old friend. I've come to talk with you again.* To prove you can stand next to the dark thing and make small talk. *How 'bout those Yankees? Nice that we're having weather. Hey, can I pour you another cup of bitter brew?* And somehow all this made me want to hug Rodney, to jump his bones, if you want to know the truth. I reached for him and told him I was about to make him late for work.

But he said not today.

Some mornings, alone in the house, I caught myself wondering which one I liked best, sex or white wine or weed or writing my play. I thought about how only one of the four involved Rodney, or really any other human being. This interested me for a while until I realized that sex was at the bottom of the list. The other three were tied for first place. You figure out things like this, and then, if you live with a psychiatrist, you understand that you don't have to tell anyone. You don't have to say it out loud. You don't, in fact, have to say anything out loud, though people are uniformly charmed if you tell them your dreams.

Most afternoons, I took the bus to Henry's house in Virginia Highlands. We talked about work. We kind of do the same thing, Henry said; a play is a lot like a map. It has location. It has directions. It has footsteps all over it. If you could draw a map of all the moves (that's called blocking I told him), what would it look like?

"Black," I said.

"Well, that's no fun."

"It's like a bedroom then."

"Backstage in the dark. A lot happens when no one is looking."

"Or when everyone is looking at something else."

"You were once a pretty good actress," Henry said. "How come you don't do that anymore?"

"I'm not sure."

"Of course you're sure. Come on, Nance."

Someday I would tell him why, but not then. I was embarrassed. The truth is that it frightened me, the way you had to be. You had to be so empty. So that the character could fill you up. Otherwise you were just playing yourself, though there was some consolation in that—at least you had a self to play. But I had been a good actress because deep down, there was just more deep down. Nothing. No self. Just responses. So that walking around in the world felt like continuous free fall. Even getting up in the morning, getting from the bed to the coffeemaker. Nearly impossible. What to hold on to? Where to hold on? You can't really say this to anyone, all those people who have jobs, careers, a family they're all the way related to, a place in the world. You can't say this because it's too crazy.

Sasha

"Come out to Long Beach for Thanksgiving," Jennie said on the phone. "You're not going home, are you?"

"I couldn't," Sasha said. She gazed around her dorm room, perched high above Broadway, the safe little crow's nest it had become. "I couldn't get on a plane."

"No," Jennie said. "Don't even talk about it."

"Are you sure your Mom wants me? Maybe it should just be you two."

Jennie made a sound like a low animal scream. Then she was quiet.

"Are you there?"

"I'm here," Jennie said. "It shouldn't be just us two. It almost never was. The tradition used to be that we went to the Jacksons'. Rodney's family. His dad cooked. I mean, he's a chef, right? Never turkey though. He'd make things like roasted butternut squash soup and pecan-crusted salmon. And there was great wine. His second wife was a sommelier."

"At Windows on the World. Rodney told me on the train that day."

"So. You know. We probably won't be going over there."

"Right. I'll come."

"Thanks," Jennie said. "I guess that's the word of the day. Thanks. And bring something nice to wear. Mom likes to dress up for the holidays. She used to anyway."

"You look great, Mom," Jennie said, when Lisa appeared downstairs in a black cocktail dress.

Sasha agreed, even though the dress made her small and pale inside of it. Her earrings and the bracelets on her wrist jangled as she moved. The heels of her shoes rang like gunshots on the dining room floor. The effect of it all was the absolute truth: a terrible injury badly covered up.

They tried to eat slowly, go easy on the wine. But still, they were done in twenty minutes. Sasha and Jennie cleared the dinner dishes and glassware, but not the crumpled napkins, the bread basket and its single roll, the crusted gravy boat, the dessert plates smeared with half-eaten pie. The sight was mildly hysterical, as if several people had had a great deal of fun eating very little. Alice in Wonderland, Sasha thought, *The Mad Tea Party.*

She had this sudden ricochet of fears in her head: what if I meet Brigid Schumann and she doesn't like me? What if I've spent all this time trying to turn into a person people might like, and she just . . . doesn't? Or vice versa. What if I don't like her? What if she's overbearing and judgmental and obsessed with appearances? Or selfish. That's pretty likely. Or just plain mean? Or bored? Bored by me. She imagined filming Brigid Schumann talking about *The Mad Tea Party.* Brigid stares directly at Sasha though the eye of the camera. And doesn't recognize her.

Lisa settled herself in the living room. She looked like a jagged black fracture in all that white.

"That was delicious," Sasha said. "Thank you."

"You're sweet," Lisa said. Tears rolled down her cheeks. Sasha could tell she was very drunk. "I think maybe I'll just go to bed."

"Not yet, Mom," Jennie said. "Please."

"What does your family do after Thanksgiving dinner, Sasha?" Lisa said.

"We used to take a walk on the golf course near our house," Sasha said. "One year, my mom said, 'How about just to be different, we take a hibachi instead?'" She started to laugh and tried to stop but couldn't. "Oh Mom," she said. "Mom, Mom, Mom. She loved Thanksgiving the best of all holidays. She always said, the Indians invented it, but then the white people brought cream of mushroom soup and that changed everything. Oh, Mom. I don't know if I'm laughing or crying."

"Go ahead, you two," Jennie said. Tears leaked from the corners of her eyes. "Go ahead. I'll hold things together here." She left the room and came back with their dinner napkins, tossed Sasha's and Lisa's into their laps. "That makes me think about Dad last year. At the Jackson's. Remember, Mom? We were just incoherent with food. And Dad started exclaiming in that hilarious voice *Riesling should be married to bouilla-baisse! Salmon needs chardonnay like a man needs a woman—or a man! There's this cakey cloud of coffee we call tiramisu!* And we couldn't stop laughing. I think that last one was the best meal of my life."

"Mine, too," Lisa said. "What was your best Thanksgiving, Sasha?"

"Best," Sasha, said. "We always said it was the year my grandfather's dog ate the turkey and we went out to dinner. There was something so abandoned about it. Like we were totally free."

"Abandoned is a weird word," Jennie said quietly. "For a good time."

"I know," Sasha said. "Seems like it would be awful."

"One year *was* awful," Lisa said. "Remember, Jennie? Rodney was not happy about his new stepmother."

"Because she was white," Jennie said.

"At first we thought he was being funny," Lisa said. "Going on about Stacey, about her enslavement, about keeping black men from the black women who need them, about wanting to do this exotic thing and try to call it love, about gold-digging."

"He missed his mom," Jennie said quietly. "And now he misses Stacey."

"Toni, his mother, was from the south," Lisa said. "From North Carolina. A town called Lowland. She told me she was part Lumbee Indian, and you could believe it. She had that strong, powerful look, high forehead, nose like a cliff."

Lisa stood up and left the room.

"Mom has this great photo," Jennie said. "She loves it. They were best friends."

Lisa returned, balancing a framed 5x7 between her open palms. "This was a couple of months before she died. God, she looks fierce."

In the photograph, Lisa had wrapped both her arms around Rodney's mother and appeared to be whispering in her ear. Rodney's mother gazed into the eye of the camera, a wisp of a smile on her lips. Fierce was a good word, Sasha thought. Aboriginal. "You can see the Indian," she said.

Lisa nodded. "And Rodney was still trying to work through it all when his dad started seeing Stacey. I don't think he really believed those awful things he said to her. Like he would never call her his stepmother."

"The oppressor," Jennie said.

"You liked that one, didn't you, Jen?" Lisa said. "She said to Rodney once, 'Well, my mom's the oppressor too, and your mom sure liked her a lot.'" She stopped abruptly, "So, who's for port or something?" She made her way into the dining room. Sasha and Jennie heard the knocking of bottles and glasses, the sound of imminent shattering. Jennie gritted her teeth, shut her eyes, then called to her mother, asked if she needed help. There was no answer. After a few minutes, Lisa returned with a tray, set it on the coffee table.

"So?" she said. "Kahlua? Crème de menthe?"

"I've always loved that green," Sasha said.

Lisa brought over a small glass and the bottle of crème de menthe. Sasha took the glass and held it out. The tremor in Lisa's hand was alarming. Sasha tried to move the glass to match it, but she couldn't.

Jennie jumped to her feet. "Mom! You're spilling it all over!"

"I'm so sorry," Sasha said. "I should have—"

"You didn't do anything," Jennie whispered.

Lisa knelt beside Sasha. "Don't worry," she said, too brightly. "The miracle of Scotchgard. Tim was a world-class spiller. Jennie, remember the strawberry-rhubarb pie? And voilà." Lisa pointed to a spot near the empty armchair. "Not a shred of evidence."

"Vaporized," Jennie said. Then she covered her face with her hands. "Oh my God."

"Jennie," Lisa said sharply, and just like that, the mood in the room changed. She looked up at Sasha. "Without the Jacksons, we were never big on Thanksgiving around here."

"He'd want us to have fun again, you know," Jennie said. "He wouldn't want us to be miserable for the rest of our lives."

"That's what people tell you," Lisa said. "But how can what he wants be so important? He can't really want anything now, can he?"

"I like to think he can," Jennie said.

"You know what I want?" Lisa said. "In the morning, I want waffles. I know. Crazy. I really want syrup and butter. The waffle is just a vessel. And we should invite Rodney. I miss him." Then she made a little noise in her throat. "Rodney, I mean. I think we're all a little in love with him."

"Mom!"

"Well, we are!" Her voice was different suddenly, a pitch higher. *Flirty* was the word, Sasha thought. "Now Sasha, why aren't you filming?"

"Are you sure?"

"Of course I'm sure!"

"Mom," Jennie said. "I really don't think—"

"We'll want this, Jen. You know we will."

Sasha hurried up to Jennie's room, mostly to be out of the way. She could hear voices, very low, maybe menacing, for just a second, then the turn of the staircase swallowed the sound. She wondered how Jennie could possibly think of coming back to school and leaving her mother alone in this house, to eat syrup and butter and change her moods that fast.

Back downstairs, she found Lisa and Jennie had moved into the kitchen, and seated themselves on opposite sides of the table staring across the middle. Something had been said and would not be repeated. Lisa looked up after a beat, "Rolling?" she said. Sasha set up the tripod, opened the lens to take in the whole table. She sat down with her back to the camera.

"The secret ingredient in the waffles is lemon peel," Lisa said, "and vanilla sugar. Old family recipe."

"From Dad," Jennie said. "From his mother."

"I think we never talked about grandparents," Sasha said.

"We didn't have time," Jennie said. "I wonder if there's some study. You can learn this much about a person in six days. Anyway, no grandparents except one who died when I was fifteen. I remember we were reading *A Death in the Family* in school, and it was too—" Jennie seemed to get the jolt of her words. "That was a dead father too. In a car wreck. He had a little bruise on his chin, and that was all. It's amazing the details you remember. Dead fathers all over the place," she continued. "It's a fucking minefield. Like every so often he *springs*." Here she pounded her fist on the table. "Up from out of nowhere. Why is that?"

"Why are you so angry?" Lisa said.

"You know why!" Jennie yelled. "I'm angry at you!"

"Should I turn this off?" Sasha said.

"No," Lisa and Jennie said, nearly in unison.

Lisa turned to face the camera. "And why, my pet, are you so angry with me?" She smiled, licked her lips, then pursed them, as if she were applying lipstick in a mirror.

"You told him to go," Jennie said. "You know you did."

"He had to go, honey," Lisa said. "He had to go to work."

"He didn't, Mom. You remember. He was trying to make it up to you. He said, 'I could go in a little later if you want me to.'"

"Jennie," Lisa said. And here she did the most amazing thing. She winked at the camera, as a girl would wink at her best friend, her accomplice. "Now, Jennie. How can you know this? You were at school. Sasha knows you were at school. You were in your room on the tenth floor of that building. I can't remember the name anymore."

Sasha knew this was true. She could close her eyes and recall it exactly, Jennie's face, agreeing to go downtown, their ride in the elevator and into the street, into the subway.

"I was at school," Jennie said. "But I talked to him before, before he went, and he told me to hold on for a minute while he asked you something, and I heard him ask if he should go in later, and I heard what you said."

Lisa's face froze for an instant, the length of a quick breath. It was the look, Sasha thought, she would take on in death. Spectacularly still. Finished. You could lose your mind this way, having your daughter know such things about what would become the end of your marriage.

"She couldn't have known, Jen," Sasha said. "It might have been any day."

"But it wasn't any day," Jennie answered. "Was it?"

"Somebody knew," Lisa said. "That's what we want to get to the bottom of, isn't it? Not this other thing. Someone told your father to go back in. That's what I heard."

"Daddy's phone," Jennie said. "What an amazing piece of machinery. It holds all the answers to all the questions. Do you think it's lying around somewhere under all the rubble? Do you think the workers will find it like they found Ron Breitweiser's wedding ring?"

"Jennie, stop it," Lisa said.

"Mom," Jennie said. "Don't you even miss him?"

This could go on for a long time, Sasha thought. They didn't know how to stop themselves. She knew she could get up and turn off the camera, but it didn't feel like her choice anymore, as if the camera now belonged to the Burgetts. The word *character* came into her head, the made-up person played by an actor, who has to understand motivation, understand everything about the person, even details that didn't seem to matter. "What was your dad's favorite kind of cake?" she asked.

"Coconut," Jennie said, and Lisa nodded.

"Color?"

"Blue."

"Season?"

"Summer."

"Holiday?"

"Christmas."

"Book?"

"He always lied about that," Jennie said. "He told people what he thought they wanted to hear."

"What would he have told me?" Sasha asked.

"The Master and Margarita," Jennie said.

"What?"

"He would have thought that suited you."

"I've never read it."

"He would have known that somehow," Lisa said. "He would be thinking you ought to read it."

"You're the director here, Sasha," Jennie said. "So direct us."

"I think the idea is that I don't direct. I think I observe."

"What do you want?" Lisa said.

"I seem to want raw," Sasha said. "Difficult. Impossible. Maybe. It's what other people think I want. *Why would you want to put these awful things on film?* But truthfully, I have no wants. I'm just a big blank waiting to be filled in by whatever you want. I'm a vessel. I'm a waffle!" She looked around the kitchen for something, she hardly knew what, an oar maybe, a floating spar. The walls were yellow, the same glistening shade as the shards of lemon peel would be in the waffles. A painting of boats in a harbor, a French Impressionist, hung behind Lisa's chair. The famous Cezanne, the tall pine trees, hung opposite, behind Jennie. The china tea service on the table was turquoise, the color of a Tiffany's box. Or bluer: impenetrable water. Water you couldn't wait to get into, though you knew you'd be way out of your depth.

It was finally winding down, this terrible fall semester. Jennie was in negotiations with her composition instructor and her French professor, who finally agreed to let her do extra work in exchange for a passing grade. Math and psychology she would have to take again, in the spring. She wrote two comp papers a week until the end of the term and signed up for three oral reports in the French class. Their room seemed alive with language. Sasha filmed the presentations, on *L'école des femmes*, *Phèdre*, and *Antigone*. "Moral ambiguity." "Passion causes disorder." "Love conquers selfishness," Jennie said over and over, staring into the camera, until the words became meaningless or very funny, or both. For extra credit, they baked madeleines in the dorm's kitchen. Sasha dreamed in French. Jennie said she did too, though she hardly slept. Nightmares, she told Sasha. Not so often now, but no less terrifying.

"My dad and I are at an open window. There's fire and smoke behind us. He's reaching for my hand, and I know he's going to ask me to go with him. I don't want to. I keep thinking there must be another way out."

"Oh, Jennie," Sasha said, "Jennie, Jennie."

"I think sometimes this dream isn't so much about Dad as it is about his and Mom's marriage. I don't know. Why would he go back in? I try to figure it out, make a timeline so there can be a minute when I see him decide. But I still don't get it. He had a wife and a kid."

"A lot of people had a wife and kids. Husband and kids."

"You're saying altruism. But he wasn't that kind of guy. Never. I mean, he was nice, but I just can't imagine."

Sasha wanted to say, *You can't imagine because it would mean that he didn't choose you.* No, she didn't want to say it. It was already there in the room with them, hanging over Jennie's head and over her own too, parents who chose according to some other, unfathomable logic.

"And the thing with your mom? Why he offered to go in later—I mean if you want to tell me."

"They weren't happy. The empty nest. It surprised them both, but Dad more than Mom. Before I left, she kept saying she would miss me, and I'd say, Mom, I'm just across the river. And she'd give me this look. Big eyes, almost hysterical. And they drank a lot. That started last summer, before I left."

"Wouldn't it be simpler if your mom was having an affair?"

"Yes," Jennie said. "I almost wish for that sometimes. But she wasn't. And I think they would have figured it out if they'd had time."

Brigid

She would paint Father Edgardo, over the next few months. Father Edgardo with long dark hair and in other costumes, a tuxedoed waiter, bread and wine on the tray he held aloft, his face twisted into something servile and cunning. Or Father Edgardo in his priest's collar and surgical scrubs, soaked in blood, a loaf of bread under his arm. All over him, that color, the cranberry. *I wish blood were really this color, not so red, not so bright,* she thought as she squeezed the last of the paint from the tube Miss O'Keeffe had given her. She was working in her parents' white bedroom, where the light was best, and there was no sign of them amid the bleached linens, though Father Edgardo had told her to make the whole house her studio. He stayed sometimes in Theo's room, but mostly at the rectory in Española. She painted him in the red robes he wore on the feast days of the martyrs. She painted him in his glorious Easter cassock, a burning cigarette in his left hand, a cigarette pack in his right, held at chest level with one finger, the way Jesus points to his sacred heart. In the middle of this painting, as she was trying to get the gold on the stole, Brigid suddenly understood that Father Edgardo was rich. How else could he afford these vestments?

He told her one night, very late, his father owned a hotel and restaurant in Santa Fe, a place the opera people had come to love.

"When I was sixteen, he said to me, 'Edgardo, things will go well for me if I have a son who is a priest.' In exchange, he said I would never want for anything. I had no calling, no vocation. But I was a realist. I thought I would come to love the church the way husbands and wives whose marriages have been arranged come to love each other."

"Have you?" Brigid asked.

"I have come to love. . . ." Father Edgardo stopped, shook his head. He made long work of opening his tobacco pouch, searching for papers, rolling a cigarette. Finally he settled back into a chair, the one that had been her father's favorite. Brigid wanted to picture her father there instead, but she couldn't.

"I have come to love doing good," Father Edgardo said. "What I think is good. Like this. Giving you a house. Your own house. I have the means to do it."

"It's very nice of you," Brigid said. She felt something unspoken between them, which frightened her.

"I may come to love God as priests are supposed to. I may come to love the Church, but I'm not sure what that is. Or love our Holy Mother, but frankly, I find her a little dull and compliant, holding everything in her heart."

They sat in silence as he smoked.

"That's someone else's picture of Mary. Usually a man's," Brigid said.

"True. Very smart. I know one thing I love, which is paintings. That I do know. Your paintings and Miss O'Keeffe's. And I love gratitude. I need it. Which is troubling."

Brigid thought she would call the Easter vestments painting "Gratitude." She would stencil that word on the package of cigarettes.

She borrowed Father Edgardo's car and drove to Santa Fe, to the university. Brigid planned to locate the art building and wander through it, to get the feel of such a place. The campus was small but complicated, and she found herself not inside the art complex but in the music building, which was inexplicably filled with children, mostly girls in church dresses. Brigid saw then that they were terrified, and that each one clutched sheets of music or slim, brightly colored music books. She followed a small dark-haired girl up a flight of stairs and into what felt and sounded like the heart of the building, to a knot of anxious parents and grim children. She stepped into a farther hallway, a warren of practice rooms, only to be engulfed in sound: horns, pianos, flutes, mourning woodwinds she could not identify separately.

She could not explain why, but she found this avalanche of music less horrifying than the parents—mostly mothers. She roamed the corridors, pausing at each door to listen to the faceless music, to wonder about the agony of each child. What she heard was lovely error: a misstep, a pause, sometimes a low, innocent curse, silence, an angry crash of keys like shouting. How to paint this? How many of these nervous children have forgotten the day, the hour, their own names? How many wish they could just disappear into a black hole of sound? She found herself back in the main hallway, as a blonde girl, about ten, Brigid guessed, emerged from the recital room. Her mother waited a few yards down the hall. The girl ran to her, and the two embraced. Brigid went to stand beside them. "No mistakes," the girl breathed into her mother's hair.

That night, Brigid asked Father Edgardo if baptizing Sasha had been part of his doing good. He nodded and then looked at the dark television as if he could see a picture there. Then he got up out of her father's chair, went into the kitchen, and poured himself a glass of wine. He stood in the doorway. Yellow light glowed around his head and shoulders. Brigid thought that was a good pose, the wine glass, the white collar and black cassock, the domestic halo.

"And her parents too," he said finally. "More do-gooding."

Brigid felt she had been knocked to the ground, that she'd entered a vacuum and her breath was gone, the blood drained from her head. She leaned forward, resting her forehead on her knees. "What do you mean?" she said. "Those people from Albuquerque?"

Father Edgardo stayed where he was. He drank from the glass. "They didn't have children. Couldn't. But they wanted to. She did especially."

Father Edgardo had moved soundlessly from the domestic halo and come to stand beside her chair. He placed his hand on her back, gently, then withdrew it as if he'd been burned. Brigid sat up.

"Why did you name her that?" he said.

"I don't know, really. I liked the name. It's different. Not Indian or Mexican."

"Maybe a little German?"

"Maybe. My mother liked it. Or she didn't mind it, I guess."

"It's a beautiful name," Father Edgardo said. "Like a dance."

"Sashay," Brigid said.

"Or it's like the sound a paintbrush makes on canvas."

Brigid didn't say anything. She didn't think he was right. She wondered suddenly if Sasha would stay Sasha. "Did they let her keep her name?"

"Yes. They did."

"How do you know?"

Father Edgardo didn't answer. He took his empty glass into the kitchen. Brigid heard the water running as he rinsed it. He called good-night and went into Theo's room and closed the door. She would have to stop thinking of it as Theo's room. She got up to turn off the lights and then returned to her chair and sat in the dark living room, staring out at the empty yard. The dry grass, illuminated by moonlight, appeared to have been turned to snow. What season is this? she wondered. How long has Sasha been gone? The time with Miss O'Keefe felt like a dream. Or all of it did, the insane, charged landscape of dreams, populated by ghosts. She felt the presence of her parents, elsewhere, asleep in their bedroom. She had to remind herself that she was living in her old house with Father Edgardo, who had just given her some small mysterious piece of information, a puzzle, a riddle to solve.

But what could she do? She had given Sasha up, she'd signed papers. But here was a little wrinkle, a crack in the wall through which something, a sound, a voice, a ray of light, might come back to her. The cry of a child, which Brigid could not remember. Did Sasha cry in Beatriz's and Francisco's house, did she know that her first mother had let her go? Did she reach out her little arms and wail for Beatriz as she turned away? Her little hands, grasping air. Such little hands, the marvel of them, Brigid remembered, how tiny and perfect, how tightly they held on.

The kitchen door had been hinged to swing into the room and out toward the rest of the house, and the next day, the day after Father Edgardo's small revelation, when Brigid touched this door, it fell off its hinges. Just like that, a single touch. She was in the house by herself, profoundly alone. No ghosts. She could have been hurt but wasn't. She moved the fallen door into the kitchen and propped it against the wall. She stared at it. Wood, painted a cream-white, its surface broken—but also not broken—by a clear plastic rectangle, attached to the wood with four white screws. The hand goes here. That would be the title: *The Hand Goes Here.* The paint on the door was thick and clean, except along the bottom on both sides where Theo or her father had sometimes kicked the door open or closed.

What lived inside that door? Brigid wondered. The slightest touch had unhinged it, sent it falling, a regular, gentle push, the door's undoing. She would sand away the old paint, then glue, gesso, more sanding until the surface felt completely smooth. This work would have to be done outside, in the garage. She should have asked Theo to build her a studio before he left. Father Edgardo could afford to hire a carpenter, but she didn't want to ask him for anything more. She didn't want to owe him. The garage would serve, especially as the days grew longer and warmer. It would be good to get out of the house. If she didn't, she might paint Father Edgardo for the rest of her life. Or babies. Sasha. The name made her ache, but she couldn't stop thinking it, saying it, like breath, exhalation.

Brigid let herself out of the back door. She hadn't really looked at the garage for a long time. Seen it, yes, but not looked. Or was it the other way around? Four flat surfaces, corrugated metal, a roof and three sides. That was all right, the open side. How else would the light come in? The open side faced east. Work in the morning, then. Colder, but then cooler into the summer. How to get the door out here? She wondered. It was heavy, inch-thick oak. A good door. Maybe she should fix it, get it back on its hinges. Maybe Father Edgardo would want it, a second opening and closing between Theo's room and the rest of the house. His house. But she wanted it more. The Hand Goes Here.

She turned and walked back into the house. She brought her towel from the bathroom, wedged it under the bottom left corner of the door and began to drag it through the kitchen. The door moved quietly. The door goes willingly, she thought. The door wants to be more than a door.

Father Edgardo's Honda turned into the drive and stopped. He got out and stood for a moment watching, then helped her move the door the last twenty feet. He didn't ask what she was doing. They leaned the door against Theo's old workbench.

"Well," Father Edgardo said, "I guess it will make a good table."

"No," Brigid said. "There's a girl inside."

It would take some time—months probably—to let the girl out. At first she simply could not be found. Every morning, Brigid sat on a low camp chair inside the open garage with a thermos of coffee, the space heater blowing at the end of its orange extension cord. She wore gloves. She waited for the girl to appear out of the cloud of door, the fog of door, the milk of it. Brigid thought if she could find the right name for the element, the girl would come. She carefully removed the plastic rectangle and laid it aside. She sanded and gessoed the door down to its cinnamon-colored wood, then built it back up again to the original creamy shade. This color was called oyster. She asked around and then bought ten cans from a man who had used it to paint his sailboat. "In the American desert!" he laughed at himself as he loaded the cans into Father Edgardo's car. He stared at them, frankly, at Father Edgardo's collar. "You two take care," he said finally.

Back in the garage, she painted the door three coats of oyster. Encasing the pearl, she thought. After the paint was dry, she put the plastic rectangle back, exactly where it had been. She pulled up the camp chair, sat down, and stared into the door as if it were a mirror.

What she saw first were the braids, dark, long, lying like snakes or the business ends of two horsewhips. For a while that was all. Images came and went, like dreaming, involuntary loss of control, pleasant. Her mother drifted by, and then her grandmother. Her father stayed away. Miss O'Keeffe too, absent. Julian Granger's wife, the actress, made a spectacular entrance, as if she were auditioning. *To be shown the door*, Brigid thought, and smiled. She almost said it aloud, *No thank you, Mrs. Granger. Next!* Mrs. Silva, the art teacher, the mothers of girls at school, the girls themselves. One classmate, Anna Sings the Dawn, who was pregnant before Brigid, and disappeared for a while. Terrible rumors about whose child it was: Anna's brother, Anna's father. Anna had come back to school, but then a month later, she and the baby girl were found dead in the family's car, shot with the gun lying in Anna's lap. The family said it was by her own hand, but other voices whispered, disagreed, then fell silent.

The last time Brigid saw her, Anna was lying on her side behind the bleachers in the gym, sleeping, her braids trailing behind her head as if she were running away. Brigid woke her up, or tried to, but Anna said, please just a little longer. Brigid walked once around the outside of the gym. But when she went back, Anna was gone.

Those were the braids she saw writhing on the oyster door, like live beings. Anna Sings the Dawn. Suddenly Brigid felt cold along her forearms, a numbness coming into her fingertips. She struggled up out of the camp chair and left the door, crossed the driveway, and let herself into the kitchen. The stove was still warm, from the rolls Father Edgardo had baked earlier, sweet round clouds from a tube he smacked on the edge of the counter. The violence had surprised her. Who had invented such packaging? She saw the oven was set to warm and the remaining rolls inside, wrapped in foil. Father Edgardo had gone to celebrate the nine o'clock Mass, his belly full of cinnamon rolls. He never fasted if he could help it.

A bun in the oven. Brigid looked at her hands, admired them. She thought of Miss O'Keeffe's hands, all those astonishing photographs. The hand goes here. By her own hand. Sleeping Anna's hands had been pressed together, the palms touching, fingers extended, drawn into her chest as if she were praying. Calmly though, not the clutched, bent-fingered prayer of desperation.

So. The braids. The hands.

What were Sasha's hands doing at this very moment? How tiny they were. Brigid could feel them, almost, grasping inside her, little fists, banging to be let out. Did she ever bang on a door now, to be let out of a room? Hard to think about. Impossible really. She would go mad thinking of Sasha locked in a room, punished by these people, their darkness looming over her. So think instead about her body with Sasha inside it. Outside, the perfectly round dome of her, like an architectural wonder, a priceless palace. And so she knew, as if the idea had been clear from the beginning: she would paint her own body, pregnant, from memory.

Father Edgardo came into the kitchen. Brigid had not even heard his car or all the doors in between opening and closing.

"What are you doing?" he asked. He was alarmed. She could see this. "That stove is hot," he said.

She had not even felt that, pressed to the oven door. "I was cold," she said. "I was thinking."

"I was thinking also," he said. "Even though I was supposed to be transubstantiating, I was thinking you ought to go to Rome. A painter should go to Rome."

Brigid laughed and shook her head. "At least in New York I know someone."

Father Edgardo poured himself a cup of coffee from the pot on the counter. He sat down at the table and spooned sugar from the bowl he kept there. Three heaping teaspoons.

"That's too much," Brigid said.

Father Edgardo seemed startled. Then he laughed. "I like having you here," he said. "I have a sister, as you probably know. In California. I miss her every day. So why would I want to send you away to Rome?" Brigid thought he was talking to himself. Finally he looked up at her. "I still know a lot of people in Rome. Mostly religious. But they could help."

"I'm not sure I want to leave," Brigid said. She fought hard to keep herself from adding *This is my house*, or words she thought might mean more: *This is my parents' house*, though those words weren't true anymore.

Father Edgardo put his head in his hands, and Brigid went out of the kitchen into her bedroom and closed the door. She'd been using the long, low bookcase below the window as a desk, and sketches of braids and hands lay scattered there. To the best pair of hands, she tried to connect arms now, four parallel lines, bent at an angle of about 110 degrees. But now she didn't want the hands together, that pose of prayer. She calculated: a woman on her back might have the right arm extended, palm up, the other arm draped across her chest. A voice inside her head whispered, *there's a nail hole*. She saw how it could work: in the right hand, in the middle of the palm. Not the left.

The arms and hands. Belly like a dome. Legs not open, but fallen to the right, below the hand. What is this woman doing?

Father Edgardo knocked on the bedroom door and called her name at the same time. She wished he would burst into the room and put his arms around her. She hadn't known it before, this wish inside her. So she said nothing. Some time passed, and Brigid thought he had given up on her and gone away to Theo's room, but then she heard a soft bump on the door and his voice, low, confused. She could tell by the sound that he had rested his forehead on the door and was speaking with his face very close, as close as possible.

"It's not me who wants you to go away. The bishop doesn't think it's right."

The voice trailed off. Brigid sketched the right shoulder, the collar bone. She couldn't draw anything else while he stood there.

"Priests have housekeepers," she called over her shoulder, to the closed door. "And cooks. Otherwise, they'd starve."

"I know," Father Edgardo said. "I can get work for you at my father's hotel."

She thought he was trying to laugh, but the sound was odd, wounded.

"I'm starving," he said.

"Father," Brigid answered, "I need to borrow your car again."

Brigid thought of those moments all the way to the Institute of American Indian Arts, what she hadn't known about herself or about Father Edgardo, that she should leave the house now, before anything happened between them. She planned to go into the administration office with one of Miss O'Keeffe's letters, but as she turned off Rancho Viejo Boulevard onto Avenida del Sol, Brigid changed her mind. She parked in the lot farthest from the campus buildings, and then walked toward an open patio set with metal tables and chairs. I would sit here, she thought. I would talk to other students. The sunshine was unrelenting but not warm. Far away, over the mountains, a storm bruised up the sky, a color that would give in, dissipate before it came anywhere near this place. If I go home now, she thought, that storm will break right on top of me. The idea was both alarming and attractive. When the woman is freed from the door, Brigid told herself, I will have to leave.

Father Edgardo's family owned the Inn of the Five Graces and another place farther out of town called Encantato, an elaborate and expensive resort, practically its own village. There was a story that a ghost haunted the main house, the first owner's wife, a white woman from the east whose husband had made a fortune during the Civil War. The wife had lost her seventh child soon after his birth and sunk into a depression and died at age fifty-two. Waitresses and barmen saw her ghost, who often caused trouble. Once a barman came to work to find sixty-six glasses broken. No guest ever reported seeing her. A woman who had lost her child. Brigid wanted to find this place, but she knew a half-breed Indian might not be allowed even to put her hand on the front door.

When she arrived back home, Father Edgardo was gone. He left a note on the kitchen table: I have gone for the month to do mission work in Chimayo. I have made arrangements with my father for you to work in the Five Graces and live in Santa Fe, beginning when I return. If that's what you want.

If that's what you want.

She would have one month to bring the woman through the door.

Nancy

Soon after we moved into the house on Candler Road, I discovered I could walk all the way to Henry's studio without crossing or even making use of a major thoroughfare. The route took me behind houses on our street and then through a park and behind houses on North Druid Hills, through back yards and along driveways of people who must have been at work. Occasionally a curtain would twitch back and a woman's face would appear out of the darkness or shadow behind her, like fish in a murky tank. Always a woman, no expression on her face, not even curiosity, maybe only a kind of showing forth: Don't even bother to wave. I exist because you walked by. You trespass, therefore I am. Something *ergo sum*. I could ask Rodney the Latin for *trespass*, but then I would have to tell him what I was doing, and I knew he wouldn't approve. And anyway, it was the kind of question Henry liked, about viewers and viewees, so I wrapped it up in my head and put it away to ask him when I got there.

There were miles of chain link fence, but I found if I walked far enough beside them, I would come to a gate, open it, and let myself into another yard. I began to understand that my path took the shape of a battlement above a castle. I remembered the word from high school: *crenellation*, a row of teeth missing every other one, someone's jaw, carefully taken apart. I wished I walked a less orderly pattern. I knew the main streets made for more meander, but I liked the privacy of cool yards, the occasional blue joy of a swimming pool, though one of the four I passed had a black bottom and sides. This was also the only pool I actually stepped into and swam the length. The pool belonged to one of the medical school deans. Rodney and I had been invited to this house early in the summer, a huge party for the residents and to celebrate the dean's sabbatical. He would be going to Italy with his family for the fall semester. We asked about renting, but his wife, a good ole girl from Huntsville, Alabama, didn't want strangers in the house. I asked Rodney what he thought she meant by "strangers." He claimed not to know.

Sunflowers, roses, crape myrtle, mimosa, daylilies, trillium ranged along my route, sounding like a poem. I tried to think how I could get an actor to say those names in that order. What would she really mean? What would she be wanting? The surprise of tomatoes still on the vine in late September. And later, pumpkins, six of them on three vines, not very big, but right there, along the side of a house. What is it about pumpkins that makes people want to steal or smash them? The color? The way they seem to lie there, reclining, half asleep, unwitting, asking for it?

Late one afternoon at the end of October, I met a child, a girl, not yet a teenager. She seemed to be expecting me, leaning on the fence beside the third gate I had to open and pass through. I wondered if she'd seen me before and had come out to catch me in the act. She held her ground, silently, when I stopped, waiting. She looked at her watch, a woman's dress watch, too large for her wrist, her mother's maybe.

"Go on," she said finally.

Not exactly an invitation. "Do you mean go away?"

"No. I mean go on and do like you always do."

"How do you know what I always do?"

"I've seen you. A couple of days I was home sick. You just walk though."

"Should I not do that?"

"It's okay with me. My mom wouldn't like it, but she's not here."

"I should get going."

"Can I walk with you a little ways?"

"I don't mind. But shouldn't you tell someone where you're going?"

"I don't know where I'm going, do I? Anyway, nobody's home."

"Didn't they teach you about talking to strangers?"

"You don't seem very strange."

I had to laugh at that. And admit to myself this was something of a disappointment to hear, though I'd suspected as much for a long time.

She walked with me through the next three yards. I found out that she was in fact twelve and her name was Olivia, and her father taught in the art history department at Emory. Her mother lived in Buenos Aires.

"The hemispheres are a problem for visiting," she said.

I liked the sound of that. Henry would like it too. I felt a little high, even though I hadn't smoked anything yet.

"Where's your dad?"

"He's tied up in a meeting."

"Who did it?"

"What do you mean?"

"Who brought the rope?"

"What?"

"To tie him up."

She stopped walking and looked up at me, not laughing. "I'm going to tell him you said that." Threatening or admiring, I couldn't tell. "I'd better go back now."

I watched Olivia walk back the way we'd come. Just before she disappeared around a hedge of boxwood, she turned to wave. I worried a little about not seeing her all the way home.

By the time I got to Henry's studio, the light would have fallen out of the trees and Henry would have stopped work for the day. He'd open beers for us and talk about how it was going. Or not talk. Either way, I loved it: the elation or the slow, sad shake of his head.

"I'm having a field problem," he said that day, the first day of Olivia, as he opened the door.

"Tell me," I said.

"Nah. It's not worth talking about."

"Can I see?" I asked. Henry shrugged, flung his arm toward the canvases. "Is one of these me?"

"No. You're the field problem. I can't quite place you."

He led me downstairs. Paula was still at work. You could tell: dirty dishes on the counter, a flat sort of light, or none. When Paula was home, she lit candles, glass votives hanging on the walls in sconces and ranged along the mantel. Then the big downstairs room came back to life.

Henry opened the refrigerator, stared inside. "Here's the thing," he said quietly, as if he were talking to the orange juice, the eggs, the cream cheese. "I think I have to go back to New York."

What's that phrase people use? The floor dropped out from under me. Floored. I needed to sit down, but all the chairs seemed to be too far away.

I could barely feel my body, as if my brain had swelled up inside my skull and somehow burst out, and that's all I was, a big thinking blob, a thought. Henry had not moved.

"You mean like for a visit?" I said.

"No," he said. "I mean like for an ever. There's no beer, Nance." He closed the refrigerator door and turned to look at me. I tried to read something in his face, but it was just Henry. He bent to open a cupboard. "Dad gave me this. I have these little glasses too. Well, really they're Paula's. She has like a hundred of them. They'll be a bitch to move." He poured the cognac. My glass was green, so the liquid inside looked strange. Mud. Sludge from the bottom of a deep river.

Anything I could say would be the wrong thing, not what I meant, so I just held onto my tiny glass.

"Paula's up for it. She says nurses can always find work."

I nodded

"So that's good," Henry said.

Rug pulled out from under me. Why don't they call that rugged? Wind taken out of my sails. Winded or sailed? I realized that with the smallest prompting, Henry would say my lines for me. We drank off the first finger of cognac and Henry refilled the glasses.

"There's just not much here for me," he said. "There's just not much here, period. A couple of decent galleries. Too few practitioners."

"Practitioners?"

"I know, that's a weird word, isn't it? I mean like the vibe is bad, the hierarchies. You remember Mom talking about it. 'Oh, you live *there*?' So polite. 'Oh, you show *there*. Well, bless my heart.' Fucking southern manners."

"I know."

"I haven't even been here six months." Now he was doing both parts of the conversation. "But sometimes you just know. You're going to say I should wait at least a year, but a year's a long time. You know I'm losing the map thing. I can't feel this place anymore. I can't see it, like from above. I could always do that, like Dustin Hoffman sees the matches when they fall out of the box. I used to be able to get it. Remember? It's like there's no *here* here. Who said that anyway? And Paula's ready. She misses the city. You can't blame her, right?

"I know."

Henry paused then, seemed to wait for me to reveal this knowledge I had.

"I was just agreeing," I said.

Henry slid his glass toward mine, made them *ping* gently. It sounded like a doorbell, and I looked over my shoulder, even though I wasn't sure they had a doorbell. Henry laughed, as if I'd made the sound into a joke on purpose.

"And you know what will happen with Rodney, don't you?" I didn't know, but I wanted to. "He's going to go back to New York for the rest of his residency. And then to practice. You get that, right?" I nodded. "You guys have probably talked about it." My head moved up and down. I didn't want Henry to know how little we'd talked about anything that mattered. "So it'll be just while he finishes this residency and then you'll be back too."

Maybe this is a dream, I thought, and someone will wake me.

And so, just like that, Paula walked in the back door. "I gave a girl three shots today," she was saying, "and she didn't cry. But her mother did." She stopped talking, and took it all in, the glasses, the cognac, the look on my face. "Henry," she said, "I told you not to tell her yet."

"That's okay," I said.

"I'll go get some beer," Henry said.

"No, no," I told them. "I need to get going."

"But I thought you were staying for dinner," Paula said. "Rodney's on his way."

Our faces, mine and Paula's, must have looked identical, struck, as if the truth was an open hand to the cheek. "I have a meeting," I said. "Didn't Rodney tell you? It's a kind of AA thing he thought I should go to."

Henry and Paula nodded. "That's good," Paula said. I could see it—the three of them discussing me and my compulsions.

"It's actually mostly for research," I said.

Something flickered around Henry's mouth; my real brother, my old ally, returned. But then it was gone. It occurred to me then that Rodney probably felt sorry for me. And beholden because he was Henry's friend.

Never before in my life had I wanted to escape from Henry. It was like being in a foreign country, or so I imagined, really foreign, India or sub-Saharan Africa. No way to understand or be understood. People crowding around you, asking for something, small people with very large eyes. They hold their hands out. It's very hot or else very cold. You're frightened. You wish you could give them what they want. You suspect it's something simple—a cup of milk or an orange. But your pockets are empty, and your wallet and your suitcase have both mysteriously disappeared. How is it that you find yourself in this strange place with nothing?

I made my way back through the yards in the dark, which I'd never done before. My feet found every rock and rut and runnel. I was sure there would be dog shit on my shoes. The top of my head felt cold, and I was acutely aware of the part in my hair. I tried to sing a little song I knew. There's flies in the kitchen, I can hear 'em there buzzing, and I ain't done nothing since I woke up today. Is it *there* buzzing or *their* or *they're*? Anyway, it was true, except for the flies. When I got to Olivia's hedge, I stopped, alarmed by the way it was lit up, like a fire burning deep inside the branches. It took me a minute to realize this was light from inside her house, surprising and frightening, the breeze making the leaves move so the light quivered like flames. Olivia and her father probably never got to see this. The thought made me sad. They owned it, all of it, the leaves and the light, but they never even knew.

I wanted to get back to my quiet house, so I gathered myself, my courage, and slid around the hedge into the light from Olivia's kitchen, a low yellow glow from lamps or candles. The top of a child's head moved across the bottom of the window glass, from left to right, slowly tumbling like something set adrift on a river. Then another drift came to me, of scent this time. I saw a small red eye on the porch and heard the whooshed-out breath of a happy smoker.

"Who's there?" a man's voice asked.

"Sorry," I said. "Just passing through."

"There's a fence," the man said.

I thought for a second, sniffed at the air. He's stoned. He'll like this. "There's a gate," I said.

The man laughed. "There's another fence," he said, "in the next yard."

"And another gate."

"Where are you going?" I told him my address and waited through another exhalation. "I see how you can do that," he said. "Walk all that way."

"Are you Olivia's dad?"

"Who are you?" He sounded angry, a little frightened maybe.

"She introduced herself when I walked by earlier. And I told her her parents might not like it, but she walked with me for a little ways, then came back. I watched to make sure she was okay."

The man sighed, dragged on the joint, held it in. "Not parents," he said hissing out the final *s*.

I realized right then that he could see me quite clearly in the kitchen light. All I could get of him was this outline: shoulders, a head above. But there was something welcome about that vague form, soothing. It's all you get of anybody at first.

"Do you want a beer?" he said.

"Not tonight. But can I take a rain check?"

"I think it's supposed to rain tomorrow," he said. I heard him groan and slap his forehead.

I laughed. I wanted to say, yeah, you're right, that was a lousy pickup line, even for a person in your condition. A condition I know quite well, by the way. "Olivia says you teach art history."

"Architecture." I heard the slide and screech of a metal chair, the sigh of cushions released. "Better get going on dinner. See you tomorrow—" He let his voice rise to mean he was asking my name.

"Nancy," I said.

"Will."

"Where there's a will there's a way."

"You have no idea how often people say that."

"Then I take it back."

"Okay," he said. "Good." He said *good* again, and then *see you tomorrow*, almost wearily, as if he'd run out of new words and was sorry to have to use the old ones.

No, I thought, as a light opened in the side of the house and Will walked into it, see you right now. I moved back, into the arms of the box-wood and shadow, and sure enough into that yellow canvas stepped a man who must have been Will, in profile, gently lit from below, as if by flames from the foot of a stage. He stood still, maybe to let me look as he spoke to Olivia. I knew he was asking the question. Did you wander around with a stranger today? He had very black hair, but his skin was so pale that I thought at any moment I might be able to see through it. I imagined blue eyes, like Olivia's, but I couldn't tell. I waited until he walked out of the frame, and then I felt my way home.

I was asleep when Rodney got home and pretended to be until he left in the morning. I lay in bed and thought about Will, how in less than twenty-four hours, I was probably going to do something very bad. I thought about my mother. A couple of times I went to our phone and pressed the numbers of hers, but not the talk button which would have connected us.

NANCY: Why did you do it?
ELLA: Do what, honey?
N: Make me.
E: I don't know.
N: That's not good enough. I know you know.
E: I'd been in love with him for a long time.
N: Before Dad?
E: Yes. Before Dad.
N: But he *is* my dad.
E: It's confusing, isn't it?
N: Not really. At least it's not hard to tell them apart.
E: It's still confusing.
N: It's black and white to me.
E: Oh, honey. Are you mad at me?
N: No. You're my role model.
E: Really? *(laughs)* Maybe that's not such a good thing.
N: Maybe. But you haven't really answered my question. Why did you sleep with him? After you'd been married to Dad and had Henry?

E: Well. I guess . . . I had to get it out of my system. To stop thinking about him.

N: Did it work?

E: No.

Sasha

"I'd like to see it again," Aaron said when Sasha felt brave enough to go to Cheim and Read and see *The Mad Tea Party*. She hadn't traveled south of Forty-second Street above ground in more than three months. The gallery was on West Twenty-fifth Street. Sasha's heart began to thud ten blocks before.

"But she won't be there," Aaron said. "Her brother would know if she was back. He would have told you."

And she didn't seem to be there. Brigid Schumann. Not in body anyway. On canvas, though, that other kind of body, skin stretched over wooden bones, she was undeniably present. Eleven canvases, five on each wall in the narrow inner room. *The Mad Tea Party* was hung by itself on the third wall, so a viewer would see it first, but from a distance, would see just color. That red. Sasha got the logic: you want to get to that painting, stand in front of it, but at the same time, you really don't. You think *crime scene*. Somehow you know you need the other paintings to let you in on the big one. So Sasha followed the numbers, lacing her way across the room like it was a shoe, or a corset, left and right, ever closer to that red, that crime, looking at it, drawn in, implicated.

In a certain way, Sasha saw, these first ten were studies, not so much of content as of theme. Brigid had called them *Mad #1, #2,* and *#3*. They depicted insanity and anger. After those, *Tea #1, #2,* and *#3*, followed of course by three *Partys*. The tenth canvas was called *Alice*, and it appeared to be more collage and mixed media than painting: crayon, paper, pencil, pastel, photographs or pieces of them, piñon needles, a swath of tan that seemed to be deer hide. In the lower right-hand corner, by itself, was a photograph cut out of its frame, a small child, a girl about two.

Sasha realized she was staring at a photograph of herself. Her uncle, Edgardo, was in the background, turned away, all black cassock. Alice. Through the Looking Glass. This painting was not a collage at all, but an illusion, a *trompe d'oeil*. Sasha spun around, expecting to see Brigid Schumann, but instead there was Aaron, very close.

"That's you," he said. "Isn't it?"

"She'll know me," Sasha said. "I'm not ready."

"She won't know you now, not if that's the image in her mind," Aaron said.

He left her then, walked right out of the room. She stood frozen.

He was back in a minute, smiling. "Don't worry," he said. "She's in Ireland. She comes back around Christmas."

They could look as long and as deeply as they liked. Aaron seemed to be in no hurry. He could concentrate on seeing, as she'd noticed before, leave the rest of the world behind.

So, Sasha wondered, how did I come to be Alice in Brigid Schumann's mythology?

Alice, Aaron said, is a blank slate, an empty girl upon whom everyone's fantasies played out. She could be large or small. She could fall down a deep hole and not be hurt. She could crash into a mirror and not be cut. She was outside time. For all that rabbit's fretting, they were never actually late for anything. She listened to everyone's tedious story. She was kind to animals. Above all, she kept her head.

This Alice was from New Mexico. Along with piñon and faux fur, Brigid Schumann had painted a dream catcher, right over the head of two-year-old Sasha. Other Navajo and Hopi symbols, sun and earth and grain, and the whitened hipbone of a deer, which must be homage to Georgia O'Keeffe. Sasha recognized all of it, as if she were looking into a photo album. Which of course she was. She wondered how this could be a study for *The Mad Tea Party*, half the room away. She moved to the next painting.

My mother is frightening me, Sasha thought. My mother wants me to feel afraid. How could such a thing be possible? What mother would desire this? What kind of mother? And what was desire anyway? The writer of the *New York Times* review used the word in her title: "Brigid Schumann: The Price of Desire." Desire was what you felt when you looked at a thing you loved. Desire for it. If the thing wasn't yours, you wanted to have it. If you had it, you wanted to be inside it, or have it inside you. How did that work with one's children? Maybe it was something like that terrifying phrase grandmothers used: I want to eat you up. That's why the big bad wolf eats the grandmother—because he's in love with her. It's a cousin to transubstantiation. You allow your body to become food. The women in *The Mad Tea Party* had an exotic air about them, dark hair gathered up into the fists of the white Indians. These women were not white, they were some darker people: Mexican, Spanish, Middle European. It was hard to say. But not white, that was very clear. And so the scene was all the more unsettling. What did the white men want the women to believe? Or was it all mockery: your own men will attack you. Your own men are the real savages. It was hard to know. Brigid had refused to say much about it in the *Times* piece, nothing more than "It's about the culture." Mostly she talked about her friendship with Larry Rivers, who drank diluted white wine all day long. "I tried that once," Brigid said in the interview, "and I was asleep by noon." When she was asked about other women painters, she talked about Georgia O'Keeffe, but admitted she wasn't close to any women painting now. "Always a lone wolf," she'd said.

What was that supposed to explain about *The Mad Tea Party*? Sasha wondered. Maybe the identity of the female figures was more important than the costuming of the men. One of these women, the most beautiful of the three, was already dead. The viewer saw that she bled profusely from the chest, her left breast that unearthly scarlet color. Her eyes were open but glazed with death, like the rabbit in a Caravaggio still life.

Sasha looked more closely and saw that in fact this woman's eyes were a kind of glass, and someone—a tiny face—stared back from inside. Sasha knew this must be Brigid. Maybe this was the price of desire: to see oneself in the eyes of the dead. *The Mad Tea Party* was one of the only paintings Brigid Schumann made without written language. Since *The Hand Goes Here*, words on canvas had defined her work. About half of the ten studies contained text. Alice had none. *Tea #1* featured the word TYPHOON, the final N added to the famous brand whose name suggested the horrors of colonization. TEA R was stenciled across the top of *Tea #2* and below the letters was an abstract violet lightning bolt. *Tea #3* read TEA T and portrayed a woman who might have been drawn by Beatrix Potter, except that she was nursing a child while an expression of terror distorted her features. Another very small line of text ran below this mother and child: They don't bite, do they? The mother bore a strong resemblance to the dead woman in *The Mad Tea Party.*

Sasha thought about all this for a minute, tried imagining it was a reference to her infant self, tried it on like an article of clothing, then took it off again. Her parents said they had adopted her when she was less than a day old. She wouldn't have had teeth enough to bite Brigid, assuming Brigid had nursed her at all. These things, these details, possible references, might never be known. But she felt the weight of them around and upon her, like deep water, the way you're pulled under, even as the body's response is to float. She understood very clearly, with these paintings encircling her, that these were the questions that would drive her into Brigid's arms one day soon. Should Brigid wish to open those arms.

Sasha saw Aaron move back in front of Alice, and she walked over to join him.

"Do you feel like they're all some kind of a message?" he said.

"You mean a message to me?"

"Just to you. You and only you."

"Maybe some of it. But if she wanted to tell me something, why this way?"

"Why not this way? This is her way."

So what's my way? Sasha wondered, but really she knew. First, though, a fan letter. Dear Ms. Schumann, I just saw *The Mad Tea Party*, and I was blown away by you. For the second time in my life.

"Tone problem," Jennie said. "That's what my comp teacher keeps writing on my papers. Maybe it's catching."

"Do I have to be nice?" Sasha said.

"Nice is too vague a word." Jennie started to laugh then, a descent into hell laughter: hearty, then uproarious, passing quickly to crazy, then bleating. "I'm supposed to invent a writing assignment for that class," she said when she could talk again, "and then do it. You can be my assignment. Letter to real mother."

"Not real."

"Okay, then what?"

"I don't know," Sasha said.

"Biological."

"Too real."

"Okay. You think about it."

"How about M apostrophe?"

"M'other?"

"Yeah."

They kept the first sentence but cut the second. The whole letter took four hours to write, over two days.

"If I got a letter like this," Jennie said, then let her voice dissolve into a sigh, the release of air after a big machine quits. Sasha waited, staring out their window. She could see into a small office in Butler Library. A woman sat at a desk. Every few seconds, she drew her left hand under her eyes. Sasha imagined the index finger sliding gently over the soft wet skin. She made the gesture herself, her hand flat, as if to salute. Jennie didn't finish the sentence.

"Good," Sasha said. It should be a mystery, she thought, what this letter would cause Brigid Schumann to do. She addressed the envelope to Brigid's gallery and slid the letter inside.

"Send her your video too," Jennie said.

"That's what I was thinking."

"Then she can't ignore the letter."

"Though she's probably seen all those images."

"You'll make her see them again. Your way."

"I can't make her do anything. But you're right."

"I know. And you should mail it right now. Before you change your mind."

They rode the elevator down to the lobby and stepped out into the afternoon chill. Sasha tried to see the woman at the desk in Butler Library, but there was no view from the ground. They crossed campus to the 116th Street gate on Morningside Drive.

"I guess you still don't have a plane ticket for Christmas," Jennie said.

"I don't," Sasha said. "What would I do there for three weeks?"

"See your dad."

"My dad?"

"He raised you."

"I know. Be on my side, okay?"

"You know I'm on your side. You can always come to my house. And bring your uncle Theo."

"He'll be gone by then. I might just stay in the dorm. I think people can do that if they live too far away. And Aaron will be there. I mean, I'll come out for Christmas Eve or something."

"Tell your dad you don't want to fly."

"That may be true for a long time."

Jennie made an awful face. "Can't think about it right now," she said.

The line in the post office wound all the way back to the door. Everyone carried stacks of boxes. The postal workers were taking a long time inspecting parcels, particularly letters. Anthrax. Still that other kind of death in the air. How much more could people take? Sasha wondered. She unzipped her coat. The post office was warm with bodies and wool, but the air actually smelled good. "Festive," Jennie said. "There's something floating around in here." A mix of gifts. People mailing cookies. Vanilla, lavender, spruce, cinnamon. Must be candles. And some other scent, like clean laundry, new sweaters, scarves and mittens. Sasha wished she had X-ray vision to see inside the packages: little pots of cheese and summer sausage from Hickory Farms, apples, clove-studded oranges, gingerbread, chocolates, rum. Close your eyes, and it's the opening scene from *The Nutcracker*, that elaborate, excessive party.

Except that the post office was quiet. Or—no. Not completely. Sasha thought someone far in the back, in the depths of the mail sorting area, had a radio. A voice rose and fell, the peaks and valleys of an announcer, accent on the wrong syllables of words to suggest good cheer, a pause, and then music. What was it? "Silent Night"? "Hark, the Herald Angels Sing"? "Once in Royal David's City"? Buried behind all that stuff hurrying out of New York, it was hard to hear any music. If you could only hear music again, you'd think it might be possible to feel better.

The idea came to her the next night. Sasha dreamed she was back in the post office on 116th Street and as the snaking line of patrons moved closer to the front, Sasha saw that her uncle Edgardo stood behind the counter, receiving packages and letters, bestowing stamps and change with the same seriousness he used at communion. In the dream, she watched his lips, wondering if he would say "Body of Christ" as he placed the stamps, the coins, the receipt onto each open palm. Uncle Edgardo in New York. That was the meaning of this dream. She would ask him and her father to come. Maybe they would want to stay past Christmas and see Brigid, negotiate a meeting. This part came to her as an afterthought, but she knew it was the true meaning of the dream.

"Your dad won't travel," her uncle Edgardo said on the phone that night. "I'll ask him, but I know the answer. He'll send me though."

"Do you want to come here?"

"Are you joking? I've been waiting three months for an invitation."

No mention of Brigid.

"That's all right," Jennie said later. "You don't have to rock the whole world at once."

"Why not?" Sasha said. "Get it over with."

"My mom will want you guys to come out. Maybe I won't tell her he's a priest."

"Then it becomes sort of an intervention, don't you think?"

"I'm leaving at the end of next week," Theo said on the phone. "Contract's expired. I'd like to say good-bye."

Sasha offered to meet him downtown, but Theo said no, he liked getting away, up where she was. Better air, buildings still had windows. Seemed like a different city, foreign almost. He liked seeing all the kids rushing back and forth, getting on with their lives. And the subway ride, one hundred blocks, the speed and the dark and then up the stairs into light, into the new world. He had something for her, he said, an early Christmas present.

That's right, Sasha thought, relatives do that. What do you get for a man? What had she ever bought for Uncle Edgardo? Her dad liked ties.

They met outside Tom's Diner, and right away it was awkward. Aaron's rooms had kept them confined, defined. There was a kind of script. But now there was too much space, too much open air and different things to do with their hands. Unfamiliar props. Aaron should be here, she thought. He would say something funny, lighten things up. Aaron, where are you? She half-believed he might appear because she wanted him to.

Theo carried a small, square bag decorated with pictures of poinsettias. Sasha had a gift bag too, stars on a blue background, tall and thin, the kind for wine bottles.

"I hope that's a tie," Theo said.

Sasha couldn't believe it. "How did you know?"

"Only one thing comes in a box like that."

Inside the poinsettia bag, Sasha found a small silver cup, engraved with the initial L.

"I think it's for mint juleps, but some people use them for martinis."

"Wow," Sasha said. It's beautiful. But *L*?"

"I bet you can figure that out. Long Night. Your name at first."

"Oh," Sasha said. "I didn't—" Then she couldn't say anything more. It was too much. It was everything all at once, another world, another life, one more person to be.

Theo touched her arm across the table. "Hey, hey. Shhh. It's okay. I'm sorry, Sasha. I didn't mean to make you cry."

"No. It's all right. It's just. . . . I haven't thought about it that way. Or I'm not used to thinking about it."

"I've been carrying that cup in my truck for a long time now, and it just sits there, and you know it seems like it should have another chance to be useful." Theo smiled. "A better chance."

"Don't you want to stay and see your sister?"

"You mean, don't I want to stay and introduce you to my sister?"

"That's what I mean."

"I would," Theo said, "but it's about money now. I'm off the payroll. And to tell you the truth, the city is getting to me. I miss the mountains. Do you ever miss that? You know, real landscape?"

It seemed like a question coming out of another universe, that whole idea of open land and scenery. "I guess I never think about it," Sasha said. "I miss different . . . the way things feel. I miss the air. I miss my mom rubbing my back at night."

"That's a nice memory."

"Open your tie. But tell me the truth. Do you ever wear a tie?"

"Every so often. Sometimes I have to go to church." Theo opened the box and slid his hand under the tie, lifted it close to his face. "What is it? A map?"

"Of Manhattan. So next time you won't get lost."

"You're thinking I'll be back."

"Hoping."

"So I can walk around looking down at my tie?"

"Come back as a tourist."

"Looking down at my tie like some art history linguistics dude."

"He's not that bad."

"He's all right. Just be careful."

"I will. But I'll still be under, you know, *avuncular* supervision."

"Edgardo's coming?"

"You should stay and see him."

"I'll see them both sometime, Sasha. Sometime. Right now, I'm just not ready for the big reunion. I should be after all this." Theo nodded his head toward the street outside Tom's. "But it just makes me want to escape. I'm not a stick-around kind of person. I never have been. Just ask my sister."

"If I ever find her."

"You will."

Brigid

A camera with a timer.

On Monday, Brigid drove to an electronics store in Taos and bought a camera with a timer. Miss O'Keeffe had one—Brigid wondered where it went—and sometimes used it to get herself into a picture. *Appear*, she'd called it. This was the first bit of the money Brigid had spent and it pleased her. She believed somewhere Miss O'Keeffe was approving: a camera, Brigid! That's perfect! The whole apparatus—camera, small tripod, flash, case—cost $85. Brigid had never spent so much money on herself—or on anyone. No one she knew, except Miss O'Keeffe, had ever handed over such a sum all at once. She tried not to like the feeling.

In the house, she set the camera on the nightstand in her bedroom. She took off her clothes and lay down on the bed, her right arm stretched out, her left folded over her chest, her legs together and fallen to the right. She practiced getting into this position quickly. And then she thought—no. Where could she go to have such pictures developed? A busy photography store in Santa Fe? Even there? She got up, dressed, and wandered out to the garage. The oyster door waited, the woman inside beginning to suffocate. She walked past it, further into the garage, wondering what was left there. A pair of snowshoes made by her grandfather, boxes of papers, schoolwork and artwork her mother had saved. A tool box. Parts of machinery, maybe a car's engine, cannibalized, her father once said. A basketball, which she kicked, so that it bounced against a broken hallway mirror, rolled back to her foot. Champion. The name smiled up at her.

Once Theo had been a very good basketball player. Hoops, he said. His height had made him what the Española coach called a threat. And the braids. Theo had refused to cut his hair, which earned him months' worth of detention, until the principal—who was a Mormon—had a revelation. One morning at assembly he announced to the whole school, God wants Theo Long Night to keep his braids. God has told me Theo's braids sometimes fly across the other players' faces, blinding them.

Brigid reached down to scoop the Champion into her arms. She caught the scent of it, rubber and mold, but also the game, palm sweat and popcorn in the gym, something sweet like spilled cola. She'd missed seeing his best year of play when she was pregnant and staying out of school.

The idea came to her then, how to arrange the photograph, how to be her own model. One or two of her father's old shirts hung in the back of her closet. She'd worn them when she got too big with Sasha. She knew they would fit now, buttoned over a Champion belly.

No one would ever confess to doing this, she thought.

All the day's light passed while she shot the rest of the film, thirty-six prints—at least one had to be good enough to paint from, the body, that dome of belly. The face in the mirror. What's that shade, that color she'd looked at all her life, so different from her father's and her mother's? Ochre, with more brown. A difficult color. So maybe the head should be turned away, so the viewer would see only a rise of cheekbone and length of throat, an ear, the braids. What was the woman doing? Sleeping? Thinking? Waiting to get up and go away, go out? She would have to paint the head first, or at least sketch it onto the door—to get to the braids. Why? Why did she want to get to the braids right away? The head comes first. Did anyone work from the bottom up, the soles of the feet, the tip of the small toe? This seemed impossible, a loss of control. The figure could turn out to be much taller, too tall, a giant woman. Why would that be so disturbing, painting a giant?

She had never painted Theo, whose skin was a shade lighter than hers, the perfect ochre. Brigid began to think about that, about Theo, missing Theo. Both senses of the word *missing*. She walked inside, to the telephone and dialed the number in Denver. The phone rang and rang, fifteen rings, like a school bell, then twenty. He told her he would buy an answering machine, but Brigid had not believed him then either.

Father Edgardo left a liter bottle of red wine in the refrigerator. Brigid wished it wasn't open, but it was, though barely touched. He'd had one glass, two nights ago, when he'd said he was starving. She opened a cabinet and brought down one of his wine glasses. She'd never held one, but now she could see the etching around the rim, triangles and a squiggle, like a wriggling serpent, vaguely Navajo, but also modern, representing nothing. Two shapes that might complement each other.

Eve, she thought suddenly, and laughed. Eve was brown.

She poured in wine up to the etching and carried the glass into the living room. Now what? Before tonight, there had been her mother and father and Theo, then just Theo, then Miss O'Keeffe, and then the relatives and then Father Edgardo. She sat very still in her father's old chair, drinking the wine. I am going to examine this room, she thought after a while, this *living room*. The armchairs, dark green and brown, large and soft, like bears without their heads. The television, the dark blue sofa, with its odd stitching, as if it were made of wrinkled skirts sewn together by a child. A long, low table, the top piled with old newspapers, the shelf below stacked with books. On top, her mother's last gift to her, *The Story of Art* by Ariane Ruskin. On the cover, this painting: a woman startled out of her reading looks at the viewer with her right eye but not her left. She wears a coat and hat, but the girl beside her is bare-armed. The air seems blue with cold, and Brigid shivered for this girl. There is something in the woman's lap, and Brigid stared at this shape for some time until she realized it is a brown and white puppy, sleeping.

How is this painting the story of art? How have I never opened this book? The ghost of her mother seemed to enter the room, giving again the gift of the book, urging Brigid to open and see.

Inside, there were annotations, in pencil. "Good test questions" and "=" and a gray dot. So her mother didn't buy this book new. The good test questions, identified by the dot, were *How did art begin? Why do early paintings appear only in small dark areas or eerie, narrow passages? Were they part of a magic spell? How could a man's soul be preserved after his death?*

All very good questions, Brigid thought, but I would have failed this test.

She finished the wine in her glass and stood up, intending to pour herself another. She knew she should have something to eat, but couldn't imagine what. Tomorrow, she would go to Taos, take the film to a store with one-hour developing. Plenty of these places in Taos, catering to impatient tourists. She would drive back through Chimayo, stop in to see Father Edgardo, ask him more about life at the Five Graces. She felt she wanted to tell him something important, but she didn't know what it was. It would be all right to visit him at the mission church, with other people, the faithful, nearby. It would be safe for both of them. Wouldn't it?

As soon as he saw her inside the church, Father Edgardo took Brigid's hand and led her into the small robing room and shut the door. The darkness was total, immense. He found her face with both his hands and touched her mouth and nose and eyes. He whispered, "We think by looking at a thing, we can see it." His thumb grazed her open eye and then both thumbs pressed against her eyelids. For one horrible moment, Brigid thought Father Edgardo would push her eyes out of their sockets.

"Don't," she said, and he was still. His hands fell away from her face, and she heard his arms drop to his sides.

"Why did you come here?" he said.

"There's something you're keeping from me."

"Why would I do that?"

"I don't know. But I want," she began, and she tried to reach past him, toward the thin line of light that must be the door. "What you said in your note. About working for your father."

"The baby is there," Father Edgardo said.

"I can't hear you in the dark. I thought you said—"

"She's there. Sasha. Francisco is my brother. The mother, the woman, Beatriz, she's very frail. She would be grateful for your help."

"No. Please. I thought they came from Albuquerque."

"I told you that because I thought you might try to find them."

"Please don't say this if it isn't true."

"She's there."

"But I'm. . . . Can I just be her mother again?"

"I can't answer that."

"She . . . Beatriz. She can't want me. Why do you want me to go there?"

"I want to know where you are."

The light flashed on and it was unreal, how they stood facing each other, enveloped on three sides by white vestments on hangers, headless seraphim, no eyes to see this spectacle, the priest and the young woman, their bodies nearly touching. Brigid would remember this moment all her life, and often dream of it, the white room, the orderly ranks of robes, Father Edgardo standing in the middle, his black cassock like a stain. Sometimes in her dreams, this was heaven's anteroom, sometimes an underground chamber. Occasionally, it was a closet full of uniforms. Always, though, Father Edgardo would be standing there, in the middle of everything, his arms at his sides. In no version of the scene could Brigid ever see herself.

Later, they ate an early supper in the churchyard, where the parish had set picnic tables. Fires burned in three metal barrels. The visiting faithful walked past them, into the church, and emerged a little while later with the holy mud dashed in copper streaks across their foreheads or clutched in plastic bags. Father Edgardo brought oranges and hard white cheese, a loaf of bread, a chocolate bar. He poured wine from a bottle covered in rope, only for himself because Brigid would have to drive. The fires kept them warm, even as the sun began to slip below the tops of the trees. Then the tourists were gone, and no one disturbed them. It seemed, in fact, that all of Chimayo, maybe all the world, had gone away. Every so often, Brigid thought she heard a car approaching, but the sound drifted into wind or evening birdsong.

"I have to finish the door," she said, "and then I'll go to Santa Fe. You'll be back at the house."

Father Edgardo nodded. He was getting drunk. "You finish the door," he said. "Then you walk through it." He reached across the table, placed his hand over Brigid's.

About seven o'clock, the blue daylight began to fade to pink. Brigid told Father Edgardo she had to leave. She asked if she could give him a ride back to the rectory, but he said no. He would stay and finish the wine. Then walk back to clear his head.

"But it will be too dark to see," she said.

"I know that," he said. He tried to smile. "I've known that all along."

The voice on the telephone nearly choked with stifled laughter. A man, who said hello and her name, both rising in pitch as questions. When she said yes, the voice let loose with a guffaw. "This is the father's father. Ernesto Hernandez!"

"Yes?" Brigid said. Relief flooded her body, as if her blood had suddenly warmed inside her veins.

"I'm so grateful!" Ernesto said. "We need you. You have no idea. We're just falling apart here. Ay yi yi! Beatriz has been in an accident. Her legs. There will be surgeries. We need you yesterday!"

Brigid thought he must be a big man, red-faced, easily delighted by his guests, by babies, by money. "But." Her resolve gave way even as she spoke the single syllable. "I can't come for a few weeks. I'm finishing some work here."

"No, no." Ernesto said. "Whatever it is, it can wait, *mija*. Or bring it with you. No problem. I'll send a van for you. Tonight! Now!" He was laughing again, still laughing.

"I'm a painter. It's a painting. It's really big."

"The van will bring it. No problem." He paused, panting. "Now. Edgardo says you have something to tell me about *la princesa*."

"Who?" Brigid said.

"The baby!" Ernesto said. "I know. What a silly thing, but that's what we call her. Now what do you have to tell me?"

It was Brigid's turn to laugh. She couldn't believe it, that Edgardo had not told his father. She heard Ernesto laughing right along with her. "Oh goodness," she wheezed. She wished she had a glass of wine, had already drunk it down. "I'm her mother. That's all."

There was a silence into which Ernesto did not laugh. "That's all?" he said. "That's all?" He paused and Brigid waited to see where this would lead. "Well, she's beautiful, I'll say that for her. And she's very . . . herself."

"Tell me," Brigid said.

"She is a force. It's her hair, crazy redhead! Like fire, a tangle of fire."

"Like my mother."

"She has a large personality for someone so small who says almost nothing. She never walks anywhere. She only runs. And fast! And my daughter-in-law can't keep up, especially not now. She wasn't prepared in the first place."

"The baby's name is Sasha," Brigid said.

"Yes! Yes! It's a good name," Ernesto said.

"Will your daughter-in-law mind that I'm . . . who I am?"

"She will. But we need you. How soon can you get here?"

"I have a project."

"And you can't bring this work?"

"It's a panel," Brigid said. "Actually, it's a door. Eight feet by three feet."

"What if I gave you a room? In the hotel. A suite. North-facing. I know all about that, the light."

"I couldn't pay for that."

"No, no!" Ernesto was laughing again, a great booming operatic laugh. "I'll pay you! The room would be part of your salary. And all your meals."

Ernesto promised he would send the van in the morning, but Brigid said no, she needed more time than that. But now, two hours later, she wondered what she would do with an entire day. She couldn't paint. Her bags were packed with Miss O'Keeffe's clothes. Her paints were sealed, brushes and palette knives cleaned and stored away in the green metal case, gesso and turpentine in a cardboard box, along with a big bottle of wine. That was all. No books, except blank ones, for sketching, for notes.

She picked out one of the sketch books, poured white wine into a jar, added ice and screwed the lid on tight. She locked the house, got into Father Edgardo's car, and drove north along the state highway. Full dark would have fallen by the time she reached Ghost Ranch. She heard the words in Miss O'Keeffe's voice: darkness never kept you out. She thought the relatives had gone, leaving the house empty but for whatever animal life could get in. Even if the place was lighted and occupied, she knew how to walk a wide ellipse toward the garden. She imagined the darkness broken only by glowing jimsonweed blooms. She would make her way through the dense juniper and piñon to the walled garden and climb in at the low side. She'd bring a blanket and the jar of wine and sleep near Miss O'Keeffe for the last time. And she'd wake in the morning surrounded by all that color: hollyhocks, the red and yellow roses, lavender, iris, thistle, poppies, and white chrysanthemums.

The house appeared to be abandoned, and Brigid was not prepared for the sadness of it as she walked the perimeter, moonshadow cast through the windows and falling on the blank walls, the empty fireplace. She saw the tables and floors cleared of books and rugs, swept clean, gleaming with a kind of pathetic hope and anticipation. She wondered if she could get in. The house was never locked unless Miss O'Keeffe was away in New York, or farther. A spare key slept under a stone, a particular stone brought from the Pyrenees thirty years ago, from one scrabbly high place to another, Miss O'Keeffe had told her. Around back, moonlight seemed to fall directly, specifically on the stone, as if there were a hand on the moon, aiming. Brigid lifted the stone, and at first thought the key was gone, but then she trailed her fingers in the dirt, making the shape of a coiled rope, and she felt it, the irregular edge, metal much colder than the earth.

This is better than luck, she thought.

Inside, she moved slowly though the familiar rooms, smaller now, sunken in like an old woman's face. She looked for the apparition, waited for the voice to come like breath over the lip of an empty bottle. She drank from the jar of wine. She remembered what Miss O'Keeffe had said when she heard the story of Sasha: *You have already had the life I missed. Keep going in that direction, the life others miss.* She had not asked about the father, as if he were unnecessary, an inconvenience.

Now Brigid spoke quietly to the house. "And so I am going in that direction, breaking into houses." In her mind the house answered. *You had the key.*

In the kitchen, moonlight streamed through the large window, making a long rectangle on the floor, wavery like a pool of water. Brigid finished the wine, wrapped herself in the blanket and lay down in this light, her head just beyond, in shadow, to sleep. Unlike her mother's house, this one made no sounds of its own. It had settled years ago, made peace. Brigid imagined herself an old woman in such a house, a native place, apart from the world. She would have to get through the world to get out of it, away from it like this. Miss O'Keeffe had taught her to love solitude, but also that deep peace and quiet had to be achieved, fought for. Tomorrow some other life would begin, a life incomprehensible but loud, full of color and heft.

The crash, the shower of scattered glass woke her from a dream she would not be able to remember, though it seemed important. The full moon appeared as if it would fly through the window on the heels of whatever had broken through. Shards of glass glittered on the blanket and along her arms. Brigid knew there was glass in her hair and probably on her face. She turned away from the window and shook her head gently, waited for movement, believing someone or something must be in the room with her now. She held still, feeling the night air driven in but nothing more, and in this moment she wondered if she'd stopped breathing, if she'd died in the explosion of glass. Then she heard it: breath, ragged and high, nearly a whine. Not hers. Not human. The shape of the window changed, moved.

Brigid carefully folded the blanket away from her legs, trapping the broken glass inside. The night air stung her cheeks and nose and lips, and she imagined tiny cuts, how she must look with diamonds of glass embedded in her face. She stood and held out her arms into the shaft of moonlight. She thought, I am a wounded glittering, and at the same time understood the movement at the window and the labored breathing: an animal, a deer or small antelope had caught its reflection in the moonwashed window, and leapt for it. The deer logic, how would it go? To find this mate. To be back inside itself. But not all the way: Brigid saw the awful failure of this deer caught on the jagged window ledge, forelegs inside, hind end outside, all four hooves in the air, wounded in the chest and belly.

As Brigid stepped closer, the deer kicked its front legs, knocking hard on the wall below the window, the sound of an urgent fist on a locked door.

"Hey, beautiful, hey, hey. Hey, beauty."

She knelt and reached out her hand and the deer dropped its head a little, dying. Brigid thought, maybe already gone. The fur on the snout was warm and wet, soft, not like anything she'd ever touched, all that known softness—cat's fur, human hair, the palm of Sasha's hand. The deer's mouth opened and the tongue lolled. Brigid swept her fingertips higher, between the deer's eyes, moving in circles, the way her mother had done to calm her and bring on sleep. Brigid looked down and saw the dark stripe of blood, running to the floor. She understood the ticking sound she heard outside was the drip of deer's blood onto the ground below. She thought the deer grew pale, as humans do, but knew this was a trick of moonlight. She put her mouth very close and smelled something like wet leaves and the coppery tang of blood. She whispered the questions she might ask herself, might have to answer later today. Why did you do this? Why did you come here? The deer blinked its near eye. Then the eye closed and breath came in long shuddering gasps. Brigid crossed the kitchen and let herself out the back door.

Outside, the desert was alive in a kind of apocalyptic dream light, in which the shimmer of objects seems to come from inside them, from what no one sees. The low brush, the small fruit trees, even the house looked like they might detach themselves from earth and fly upward, to be pulled through the moon as if it were an opening in the sky. Brigid made her way to the kitchen window and the sight was astonishing, surreal, the back end of a large deer hanging out the window, as swath of blood ran down the adobe, identical to the one inside, as if leached through the wall.

The deer kicked once, the sound like gunfire. Brigid knew she would have to do something, free this deer. This was a large, strong animal. She might survive. Her hind legs hung about six inches off the ground. Gravity would be a help.

In the garage, there would be a ladder, drop cloths, towels, the gloves Miss O'Keeffe used to work in the garden. Brigid found all this without much trouble, brought it back to the smashed window and hurried inside, where the deer waited, eyes wide now and following Brigid as she opened a cupboard, took down a bowl and ran water in it. She used a cloth to wet the deer's face, and the great black tongue moved to catch what ran off her snout. Then the legs kicked, inside and out.

"I'm going to lift you out, backwards," Brigid said. "You'll fall to the ground. We both will. The ground is sand. It will hurt, but not as much as this."

Brigid and Miss O'Keefe had made the ladder together, out of cedar. She leaned it against the house, beside the window. The deer could kick it over if she had a mind to. Brigid eased her fingers into the gloves and tucked the largest drop cloth under her arm. The ladder creaked but held her weight.

The window track was a canal of deer's blood. The animal herself seemed unnaturally still. Brigid drew one gloved hand along the deer's backbone and felt a quiver. Then a sound came from the deer's throat, projected forward into the house, like a girl's scream, heard at a distance.

Brigid began to thread the drop cloth under the deer, just behind the forelegs. The deer bore this patiently. She could not see the deer's head, which drooped now, below the window ledge. Once there was a shudder and Brigid felt a stiffening come into the deer's body, and she thought it was done, but then this sensation lessened, the deer trembled and made again the small, shrill cry. She held both ends of the cloth now, like reins, and she stopped to think how this maneuver would actually work. She had envisioned pulling the drop cloth toward herself and dragging the deer over and out the window. She knew the physics of it would bring her to the ground too unless she stepped down the ladder, but then she wouldn't be able to hold both ends of the cloth. She wondered if she could let go at exactly the right instant and manage to stay on the ladder and out of the deer's way. The deer would try to run. She would be terribly frightened. The fall wouldn't hurt either of them, but they might hurt each other. She leaned into the deer, reached her arm over her back. She saw that the hide and her own skin were the same shade, that impossible ochre.

And then they were in the air. Brigid had given the cloth a mighty tug or else the deer had thrown herself backward, or maybe both at once. The deer's wet nose grazed Brigid's cheek and then her entire glimmering body slipped out of view, behind Brigid's field of vision. She heard the deer land, a thud and a sharp crack, and then Brigid landed too, her head and left shoulder pillowed against the deer's belly, her cheek against the lowest ribs. She put out her hand and felt for blood and found a deep gash, almost slipped her hand inside it. She heard a heartbeat, or felt it—this close, hearing and feeling were the same. They lay still, awash in moonlight. Brigid pressed her hand very gently against the deer's wound, though she did not believe she could stop the flow of blood. The air was still, the night utterly silent.

When I get up, Brigid thought, I will have to go back into the world. Even if the deer does not die in this spot, even if she gets up and runs off into the scrub, something will have to be done about the broken window, someone will have to be told. Otherwise the whole world could get in. And how Miss O'Keeffe would hate that, not the animal life so much, not really, but the trespassing humans. And I will have to go, to Santa Fe, to work in the hotel, to face whatever sort of strange Sasha and I will be to one another.

She did not want to do any of this, not yet. She pushed her hand deeper into the deer's belly. Blood had stopped flowing down her wrist.

The deer must have a strong heart. The muscle that makes its name: *hart*. This deer must have something to live for.

Nancy

Three o'clock is too early for beer in Atlanta, and that's why I went. Will was just coming out of the house.

"Oh," he said, "Nancy. I was thinking a little later."

"I know," I said, and didn't move. I didn't know what to do next.

"I was just going to the office."

"Okay," I said, stupidly. I noticed Will didn't move either.

"You haven't been standing out here all night, have you?" he said.

"I'm not sure. I think maybe in my head I have been."

He was staring at me. The word is *bemused*. I thought about the difference in our ages.

"You say things people aren't supposed to say."

Might as well prove him right. "Can I come with you to your office? But you probably want to work."

"Not really. I have to pick up papers. Check on a couple of things. Nothing much." He touched my elbow, directed me down the driveway and onto the sidewalk. I felt a kind of sudden exposure, what happens on film inside a camera when the light is let in, but the sensation went from full-body down to a tiny point between my shoulder blades. It wasn't like walking with Rodney.

"Nancy what?" Will said.

"Diamond."

"Great name."

"Thanks. I didn't do it."

"Are you from Atlanta?"

"Born and raised."

"You don't have much of an accent."

"My parents are from Chicago." Not exactly true, but we'll get to that later when he asks if I'm Puerto Rican or Korean. "How about you?"

"Massachusetts."

"How did you get here?"

"I drove."

"Ha ha."

"Sorry. The job. You go where the job is."

"Do you like it?"

"I like it fine. My wife didn't care for it."

"Olivia says she's in Argentina."

"Yep."

We walked on. Sidelong view: running shoes, khaki pants, fleece jacket, blue backpack slung over the far shoulder, held there by one pale fist. This is the man all white girls in Atlanta would like to end up with. Clean, white, good job, not dangerous. White. Articulate. Did I mention white?

No one paid us any attention. What color am I against this background? I felt white. I loved my white self.

Will's office, in the Michael Carlos Museum, was the least occupied space I'd ever seen. Blonde wood. IKEA. The only papers were on the floor just inside the door, four or five, stapled, which he stepped on but did not pick up. I stepped over them.

The books on the shelves were so perfectly arranged I had to touch them to make sure they were real. "You have no idea how many people do that," Will said.

"I seem to do what a lot of people do."

Will looked at me as if I'd said something in an unknown language.

"What do you teach?" I said.

"East Asian. Buddhist religious art. But I do theory too. I'm interested in the architecture of imaginary places."

I tried to remember if I'd smoked any weed earlier in the day. "Can you explain that?" I said.

"That's what I work on," he said. "I'll tell you."

Avalon, where Joseph of Aramathea, that rich and elusive hero, built a church. Eldorado, where once a year the king is covered in oil and powdered with gold dust. Leonia, a city in Asia that is made perfectly clean every day. Balribarbi, where architects are working on building houses from the roof down. Also, Philosopher's Island, where the inhabitants construct vast buildings, called systems, starting with the ridge piece of the roof. While they wait for the foundation to be laid, the building generally collapses, killing the architect.

"You're crazy," I told him.

"Let's just say nobody gives me much grant money."

"I guess not."

"Actually, I'm a pretty normal divorced guy."

Notice the props surrounding the people. Here was hardly anything to notice. Something about the emptiness of this office made me feel suddenly awake. Like I recognized him, like this office was a mirror and when I looked into it, I saw both of us. I think my eyes flew open in that cartoon gesture of realization. Will got it. "Come on," he said. "I'll take you on a tour of campus."

"I've been," I said. "It's nice and all, but once is enough."

Turning, I saw the one prop, hung on the back of the door, a photograph, enlarged and matted on foam core. Olivia in the arms of a woman whose face was turned completely away from the camera, as if she were about to, as if she could, leave the frame, or as if her head had just then been disconnected from her shoulders but not yet flown off.

When we got back, Will's house was quiet. A note on the counter, large letters in red ink: the sitter had taken Olivia to the library. "History project," Will said.

I don't know that he kissed me right away. I thought about that later. What I remember were his hands taking off my coat, his hands on the back of my neck, under my shirt, below the waistband of my jeans, everywhere at once, though of course that isn't possible. And cold—the fingers like points of ice, pinpoints of cold light. We didn't quite make it to the sofa in the next room. I had the feeling I was underwater—floating and not breathing, a voice inside my head like a flight attendant's, saying that breath was unavailable at the present time, but would be again, so not to worry. Some little animal was cooing nearby, or maybe it was me or Will, I wasn't sure. I didn't have time to listen. Then I was falling, a long fall towards nothing, just the fall itself, my heart grown to fill up my body, filling it like water inside a jar, waves beating everywhere at once.

"Did you mean for that to happen?" I said when I could talk again.

"I think so," Will said. "Did you?"

"Yes. Maybe not today, but yes."

We lay side by side on the floor. Somehow my legs were under the sofa. The rug looked just bought, a pattern of squares the color of the birthstones I knew, vivid and hard: garnet, amethyst, topaz. The rest of the room was nearly empty, not much different from the office, a table and two chairs, the sofa, which I realized was a futon. Maybe the ex-wife took the real furniture. All the way to Argentina. Will rolled onto his side. I felt something serious looming, a question.

I would swat it away. "Can we do that again?" I said.

Will smiled. "It's been kind of a long time."

Replies came into my head: It's like riding a bicycle. Glad I could help out. "I said something kind of bad to Olivia." Will put his hand over his eyes. I was harshing the mellow, all of a sudden. "She told me you were tied up in a meeting, and I asked who brought the rope."

"Did she get it?"

"No."

"Are you into that? Tied up?"

"I don't think so."

We heard voices outside then, Olivia laughing, calling "Dad?" We sat up, stood, adjusting our clothing, not much of which had come off. Will moved quickly away from me, into the kitchen. I pretended to be interested in the prints on the wall. Actually I was interested. They were Bruegel's *Tower of Babel* and *The Garden of Earthly Delights* by Bosch. Imagine seeing these every day of your preteen years. I wanted to know how Olivia would turn out. I imagined for a moment I could stick around and watch.

The sitter walked in to get her car keys, and at first she didn't see me. I was behind her, pressed close to Babel. She was a large black woman with dreadlocks, mid-forties. She jumped when she turned around to go, pressed her hand to her massive bosom. "Honey," she said, "you like to. . . ." And then she got it, caught the scent, saw some dishevelment I'd missed. I glanced down to see if I'd forgotten to zip my jeans. I thought about asking *like to what?*

"Mmmm mmm," she half-whispered, half-sang. "Next time, let me know."

"I will," I said. "Will will."

She threw back her head and let out a deep laugh. She reminded me of Clarence Clemmons. "Good for you," she said. "And good for him."

INT: Kitchen. Huge. Mostly unused because the resident in psychiatry is never home. But when he is, he likes to occupy the space.

RODNEY: I think you're seeing someone else.
(Nancy looks down at her hands, then stands up and crosses to the doorway. Stops.)
RODNEY: You can't even defend yourself. Can you?
(Nancy shakes her head, walks back to the stove, turns on the gas under a pot. Moves to the refrigerator and opens it, removes an onion, peels it, chops it, wipes her eyes.)
RODNEY: Should I leave?
(Nancy shakes her head no, finishes the onions, slides them into the pan. She takes a wooden spatula from a jar of cooking utensils, begins to move the onions back and forth.)
RODNEY: I'll leave.
(Nancy shrugs, turns away toward a high cabinet, opens it, and lifts down a jar of rice. Obviously the jar is heavy and awkward, but Rodney makes no move to help her. She opens the jar and pours rice into the pan. She stirs the rice, lifts the lid off a second pan and begins to ladle broth into the rice and onions.)
RODNEY: You couldn't afford to live here if I left.
(Nancy nods slowly, ladles, stirs.)
RODNEY: You love this house.
(Nancy lifts her head, gazes out the kitchen window.)
RODNEY: You forgot the wine.
(Nancy turns to the refrigerator, opens it, draws out a bottle of wine, glugs some into the pan.)
RODNEY: How come you never measure anything? *(He sits down at the kitchen table, opens the newspaper, flips through it, finds the puzzle, takes up a pencil and begins to write.)*
(Behind him, Nancy raises the wine bottle to her lips and swallows noisily.)

RODNEY: You want me to deliver you from something, but I don't
    know what it is.
(Behind him, Nancy nods.)

"It's all *trompe d'oeil*," Henry was saying. "I'm not sure why anybody makes
a distinction." He was holding a postcard, Vermeer's *The Kitchen Maid*.
"This, for example. We're supposed to believe in the shadows, in that
stream of milk." We were trying to decide what to cook for dinner, but
nobody was hungry. There was a certain wretchedness in the room. I had
the urge to sniff the air to find out what had spoiled.

"What does she say?" Paula asked.

Henry looked up quickly, confused, shaken even. "Say?"

"I mean Ann. What does Ann say on the postcard?"

Rodney and I pretended not to listen. Maybe I was the only one pre-
tending. I'd been doing a lot of that lately. Rodney paged through the L. L.
Bean catalog, pausing over the deck shoes, the waterproof sandals, press-
ing his index finger against the pictures, as if he could bend the leather,
the polystyrene, the soft, tanned hide. I looked over his shoulder and
thought of Will's Nikes, kicked under the bed or across the room, laces
still tied. I placed my hands gently on Rodney's shoulders, whispered in
his ear, "Which ones do you like?"

"You can read it for yourself," Henry said to Paula. He handed her
the postcard, and she took it like you would a photograph you didn't want
to smudge, the diagonally opposite corners appearing to pierce the soft
pads of her index fingers. Held this way, the kitchen maid revolved slowly,
exchanging herself for words, then reappearing. I thought of the Calder
mobile in the High Museum downtown, a Möbius strip, an endless gleam,
with a twist.

"'Dear Henry,'" Paula read, "'this is the best news I've had in a long
time.'" She looked up at Henry, smiled the way women do when they're
thinking, *should I fuck you or kill you?* "'I know of some good studio spaces
for rent. One of them is in my building.' Hmmm." Paula drew out this last
sound elaborately, so that it rose finally into a question.

"She lives too far uptown," Henry said.

"Too far for what?" Paula said.

She didn't read any more out loud. We watched her, saw her eyebrows rise once. Henry exhaled loudly, turned away, turned back. It was riveting somehow. *Woman Reading.* Vermeer painted one of those too, but not this way. Not busy enough. He'd painted the woman writing too. I pictured the smile on Ann's face as she thought about Henry returning to New York.

Paula placed the postcard gently on the counter, the kitchen maid face up, still intent upon her work of pouring milk. The pitcher is heavy. She has been doing this for a long time. When the pitcher runs dry, Vermeer fills it up again, steps back, waits for his model to compose herself back into stillness and concentration.

"It sure is all *trompe d'oeil*," Paula said. "You must not have told her I was coming."

"I thought I did," Henry said.

"Lame ass," Rodney whispered, but we all heard.

This was the play I should be writing. Ann and Will would have to make appearances, separately and together. Paula picked up the postcard again.

"Just let it go," Henry said.

"No," Paula said. "Look. This is weird." She tapped her finger above the kitchen maid's head. "There's a nail in the wall. But it's not holding anything up."

"Look at it," Henry said. "You can see the outline of what used to be there."

"I don't see anything," Rodney said.

"Are you Korean?" Will asked, finally. I explained. I used the term *biological father,* which shaved off a few corners, saved some painful meandering. "There's a story there," Will said. We'd gone to the Emory Library, wandered down into the subterranean stacks, the catacombs, Will called it. It was pretty quiet.

"I used to think there was," I said. "But then one day I realized it's kind of the same old story."

"Do you see him?"

"No."

"Do you want to?"

"Not really. Sometimes. But I can't imagine the conversation we would have."

We were sitting side by side on the floor, turning the glossy pages of large-format art books, pictures of Buddhist temples. Will had just said it was nice of me to pretend to be interested, and I told him I really was interested, but I could tell he didn't believe me. We had been there for a couple of hours, I think, I thought then. Time had become something else, taken on a sort of personality. If I describe it now, I would say that time seemed like an edge that never receded, never shifted away from parallel, like the horizon if you're walking on a beach. I guess people use the phrase *living in the moment*, but that suggests a person can escape from the moment, and maybe some people can. I couldn't. The edge of Will, the edge of Rodney. The edge of discovery, all of them constant, present.

"You should meet my brother," I said.

Will looked at me as if I'd suggested a rendezvous with the Queen of England.

"You have a brother?"

"Yes," I said. "Do you?"

"I do, actually, but he's in San Diego."

"Oh." For a second, I forgot what should come next. Actually, that's also what I mean about time—it kept stopping and starting again, like an electric light switched off then on then off by an angry child.

GEORGIA: Do you think electricity changed painting forever?

VERMEER: Now how would I know about that?

G: I thought you might have the long view.

V: Sorry.

G: So what about that empty nail in *The Kitchen Maid?*

V: I liked the shadow it cast.

G: I don't buy it.

V: Wise woman.

G: So?

V: The crucifix. It was in the way. Too much meaning. Or not
   enough. Think how all eyes would have gone to that detail.

Think how a crucifix looms. What sort of shadow it casts. The poor girl—she is just trying to make a custard out of dry bread. Surely there's enough resurrection in that.

G: Sometimes the looming is what you want. Sometimes you want that dark abstraction.

V: You have it by putting it in. I have it by taking it out.

G: Ah.

"I was thinking about meetings too," Will said. "I was wondering if you wanted to come over for Christmas dinner. Meet my parents."

I almost laughed out loud. I could do it. My parents liked Christmas Eve for that sort of thing. Rodney was flying to New York Christmas morning. I had not been invited. I'd planned to watch twelve straight hours of *It's a Wonderful Life* with Henry and Paula since they wouldn't be talking to each other. Paula said if I was there, they might not fight.

"What time?"

"It's lunch," Will said. "Noon."

We had got to that stage where making love was anywhere except a bed. We were that couple in the library. We were that couple in the unisex bathroom at *I Fratelli*. We were in that car at the Brookhaven MARTA station, the far end of the parking lot, the car that seemed to be shaking. You looked back, not sure what you saw, then you knew and looked away, smiled to yourself, felt a little cold blade of envy. You know: airplane lavatory, heated swimming pool, hammock with a blanket, high school stairwell, any stairwell.

Well. Ahem.

And it just wasn't happening with Rodney for whatever reason. We didn't talk about it. Maybe the problem was my age, my skin color, another woman. Our schedules. Rodney's schedule. The only times we saw each other, our eyes were closed. So I told myself it was okay. It was only a matter of time. Will wasn't my back-door man, he was waiting in the wings, my wing man. I thought about what Henry had said, that Rodney was headed back to New York. Maybe he'd decided to leave me behind. Maybe he knew there was a Will, a wing man, and it just didn't matter because he was already halfway gone. He let me have a Will because he was already away.

Which brings us to Christmas Eve.

Allow me to set the stage.

We are in the geodesic dome my father designed and built, with its five interior walls, one of them a curved circle, the curvature gradual so that paintings hanging on it make contact only at their very edges. The public rooms ease one into the next; moving between them feels like passing between railroad cars when the train comes into a roundabout turnstile. The kitchen is between the living room and the dining room. My father's office is connected but invisible. *I'm behind the curve*, he liked to say. The bedrooms and bathroom are hidden inside. It's a metaphor.

Tonight, votive candles flicker in red and green glass cups set on the bookshelves, the kitchen counter, the tables. No tree. Ornaments hang from tiny nails in the walls so that the whole house becomes the tree. Every year, there's a theme, and this year seems to be stars. Snowflakes like stars, animals holding stars, mermaids with starfish, angels swinging on stars, manger scenes dwarfed by the wise men's star. Stars made out of beads, fabric, mirrors, raffia, glitter. It's like being in the heavens. This may be my favorite theme of all time, and I tell my mother so. She says it's hers too. Rodney and I have arrived before Henry and Paula. Dad pours glasses of wine.

I've let myself into the present tense, via the front door, and I think I'll stay awhile.

Mom has made *gougères*. Rodney is wearing a suit, which Dad eyes, appreciatively, his gaze lingering on the red and green silk tie. Dad has on a red bow tie, which makes him look like a waiter. Some men can carry off the bow tie, but my dad can't. Mom is wearing a top and a long skirt in a color she calls winter white. It's like blank canvas. I'm wearing a black dress edged with an inch of floaty black chiffon. I found it at Goodwill. I have the giddy sense that we're in a photo shoot for *Food and Wine* or *Bon Appétit*. The *gougères* are perfect, flecked with thyme. The wine glasses stay completely clean, as if an invisible food stylist polishes them after every sip.

My mother takes my hand and leads me over to the oven, opens the door. We bend to look in. There's a green pot. She doesn't move to uncover it. Instead, she whispers, "I know a secret." She tilts her head to look at me, smiles crazily, heat from the oven charging out at our faces. She's not really seeing me though, she's thinking about something beyond us. I realize she's been at the wine for a while now.

"Tell me," I whisper back.

She shakes her head. No. "Don't worry. You'll find out soon enough." She unbends herself to close the oven door. I find I'm deeply relieved to understand the secret is not about me.

Outside the sound of car doors, murmuring voices. That's good, I think, at least they're talking, or acting like it. They come into the house in a kind of shimmer. Some of this is real: Paula wearing a dress covered in sequins, little stars all over her, and on the jacket she's carrying. She matches the house. She is joined to it visually in a way that startles me. I feel a fog dispersing, like when you wake up in a strange bedroom, and at first it's frightening, but then you sort of float up into the sense of where you are and how you got there.

Henry's shimmer is more of a daze. He kisses Mom, hugs Dad, shakes Rodney's hand, which puzzles everyone but then they embrace, and it's all right. Then it's my turn. I get a long, tight hug. Henry breathes into my ear. "Oh boy, Nance," he says, but I don't know what he means. Dad's pouring wine, handing the glasses around. Paula reaches toward him, and I see it. Another diamond. In all senses.

When everyone's got a glass, Henry clears his throat. "So," he says. He looks at Paula as if he's forgotten her name. She stares back, smiling, but giving him no help at all. There's absolute stillness. Then she nods and Henry comes back into the world. "I asked Paula to marry me, and she said, hell no. Then she changed her mind." I understand from the tone of his voice that this is exactly how it happened. Mom and Dad put down their glasses and applaud, then put their four arms around Paula. It makes a pretty scary picture, I have to say, as she's engulfed by them. Swallowed up. Completely disappeared. Good thing they're moving back to New York. Suddenly I see it, the huddle of white people, with Rodney and me waiting outside.

Then Rodney slaps Henry on the back. He asks when, and Henry tells him, next week, at City Hall. My mother smiles and nods, then glances at Paula and adjusts her expression. "What about your parents?" she says.

Paula explains they're fine with it, maybe even relieved. They'll do a party at their house in New York sometime. "You'll be invited of course," she adds. Mom and Dad look at each other, but I can't read them. Time's changed itself again: I feel like they're sailing backward through time, like this is the last Christmas I'll have with them.

The dinner was got through. I'm using the passive voice on purpose. There was some sort of stew out of the green pot, orange peel floating in it, vivid red tablecloth and napkins, wine in amethyst-colored goblets, something my mother called chocolate volcano that sent everyone into a stupor. But before that, talking and laughing. Somewhere in the middle of this, though, I realized that everyone was going to New York, and I would be left behind. I listened to them, watched their glitter, and then decided, no, I wouldn't be left. I'd just have to take that leap.

A strange memory came to me. I was a little girl, four or five. I was lying on a mound of blankets in a long cold room full of paintings and the smell of them, the metallic shock of turpentine up your nose. My mother had just covered me with a quilt and turned away. She was whispering to someone that yes, I would stay asleep, so I closed my eyes, just for a minute. When I couldn't feel her nearby anymore, I opened my eyes, gazed around without moving my head. I looked up, and there above me, a little to my left, was a square cage. A small bird, green and yellow, hopped and twittered inside. I remember that my mother had told me her friend had a canary in his studio. The bird seemed agitated, though it did not sing; it hopped and fluttered and ran up against the sides of the cage. I thought my mother must have left the room because otherwise she would come back and comfort the bird. As I lay there, I saw the little door on the front of the cage swing out. Then the bird appeared in the opening. He stopped—I think his name was Simon too—and stood there. "Don't," I whispered. But Simon didn't listen. He moved forward and fell headfirst without even trying to fly. This made me furious, that he didn't flap his wings, not once. He landed a foot away on the cement floor.

"Mom," I said, interrupting Rodney's story about the chief resident. "Do you remember the bird named Simon falling out of the cage? Where was that?"

Dad looked at me, his eyes huge, wet, and angry. It was like he was willing me to fall into his eyes and drown.

LOU: When I was four my father traced the outline of his hand and then traced my little hand inside his.

EMILY: Stolen—Captured—Saved.

LOU: It's in his notebook from that year. Still there for the world to see.

EMILY: It must look like two birds making their own cage.

LOU: It does. Exactly. My hand caught inside. Guarded. Restrained. He never really loved me until I became an invalid. Then I could be controlled.

EMILY: Burglar—Banker—Father.

LOU: I am poor once more.

Sasha

After Jennie's last exam, they met Rodney at the West End. Most Columbia and Barnard students had finished and left the day before. The campuses and Broadway lay under a new dusting of snow, empty and still. But the whole place seems relieved, Sasha thought, every cluster of buildings and courtyards open and expansive rather than shut down and sad, the way all these places had felt since September.

When they'd settled into their first pitcher, Rodney got quiet. Then he left the table abruptly, walked to the bar, signaled the bartender. Rodney spoke to her, explaining something in great detail, then opened his wallet and handed over some cash. All the while, the bartender gazed at Jennie and Sasha, nodding and tapping her index finger on Rodney's sleeve. She disappeared and then the music got much louder. The Rolling Stones. "Beast of Burden."

"Did you do that?" Jennie said.

"It's my favorite," Rodney shouted back.

They were all Rodney's favorites: Elvis Costello, Cyndi Lauper, Bryan Adams, Robert Palmer.

"Some kind of '80s night," Jennie said.

"What?" Sasha yelled. She leaned into Rodney. "You can tell her to turn it down now."

"What?" Rodney said.

"It's too loud."

"What?"

Sasha gave up. The bartender brought them another pitcher. Jennie pointed to the ceiling and covered her ears. The bartender shrugged and walked away.

"She thinks you want to hear from God," Sasha said.

"I do," Jennie yelled back. "I'd like an explanation."

Rodney ignored them. He looked, Sasha thought, like someone had turned him completely inside out, as if he was living a fully animated life under his skin, and the exposed part of him, the Rodney they saw, was the mechanical, visceral, automatic, involuntary part, the heartbeat, the blood moving, the lungs as they filled and emptied, the nerves twitching. She imagined a science textbook: the cross-section inverted. Instead of all that machinery inside, there would be something like Hieronymus Bosch. *The Garden of Earthly Delights*. She had a crazy thought: Bosch: the movie.

Jennie leaned toward Sasha. "Christmas is going to be harder than Thanksgiving," she said and nodded across the table at Rodney, who nodded back as if acknowledging a stranger on the subway.

Suddenly Sasha wished her Uncle Edgardo had already arrived, or that she was on a plane back to Santa Fe. "I've never spent Christmas without my mother," she said. She knew neither Jennie nor Rodney could hear her. Maybe that was Rodney's point with the music. They could all say these sorts of things, near but not to each other. Bodies need bodies, sometimes, just the hulk and heft. Not the voice.

When they'd finished the second pitcher, Rodney stretched his arms around Jennie's shoulder and pulled her close, so that their faces touched. Then he reached across the table and dipped his index finger inside the collar of Sasha's jacket. "I want to see the river," he yelled.

"I haven't thought about the river in months," Jennie said.

"I know," Sasha said. "It's strange. How can you live so close to such a big body of water and never think about it? Especially with our view. I ran along Riverside Drive exactly once. September 10."

"The day of last things," Rodney said. The music softened as he said this, as if his words had turned a dial somewhere.

They heard the bartender call, "Okay, that's enough."

"I used to see the river from my apartment," he continued. "But now, I'm never even in the city. Actually, that's a lie."

Rodney told them he had used an old army connection to get into the Frozen Zone and then to his apartment on Church Street. He found an unlocked basement door. It was like a whole lost world, he said.

"You remember the day: so beautiful, cool, and clear. Everyone had their windows open. And so the whole building is full of ash, ash gray furniture, ash banked against the walls. Like a new kind of snow. People left so fast, all the doors are open. No, I guess a few are locked, but not many. Everybody seemed to think they were coming right back. Just five minutes.

"It was like I was sleepwalking. I was relentless. I tried every door on all six floors. I went in and looked around. I didn't touch anything. That wasn't the deal. But you know what was so strange?" Rodney's voice pitched itself higher—as if reaching for a note—but not louder. He waited for them to answer.

"What?" Jennie whispered.

"Every office, every apartment looked exactly the same, just these drifts of gray. There was always a desk, a couch, a bed, a small kitchen. All the same. After a while it was like that dream where you keep doing the same thing over and over. Because you can't *learn*. But I couldn't stop myself. And I felt angry when I found a locked door and couldn't go in. I needed to see it again, the desk, the couch, the bed, the gray. I needed it like a fix.

"Then I went to my office, which is also where I lived. Same scene. I didn't recognize my stuff. I could have been in any one of those apartments. And this terrible thing occurred to me then, as I stood in my own kitchen, not quite knowing where I was. All that time, in every apartment, I'd really been looking for bodies."

"Oh, Rodney," Jennie said.

Sasha felt frightened for him. This seemed like it might be the moment of his caving in. The canary stopped singing. Jennie took his hand and pulled him closer. "Whose body, Rodney?"

"Anyone's. Someone I knew. I knew half the people in the building."

"Why would there have been any bodies inside?"

"I don't know. I just don't know." He let go of her hand. "People die of fright. They just die. You don't have to have a reason. I mean, can you think of anything more heart-stopping than the sight of those planes? Those buildings going down?"

Jennie shook her head. "I can't."

"Let's go," Rodney said. "I need to go."

They rose from the table and filed out of the bar, turned west on 114th Street and started down the hill. The sidewalk was icy in patches.

"Does the river turn to ice?" Sasha said.

"Everything turns to ice," Rodney told them. He stumbled away, caught himself on a garbage can. It occurred to Sasha he might have been drinking all afternoon. She nudged Jennie.

"We could go back to the dorm if you want," Jennie said.

"I have to see the river!" Rodney shouted.

"Not too close," Sasha said.

"No!" Rodney said. "Too close! And closer. And faster. Before we freeze to death." They crossed West End Avenue, running, breathless. "Don't you just love gravity?"

Riverside Drive stretched empty in both directions, and the park beyond it too, dark and still. The West Side Highway hummed below, the river still lower, a black ribbon bordered by glowing strips where it had frozen. "If you cross the highway, there's some grass. We used to have picnics." He stopped to breathe. "That was a long time ago."

They had come to a chain link fence. "End of the line," Sasha said.

"Oh shit," Rodney said. "I forgot about the fence."

"This is far enough," Jennie said. "And I'm freezing. You can't really see the river anyway."

"Maybe you can hear it," Sasha said.

"Are you fucking kidding me?" Rodney said. "Watch. Your foot goes here. Your hands go here."

"That's what Brigid Schumann thought," Sasha said.

"What?" Rodney said.

"Her famous painting," Jennie said. "The woman on the door."

Rodney helped Jennie and Sasha over the fence and dropped down beside them. The lights of Fort Lee were another planet, and there was all this empty universe in between. It was hard to see where one world ended and the next began. Sasha wished she'd brought her camera. Rodney walked to the drop-off and sat down, arranging the tail of his coat in an oddly fastidious way, as if he were going to be filmed.

"It's too cold for sitting," Jennie said. "It is pretty though. Pretty dramatic. But it's too dark, Rodney. Come on. Let's go back." She stepped close behind him, reached down for his hand.

Sasha thought she would see the end now, Rodney pulling Jennie forward, both of them tumbling over the edge and down into the river. A scream, a splash, silence. Her body flushed and tingled with adrenalin. But Rodney didn't touch Jennie. He patted the grass.

"Please," he said. "How about some body heat? Huddle in."

"Just for a minute," Jennie said and eased down next to Rodney.

"All right," Sasha said and crouched down beside them.

"I have to tell you something," Rodney said. "Before I forget. But I won't forget. More like the door will close. Something like that. There was this woman. I met her at a wedding. She was young. Younger than me. Your age. She did temp work at Marsh. She was in the North Tower."

"Who are you talking about?" Jennie said. The question seemed to rattle around then, bouncing off the lights of Fort Lee and zooming back.

"This girl," Rodney said. "Woman. My friend Henry Diamond—"

"Oh no," Sasha said. "She's in my film."

"I know," Rodney said. "He told me. I saw it. Yesterday. I finally got the nerve. And it's amazing, Sasha. Awful. To see her again like that. She came here for me. And then I dumped her."

"She wasn't in the north tower because you dumped her."

"I think she was."

"No," Sasha said.

"She might have been in a thousand other places."

"We all might have been a thousand other places," Jennie said.

"Why do you want to make me feel better?" Rodney said.

"That's a good question." Jennie said. "But you of all people shouldn't have to ask. I don't know why. Maybe it's just what people do, and there doesn't have to be a reason."

"Do you miss her?" Sasha said. She lay back and closed her eyes against the few dim stars.

"I don't know," Rodney said. "I don't think I knew her very well."

"Oh, bullshit," Sasha said. "Either you miss people or you don't. Sometimes you lie about it. Or you miss something about them. The thing I miss about my mother, Beatriz, my real mother, is that she could be completely calm. You'd sit next to her and you'd literally feel your pulse rate slow down. She'd get nervous sometimes, and she always had to plan everything, carefully map out her own stuff, but for other people, she could get still. Or act still, anyway."

"I do miss her," Rodney said. "I miss them both."

"It's dumb," Jennie said, "but I want to know where they go. All those people. Where do they go?"

"There's a fold in the universe," Sasha said. "They're all in there."

"Like hiding behind a curtain," Jennie said. "The northern lights. We saw it once in Alaska. That's the curtain. It's perfectly gorgeous. That's where they are. I just figured it out."

"Stacey my stepmother used to tell a story," Rodney said.

Then he stopped talking. There it is, Sasha thought. He said it.

"About four months after her father died," Rodney said, "this happened. She called it a visitation. Early in the morning, she heard this thump on the front porch, and then again a couple hours later when she was home alone. She opened the front door to see a skinny brown dog, all ribs, long nose, big ears. What people would say to describe her father. This dog was curled up in a corner on the porch, looking up at her, wanting something. No collar. Wanted to come in the house. She gave him some dog bones. She went out the side door and he came down off the porch, wanting to go in there or meet her there or something. He ate the bones, stayed for a little while, then left the porch, disappeared into the bushes and was just gone. She'd never seen him before and never saw him again."

"He went back behind the curtain," Jennie said.

"Are you wanting your visitation, Rodney?" Sasha said.

"Yes," he said. "Aren't you?"

"Sometimes I think Theo Long Night was it," Sasha said. "My mother come back as my other mother's brother. God, that's insane. But maybe that's part of the deal. No logic to it."

"I'm afraid I'll miss it," Jennie said. "Is it always an animal? Is it ever a thing?"

"I don't know," Rodney said.

"We could ask," Sasha said. "*Is it ever a thing?*" she yelled, as loud as she could.

They waited. Somewhere north, up Riverside Drive, a siren began.

"There you go," Jennie said.

"But is that a yes or a no?" Sasha said.

"It's an emergency," Rodney answered.

Edgardo liked to travel "dressed out," as Sasha called it. Always the collar, sometimes the cassock. "It's warmer," he said. "Airplanes are always so cold, even in the summer." He had imagined that on this trip, full regalia would speed his way through airport security. Not so, he told her in the taxi from LaGuardia. "A single man with brown skin is still a single man with brown skin, even if he's discovered to be travelling with consecrated hosts."

"You are?" she said. "I'm sure there's a few in New York City."

"Superstition," Edgardo said. He glanced at the taxi driver, read the license. Arnold Patel. "Fear."

"Like a bullet-proof vest."

The driver did not look at them, but he sped up through the northward bend of Grand Central Parkway.

"I'm sorry your dad didn't want to travel."

"I can understand," Sasha said, "I didn't either. How was it anyway?"

"Alarming. I haven't ever felt claustrophobic on an airplane, but this time. . . . There was a certain resignation. You could tell everybody felt it. You're in the plane now. There's nothing you can do. And then you look in the cockpit and think about—all of it."

Sasha shook her head and turned away. The sky was brilliantly blue, cloudless, brittle in the cold.

"I might rent a car to drive back," Edgardo continued. "Or maybe I'll just stay until summer and drive you home."

He laughed, but Sasha knew it was entirely possible. "A lot could happen," she said.

"There's no doubt about that. Do you have a plan?"

"Not a good one. I know she comes back right around Christmas Day."

"I haven't seen her in a long time," Edgardo said.

"How long?"

"How old are you? Eighteen?" Sasha nodded. "Fifteen years then."

"I keep trying to remember," Sasha said. "Her face. Where she might have stood in my room. But I can't get it. Not all the way. Almost like I can see the shadow she cast, but never the body making the shadow. I remember her singing 'Twinkle, twinkle, little star.' I remember a door off its hinges."

"*The Hand Goes Here.*"

"Right. But I've seen it so often in books, I don't know if it's really my memory. That's a funny thing, to think your memory really belongs to some editor."

"Maybe that's the world now."

The girl and the priest dissecting the culture. The cabbie turned his radio down, listening, speeding through Queens, then into the Holland Tunnel. "I'm sorry I was so hateful when Dad told me about her."

"It's all right. He's forgiven you. They shouldn't have waited so long. I thought your mom would tell you."

"Not Dad?"

"No. You know that, Sasha. Or maybe you don't. He loves you so much. He can't stand the thought of losing you. He thinks of himself as your real father."

"Is he?"

Edgardo turned to look at her so quickly and sharply that she winced, thinking he must certainly have wrenched his neck. "No," he said.

"Do you know who . . . ?"

"I don't know."

"I think you're lying."

"I'm a priest!"

The cab driver hit the brakes hard. He seemed to be taking a circuitous, erroneous route through Lower Manhattan, orange cones and barricades at every turn.

"Oh, come on," Sasha said. "Don't pull that."

"It's Christmas, Sasha. Let's not start this way."

"What do you mean, *this way*? Like with the truth?"

"She'll tell you herself if she wants you to know."

"Why is it up to her?"

"Who else would it be up to?"

"I don't know. I'm just. . . . It feels urgent. Somehow it's more real now that you're here. She's more real. For six months, she's been paintings and sculpture. She's been—I don't know—still. But it feels like she's starting to move around."

"But that would be more your sort of thing, though, moving around."

"True."

"Are you going to film my whole visit?"

"Pretty much."

"Is this where I make the Mr. DeMille I'm ready for my close-up joke?

"I wish you wouldn't."

They rode in silence, listening to Arnold Patel's music, jumpy Bolly-wood. Sasha imagined the soundtrack for a frenetic love story.

"Will you show me your film?" Edgardo asked.

"It's hard to watch."

"I've seen some photographs. The man in the jacket."

"I was going to say it's hard to watch all the way through. Almost everybody's seen an image or two, or heard the sound, but together. . . . It's worse."

"You were brilliant at that sort of thing in school. Seeing what nobody else saw. You get that from your mother."

"Which one?"

"Both, really. Your mother—"

"I'm sorry, but it makes me crazy when you say that and I don't know which one you mean." Sasha looked away from her uncle at the bright slice of the Hudson. The low winter sun had turned the river pink like the nick of the razor in the bath, that faint tinge.

"It's my eyesight," she said. "I don't see what's there. I don't care what's there. That building, for instance." She pointed out the window.

"Which one?"

"It doesn't matter. That building is pink, with a shadow of very light purple. You know like if something's wrong with the air, a storm coming maybe, the light turns a sort of pale lavender."

"It does?"

She glanced at her uncle, then away, out the side window. "My air does. Also, people's faces have a streak of green, like an old bruise. That's what I see."

"My face?"

"Especially yours," she said. "A very old bruise."

"That's Beatriz," Edgardo said. "What she saw in faces. And the weather. Noticing it almost obsessively. You get that from her."

"That makes me so happy. To hear you say that I'm part her too. It's like having her back, a little. That's what somebody said to me about seeing his sister in my film. 'Thanks for giving her back to me.'"

Brigid

In Santa Fe, at the Inn, Brigid thought the silence was awful. People liked it though; that's why they came to the Five Graces, for the peace and quiet, to get away from noise and bustle of the city. Even the baby is quiet, the guests told one another, whispered back and forth between the tables at dinner, although she never stops moving. Here she comes, they said, as Sasha darted through the dining room. Look at her, they said in the lobby where Sasha played on the rug in front of the fireplace. Have you ever seen anything like that hair? And the pale skin, like cream. In her kitchen, Beatriz had a casta painting, their very likeness, a light brown mother holding a white baby. Writing on the canvas explained the equation: *De Espanol Y Morisca Produce Albino.* Around here, Brigid thought, I look exactly like her mother, the mother everyone is accustomed to seeing.

They were walking through town, Brigid half-guiding Beatriz on her crutches, pushing Sasha in her stroller, when Beatriz stopped, bent and whispered in Sasha's ear.

"I do this a few times a day," Beatriz explained, "say the words she ought to be saying."

"What is *ought*?" Brigid said.

Beatriz shrugged. "Anything. Any words. Her hearing is normal, but there are other tests," Beatriz said. "One doctor is calling it aphasia. But usually there's been brain injury. Could she have fallen without anyone knowing?"

"I had her for one day. If she fell, it would have happened here."

"She didn't fall here."

Sasha the baby looked at them, up at Beatriz and across to Brigid, as if she understood everything they said. Then she put her little face into the wind, and opened her mouth very wide, trying to swallow the sky. Brigid waited for her to spit it all back as words.

"Sometimes," Brigid said, "I think about those weeks before she was born. My father and mother both died. It was a very hard time." She shut her eyes against the memory, which only caused her to see it more clearly. The red of her mother's hair almost matching the color of blood spreading across the front of her blouse, the two men lying on either side, both faces half gone, blood and flesh shining on the tile floor, spatters on the walls, as if shaken out of a brush. Theo's vivid plum-colored shirt, a bruise blooming among wounds as he ran between the three bodies like a trapped animal, his arms held out as if he could hold something or carry it away. She looked up at Beatriz. "I have this idea that babies are born knowing everything. And little by little, they forget."

"She won't forget," Beatriz said. "I've decided she has a photographic memory. That's why she doesn't need to talk."

"I don't understand what you mean."

"Sometimes I think people only talk to remind themselves of what they already know or to get somebody else to agree with them."

"That's interesting."

"Can we go back now?" Beatriz said. "I haven't really got the hang of these yet."

"Of course," Brigid said. "Do you hate having me here?"

"I don't hate it. I know I sound so . . . angry. But the truth is I'm very grateful to you. And so is Francisco. But can I ask why you gave her up?"

"I was told I had to."

"By whom? You said your parents were dead."

"She could have a better life."

"I have to think that's true."

"We both have to."

Brigid felt that if this conversation went on much longer, it would kill her, her heart sliced to ribbons by all this talk of giving up. With the noise of it in her head, she would not be able to work. The woman in the door insisted, called out from the large white north-facing room. The Hand Goes Here ticked like a clock, the way a clock both measures time and is time. If she didn't finish this painting, she would never get to New York.

"I need to get back to work," she said.

"One more thing," Beatriz said. "I think it will be too strange for her to know you lived here, in this house, so close to her with so much. . . ."

"Knowledge."

"Yes. I wasn't planning to tell her your name."

Brigid cast her mind forward to a time when Sasha might try to find her. It seemed the pain and uproar of that day, amplified by years, would be far worse than this. "No," she said. "Please don't."

After a few weeks, Sasha's silence stopped being strange. She loved Brigid. Sometimes they were together all day, in the hotel lobby and kitchen, or in Brigid's rooms. They shared a secret language. Sasha liked to be read to, and she seemed to prefer rhymes. When Brigid held her and read a rhyme, or sang, she could feel the little body relax. After a minute, she would start to roll her head from side to side against Brigid's chest, in time with the words.

There was a little boy, about five, who came to the hotel with his mother sometimes when she delivered produce to the kitchen. One day, he asked everyone to speak more quietly because Sasha was sleeping. Quiet, please! he whispered, Sasha is asleep! Brigid thought at first this was a kind of joke, as Sasha was usually standing right next to this boy, even holding his hand, very clearly not asleep. A metaphor then, Ernesto said, a message. Sasha does not want to be disturbed! She is resting! She is gathering strength for a fantastic talking debut!

That summer she played or napped sometimes in the next room while Brigid worked on the door. She was not a good sleeper. Fifteen minutes after Brigid had put her into bed, she would feel Sasha's soft little hand on her back, and she would walk around the worktable, then climb up to sit on the high stool. Brigid whispered to Sasha, the words for colors, for the tools that lay beside the tubes of paint, slowly, as if Sasha were an audience, a conscience, as if she were the woman inside the door. Then there weren't any more words, just the work. Sasha watched and Brigid went on with it. Sometimes she fell asleep there, finally, leaning against Brigid's arm as it moved with her hand.

Of all the pictures in her studio, the print of Miss O'Keeffe's *Black Abstraction* seemed to capture Sasha's attention. She could see it clearly from her little bed. Sometimes she put her hands toward it as if she could grasp the white sphere, like a pearl, balanced in the middle of two dark rectangular shapes. They made a right angle, like the arm of a chair, as if that pearly glow came from a person sitting there, just out of sight. The light a body hides. The light that would replace the body. The light inside the body.

One day, as Brigid watched, Sasha began to laugh. Brigid tapped her fingernail on the sphere and Sasha laughed harder. "It's funny," she said to Sasha. "Why is it funny? Miss O'Keeffe didn't think it was funny." Or maybe she did, Brigid thought. Why should art be so serious and grim? Why shouldn't it make you laugh?

Sasha turned two. Her hair was like a halo of fire. Her hair is very loud, Brigid thought. No wonder she doesn't need to talk. Sometimes she said "no," but that was all. Beatriz and Francisco started to worry that Sasha might depend too much on Brigid. They thought they should be separated, each in her proper rooms, at least for the night. For Sasha, this was horrible. She sobbed. She wouldn't eat. She ran to the door of Brigid's room and flung herself there, her face pressed to the gap along the bottom. Brigid let her in and Sasha climbed up on the stool.

"Can you help me?" Brigid said.

Sasha didn't answer.

"In the paints," Brigid said. "Can you find the ochre?"

Sasha's little hand moved over the tubes ranged along the side of the table. She turned them over carefully, with her index finger, like somebody much older, Brigid thought, a grownup, picking through loose stones, looking for the precious ones. Then she found the right tube, held it up, the color of the hills beyond Ghost Ranch.

"Very good," Brigid said.

This color, the ochre, caused another piece to begin to take shape in her mind. The deer that crashed through Miss O'Keeffe's window, she knew the deer suffered a moment of visceral and horrified recognition: *In this house once lived a woman who had intimate knowledge with the bones of my kind, the empty space of my os coxae, which even now pulls me*

toward the earth and the peeling back of my brown skin to that whiteness
and eventually to dust.

Not a painting, though. It would have to move, stay alive, as the deer
did. Call it Red Sky/White Doe.

Sasha handed Brigid the paint. "Thank you. Someday I might need
an assistant."

Nancy

The second Christmas, Christmas Day, with Will. His parents turned out to be very rich Episcopalians emigrated from Massachusetts to live near their son. They adored Olivia. They were glad to be rid of that South American wife, his mother told me when we had a moment alone in the kitchen. She was very blunt. "You're the rebound," she said. "And you're too young. You know that, don't you?" I did. I wanted to say, "And you should know that your son is helping me get over my black lover. Who will someday be a psychiatrist in New York, and women like you will pay him hundreds of dollars to nod and offer Kleenex. What you call tissues."

God, I sound so angry sometimes. I'm really not. I'm just reporting.

"Are you Puerto Rican?" she asked.

"No," I said. "My father is black."

"Oh!" she said. "Well, you're a beautiful young woman." The word *anyway* drifted above her head. I watched it, a mote, a tiny feather, a spider spinning, until she looked up. But it had long since become part of the invisible air.

And that meal was got through too. I went home to my empty house. Rodney's house. He'd left a message on the phone: "I'm here at the Admiral's. Merry Christmas. Talk to you later." About what? What would we talk about later?

As if I didn't know. It was going to be one of those earth-shattering one-word conversations beginning with *good* and ending with *bye*.

I thought about inviting Will over, but instead, I called Henry.

"So what kind of work could I get in New York?"

"Temping. No problem."

It seemed settled. The rest of my life, the shell of it, waiting to be filled in. The map without my face. Or was it the other way around? No map. I was nowhere. No direction. Or I was in the afterlife with the chattering dead.

GEORGIA: They call you the Sphinx of Delft.

VERMEER: *(says nothing)*

G: That's a good one.

V: What was that? Did you just hear that sound?

G: A bell, I think. I remember it from the church in Ward, Colorado.

V: A bird?

G: Sometimes birds got into my house.

V: In mine too.

G: Not in the paintings though.

V: No. Only women in the pictures. I had eight daughters.

G: Listen. It's a girl singing. What's that song?

V: It's a bell.

G: Morning matins. Or maybe your mother-in-law?

V: That window should be open.

G: I've been thinking about windows. I've been wondering what they're for, exactly. Why not just have doors?

V: Prettier.

G: Why is that?

V: The bottom is in shadow. That bird again. Listen.

G: A girl this time.

   (time passes)

V: How did the work go, Georgia?

G: It's late now, isn't it?

V: Later.

G: How much?

V: Can't you tell? Read the light.

G: Someone closed the window.

V: Is that the clock? It's louder now.

G: The sound got bigger. When the window closes, the sounds inside get bigger.

V: I'm not a fan of this clock. It's saying I haven't done enough today. To tell you the truth, I haven't done anything at all.

G: Why is that?

V: I'm not sure how to work in the absence of my daughters.

G: A girl's voice.

V: Yes.

G: A girl's voice singing turns into a clock. How does that happen?

V: She grows up.

Henry and Paula got married, on New Year's Day, 2001, not at City Hall but in the amphitheater at the south end of Centennial Park. Henry arranged this to please our dad, to redeem the Park, reinvent it, take it back from the murder and mayhem of July 27, 1996. Nobody mentioned Alice Hawthorne, but she was there, an invited guest, first on the list. It was mostly just like old times: Rodney was the best man and I was stoned. Though there were no crossed swords, Henry looked frightened. But when it came time to say the vows, he got choked up, and Paula gazed at him as if he was the sweetest thing in the world.

Paula said, "I ask you to be the guardian of my solitude. I ask you to recognize that even between the closest people infinite distances exist. I ask you to love the expanse between us." Henry said those same words back.

There was a kind of stunned silence after that, everybody thinking about solitude and distance as the starting place for a marriage. A pair of runners flew by, streaks of red and blue, a couple pushing a huge stroller, joggers next, in paint-stained sweats, slowing down to give Paula and Henry the thumbs up. Finally, an old woman creaked slowly past on a rusty bicycle. We all took it in, the progress of life, a pageant enacted for the happy couple, a little play. No need for dialogue. The twenty people gathered there to witness let out their breaths. Our parents clasped and then unclasped hands, guarding each other's solitude. The minister pronounced.

The end of Rodney and me arrived in the form of Buddhist monks. As part of a university conference on healing, a pack of monks came to Atlanta to make a mandala on campus, and they needed a place to stay. Of course, they weren't called a pack, I knew that, and I started to think about what a group of monks should be called. The university said "a cohort," but the way they floated about the room with their bowls of colored sand made me think of birds building nests—or something less purposeful, because what happens to the finished mandala is that it's poured into a moving body of water. All that work. Drowned. It makes you think. It makes you feel stupid for wanting anything, ever.

The monks stayed with Henry and Paula because monks' hosts had to be married. So even though Emory's Psychiatry Department was partly sponsoring the visit and we had plenty of room in the house on Candler Road, we couldn't have them. The dean of the medical school and the head of Religious Studies explained it to us, both of us, in the dean's office, as if we'd misbehaved. I understood this was really the dissolution, the conclusion. Rodney stared straight ahead and then left the office before I'd had a chance to stand up. Even the dean looked surprised. The head of Religious Studies wrinkled his brow in the do-you-need-to-talk-about-it look. He handed me his card. I read that he had a master's degree in social work.

When I caught up to Rodney in the parking lot, I said that I was sorry, that I didn't know it meant that much to him.

"I didn't know either," he said, sounding really young and truly surprised.

"You can hang out with them at Henry's."

"It's not the same."

Healing was his deal, he said. He wanted to learn from the monks, observe their daily practice. I thought about offering to move out. I almost said, *I know somebody in the Art Department I could stay with,* but I didn't. Didn't say it, that is.

"You get to meet them at the president's reception."

"How do you know that?"

"I saw the invitation."

"On my desk?"

"Yes."

Rodney sighed and grasped my arm under the elbow, harder than he needed to. Healing, I thought, how funny.

At the university president's house, there were six monks altogether, five young, small and thin, one older, jovial, with a soft paunch. They all wore sleeveless, saffron-colored robes, and I tried not to stare at their impressively toned arms. They did not speak any English. They didn't seem to need language—eyes and smiles and hands were enough. I noticed they hardly looked at one another, but they took in every detail of the president's huge living room without seeming to. It must have been baffling, all those tapestries and statues, paintings of horses and Civil War battles, tiny pecan pies and cheese straws, men and women in suits who held out their hands to be shaken. I reminded myself that, no, this was the traveling team, they were used to American excess. Still, there was a strange hesitation in the room, suspended time, a parlor trick the monks had performed, a spell.

Will arrived late, breathless. It took me a minute to realize he was the monks' translator. We had all been waiting for him. The monks seemed suddenly to breathe again. Everybody woke up, as if from a nap, refreshed. The president could now speak his welcome, offer a toast. People stopped staring at the monks, took bites of their little pecan tarts, and crumbs fell to the floor. A woman spilled her drink. I thought the word *disenchanted*.

Then there was a clatter and rustle in the president's front hallway. Guests moved out of the way, and I moved closer to Will, who did not appear surprised to see me. He cleared his throat and began to speak, announcing that local monks, from the Drepung Loseling monastery across town, had prepared a chan dance to welcome their foreign brothers, for good luck and health. These monks, ten of them, moved into the room in a kind of electric slide. The costumes were blindingly gorgeous: embroidered silk robes, pink and orange and green, impossible headdresses that reminded you of the Incas and of the Ascot opening day number in *My Fair Lady* and of southern black women on Sunday. I whispered this to Will and he looked at me and nodded like that was a normal thought to have. I wanted to ask him about the story, the plot of this dance, but after a few minutes, I realized that plot wasn't the point. The word probably didn't exist in their language. That's what I would ask Will later. As the dance ended, I watched Rodney slip out of the room, his head down, his jaw set. Will turned to the visiting monks, who had been joined by the president. I listened to what was being said in both languages. I wondered if anything really made it whole from one tongue to the other.

The older monk, not so lithe and muscular—I could see this now, up close—had glimmers of silver in his hair. He bowed toward me and said a few words to Will. Will spoke back, shaking his head to mean yes. All the monks were now looking at me and smiling warmly. The older monk spoke again, opening his empty hand, palm up, as if he'd just made something disappear. There was some evidence of surprise. Someone touched my shoulder. I expected Rodney, but instead there were Henry and Paula.

"You're probably going to need a ride," Henry said. "Rodney had to go."

"Thanks," I said, and turned to Will. "Say good-bye for me."

"Just bow," Will said.

I did, and the monks returned the gesture. Their smiles were electrifying and beautiful.

"They're so happy," I said.

"They wanted to know if you're Korean," Will whispered. "I told them you are."

The next morning at nine o'clock, in the Carlos Museum, the monks unpacked four very American-looking blue plastic storage bins. Out of these they lifted white porcelain bowls and Ziploc bags of colored sand, a roll of thin white twine, chalk, small pillows the same shade as their robes, and a large black Masonite board. Two tables had been arranged for them, larger and smaller, one for the board and the other for supplies. Immediately, the monks began to stretch a length of twine over the board, marking sections, tracing the twine with chalk, then tapping the twine so that the chalk fell to the dark surface of the board. Four monks worked at once without speaking, marking lines in this way, no mistakes, no erasures, no hesitation. There was no one in the world I could work with like this. Not even Henry.

It's a map, a map in real time, a map to spiritual concentration. They're making it up as they need it. They already know what they need. So it's not really subject to time, except that it takes time, that's what Henry said.

Watching them work, it was like looking at a body of water, a river, an ocean, current, or tide; constant, steady motion, a sound that's not quite whisper, not quite song. Which is actually the monks' chanting. It's mesmerizing. No. That's too hostile and controlling. It's soothing. You could do this completely pointless thing for a long time. Until someone drags you away. It's cosmic, really. I'd become some sort of heavenly body, and my men revolved toward and away. All of them, except Simon Anderson, the dark star, appeared at different times during the hours I watched the monks. Henry. Rodney. Will. Even my dad, who had a hard time with the whole notion of building something only to destroy it.

But three days later, that was the part he came to watch. He called it the bitter end: the briefest pause and a photo op with students and faculty, one of the vice chancellors, a state senator. The monks turned their backs, not in protest, I don't think, but away from the noise, the flash. I think they were saying good-bye. Then, out of nowhere, out of the folds of their robes, they brought out little brushes and swept the sand into a pile, then into a metal urn. This took about twenty seconds. A voice across the room breathed a little protest: *oh no.*

Dad clucked and shook his head. He said, "I have to see it," and we joined the monks' procession across campus to the little trickle of Nancy Creek that runs under the student union.

"It's like the sand is you," somebody behind me said. I turned to see a woman in her thirties, probably a graduate student. She looked at me, took my measure. "Don't you think?" she said. "You give up a little piece of yourself by watching."

"I never thought of it like that," I said.

My dad caught my arm and dragged me forward, as if I were talking to a person he suspected would turn out to be a bad influence. And I have to admit I liked this a lot, his taking charge of me that way. Protecting, keeping me from going the way of the mandala. He lowered his head like somebody walking into a fierce wind. His breath came in little gasps through clenched teeth. I wondered if he was hatching a plan to save the sand. Or save me. I would have to remind him that the harm was already done, everything swept away into chaos.

Onward we marched, following the monks' warble, crossing streets, threading in and out of the shadows of buildings, passing students who smiled or stared or rolled their eyes heavenward. Occasionally, the monk carrying the urn of sand lifted it high above his head, a tour guide with his umbrella or stick or sign to keep us all together. If you get lost, look for this. It's your sign. You're in here, like the woman said. And I was, on my way to Nancy Creek. Nancy to Nancy, dust to dust.

"I don't think I can look," my dad said. The monks had stopped on the north campus bridge. The older one leaned over the railing to peer into the water. "It's like an execution."

"Where's Mom?"

"In her studio. She said she didn't need to see it."

"But you did."

My father looked at me closely, considering, weighing his admission. "I kind of admire these monks," he said finally. "The way they let go. And you know what I heard?"

"What?"

"The monks really like basketball. Henry said that. I don't know how he knows."

We watched the monks balance the urn on the railing, all six touching it, their fingers intertwined. Their voices rose, and then went silent. Then they carefully poured the sand over the side of the bridge. A stream of sand, elements exchanging themselves. There's a play in there, but without characters. I hadn't thought to see so much sand, and it all caught the afternoon light, the pink and green and red sand especially vivid. You tried to see a pattern, you wanted to see the mandala making itself whole again, a last gasp, as it fell. A puff of wind came out of nowhere and carried some of the sand away from the creek, into the trees. I wondered if that was good or bad, and I turned to ask my dad. He was watching the escape, the sand that got away. He was smiling.

I thought about that moment often, later. Dad and the renegade sand.

Sudden silence: a hundred people waiting for what would happen next. What would the monks do, now that they had no real function? You could almost hear the creak and rattle, as some balance of power shifted. A minute ago, the monks had us under their spell. We would have followed them anywhere. But now, not now. All they could offer us was an empty urn and an impossible lesson. Not impossible. Difficult. Distasteful. Un-American. The crowd began to untangle itself, drift away. The dean of the medical school offered to shake hands with the monks, and they returned the gesture, though you could tell they didn't want to. They tried to bow at the same time, so it looked like they would kiss the dean's large class ring. The older monk gripped the urn with both hands. The dean said something about a meeting, turned and walked away. I wondered if the monks would be left standing on the bridge. The youngest monk caught my eye: *Korean girl, please help us.*

Will appeared from the fraying edge of the crowd and spoke to the monks. Everyone bowed and nodded and smiled. The woman who had compared us to the sand joined them, and Will introduced her to the monks, which made me feel strangely sad. And jealous. I asked my dad if he wanted to go get a beer.

"It's too early," he said. "Walk me back to the parking lot, will you? I'm not sure where I am."

"Neither am I, to tell the truth."

Will and the monks and the sand-is-you woman had moved off together, not the way we'd come, without speaking to us. I told myself that Will hadn't seen me, that it was his duty to guide the monks, that maybe he did see me and wondered who my dad was the same way I wondered about the woman. You're not the center of the universe, a little voice inside me said. Didn't you learn anything from those monks just now?

Not hardly.

What do people mean by *not hardly?*

So I strolled with my dad. It was clear he did not want to go back to work right away. The day was good for that, the kind of day I liked for its strangeness: January, but close to 70 degrees, so that the light is all wrong for the temperature, slanting in from the wrong angle. Light behind us instead of beside or in front, so that we kept walking into our own shadows.

"How's your play, Nance?" my dad said.

"Coming along," I told him. "I'm not sure I'm doing it right."

This made him laugh in a kind of terrified way. "What's right?"

"I feel like there should be more to it."

"Harder?"

"Bigger. Right now, it's just two dead people talking to each other."

"Hmmm," my dad said. "Could you show it to somebody?"

"Not yet."

He nodded. "We're big on showing in my line of work."

"That makes me nervous," I said. I'd been watching our shadows, following our shadows, and now I looked up and realized I had no idea where we were. Oh well. Sooner or later, we would come to a road. That's how it always worked.

"So what will you do when everybody goes back to New York?" he said.

"Not sure. Move in with you and Mom again?"

"That would be okay. You'd hate it though."

"Get a job?" I said. Move in with Will? Not that Will had asked. I wondered if I could keep doing this for the rest of my life, live off of guys. Of all the things to think about while walking with your father. "Maybe I'll go with them."

"I'd miss you," he said. "*You-ou, my brown-eyed girl.*"

"You would? I'm a lot of trouble."

"But you're my trouble. All mine."

God, how I loved hearing him say that.

The path we were on ended suddenly, right in front of us, at the side door to the gym. I confessed to Dad that I was lost, but Newton's first law was at work, and we were bodies in motion, so we pushed the glass doors open and stepped inside.

"I'll ask somebody," I said.

"There's probably a map," my dad said.

We'd come in to a hallway of offices, silent, doors all closed. "Baseball wing," Dad said. "Off-season." We could hear the faint thud, thud, thud of a basketball, then a moment's silence and the clatter of the ball against the rim of the basket. Or longer silence. "Nothing but net," my dad said. "That's too slow to be a game." The sound drew us on, down another hallway, toward another set of doors, blue metal, small glass windows at eye level.

As long as I live, I will never forget the sight of the monks in their robes at the free-throw line, four of them, waiting their turn. Something about the saffron color caused the basketball to look like a huge piece of fruit, maybe an orange or a pumpkin, but more likely some exotica you'd never heard of before and certainly never tasted. Forbidden maybe. But still—those colors together, the word that came to mind was *edible*. My dad and I watched, stupefied, as each one of the monks bounced the basketball a few times and then took a shot. They hardly ever missed. They smiled but didn't speak. I noticed that when the monks crouched and sprung into a shot, they stood on the very tips of their toes, balancing in a way that didn't seem possible.

Suddenly Will's face appeared in the glass like a reflection, the door opened, and he ushered us onto the court. The monks did not seem to notice.

"They do this to relax," Will said. "They would play, but we're an odd number. So I made a couple of phone calls."

And there they were, summoned just like magic, my brother and my lover. My other lover. With Will and my dad, they make eight. I climbed into the stands.

"I'll take that beer now," my dad said.

I told him no, he had to play. He paused, then took off his watch, handed it to me, and I put it on. I liked the way it looked, too large on my skinny wrist. Time is big. Timing is everything.

Love is not the international language, I discovered. Basketball is.

The teams were Henry and Dad, Rodney and Will and two monks each. In the air, for lay-ups and rebounds, the monks looked like red and orange flames, shot from the floor, gleaming, blossoming, and then falling back to earth. Flames in the air, man-shaped, tear-shaped as their robes puff away from their bodies, their feet and legs tucked up inside, invisible. Among and below them, regular, earthly men seemed confused, running and chasing and calling out to one another, as if they'd lost their sight, blinded by smoke. Over here, one said, then another. The monks didn't speak, except for the two on Will's team, who called his name. *Wheel*, it sounded like.

I thought about how my mother would love this and opened my Dad's cell phone to call her. She said okay she'd be over, but I doubted she'd make it in time. I called her back and told her to hurry. I tried to keep score, but then I was ashamed of myself. The monks weren't keeping score. It wasn't about that, you could tell by watching; it was about the seconds between half-court and the basket, how to get there, how to get in the air. I wondered if the monks used the word goal, if the word exists in the language of their belief.

My dad's in great shape for sixty-six, but he's slowing down now, breathing heavily, and the monks notice this. They walk the ball down the court, pass less. The game begins to take place less in the air. They play zone defense instead of man-to-man. More stillness. Less chasing after the illusions of this world. After a few minutes, Dad doesn't look quite so haggard.

The monks' basketball has no personal fouls, no whistle, no time outs, no out of bounds, no three-second rule, no referees. No traveling, except that it's all traveling, a sort of hypnotic up and down the court, back and forth. It's lulling, like the ocean. Even the swish of the ball though the net sounds like the hiss of waves on sand. I'm tempted to lie down, stretch out in the bleachers, and close my eyes. But then I'd miss the spectacle.

My mother arrives in a swirl of brick-colored cape and a hammering of clogs. My dad looks up and waves, shyly, it seems, a gesture from twenty-five years ago. The game resumes. We watch in silence through a couple of plays, and then my mother says, very quietly, almost a whisper, "I get it." She glances at me, and I must look puzzled, because she smiles and reaches her arm around my shoulder, drags me closer. "Why you wanted me to see it." I think I'm going to cry, right there, leaning against my mother, cry like I was nine years old and someone had been mean to me at school, or maybe like I was older and couldn't figure out how the world was supposed to work. But I don't, because if I start crying now, I might never stop. "Dad looks pretty good out there," she says. "Who's the other guy?"

"He's in the Art Department."

"Oh?" she says, like there should be more to tell.

"He lives in our neighborhood. Mine and Rodney's."

"What's he teach?"

"Architecture."

"Oh!" she says, different this time. "Does he know Dad?"

"I'm not sure. I just met him. His work is in imaginary places." I am saying all this into the blood-red shoulder of my mother's cape. The regular pounding of the basketball is that heartbeat sound effect in a movie, not the real thing, but telling you what to feel. Frightened.

"Nance," she says, "why don't you go to New York too? Dad and I will help you get set up. Though Henry thinks you'll find work right away. And you can take some classes. Get on your feet." I'm nodding into her shoulder, whispering *okay okay okay*, making up my mind. I open my eyes and all I see is red, like what happens when you stare at the sun too long.

Just then, in the mighty twirl of a rebound, Rodney falls and takes one of the monks down with him. Both lie still, not really hurt, trying to catch their breath, smiling a little, glad for the forced break. But this gives me time to see them. The spread of the monk's robe over Rodney's leg looks like blood, a hideous injury, amputation. My hand flies to my mouth, even though I know nothing's wrong. They can't see it, the men. They're too close. I'm suddenly quite sure I love Rodney, and I also love Will, and that these loves are going to cause me terrible pain sometime very soon. Then the monk rolls away, and it's miraculous: Rodney's legs are restored, just as they were before his fall. The monk rises, turns, extends his arm. Rodney sits up, clasps the monk's hand, smiles broadly. His teeth gleam. I swear they twinkle, like in cartoons. The monk's small brown hand inside Rodney's looks like it could be mine. Will puts his arms around both of them, asks if they're all right. They're a gorgeous trio. They're an ad for something you know you need even though you can't name it and you're not sure if it's even been invented yet.

Sasha

Sasha slid the tape into the VCR. The common room in Carman still smelled like spilled beer and the inside of a microwave oven, old popcorn, pizza snacks, ramen noodles. Strangely comforting. The quiet, though, was surreal. Edgardo dragged his chair closer to the television. Sasha sat down on the coffee table beside him. The first image snapped into focus as if the viewer's eyes had opened onto it. A woman in the air, a mass of blond hair above her. She seems to float and then, like the hands of a clock going around, her legs rise and her head moves back. She seems to recline very slowly. There is nothing else in the shot except a streak of silver running down the left side of the screen.

Sasha pointed to it. "That's the North Tower."

"The building?"

"I've slowed the image."

"It's awful," Edgardo said. "But not."

"It is. There's more."

"How many?"

"Fourteen. And then the two women holding hands. That's the strangest one. It's at the end."

"Oh my God," Edgardo said. "So many of them have their coats on."

"Like they're leaving."

The body language—every one was different—you could almost hear each one of these people thinking: defiant, resigned, almost peaceful, like they were about to fall asleep, concentrating, holding an image in their mind's eye: a child, a spouse, a parent, God, heaven. Awe. A man pumped his arms and legs as if he'd just let go of a tire swing over a lazy river in July. A woman opened her arms. What made one body fall in stillness while another spun or turned head over foot? What sort of interior chemistry or particular body mass or sense of privacy informed this last passage? These images, Sasha thought, were so specific, so telling. It was not surprising that some family members watched them over and over. "That's so him," one man's sister had said.

"Oh, Sasha," Edgardo said. "That sound."

"I know," Sasha said.

"How did you make music out of it?"

"I just heard it that way. It sounded that way."

"That's the bodies landing."

Sasha nodded.

"But you made it. . . . I don't know what to call it. Symphonic."

"That's the part some people hate. The music's too pretty."

"Did you talk to the families?"

"I tried to. But not all of them were interested, and some of them were flat out furious. They may feel different later. But they may not."

"The only thing that makes it bearable," Edgardo said, "is how slow it is. So it's like they're floating. Like there's some magic at work and in the end nothing bad will happen to them."

"Maybe."

"Brigid told us this story, when she first came to Santa Fe, about a deer crashing through the window at Georgia O'Keeffe's house, hanging there. That became *Red Sky/White Doe*. Your film has the same feel."

"A world without gravity," Sasha said.

They sat motionless. The common room darkened. When the sky began to glow pink, Sasha left her uncle and rode the elevator to her room, retrieved the bottle of rum from the floor of her closet. She left the room without locking it. No reason to. No one was around. And what was there to take anyway?

When the elevator opened in the lobby, she heard Edgardo's laugh. He was standing with Aaron, who held three small glasses from the dining hall, the squat size used for milk or juice. "Your uncle invited me," he said. "I can't stay long." Edgardo took the bottle of rum from Sasha and they moved back into the common room. Edgardo asked Aaron if he was going home. "I'm going to my parents' house. This is home," Aaron said. "Though it's a little creepy right now, all by myself."

"Sasha's here," Edgardo said. He poured rum into the three glasses.

"But she's way upstairs." He turned to Sasha. "I thought I was looking out for you, but I think you guys have been looking out for me all semester."

"It must be a little bit nice to have us all gone."

"It reminds me of the first couple of times my parents left me alone in the house. The quiet. All those empty rooms to explore. My parents' room and their dressers and closets. The temptation. Sorry, Father. Not really. Though I do have a master key. As you know." He said this to Sasha.

"I didn't."

"I thought Jennie told you. But no, now that I think about it, she wouldn't have."

Sasha took a gulp of rum. "Careful," Edgardo said, but she wasn't sure he was talking to her. Revelation has a certain sound or smell or taste, she thought. This is about to be it. Aaron swallowed the last of his rum. It smells like this, she thought, revelation does. Like rum suddenly in a glass that's always contained milk.

"She had this weird idea," Aaron said. "Jennie. Actually two weird ideas, on two different days, when she was home in Long Beach. You were in class. First, she thought her dad might have gone to her room. She said maybe he was lost or crazy or got hit on the head. And she wanted me to check. And so—it wasn't a big deal for me. And you know I just wanted to help her. Make her feel better, though of course, he. . . . Well, you know."

"Poor Jennie," Edgardo said.

"I think she's getting along," Aaron said. He handed his glass to Edgardo. "Because of Sasha. It was a really good thing putting them together. Sometimes you can see so clearly who's going to work out well. Okay, thanks for the drink. I'll be back later."

"Wait," Sasha said. "What was the second weird idea?"

"Oh." Aaron sighed heavily. "It was just . . . your. . . . Brigid Schumann. Jennie thought she might be in there. She might have come here to wait for you or something."

"I had no idea."

"She could hardly think straight. Jennie."

"And she wasn't in there, right? Brigid Schumann?"

"No, she wasn't. She couldn't have gotten in the front door with all the security."

"How could she have got in the door?" Edgardo said. He swept his hands in front of his face as if he were trying to clear something away.

"That's what I said." Aaron stepped closer to Edgardo, as if to catch him. "What do you mean?"

"I remember," Edgardo said, "when she was just starting to work on *The Hand Goes Here*. She talked about getting the woman to come out of the door. I think about that all the time. It seems so logical, the idea that something already exists inside the raw material. Or continues to exist."

Aaron nodded. "Given all the talk about souls." He pointed to Sasha, "She's really her daughter?"

"She is," Edgardo said.

"I honestly do have to go now," Aaron said. "My mother thinks on time is ten minutes early." His gaze drifted to Sasha. "See you later?"

"I'll be back after dinner," Sasha said.

"Nice to meet you, Father," Aaron said. He seemed to be studying Edgardo's face. "I could listen to Brigid Schumann stories all day."

"I've got them," Edgardo said. "All true." He made the cross-your-heart gesture, and Aaron returned it. Seeing this cause a little window to open inside Sasha's chest, and let in a pinpoint of light. Brigid Schumann moving in closer, conjured. By Aaron. She wondered if she'd been falling in love with Aaron Fisk all this time.

"I tried looking at the paintings," Sasha said. "I mean, I did look at them. At her gallery."

"And?" Edgardo said. They were eating dinner at Carmine's, of all places. Sasha decided she'd had enough quiet and privacy for one day, and she imagined it would be vaguely hilarious to be shouting about Brigid Schumann across a table to a priest. Why did people stare at priests? Looking for the flaw, the slip of the mask, the secret sin. But Carmine's was nearly empty.

"And I tried to read about them. Art criticism. That sort of helped, in a weird way. Some people hate her work. That makes me feel better. I feel like, okay, so she hasn't had this totally idyllic life being celebrated and applauded. And I also want to defend her. Sometimes I want to bite back. 'You're just mad that she thought of it before you did!' or 'You don't get it because you're a man!'"

The family at the next table looked up from their plates, their five heads turning in unison, mechanized tourist dolls, all but the father who was frowning, clearly unhappy that this brazen young woman was yelling at a priest. "Don't worry," Sasha called to them. "He's my dad."

"Oh, Sasha," Edgardo said. "I'm really not. You understand that, don't you?"

"I guess."

"You guess?" Edgardo sighed, made some small business out of balancing his fork on the side of the massive plate of spaghetti Bolognese. It looked funny there, Sasha thought. Like a toy. Useless. It had laid itself down in defeat. Edgardo poured more wine, seemed to admire its color, sipped from the glass. "I admit I was a little in love with her," he said finally.

"You were?"

"Everyone was. She was just so different. And determined."

"Can I film you talking about that?"

"No."

"Have some more wine."

"All right."

"All right which?" Edgardo smiled. Sasha watched him. "You're thinking about it."

"About what?" Edgardo asked.

"Being filmed. Your fifteen minutes."

There were two projects in her head, she told him. "Strange and Forbidden Love" was the first film she wanted Edgardo to sit for. People talking about their forbidden or impossible loves, no faces though, just their hands or their feet or some kind of prop. A woman's finger moving across a road map, tracing the route between her house and her married lover's house. Edgardo's collar. All monologues, starting with a woman Jennie met in grief counseling. This woman talked about flying to New York from Ohio two days after. Her father was in the South Tower. She talked about a guy who sat in her row on this flight, when she knew her father was dead and she was in midair. *This is why I love Nicholas Colby Austin, she said, because he slept through my grief.* She was in the bulkhead seat, on the aisle, two empty seats beside her. At the last minute, this vision boarded, a black man in his twenties, black jeans, black sweatshirt, black shoes. He took the window seat, pulled up the hood of his sweatshirt and slept through the entire flight while she looked out at the clouds and wondered where her dad was. Nicholas Colby Austin woke up as they landed, and she told him he was a good sleeper. He had been clutching his boarding pass, she said, and his name was right there. She said it seemed important to name him.

Sasha thought she might film Edgardo with Brigid and their segment would come last and the only face in the entire piece would be Brigid's. She didn't say this to Edgardo.

The second project she was calling "Centaur and Mermaid." The idea came to her when she heard a woman talk about her black father and white mother. The woman said she believed this parentage made her an exotic, fantastical creature, an enchanted thing, like a mermaid. Like Brigid. Like me, Sasha thought. So if you can't talk to her, Jennie had said, and you can't stop thinking about her, you can talk *about* her, make her into art. Sasha thought of an oyster, the grain of sand, the pearl.

"Aaron?" she asked that night, in his room, "do you have a forbidden love?"

"I do now," Aaron said. "May I kiss you?"

Why didn't I ever have time for this before? Sasha thought. Why did I never want to be the subject?

"Your uncle," Aaron said later, "I recognized him right away. She painted him, Brigid did. Six studies. He was in costume sometimes, dressed like a waiter, a doctor, a lawyer."

"Indian chief?"

"There's one of those too. One of them was the first painting she did with words. A word. *Gratitude.*"

"Her first word was gratitude? That's encouraging."

"It is," Aaron said.

"Gratitude," Sasha whispered. *Gratitude, gratitude.* Aaron's dark sitting room warmed with their breaths, the air from the ticking radiator, the glow of the streetlight outside his window. She felt like maybe they were bringing it back, gratitude, into this place of sadness and fear, breath by breath, little by little.

She is arguably the most famous American woman artist alive, Henry Diamond's interview began, partly because she's never where you expect her to be, never doing what you expect her to do.

Like sitting right here, Sasha thought. Can you freaking believe it? In the Cornelia Street Café. Where I've come to be alone. And it appears Brigid Schumann had too. Separated by about twenty feet of bar. Brigid Schumann, quite a small person in the flesh, rail thin, her skin the color of fallen oak leaves, looking older than she was, and tired. Before her a glass of wine. She was reading a book. She'd slung her coat over the seat beside her. Might as well be a sign: don't you dare talk to me. Every so often she looked up, at nothing. She's probably jet-lagged, Sasha thought. Maybe she hasn't collected her mail at the gallery, hasn't read the letter or watched the film. Doesn't have any idea what's in store. Sasha marveled. All these years Brigid had known Sasha's whereabouts, but now it was the other way around. Sasha wanted to stand still for a minute and just watch. The late afternoon light above Brigid's head was full of dust. Sasha thought the word *curdled*.

Sasha pretended to read the menu posted on the wall beside her. She told the hostess she was waiting for someone. And it was true. She was waiting for someone to take the seat beside Brigid, fill it up, maybe fill out this scene with an old friend: this person would start talking, and Sasha would slide in a couple of seats over and listen. Brigid would say, Yes, long-as-hell flight. Strange to be back. The air's awful, isn't it? Still full of rotting and burning. How to paint that? That stench. No I haven't been back since. Left in May. No words for it.

And then she would take the hand of her friend, Brigid Schumann would, grip that hand and lean in close. She would say the words, and even if Sasha couldn't hear, she could read Brigid's lips: I got a letter from my daughter. Or: I got this letter from a girl who says she's my daughter. Or: remember the child I had in New Mexico? And the friend would do that thing people do, which is raise the eyebrows or blink slowly and say wow or shit or no fucking way.

But such a person did not appear, and Brigid Schumann continued to read her book and sip at her wine while the dusty light swam and dimmed, and finally there was nothing left for Sasha to do, no more waiting. She wound her way around the bar and took the seat two over from Brigid, who did not look up.

Stillness and light. Linger in it. Sasha imagined she felt a current of warmth running along the left side of her body, viscera finding and seeking their oldest connection. She almost laughed out loud. What a crock of shit. She saw what the camera would see. Two women, one dark haired, one a redhead, one older. Something odd about Brigid's hair though, as she glimpsed it sidelong, some kind of chestnut rinse, maroon really, a little like a paint can tipped over and she tried hard to wash it away, without much luck or soap. The light from the window behind the bar dazzled into her glass as if the wine inside were some phosphorescent potion.

Brigid Schumann sighed and turned a page in her book. Sasha tried to see what she was reading, couldn't, tried to imagine. An Irish novel maybe, since she'd just been there and probably hadn't wanted to leave. Brigid took a sip of her wine, coughed delicately, a little *ahem*, the sound people make when they're about to say something mildly unpleasant. Sasha waited.

The bartender smiled from the other end of the bar and held up two fingers. Give me two minutes, two seconds, two something, two more. Sasha had no idea what he meant. She wondered what she could order that would cause Brigid to recognize her. Anything from New Mexico. Typhoo tea. I'll have what she's having. She could turn to Brigid and ask if the wine was any good. Nobody really did that. It sounded like a pickup line. Then there he was, smiling, coming toward her, the bartender who was probably an aspiring actor, who obviously spent a lot of time at the gym. Sasha felt a strange, piercing rush, a flood of happiness. It really does come in a flood, she thought. New York will be okay because painters could still sit quietly in bars, and guys like this could still work and audition and perfect themselves and look so buff and so hopeful.

Bushmills on the rocks. Right, the bartender said, I remember. Sasha sensed a flutter of attention from Brigid. She started to tell the bartender she'd never had a drink here before, but what did it matter? He brought her the Bushmills and moved away again. How to do it? Leave the wallet lying open. Brigid turned a page. She was a slow reader, or maybe just tired. Her wine glass was still more than half full, maybe, depending on the pour.

There was a commotion then, behind them, at the door. A woman laughing so hard she couldn't speak, but trying to. Finally, she managed to yell, "You mean it's not New Year's Eve yet?" The small crowd with her shook their heads, howled back "Nooooo," and the woman said, "Will this year ever end? Please let this year just fucking end."

"Amen to that," Brigid Schumann said quietly.

It was a good enough opening. Sasha turned, took in fully the face of this mother. "Yeah," she said. The next words came without conscious thought. "Excuse me, but are you Brigid Schumann?"

Brigid looked at her for a second, a face seeing another face, no more than that. "No," she said and smiled, a tight, sad, secret smile, code for *people ask me that all the time.* She stared back down into her book. Her eyes, Sasha noticed, were still. She was not reading.

"People probably ask you that all the time," Sasha said. She took a big gulp of whiskey.

"Not really."

"Do you know her work? I guess everybody knows her work."

"Probably not everybody."

"That's true," Sasha said. "Do you like it?"

"Please, honey." Brigid lifted her chin and stared straight ahead. "I came here to read."

"Sorry," Sasha said, but she wasn't sorry. The game was enthralling. "It's just that she's my mom, and, you know, I haven't seen her since I was little, and well. . . ." She held up the whiskey glass, swung it like a bell. "You know."

"And what's your name?"

"Sasha."

Brigid was a pretty good actress, but not great. She drained her wine glass, opened her wallet and took out a ten-dollar bill, slapped it on the bar. She placed her right hand on Sasha's wrist, curled it around, a brown bracelet. Skin to skin, the touch was electric. She wondered if Brigid felt it. "You should write her a letter," she said, easing off the barstool.

"I did," Sasha said.

"Well then," Brigid said. "Good luck."

Even after she'd been gone ten, fifteen, twenty minutes, Sasha thought Brigid would come back. She could picture it. The determined march down Cornelia Street, the gradual slowing, the pause, the turn, the reentry. Cinema. Bad Hollywood. The worst sentimental shit.

Later, Aaron came to get her. "Brave girl," he said. "Not everyone is good. As good as you are. Not everybody gets a happy ending."

"I'm not good," Sasha said, "and it's not the ending."

Nancy

LOU: Our fathers loved us—
EMILY: According to their abilities.
LOU: That's not what I was going to say.
EMILY: I know. I was saving you from sentimentality.
LOU: Listening to my father talk was like going to heaven in a swing.
EMILY: I never learned to tell time by the clock until I was fifteen. My father taught me ten years earlier, but I didn't understand and was always afraid to ask him to explain.
LOU: Their hearts were terrible and pure.
EMILY: The world wronged them and we were the recompense.
LOU: They didn't want to let us go.

"You really can stay here, Nancy," my dad said. "But my friend Tim says he can use you in his office. He said, 'any kid of yours, Mark.'"

Any kid of yours.

So it was a done deal, my following Henry and Rodney out of Atlanta. And thus the idea of New York kept me going as I helped Rodney and Henry and Paula pack up their two households and load the trailer. They crowded onto the bench seat and Rodney turned the key.

"Where's the map?" he asked.

Henry opened the road atlas, the two-page spread of America, over his lap and Paula's. He traced their route with his pinky, an elaborate sweep up the East Coast. Then he circled his thumb and first finger around the city of New York. "Here there be dragons," he said. "See you in a couple weeks, Nance."

I noticed how Will's house was much smaller than its neighbors, set farther back from the street, shrunk in at the sides, inhaling, in order to avoid contact, to keep from overhearing or being overheard. Long stiff hedges rose on both sides, harshly squared boxwood. I'd never seen boxwood grow so tall. The lawn was a little less groomed than the others on the block, with no shrubbery planted close to the house, not flowers or other adornment. Here was a house, you thought, I thought, that had lost interest in itself, or maybe its life only went on in secret, on the inside. Except for the girl's bicycle at the upper end of the driveway, and Olivia standing next to it, holding onto the handlebars, watching me. She was too tall for the bike, and had seemed, before she heard my step and looked up, to be making her peace with it, with the end of this bike, measuring it against her hip, shaking her head. She would need a new one. It was a small simple thing in a girl's life. The next move. It was nearly her thirteenth birthday. I imagined she was thinking about what she wanted, what she would ask for, what color. A mountain bike maybe. She could probably ride a lot farther now than when she first got this bike, she could pedal miles and miles away, and when she looked up toward that distance, she saw me walking to the driveway from this different direction, alone, not somebody she really knew, not of an age she understood, not a kid like herself, not an old woman. Closer to her mother's age. Like her mother, somebody partly lost.

I smiled and held up my hand, and she did too, and I kept walking to the end of the block, six or seven houses to an intersection with the same kind of quiet street. I could cross and keep on going, walking into the whiteness, the plain Saturday noon of Atlanta, the heart of its quiet relief that there would be no work today, and not tomorrow either. I stopped there and looked up at the street signs, but they were no help, so I turned and started back toward Olivia. She was still standing in the same spot on her driveway, waiting, I think now, for her life to fall open, neatly, into two clean halves, waiting for the sounds of the world to rush back in. It had been so quiet in her house this past year. Nobody talked much, except the people on television. Her face looked frozen, the exact twin, I guessed, of mine. Like me, she was falling into the middle of something she didn't understand.

When I told Will I was going, his eyes filled with tears. "Oh," he sighed, "you'll be great there. That city. It's magic. I'm so jealous." He started to talk about how summer was his favorite season in New York City, how the days begin in sunshine and silence, and everybody's got those blue paper coffee cups, the same blue as the sky, so it looks like they're all holding a piece of it in their hands. Men in pressed suits. Women in sneakers and ankle socks below their summer frocks. Silence in the subway, plenty of noise, but no voices. Nobody's a morning person, nobody who actually gets dressed and sets foot outside. Little by little the day speaks, asks for a handout, offers a hot dog, a pretzel, tips its hat to you, winks, blows you a kiss. You're going to fall in love with it, he said. Fall. Hopelessly. In love.

GEORGIA: This is an improbable conversation, isn't it?

VERMEER: That's an understatement. There is no word for understatement in Dutch.

G: In American: silence. But who's to say the dead don't speak to each other?

V: Who's to say?

G: Who's to say people don't all have wings, and it's just that no one can see them?

V: How else do you account for the way human figures seem to float in certain paintings?

G: How else? *(beat)* I think, Jan, if we'd met in life, I would have fallen in love with you.

V: You like older men.

G: I do.

V: You would have had babies.

G: I wanted to have babies.

V: Sixteen?

G: Maybe not sixteen.

V: And you like photographers.

G: So it's true about the *camera obscura*? That you invented it? People have started to whisper, you know.

V: I'm not saying.

G: All right. But let's go back to improbable.

V: I'm enjoying all this talk about love.

G: That's fine. But first the other.

V (*overlapping*): Improbable how?

G: I'm outside. You're inside.

(*wild laughter*)

G: I didn't mean it that way.

V: And all those flowers, you didn't mean those *that way* either. And when you said, "It's hard to paint a slit in nothing," you didn't mean—

G: Honestly, I don't know what I meant by that. But *before*, I meant I never painted people in rooms. Doing things. Tasks. I never painted faces. At least not after I left school. People in motion. Forever pouring the milk, reading the letter, playing the piano, learning a song that nobody will ever hear.

V: The canna forever in bloom.

G: The deer forever dead, bleached to bone.

V: We don't choose our subjects.

G: Maybe not, but I don't like it the other way around either, that dreamy idea: our subjects choose us. It doesn't happen. The sky doesn't say paint me, the hill doesn't say, oh, Georgia, please make me the most famous hill in New Mexico.

V: The hill calls out to you.

G: That's what a man would say. And then he would paint a dismal, low-toned hill and call it the Great American Hill.

V: I think you're falling out of love with me.

G: I might be, just a little, just for a second.

V: A second can last a long time around here.

G: We digress.

V: It's the business of the dead to digress. It's the exact definition of death, isn't it?

G: How did you choose your subjects?

V: They were right there. A house full of women. Everywhere I turned, a woman busy, by an open window, to see something more clearly in those dark, cold rooms. A woman lit up. No story. No thoughts of her own.

G: You don't think so?

V: That was the perception. But if you look closely, you see the thoughts are turning, grinding over one another, or the hands are red from hot water or cold water. You can see the life, the little questions, hopes, embarrassments, indignities. The image deserves a story, a history. It's not a single frozen moment, it's a series of choices and accidents that got her to this pose. The painter has to either imagine that or know it.

G: Flowers and rocks and bones are not so much trouble.

V: I expect not. That's why you make them look so much like bodies.

G: Aren't you clever?

V: We're two sphinxes. What do you say to that?

G: *(silence)*

V: Exactly.

G: How did we begin this anyway?

V: With a love child.

G: And how will it end?

V: In fire.

Sasha

At first they were quiet, Sasha and Edgardo, Jennie and her mother, staring out at the Atlantic. They were going to meet Rodney and his friend, Henry Diamond, who wanted to talk to Sasha, and Edgardo wanted to see the ocean, this ocean, so they had walked over to the beach from Lisa's house, walked into Eddie's Burger, which was deserted, ordered coffee and arranged four chairs in a row in front of the big plate glass window. "In forty years," Edgardo said. "I haven't seen the Atlantic except to fly over it."

"Going where?" Lisa asked.

"Rome," Edgardo said.

"Of course," Jennie said. "Did you meet the pope?"

"I did," Edgardo said. "PJP."

"You called him that?" Sasha said.

"Not to his face. But he's miraculous. Just like people say. He glows from within. He speaks perfect English. We talked about skiing. But this. . . ." Edgardo nodded toward the ocean. "I forgot how uncomplicated it is. No rocks, no cliffs. No intermediaries."

The slate gray expanse before them seemed not to move at all until the little waves arrived and broke, ruffles at the bottom of a dress or the hem of a quilt on an enormous bed. Sweet waves, almost apologizing for themselves. Sorry we're not more mighty, more crashing, not what you expected. Waves like toddlers at a funeral, Sasha thought. They don't understand what's happening.

"I could sit here all day," Jennie said.

"Sometimes we do," Lisa said. She reached over and held Jennie's hand. Sasha wanted to film Lisa right then, in all her unkempt beauty. She wore a lilac-colored sweater that brought out the olive tint in her skin, making her look almost suntanned. Her hair hung loose around her shoulders and down her back, so black it was almost blue, shot here and there with silver strands. Sasha had not ever seen her this way—without makeup and seeming to be fresh from sleep, a cheerful swelling around her eyes and mouth, as if she'd been sleeping with her face pressed into the pillow. Not crying. Sleeping. Long, deep, dreamless. She remembered a picture of Marilyn Monroe, framed in a window in the same open disarray. Norma Jeanne again, and relieved.

"There's a rumor they need people to work the bucket brigade at night, from the crater to Chambers Street. And you help dig through," Jennie was saying. "It's not really helping. I don't know what it is. They relax the rules for some people."

"For who?" Edgardo said.

"Relatives mostly. The most pissed-off relatives, the ones who feel like it's going too slowly. People's kids."

"Like you," Sasha said, and Jennie nodded.

"You can kind of wander around a little more at night."

"What if you get caught?" Edgardo said.

"Nobody wants to catch people like us. The cops sympathize. A lot of them have friends buried in there."

"So you just turn on your flashlight and start sifting through the pile?" Sasha asked.

"How do you know where to look?" Edgardo said. "It's sixteen square miles."

Jennie shrugged, stared out at the water.

"They think there's some kind of magic working," Lisa said.

"You have to see it," Jennie said. "Film it."

The silence grew around them, attenuated, thoughtful, almost comfortable, like the arms of the people we're missing, Sasha thought, tentacles, but soft not frightening. A kind of quiet that had not been possible the last four months. Uncle Theo should be here too. Uncle Theo should be witness to what would come next.

"I met her," Sasha said and told them the story.

"I was wondering why you stopped talking about her lately," Edgardo said.

"Maybe she really doesn't know she's Brigid Schumann," Jennie said.

"I think she knows all too well," Lisa said. "Probably she'd like to forget for a while."

"So what do I do now?" Sasha said.

"I'll call her," Edgardo said. "You should have let me do that first. Now maybe she'll be mad."

"Mad?" Sasha said. "The mother who. . . . Mad? That's a good one."

"She'll watch the video," Jennie said. "And then she'll call you. You know she will."

"That's what I wish would happen." Sasha turned to Edgardo. "So please don't call. Not yet."

"What was she like at the bar?" Lisa asked.

"Cold," Sasha said. "But, like, *royal* too. The Snow Queen. Like she could slip a little piece of ice into your heart."

The string of bells over Eddie's front door rattled. A gust of cold air brought with it Rodney and Henry Diamond.

"Here's somebody who would know about that," Jennie said. "About what she's like."

"The guy who hates my video," Sasha said.

"Not *hates*," Jennie said.

"No. You're right," Sasha said.

"I'm not sure there's a word for how he feels about it," Edgardo said.

"The Snow Queen," Henry Diamond said two nights later as they walked past the National Guard on Fourteenth Street. "I can see that. The third kiss would kill you. And she likes spelling. Hard to believe she's anybody's mother."

Sasha wondered about that. Had she ever known a woman who looked and acted definitely like somebody's mother? She wasn't even sure what her own question meant. Her mother, Beatriz. The word *mother*. What did it even signify if you could have two? Your real mother and your mother of invention, Henry Diamond called them. Henry Diamond whose wife, he'd said, was going to become a mother any day now. And yet here he was, talking about how they could get in to roam the stinking wreckage of the Frozen Zone in the dead of a winter's night. That's a title, she thought, the dead of winter. She was following Henry and Jennie, a step or two behind, carrying her own pack. Henry seemed in a hurry to get digging.

Sasha would film from outside. She wanted the distance for all kinds of reasons: the texture of a chain link fence, the view through, the enormity of the ash pile, the quiet frenzy of all those anonymous diggers, the crazy play of their flashlights.

"Don't let me get lost," Jennie said.

That's the opening line, Sasha thought. That's it. Perfect.

They seemed to come out of the night like the animals they been turned into, the victims' families, made feral by waiting. Gloved, faces masked, carrying backpacks. And that was the first sound, the zip of opening a pack, the click of the headlamp, the hum of GPS, the clink of the rakes and the trowels. Then breathing, breathing, the sheer effort of it here because of the air, because of the work, because they still could.

Sasha had asked, What happens if you find something? You send it all to Staten Island, they were told. People have found bones, teeth, parts, wedding rings, jewelry, halves of wallets. And there's no stealing. If you steal, you'd be killed. The vigilante justice of a thousand little shovels. They'd make sure it hurt for a long time.

Here Sasha would say stop, and she would suddenly think of her mother's body, how it was both like and unlike the bodies under all this ash, still knit together, but just as gone. Her real mother, many years' mother, dead mother. What to call her?

The question was how to get this scene on film, from this distance. The spots of trembling light, the ragged breathing, the indecipherable landscape. Shapes that might be human but might be ghosts, the idea that ghosts were here. How to make the images talk? That was always the question, Wayne had said this to the high school film class in Santa Fe, how to close the gap between what you wanted to make and what you could make. Between your vision and your—what?—Sasha couldn't remember the other word, the lesser thing. But that was the point, the attempt to close the gap. That was the work and the art.

Sasha thought about Brigid Schumann. The mother of invention. And it occurred to her suddenly that Brigid Schumann cheated. All that text in her paintings. THE HAND GOES HERE. KACHINA. INERTIA. Brigid Schumann wrote the vision on top of the other thing. Maybe she was missing the point. Maybe she wasn't doing the work. Like Henry

Diamond said to her in the interview: you try to tell people what to think. And Brigid had replied, that's one way to look at it, I guess. But doesn't the title do the same thing? That little card on the wall, that little plaque on the ground. People's names. Your name, Henry Diamond?

In the camera's eye, Sasha saw Jennie, her miner's headlamp like a white hole in her forehead, scrambling towards her, holding up a piece of paper about the size of her hand. She drew her index finger across her throat: stop filming. Sasha straightened up and stepped away from the tripod.

"Look at this," Jennie said. "It might not be his, but still." She bent her head to illuminate the page, which seemed to be the end of a typed letter. Two words: *Love, Tim.* "I'm going to keep it," she said. "Even though. . . ." Her voice trailed away.

"A lot of people named Tim," Sasha said and gestured toward the blank, dark sky.

"I know. But it might be."

You need it to be, Sasha thought, and that's all right. So it is. She watched Jennie fold up the paper and slip it into her pack, then take it out again. "I can't," Jennie said. "I'm going to get back in line. You okay?"

"I think I'll walk around a little. Warm up."

Jennie nodded and turned, moved away to become shadow and unsteady light.

You could get closest to the ruined plaza at Church Street, and to the object that had lured her downtown three and a half months ago. You're writing about her, Aaron had said that Tuesday morning. You should go see it. *Red Sky/White Doe.* It's a strange piece, he said, and Sasha agreed. She'd only just met Aaron the day before. He seemed too young to be their resident adviser. But worldly somehow. Sasha could tell he didn't quite believe her then, that Brigid Schumann was her mother.

That word again, the wreckage of it. M'other. She planned to spell it that way in the essay, if it ever finally got written.

The people from the Port Authority thought some of the art from the plaza might eventually be recovered. Most of it was metal, so it would possibly not be recognizable. But you never know, they said. It may have been protected by ash and by who can imagine what else. Bodies. Carpet. An upside down cubicle. With a GPS, you could plot almost exactly where the piece had been. You could probably stand right on top of Brigid's masterwork, Aaron said. Latitude 40.7118 degrees N. Longitude 74.0124 degrees W. He had a map. There was something about completing the errand. Because that had been the idea back in September: go there, see it, and then call her. Because then they would have something to talk about, Sasha and Brigid, something concrete.

The darkness here was a riddle. All these klieg lights, and yet you still couldn't see much. The particular, illuminated mound of ash, but that wasn't ever what you needed to see—not that place, but the place just beyond. Light was so specific and insistent. It was childish. I want *this*, it said. *Here*, it said, stamping its bright foot. Painters loved it, understood it. Children, all of them.

A memory came to Sasha then, from out of that darkness, a black flower, another shape that seemed to be an armchair, also black, a small white pearl balanced in the crook, where the back meets the arm. Wondering if there was light shining on the pearl or if the pearl was the light. And was anyone sitting in the chair, or hiding there, hoping not to be noticed? The curve of shoulder, down to the elbow, to the outstretched arm. The same idea though; the pearl was a kind of a decoy, it drew your attention away from the thing you must not see, the person in the chair, the body. It was like hide and seek. When you found her, you laughed for a long time to cover how frightened you'd been. "Mother," Sasha said, and the memory closed up like a fist, a shadow moved away.

Then she knew she was standing right on top of it, the remains of *Red Sky/White Doe*, a rectangular frame through which a deer was caught mid-leap, a six-foot square metal piece that made its own balance with weights and pulleys. If you stood on the other side of it, in the imaginary room, you saw the deer had a woman's face and shoulders. And her expression—well, people described it differently. "Surprise," Henry Diamond had called it, "sort of." Wonder, power, amazement, awe. You have to see it for yourself, the Frommer's guidebook said. That face.

And now you couldn't.

Except maybe.

Sasha snapped open the tripod and fixed the camera on top. She stepped back into 40.7 degrees latitude and 74 degrees longitude, pointed her toe like a dancer and spun slowly, drawing a circle in the ash. The circumference of M'other. Of us. Then she stepped outside the circle, sighted the camera, turned it on, walked into the frame. Two frames, one on the earth, the other in the machine.

"What do I do now?" she said to the camera. "Below me, somewhere, is Brigid Schumann's hart."

Then she knelt and began to dig.

Strange and Forbidden Love

(*blurred image resolves to a map of Lower Manhattan, while a man's voice speaks*)

Nancy Diamond might have made a sad joke, she might have called my name. Will! Or said something like, Where there's a will there's a way, so where the hell are you, Will? She might have said, a *jumper* is what girls wear in kindergarten, so don't go calling me that. There was a woman standing beside her, and Nancy held out her hand, and the woman took it, and there you have it.

They didn't say much. I don't know if they really looked at each other. I think Nancy had her eyes open. She has them open now. The building was on fire, above and below. I call it a building, as if such a configuration, such a simple place existed then. It was hell, the fire and brimstone they teach you in church. Bodies everywhere, or parts of bodies. She could hear voices but couldn't tell where they were coming from. She sort of decided they were in her head.

I've come to believe the other girl's name was Angie. Nancy knew her only a little bit.

She worked two floors down, so Nancy wondered at first what she was doing standing right next to her. She actually took time to think about that, to decide Angie had brought up some papers for her boss, Tim Burgett, to sign—or something like that. What I mean is Nancy considered her intent, her reason for being so close right then, and she made a decision. Second-to-the-last one, or third, I guess. And right then, like Angie could read her mind, she said to Nancy, *I don't know how I got here. I think I flew.* Angie, Angela, Angel, like her name, she flew up to the ninety-third floor to hold out her hand. Her coat was unbuttoned and perfect, not a single mark on it, no rips or tears, really not a hair out of place. Both shoes still on. Low heels. Dark blue. Made Nancy think of Delta Airlines flight attendants. That shade of blue.

So I'm going to make it up, since we didn't talk at the end. Because we should have. Talked. I'm going to invent, since I'm the architect of imaginary places. That's what Nancy said: Will, your work is in imaginary places.

Then they took it all in for a little while, probably not an entire minute, Nancy's clothes, Angie's clothes, the wall of heat and smoke behind then. Angie held up her cell phone.

"It's really, really bad," she said, and then she told Nancy how bad. Words I can't understand, a new kind of obscenity, words brought into the language just that morning. They looked out the window, even though there wasn't very much to see besides smoke. "Open it," Angie said. "We've got to get some air in here." Nancy did, and they pushed a desk over to the window and climbed on top. "On my floor," she said, "the windows are sealed."

"That sucks," Nancy said, and Angie looked momentarily scared or horrified or something. Anyway, her face changed.

I'm making this up, but even the architect of imaginary places has his limitations.

"How old are you?" Angie said, and Nancy told her she was twenty, which was the truth at the time. She pointed to the cell phone in Nancy's hand. "Who do you need to call?"

And Nancy just kind of drew a blank. She started to ask why. It sounded like Angie meant call somebody to come get her, as if her mom could show up in the station wagon, and Nancy could take the elevator down, and there her mom would be right there, going, Did you have a nice day, Nance?

No, I did not, Mom, she would say. I did not have anything remotely resembling a nice day, and it's only—she checked her watch, her Dad's. He gave it to her when she left Atlanta—only nine in the morning.

So she just stood there until Angie reached over and gripped her shoulder and shook it. "To say good-bye," she said. "Who?"

Nancy said, I can't call my parents. They'd be too upset. Especially my dad. They wouldn't be helpful. They didn't really do helpful in the usual way. They'd probably just started telling themselves I was going to be all right, and now, well, just look at how not all right I'm going to be.

She tried to think, but the smoke was getting to her, and she felt like lying down on the desk and going to sleep. *Who, who,* Angie kept saying, like an owl, and shaking Nancy's shoulder very slowly and gently, as if she were made of something breakable. "Do you have sisters? Brothers?"

"I have a brother," Nancy said. "He's here. But he sleeps late."

"Then you'll wake him up," Angie said.

But she didn't have to.

"Henry," Nancy said when he answered. "Is this you?"

"Nance!" Henry said. "God, you're okay, You're okay. I'm down here. On Greenwich. We're seeing it. Oh my God. But you're okay."

"I'm inside," Nancy said. "But someone's with me."

"That's good," Henry said. "You'll be okay."

"No, Henry," Nancy said. "I don't think so."

She wouldn't have wanted to tell him she was so far up, though he knew this. She wouldn't have wanted to tell him about the fire. He didn't need to know. He didn't need to think about fire and brimstone right then. There would be plenty of time after.

I'm making it up for Nancy and for Henry. I'm inventing it to make sense, to help you grapple with your fears. Make it up, Will, make it up:

"Henry," Nancy said, "I just wanted to tell you that I loved your wedding. I love it that you and Paula found each other." Henry laughed or sobbed or something. "Keep thinking about me, okay? That helps, just to know you'll be thinking of me."

"Always. Every second of every day." He could barely get the words out.

"And please tell Mom and Dad. . . ." She couldn't think what, until Angie said it, her mouth right beside Nancy's face.

"Tell them what you think they need to hear."

So Nancy repeated this to Henry. She could make out Paula's voice, amid the yelling and sirens in the background, asking what she'd said, where she was. "Henry. Let me talk to Paula," she said.

Angie had moved away, closer to the window, and almost entirely disappeared in the smoke. Nancy had this strange feeling that they had lots of time.

I'm giving Nancy a moment here. Because that's what she would have said: Will you give me a moment?

"Nance?" Paula said. She was entirely composed. I'm imagining she was always better at this kind of thing than Henry was. At their wedding, even. He cried like a baby, and she just looked at him, smiling, kind of the way you'd look at a baby. *Oh, you adorable little sweetheart* was what her face said the whole time. And now she was that Paula. "We love you, Nance," she said. Her voice was very clear through the phone, through the smoke and mayhem. "We're going to have a baby, Nancy. We weren't telling anyone yet, but we know it's a girl, and we're going to name her after you. So there will still be a Nancy Diamond."

Paula said *still* because she knew.

"That's good," Nancy said. "Henry will be a great father. He knows how."

"He does," Paula said. "Do you want to keep talking?"

"Can you see me, up here in the window? I'm waving."

"I think I can see you. Yes. There you are." And she asked again, "Do you want to keep talking?" and Nancy told her she didn't think so, that she was ready for whatever would happen next, that she loved Paula and Henry and the new, pure white Nancy Diamond. She felt like she was a million years old, like she'd lived a long life. Kind of tired. She closed the phone and looked around.

Angie was standing at the open window staring down. The light on her face was gray and brown. Nancy remembered the word from playwriting class: *sepia*. She thought at the time, *That's the right word, that's the color of my skin. So there is a word for it!* She found this class at the New School, she told me, and it seemed good. The teacher was also a portrait photographer who used only natural light to photograph writers. She talked about how to get color into words. *Color into words, imagine that!* Nancy had said. Angie looked over her shoulder, and Nancy found it amazing that she knew exactly where to look through all that smoke.

"People are in the air," Angie said. Nancy stepped closer and tried to hand her the cell phone. "Just leave it," Angie said, and Nancy put it on the windowsill, where it instantly began to vibrate. "Possessed," Angie said.

That was me calling. I'm going to imagine that was me, though it couldn't have been. I was calling her apartment, ninety blocks uptown.

Pick up Nancy Diamond, I was saying, please pick up. Olivia was watching me, her face a mask.

"I don't know if I can do that," Nancy would have said. "Be in the air."

Angie glanced over her shoulder into the smoke behind them, lifted her chin, meaning *get a load of that*. "It will be worse if you don't." The knowledge in her voice was terrible and calm. Serene. "Just climb up here and take a look," she said.

The air outside the window had gone pillowy with smoke. Every so often a rogue wind would open the view down to the street, which seemed like a clutter of toys: little moving dolls and tiny fire trucks. She wanted the view to go away, the air to close up. "It won't hurt," Angie was saying. Nancy thought Angie might push her, so she moved back, away from the ledge. "Pain comes with consciousness," she said, "and you won't have consciousness at the end, ergo. . . ."

"*Ergo?*"

"Therefore."

"How did I end up alone?" Nancy said, gazing out the window. "On this island."

"Do you mean today? Or do you mean, you know, the big picture?"

"When I first said it, I meant today. But now I mean both."

"Everyone else died is how," Angie said. "Isn't that right?"

"Must be," Nancy said. "I'm feeling a little numb."

The room had grown hotter. And louder, alarms wailing, screaming, wires popping and snapping.

"I think the whole floor is about to go," Angie said. "Don't you want to be in charge of your own destiny?"

That made Nancy laugh. They stepped up on to the window ledge.

"Here," Angie said, and she held out her hand, but there seemed to be only emptiness between them. "Here."

"I don't know what to do."

"Put your hand in mine. Your hand goes here."

That's why Henry was crying, Nancy thought, gripping Angie's hand. He remembered saying that he wanted to save someone from a burning building. Every so often, the smoke drifted, and she got a view of Staten Island, Lady Liberty, a kind of side glimpse, or intermittent, like when you drift in and out of sleep. She thought—I know she did—of all the fish out there in the harbor and how safe they were and how much she wanted to be a fish, and now this was just another of the thousand things she'd never get to be.

She wondered if somehow the rules of the universe had changed enough to permit her to leap from here and land on something soft. If forces were so altered that airplanes could crash through buildings, then maybe, who knew? She could try. Maybe there was some magic at work. Enchantment. She might land in Henry's arms. Or mine. Hello, Will, she'd say. No explanation would be necessary. In fact, I'd be expecting her, checking the time every few minutes, scanning the sky, waiting for the ashes to gather themselves, coalesce into the form of Nancy Diamond.

I was, in fact, checking the time.

Olivia said, "Is she all right? Are you all right, Daddy?" Olivia asked, and I held her close.

This next part is difficult for me.

"Is that Governor's Island?" Nancy asked Angie. She tried to free her hand to point, but Angie wouldn't let go, only smiled and nodded, and Nancy thought she must know something. Had she mentioned Rodney? The smoke was making her dizzy. It was hard to remember certain parts of the past. Or was it hard to think about them?

Don't look down, Angie was saying, you can't see anything anyway. Nancy didn't have to look down. She'd spent the last three months looking down for the sheer horror of it. Imagine that, Will, she told me. To scare herself, she'd press her face up against a window that wouldn't open and try to look down. What absolute idiocy. But everybody did it, all the temps and interns. It was like they were trying to find something in the street, she said, something disguised, like that game "Where's Waldo?" Or the idea of something. Or the definition of down. Your supervisor took you to Windows on the World for lunch, and that was even more of a challenge, to look down from there. And if your supervisor was cool—mine was, Nancy said—he led you through the kitchen where he said hi to the cooks and the sommelier, and past the walk-ins and through the storerooms—Jesus, how did they get all those groceries up there?—to the roof. The roof! Like a horror movie and a trip to paradise combined, that's how it felt. She could see the lost wilderness of Governor's Island, she could see the curve of the earth, she could see the ocean, halfway to England. But she was scared out of her mind. One of the other interns said, I bet people sneak up here all the time to have sex. And the supervisor went sort of theatrically quiet. Nancy was pretty sure he'd never done it. She wanted to laugh, but she was afraid her laughter would shake her too close to the edge. And she was afraid how inviting Rodney to the roof of the WTC that time seemed like the only way to get him back.

I know this, even though it hurts me. I know she loved him. I know he made her feel less alone, less strange in the world.

She wondered, just for a second, if there was some way she could turn around and look down and see right into Rodney's present apartment on Church Street. By now, she reasoned, he knew or had some idea of what was happening. She thought at this moment she should be allowed some kind of power, some sort of extraordinary vision. Wouldn't that be a fair trade? All she wanted was to look into Rodney's eyes and say thank you. Because Nancy knew, finally, at that moment, holding Angie's hand, which pulsed around hers, as if she were keeping her heart beating, Nancy knew she was going to die. So she thought her last words should be to Rodney, a little whisper, a little breath to reassure him that none of this was his fault.

"Daddy," Olivia was saying, "don't cry."

I wonder, Nancy said to Angie, if people will be rescued from the roof. Helicopters with ladders, with cables. Like the French acrobat again, only this time in a different direction, this time ascension. Angie shook her head no. She didn't look at Nancy.

"Nobody lives on Governor's Island anymore," Angie said. Had Nancy mentioned Governor's Island? She didn't remember. She wondered again if Angie was really there. The smoke was making it difficult to see, though she could feel the pulse of blood in her wrist up into the palm of her hand. "It's an enchanted forest now."

"I know," Nancy said. "I knew the last person to leave. They left him there as a sort of lifeguard. By himself. Like a guy in a firetower."

"Like you," Angie said. "Right now."

"Me?"

"You."

"Are you really here?"

"Do you want me to be?"

"Yes."

"Hold my hand then."

Long on prologue. Short on denouement.

I will give up this moment to someone who deserves it. Henry. Let's imagine Henry could see Nancy. Henry saw her in the jagged window frame on the ninety-third floor, waving to him. Henry saw her in the air. He knew her, his darker sister, going now into deeper darkness.

How can I be telling this? How can I not be? I'm the architect of imaginary places. Still, you say, this whole story must be against some kind of law. But what kind of person are you, that you'd deny me my version of events? What law, what rules do you live by? What stupid fucking rules for living? Who says you get to make the rules anyway? Her whole life story in between two sentences. Once upon a time. They lived happily ever after. Two sentences. Only one of them true.

Sasha

Brigid Schumann lived on the eighth floor of a building on Hubert Street, the neatly typed card informed Sasha. *Please come to see me at home. 6 p.m. on January 5.* That was all. No telephone number, no sense of what might be said or not said, no closing tenderness, just the name and address.

Start slow, Jennie had advised, start with something easy.

I can't go with you, Uncle Edgardo said as he climbed into the taxi. He had decided to fly back to Santa Fe. I wouldn't be any help.

And on the appointed day at the appointed hour, there she was, Brigid Schumann framed in the open door of her apartment, waiting as Sasha walked toward her from the elevator. The light blared in the hallway between them like a kind of alarm, a shining guard dog. She wore black trousers and a billowy white shirt, her maroon-colored hair gathered into a tight knot at the nape of her neck. Sasha didn't know if the expression she wore was happiness or curiosity, but maybe for Brigid Schumann there wasn't much difference between the two. The space between them seemed not to diminish, and then suddenly, it was gone, and they were face to face, Sasha two inches taller. "We don't see eye to eye," Brigid said and led Sasha inside.

The loft was magnificent and industrial at the same time, a factory extravagantly decorated for an unspecified but glorious holiday. Sasha counted seven tall windows, took in the north view and the luminous shimmering inside and out: white Christmas lights glittering from the ceiling, and beyond, the city and the George Washington Bridge winking off to the left. The silvery kitchen reflected all this so that Sasha felt she was inside a cage of light, but not blinded. Actually, she thought, it felt safe. No shadows. Everything out in the open. A long white sofa and two armchairs faced the windows. The walls were painted white. Brigid had not hung a single painting or photograph. Sasha took note of the sheer

curtain, which she finally understood was an opened parachute, separat-
ing the living space from the studio.

"It's a mess in there," Brigid said.

"That's probably a good thing."

This made Brigid step closer, study Sasha's face. "Usually," she said.
"You do look like my mother."

"That's what Theo said."

Brigid nodded. "He left a note at the gallery. I got yours and his on the
same day, but I read them in the wrong order."

Sasha felt afraid to ask what the right order would have been or what
else Theo's note might have said. She remembered the first time she saw
Theo in the Carman lobby and how she thought he looked caught, frozen. She felt just that way now. She wished Brigid Schumann would touch
her. She thought it might break the same kind of spell.

"Where do we start?" Brigid said. "We could sit down." She moved
toward the windows, settled herself into a corner of the sofa and patted the
seat of the closest chair.

I know the color, Sasha thought. "Ochre."

"That's right," Brigid said. Sasha saw a brightness come into her eyes.
"You must want to ask me some questions."

Jennie said start with something easy.

"I tried to find *Red Sky/White Doe.*"

Brigid closed her eyes, leaned her head back. "My God. How would
you do that?"

"Digging."

"Really? Well, thank you, but. . . . I don't know. There may be nothing
to recover."

"Uncle Edgardo told me the story of it."

"And how is Edgardo?"

Still in love with you, Sasha wanted to say. "He was here for Christmas."

"But he's gone home?"

"Last week. I'm sure he'll be back though."

Sasha didn't want to talk about Edgardo. She wondered if maybe she
should leave the past alone, but it seemed like there was no way to get to

the present without going through the door of the past. They sat in an odd silence. It was like having cotton in your ears, Sasha thought. Maybe city noise couldn't rise this high.

"Start with the hardest part," Brigid said. "That's what I would do."

"All right." It was all the hardest part. "Why did you give me up?"

Brigid sighed, maybe a bit theatrically. "I gave you up so I could be this person now to have you back."

Rehearsed, Sasha thought. "I don't know what that means."

"I think it means I didn't know what I wanted."

"But you knew what you didn't want?"

Brigid stood up from the sofa, crossed behind to the refrigerator, opened the silvery door, and drew out a bottle of wine. She reached toward a cupboard over her head, and rows of glasses were instantly illuminated. She chose two and turned back to face Sasha. She poured wine into the glasses and paused, rested her palms on the counter.

"Because other people told me to," she said. "Because I was too young. Because you didn't make any noise, and that scared me. Because I was afraid of what people who seemed to love each other were capable of."

"I don't know what that means either."

"All right," Brigid said. She sounded like she'd been told to snap out of it. Chastened. "All right."

Brigid brought the wine glasses back to the sofa and chairs by the window, handed one to Sasha. She's not used to asking permission, Sasha thought. Brigid moved back into the corner of the sofa but leaned very close to Sasha. She gazed out at the lights of Manhattan. "Because you were going to be a burden," she said. "You were a burden. Because I wanted to do something else with my life."

"I'm sorry."

"It wasn't your fault."

Sasha realized she knew all this. She had come here for information she didn't already have. She glanced to the coffee table, the sideboard, a bookshelf by the door. No photographs. No evidence of a life outside this enormous, illuminated room.

"Can I ask about my father?"

"No. Not now."

"Why not?"

"I'm just not prepared for that. Maybe later."

"Just one question. I won't ask who."

"What other question is there?"

"Did you love him?"

"Ah, *that* other question." Brigid sipped her wine. "I thought I did. I loved . . . the way he was a kind of magic mirror. And when I stood in front of him, I saw not what I looked like, but what I wanted to be. What I was going to be. A painter. I loved that."

"Does he know about me?"

"No."

"Why not?"

"There was a point when I might have told him, but then I realized I wanted you all to myself."

"But then you gave me away."

"Think of it this way," Brigid said. She sighed but did not seem annoyed. "It's like a painting—or maybe any kind of art. You don't want to admit it's a collaboration. You want to be, as they say, the sole proprietor. And then you want other people to have it."

Sasha wanted to laugh. "That's about making money," she said.

"Not always. What about your film? You didn't do that to make money. Why did you do it?"

"I think I did it to explain something to myself. To understand what was happening."

"Why do you want people to see it?"

"There must be other people who want to understand it too."

"Right."

"I think you just totally rerouted the conversation."

"I did. But isn't this a better conversation to be having? Wouldn't you rather talk about art than about mistakes I made when I was too young to know anything?"

"Why did you come to Santa Fe when I was little?"

"I thought Edgardo would have explained that to you. I didn't have anywhere else to go. My parents' house was sold. And I wanted to see you."

Sasha had been staring out at the bright confusion of city lights, and the break in Brigid's voice struck her as the sound those lights would make, a gleam, a piercing.

"I wanted to make sure you were happy. And you were. A lot happier than I could have made you. They loved you so much. I was sorry to hear about your mother. I know it was an awful time, just before leaving home."

"Thank you. It was awful. But. . . . Is it strange for you to call her that?"

"No. It's what she was."

Sasha tried to find some revelation in that last word. "Was," she said. "*Was* is sort of wrong. She'll never not be my mother. Death doesn't change things like that, does it?"

"It sort of expands the universe, I think. Pushes out a wall. Shows you a place you never knew was there. Which brings me back to your film."

"What did you think?"

"It gave me an image."

"That must mean you liked it."

"You'll learn that *liked it* is less important than *took it seriously*."

"If there's anything I've learned, it's that. Can you talk about the image?"

"Something about gravity and dust. It involves climbing on top of a church and a magic trick, old school. A woman is made to disappear. But actually to be transformed. Part performance, part object, so the best of both art worlds. Think of the mirrored ball dropping in Times Square on New Year's Eve. How it's a symbol and it's abstract at the same time. Why should a mirrored ball stand for the moment an old thing passes away and a new thing begins? Why shouldn't it? Mirror. You have to look at yourself. And you wait for it every year. You stay up late. Like that, but. . . ."

"Better?"

"Other."

Brigid

An installation, over the central doors of the Cathedral of St. John the Divine.

Begin with a profusion of wings, beating, descending, ecstatic. Barely visible beside or beneath these wings are two women. Soon enough, the wings explode into a shower of strobe light and glitter, smoke, sequins, tympani, bits of colored glass, rose petals, discs of pressed sugar, water droplets, diamonds. Then they fall. It's like flying and like swimming and like sleep, all rolled together. The falling seems to last forever. Lighted words appear on the façade of the Cathedral. They say

A TERRIBLE BEAUTY
A VESSEL FOR THE CHAOS
SUFFERING IS INFINITELY ABSURD
WRENCHED FROM COMMERCE AND MADE USEFUL
STARE WITHOUT FLINCHING

And the woman? What happens to her? They're not sure yet. It's a work in progress. How could Brigid explain it? The woman is light. The light a body blocks. The light a body hides. The light that would replace the body. The darkness bodies make. If you could get rid of the body, what light would be found there, in its place? The light behind the body, the light underneath the body. Not shadow. And not the light inside the body. That's something else, the soul maybe. If you could show the body without the body actually being there. Think of the way words work. The word *body* is not the body but the space it occupies. The light it gets in the way of.

In the making of this performance object, there was an accident, but no one was badly hurt. Brigid and Sasha had been working at the bottom of the Cathedral's rose window. It was late in the summer, the sun just beginning to set. Brigid saw what would happen before it did happen, she saw in her mind's eye the step Sasha would take, the wrong step, the placement of her left foot so that the right would have to fall too close to the steepest pitch of the roof, and then slide, and cause Sasha's weight to be thrown behind. Into the unloving arms of gravity, was what Brigid said.

So when Sasha began to fall, Brigid had already maneuvered her upper body directly beneath, on the open part of the scaffold. And so Brigid caught Sasha, and only for a moment, a few seconds really, she held her daughter in her arms. The scaffold was very narrow in this place, and Sasha's greater weight tipped a board, and Brigid began to fall too, slowly, with Sasha clasped to her, as if they were dancing or fighting.

Or both, Brigid said. She started to fight me then, Sasha did, without words, with only her eyes, which told me to let her go, to save myself. But I wouldn't do that, she said. I wore a safety harness. Brigid always wore this harness, but Sasha, she said, sometimes did not. The arrogance of youth: the belief that you will never die. Brigid would be all right, even if she fell, and so she knew she would fall, down before the façade of the Cathedral. She knew her safety line would drop her about three feet above ground level, and so the only thing she had to do would be to hold on to Sasha, her daughter, who weighed maybe a quarter again as much as she.

The drop seemed to take years, the way it always does for the earth to come nearer to another celestial body. Brigid did not close her eyes, though she felt at first that she wanted to. She gazed into Sasha's face, and Sasha looked back. Sasha slipped and Brigid found she was looking down, and Sasha gazing up at her, a relation they had, for only a few days in life twenty years before, ever found themselves in. Sasha slipped a little lower, so that when the harness ran out of line, she was standing on the ground, just in front of the Cathedral. She absorbed some of the shock with her feet and ankles, but stood still for a moment, as if she were holding Brigid aloft, on display.

Many people surrounded them, mostly tourists. There was a rush of languages, Brigid said. People asked Sasha whether she was in pain, but she didn't answer. Someone called an ambulance, and Brigid went with Sasha to St. Luke's. It turned out Sasha's left ankle was broken, a very small, simple fracture. Although there is a cast, she can walk without crutches. Because really, Brigid said, her voice halting now, breaking, she has such good balance.

One of these tourists, in a very strange state of mind, thought to raise his video camera to his eye—or perhaps he was already filming—and record the descent. You wouldn't want to call it a fall. Sasha has not seen this film, but Brigid has, and she says there is something intensely private about the moment, but also very choreographed, as if she and Sasha were performing a stunt. Others outside the Cathedral believed this as well, and took still photographs. You may have seen these, but they are blurry. You stare at the image, though, for nearly a minute, waiting for the mother and the daughter to resolve themselves, to take shape out of the mist.

Sasha

One of the reviewers will say this: In the Navajo language, verbs distinguish between the object's manner of movement. Verb stems are grouped into three different categories. *Handling* includes actions such as carrying, lowering, and taking. *Propelling* includes tossing, dropping, and throwing. *Free flight* includes falling and flying through space. In other words, *keeping close*, *sending away*, and *having no control over*. These are the three ways in which humans may treat each other. These are the three means by which people come to know who it is that they love.

Privately, Aaron Fisk will make a joke. But not the kind you laugh at. More like a frightened art history joke. More like months of clenched fright finally letting go. He will say Brigid Schumann should call it *In the Sky with Diamond* or *The Girl with Kaleidoscope Eyes*. And Sasha will tell him, I love you, but that's why you're the critic and not the artist. It's okay. There, there. Hush. Don't cry. I love you.

Centaur and Mermaid

(blurred image resolves to a map of Lower Manhattan, while a woman's voice speaks)

I, Nancy Diamond, know some things now, from my particular and unruly vantage point.

I know the world is made of paper, down here between West and Church. Memos and checks, business cards, blueprints, users' manuals, Post-it notes, file folders, newsletters. Torn yellow legal popping up everywhere, like misshaped dandelions.

This world is ink and lead. Pens and pencils bent and stretched by fire and velocity and collision. So many ways to write a sentence that would never be read by anyone. So many last sentences. Client can't be reached, call back tomorrow. Numbers don't add up. Lunch specials today. What the hell is the market up to? Want to meet for coffee? Could you send this to the dry cleaner's? My kid started school today.

And the world is shiny, even in the dark. Slabs of incongruous metal, corners of desks, shards of telephone, chair legs, drawer pulls, motherboard, coffee maker, picture frame. Think of all the pictures on all the desks, thumbtacked up in all the cubicles. Painted portraits and one-hour developed and Coney Island booth with the whole team piled in. Weddings and birthdays, bar mitzvah and graduation, first communion and first lost tooth.

Teeth. Oh God. This world is made of bone. A jawbone, with fillings. Small teeth, like pearls, the white of life without coffee, cigarettes, or red wine. That's when you remembered the children, a class on a field trip, a toddler visiting Mom at work, an afternoon kindergartner who never made it to the first day of school. Long bones, tibia that could not outrun the moment, a shoulder, a wrist with a watch, fingers with rings.

A man's watch arrived with the glass face shattered but otherwise mostly unharmed in a bag at the medical examiner's office on Thirtieth Street.

In Theo Long Night's two hundred and seventh load of debris, the federal agents in hazmat suits on Muldoon Hill found a wedding ring. Inscribed on the inside and still legible were the initials T. L. Tim. Lisa.

No one named Angela worked at Marsh and McClennon, no one who didn't get out, that is.

I know that I am responsible for their reunion, that I caused them to be resolved, as my body took and then changed shape. I said this some time ago, that I wanted to meet Brigid Schumann. I wanted her to walk into her exhibit, stare at my face and then paint it. Then I could look at her rendering and know for once and for all who I really was. Now I know. I know that I gave them their dark masterpiece.

And this too: I now know something about angels, and so I reject Swedenborg's heaven, in which the angels are perfect and white, and two people in love make a single angel. Because why should love make us lose ourselves? Become less? And when have you ever known love so neat as that? Two people, forever? Swedenborg, I'm sorry to tell you, you are an idiot. And then this part: everywhere the angels look—north, south, east, and west—they see the face of God. I reject that too. Who would go to heaven for such a limited view, for such tedious landscape?

I reject any heaven in which there are no bodies. There will always be bodies, broken, smashed, rent, the variously colored bodies and the blank ones, so much indecipherable language of flesh and bone, bodies demanding a voice, because there is always more more *more* to say.

And yet.

So many last sentences. Here is a sampling:

Now comes the mystery.

How were the receipts today at Madison Square Garden?

Ah. That tastes nice. Thank you.

Called back.

It's very beautiful over there.
I have not told half of what I saw.
All right then, I'll say it. Dante makes me sick.
The show looks good! The show looks good!

And these are mine, my last, the last of Nancy Diamond:

(And because drama is supposed to be the intersection of bodies and language, there would be a touch as well, and revelation of course. Questions asked and answered. Truth. Two people helping each other find a way to live in a world in which they will surely die.)

BRIGID: Sasha, my baby, my daughter. You have to tell me the truth. Did I miss anything?

SASHA *(beat, tilts her head into a bright light)*: No. *(beat)* Nothing.

BRIGID: Nothing?

SASHA: Actually, the answer is yes. Yes, you did. You missed quite a bit. A hell of a lot, really. But not everything. And if you hurry, you can catch up.

BRIGID: All right. *(glances over her shoulder, then into the darkness before them)* I guess I could use some direction.

SASHA: Couldn't we all? Start with this. *(embraces Brigid)* Start here.